The L

Ka

When their mother died, Lauren took her place and raised her younger sisters. Now with the help of one special man, Lauren will find her own place in the world—and in his life. . . .

"ARDATH"

Anne Stuart

A fiery artist, Ardath is still haunted by her mother's death. But when she finds the man who broke her mother's heart, will she be in danger of losing her own?

"DINAH"

Donna Julian

On the anniversary of her mother's death, Dinah is caught in a life-and-death crisis of her own. But the skills that made her a successful lawyer will serve her well—and turn near-tragedy into true love. . . .

"YARDLEY"

Jodie Larsen

The youngest Smith sister, Yardley is also the most romantic. Yet her sentimental nature conceals a strength of character that would have made her mother proud, especially when it comes to matters of the heart. . . .

SISTERS AND SECRETS

A NOVEL IN FOUR PARTS

BY
KATHERINE STONE
ANNE STUART
DONNA JULIAN
JODIE LARSEN

AN ONYX BOOK

ONYX
Published by the Penguin Group
Penguin Putnam Inc., 375 Hudson Street,
New York, New York 10014, U.S.A.
Penguin Books Ltd, 27 Wrights Lane,
London W8 5TZ, England
Penguin Books Australia Ltd, Ringwood,
Victoria, Australia
Penguin Books Canada Ltd, 10 Alcorn Avenue,
Toronto, Ontario, Canada M4V 3B2
Penguin Books (N.Z.) Ltd, 182–190 Wairau Road,
Auckland 10, New Zealand

Penguin Books Ltd, Registered Offices:
Harmondsworth, Middlesex, England

First published by Onyx, an imprint of Dutton Signet,
a member of Penguin Putnam Inc.

First Printing, March, 1998
10 9 8 7 6 5 4 3 2 1

 REGISTERED TRADEMARK—MARCA REGISTRADA

Printed in the United States of America

PUBLISHER'S NOTE
These are works of fiction. Names, characters, places, and incidents either
are the product of the authors' imaginations or are used fictiously, and
any resemblance to actual persons, living or dead, events, or locales is
entirely coincidental.

To Audrey LaFehr, whose insight,
enthusiasm, and tenacity brought new
and old friends together to make this one
happen. We thank you.

Prologue

❧

Christmas Eve, 1977

"Does Santa's sleigh have pretty red and blue lights like those?" four-year-old Yardley asked in a lisping, dramatic, baby-sweet voice. Her button nose pressed against the windowpane, she knelt on the cushion in the dormer, watching the excitement below. Her blond, waist-length, spiraled curls bounced with the energy and restlessness peculiar to the very young.

The question had been posed to Lauren, the oldest of her three sisters, who sat beside the "baby," somberly watching the commotion of police and paramedics as they finished up their investigation, which had begun just before nightfall. At fourteen, Lauren Smith's face had begun the process of shedding the remnants of childhood. With a complexion as flawless and fair as alabaster, eyes the deep true blue of sapphires, and hair as black and glossy as jet—she held the promise of great beauty. To-night, however, every extraordinary feature was di-minished by a profound sadness her young years hadn't prepared her to disguise.

"Lauren!" Yardley demanded.

"No, sweetie," Lauren said, her voice hardly loud enough to be heard over the din below.

"You're a dope, Yardley." This from Ardath, who at twelve was old enough to comprehend the im-port of the shrouded gurney two ambulance atten-dants were guiding over the cobbled courtyard.

"Am not!" Yardley cried. Tears dribbled from her eyes, which were as blue as her eldest sister's, though shades lighter. "Eberbody knows it's Cwiss-mas Eve, dummy. Santa Cwaus is comin'. He might have lights like those, huh, Lawen?"

Lauren nodded absently, her agreement to any question from the baby as automatic to her as draw-ing breath. Now, though, her attention was focused on her father sitting on a bench at the far end of the courtyard, his shoulders heaving, his back to the scene he couldn't bare to witness.

Ardath leaned against the sill, her expression a conflict of belligerence and pain. "Jesus Chr—"

Lauren turned on her sister, her gaze almost as dark as the falling night in her sudden, uncharac-teristic anger. "Don't you dare, Ardath! Don't you talk about the Lord that way!"

"Yeah," Yardley agreed. "He's just a little baby, and tomorrow's His birfday."

Ardath ignored her, turning on Lauren with a glare. "Oh, what ya gonna do, smarty-pants? Tell Mom?"

Lauren slapped her.

All four sisters—even seven-year-old Dinah, who
sat in the far corner of the room, a thumb stuck in
her mouth for the first time in five years—gasped
with shock at the uncharacteristic display of temper.

Tears of chagrin filled Lauren's eyes. "Oh, Ardath, I'm sorry! Please don't be mad."

But the twelve-year-old's eyes glittered like green
shards of a broken bottle behind her tears, and her
face, normally as fair as Lauren's, was infused with
red-hot anger. "Leave me alone, Lauren!" she yelled,
spinning away on her heel and darting for the door.
She stopped just short of leaving to turn back and
face the others, and in the shadows of the darkened
hallway, the thick red hair that framed her pretty
face looked for an instant like a halo of fire. "In fact,
why don't you all go away just like she did!"

Dinah drew her legs up under her chin as tears
filled her eyes. "You're just plain mean, Ardath
Smith! Mama didn't want to go away! She . . .
she . . . had an accident, didn't she, Lauren?"

"Yes," the oldest girl replied quietly, her own
eyes swimming behind a blur of tears. "It was a terrible, terrible accident."

Dinah nodded solemnly, her tiny heart-shaped
face and big gray eyes as serious as her heroine's,
the oldest of the four Smith girls. Her hair, too, was
as black as the night that had settled fully over the
house, now that the last of the flashing, whirling
blue and red lights had disappeared in a procession
down the long private drive away from the Chestnut Hills estate. "Ardath's just being bad 'cause she
doesn't understand, huh?"

"I understand, you little idiot! Mama's *dead*!"

All four of the girls—"the beautiful little ladies

Smith" as their mama had called them just today when they'd posed together in front of the Christmas tree in their Sunday best for Daddy to take their picture—began to cry.

"Is Santa still comin' tonight?" Yardley asked on a tear-clogged hiccup.

PART ONE

Lauren

BY
KATHERINE STONE

Chapter One

~

Summer 1997

"Aloha, big sister. Have a *fabulous* time in paradise, but don't you *dare* get married without us. Oh, and regards, of course, to the hunk!"

Lauren had long since erased Dinah's voice-mail message. But the message, as well as her sister's irrepressible—and irrepressibly irreverent—spirit, resonated still.

Lauren was not in Hawaii with John, the heart surgeon "hunk." John was in paradise, however, with Stephanie, a tropical holiday from which he might well return happily wed. Married or not, John was deliriously happy with Stephanie. Everyone at Cascade Medical Center had borne witness to their fairy-tale romance—just as the entire hospital staff had witnessed its impact *on her*.

Lauren never wore her heart on her shirtsleeve, nor on the crisp white fabric of her physician's coat.

During the four months since John had summarily ended their relationship, she had maintained her cheerful facade, the consummate professional, always. But it was impossible to hide the weight loss, the dark circles, the haunted sadness beneath the valiant veneer.

No one knew, because no one really knew her, that John was far from her first failed love affair—hardly the first man whose interest Lauren had been unable to sustain. Men *were* interested—at first; fascinated by her intelligence, intrigued by her demure reserve. Such modesty in the face of her brilliance was mysterious, enticing, and sent the false yet captivating promise of a rare and secret wisdom.

Dr. Lauren Smith *did* possess something rare, a talent for reading X rays—and angiograms, ultrasounds, and MRIs—in a way that defied all logic. She saw shadows that no one else could see—shadows that led to early diagnoses, to life-saving cures.

Because her gift verged on clairvoyance, Lauren was viewed as a priestess of sorts, a prophetess. Her mystical reputation preceded her to Seattle and piqued interest even before she arrived. John wasn't the only bewitched male. But the handsome heart surgeon was the hospital's golden boy. What John wanted John got. Only a fool would compete with him where women were concerned.

For a few glorious months, Lauren spun in John's orbit, basked in his dazzling light. She was an inconsequential moon, illuminated only by him, a radiance so brilliant that, for that glittering time, even he was blinded to the truth.

Lauren should have known better. She *did* know better. At least the scientist within her knew. But the woman, the *woman*, ignored the mountain of evidence: her lifelong failure with men.

Lauren even broke her own cardinal rule. During Dinah's visit in February, she introduced her sister to John. It seemed safe. She and John had been involved for several months, and they had made plans into the future, including the romantic vacation in paradise slated for June.

They shared those sun-drenched plans with Dinah, who insisted on documenting their happiness on film. Then, with typical Dinah enthusiasm, she sent copies of the photos to Ardath and Yardley, accompanied by rave reviews of Lauren's *man* and the buoyant prediction that wedding bells would be chiming in the very near future.

But even as Dinah was forecasting joy—at last—for the most serious of the sisters, the fantasy was shattering. Lauren should have simply let John go without asking *why*. Lauren *knew* why—reasons that had little to do with Stephanie and everything to do with her. Some punishing impulse, however—some authentically inherited proclivity for self-destruction—compelled Lauren to force him to speak the devastating truth.

John had willingly complied. Unaccustomed to being pushed, to being trapped, he responded with cruel fury, the gifted surgeon wielding scalpels in both hands, slashing without mercy her already wounded heart.

"I *never* loved you, Lauren. How could I? There's nothing *to* love. You're ice, in bed, out of bed. I kept telling myself there had to be something more—warmth, sensuality, something. But there isn't. I wasted way too much time looking for that non-existent something, and I sure as hell don't want to waste any more time explaining *your* problems to *you*."

The priestess became a pariah. The gracious welcome that had been hers, because of John, vanished the moment he no longer wanted her. Lauren's medical colleagues noticed her, however. How could they not? She was a corpse wandering in their midst.

To her co-workers Lauren's despair seemed extreme. True, she had been jilted by John, a significant blow to any woman. But Lauren's reaction was extreme. She realized it finally, recognizing in herself the classic symptoms of depression: loss of appetite, insomnia, a sense of estrangement from oneself and from the world.

John had been the catalyst, that weightiest of last straws, but her despair was cumulative, a lifetime of failure, of running away. Dr. Lauren Smith knew something else as well, a wise insight despite her sleep-starved brain: I must get a grip—I *will*.

While John and Stephanie were luxuriating on the white sands of the Hawaiian Islands, she would be in her condominium on Queen Anne Hill, confronting her past. The past was there in the tightly sealed boxes that had traveled with her from place to place. She would open those ancient boxes, and she would face the tangible reminders of who she was—the serious sister, the responsible one; a failure socially, with men, but professionally a superstar, a shadow-gazer extraordinaire.

Aloha, big sister, Dinah had enthused into the

netherworld of voice mail. Aloha: in Hawaiian it meant hello *and* good-bye.

Aloha, John. Good riddance. Good-bye. And aloha, Lauren. Hello. *Hello.*

By the end of the week she would be Lauren again—capable, competent, cheerful, crisp. Aloha, little sister, she would greet when, at last, she returned Dinah's call. And although she wasn't in paradise, her voice would be as warm and breezy as a tropical zephyr. The relationship with the hunk had faltered, she would confess. But it was *fine,* she would reassure, of no consequence at all. She was busy, happy, reading shadows.

Lauren was in the third day of her self-imposed journey into the past. It was a sluggish journey, a slow-motion pantomime of frail limbs through weighted air. Finally, only one box remained—*that* box, the one most tightly sealed and sealed the longest.

The contents of the other cartons lay on the floor, fully exposed, but not yet triaged. Letters, photographs, matchbooks, and ticket stubs surrounded her in tidy stacks—discreet, precise, compulsively assembled bundles: meticulous proof of her depression.

I'm really in trouble, Lauren realized. The vague awareness was sharply embellished by the physician within. *Get help,* that doctor warned. Get help now.

But the shadow woman resisted the urgent command. She would handle this on her own, as always. She was Lauren, the pillar upon whom others leaned, and who never swayed herself. It was her fault, her failure, that John's rejection was effecting her so. She'd been jilted—so what else was new?

She, and she alone, was responsible for digging her-self out of the emotional hole.

Fine, the physician acquiesced. Dig yourself out. But not here. These oh-so-neat piles of memories have buried you even deeper. Before journeying even further, even deeper, you must spend a little time in neutral territory, a place with no memories at all. Go away for a few days, just long enough to become Lauren again. It will be so easy upon your return to dispense with these fastidiously ordered little stacks.

The Pacific Northwest afforded myriad pic-turesque destinations. The most familiar ones, how-ever, were already tainted by failure, by John—places they had been, or planned to go. Lauren needed a spot that was hers only, where she could be alone, without taunting memories, past or future.

Rhododendron Manor. The name danced with amaz-ing lightness, twirling defiantly amid her dispirited gloom. Lauren had learned of the lakeside lodge from radio ads—enticing invitations to elegance and tranquility, to paradise, Northwest style.

Aloha, Lauren. *Aloha.*

Rhododendron Manor was located on the shores of Lake Hoquiam on the Olympic Peninsula, a three-hour drive. In just those few short hours she could see for herself the towering evergreens, ma-jestic monarchs of the rain forest. She could listen to the cheerful chatter of silvery waterfalls and inhale the fragrance of cedar and roses.

Eagles soared overhead, the radio ads promised, and there were deer, hundreds of them, frolick-ing fawns with their ever-vigilant parents. And the Manor itself? Rustic elegance, the radio proclaimed—

five-star luxury within hand-hewn cedar walls. The spacious guest rooms, most of which were suites, offered breathtaking vistas of lake, of forest, of the bountiful gardens for which the estate was named.

The rhododendron collection, one of the most extensive on earth, was reason enough to visit the manor. But there were other blossoms, too—azaleas, lilacs, camellias, roses. The gardens were abloom, ablaze with color, and the June air was an intoxication of floral perfumes.

Come, the radio voice urged. *Come see the flowers.*

The radio ads ran frequently throughout the night, Lauren knew, for it was during her hours of wakefulness that she reached for the companionship of the radio, a respite from her nocturnal solitude. Was Rhododendron Manor a refuge for fellow insomniacs, lonely depressives such as she? Or was it a glittering retreat for the ultrasuccessful, those with such energy, such enthusiasm, that they slept only grudgingly—why waste any precious moments of life?—awakening long before dawn to greet the newborn day?

She would find out. Even now her fingers were dialing the 800 number, which, after all these months of listening, was etched in her mind.

This June day was not yet fully born. But the receptionist at Rhododendron Manor, Gertrude, sounded wide awake, then surprised, then somewhat apologetic. One did not, apparently, call for same-day reservations at the lodge, even on a Monday. As it happened, though, Lauren was in luck, sort of.

There was one vacancy. A small room, Gertrude

warned, the back bedroom of a lakefront suite, specifically designed for a child. The bed was a twin, and the outside door, which was rarely used, opened to forest not to lake, and the bedroom's only window was both meager and opaque, purposefully fashioned to enable young guests to take undistracted naps.

Lauren was welcome to the modest room if she wanted it.

Yes, she said—a calm assertion silently embellished by a somewhat urgent *please*. It suddenly seemed necessary, essential really, that she journey to the Manor. A few days in a springtime garden would leave her feeling refreshed, restored.

On her return she would summarily dispense with the mementos she should not keep, and display the ones she should. It was time, after almost a year in the condo, to personalize her home. Perhaps there were knickknacks for sale at the elegant lodge, framed watercolors of rhododendron blossoms, or an appealing assortment of ceramics—trivets, vases, mugs emblazoned with lilacs and roses.

As Lauren imagined her home bright with floral souvenirs, she felt a faint but real frisson of hope. She loved flowers. She always had. They seemed so courageous, fragile yet bold. In the bitter cold climates where she had lived, the delicate blooms spent most of their lives in hiding. But they endured the harsh winters—endured and then flourished, blossoming with joy as their delicate petals smiled toward the sun.

Come see the flowers, the radio urged.

Leave right now, her own inner voice, that sage M.D., advised.

Lauren ignored the wise counsel. There was that final box, and it had to be opened before she left, its contents compulsively placed in their own small yet monumental stacks.

Lauren had filled the box—compulsively, methodically—years ago, before she left for college. For a long time the carton had lived, a sealed coffin of childhood, in her family home. But when that house became another family's home, the box became hers, a silent yet constant companion.

Now, after all this time, she was going to open it, was opening it . . .

She had forgotten about the photographs. There were so many, brilliant images that had faded from her mind, portraits of happy times so shadowed in her memory that even the gifted reader of shadows could not see the joy in the veiled depths.

But here were her sisters, mercifully younger than she, too young to really know; and her father, so much in love he was blind to the truth; and her mother, smiling, seeming to smile, with love, with wonder at her daughters.

Most of the photographs were within albums, lovingly displayed. Lovingly? Lauren wondered, or merely meticulously, by fingers as slow, as weighted as her own?

One batch of photographs, that final batch, never found a home within the albums. The roll had been developed months after that life-shattering Christmas Eve, and even now those poses remained within their bright yellow envelope.

Don't look at them now, the inner voice warned. *Don't even begin to open the envelope—*

But she couldn't help it. She had to see that final photograph of her mother. *Had to.* And when she did, Lauren saw her mother's image as never before—the lips curved in a smile that was laden, weighted, false; and the dark blue eyes, so like Lauren's own, sunken, haunted . . . and then suddenly alive, intense, staring at Lauren, daring her.

Daring her.

Lauren put the photograph on the floor, apart from all the others. This image of her mother, this image of herself, was a monumental hurdle unto itself, an immense mountain to be faced upon her return.

The carton was almost empty. Her girlhood diaries remained, earnest pages of youthful optimism with wildflowers pressed in between—a girl's attempt to preserve the blossoms forever . . . before she learned such perishable fragility could not be saved. Beneath the diaries lay the carved wooden box, and within, loaded still, *loaded still,* was the gun.

All right, that's it, that's all, the carton is empty. Leave the gun right there in its purple satin nest, and drive like the wind toward the flowers.

Do not, *do not,* put the gun in your suitcase. You're leaving your memories behind, remember? It must be you, just you, who wanders in the gardens beside the lake.

Just you, just Lauren.

But this gun, this Lady Smith, *is* me—my heart, my soul, my very life.

Chapter Two

~

Peter Cain was a restless man, always. His smoldering impatience was a positive force, a powerful one, a fierceness that propelled him to stratospheric success. Peter welcomed his brooding restlessness, surrendered willingly to the relentless mandate that he confront and master every challenge.

At the moment both the man and his restlessness were trapped, caged, and it was driving him crazy. Admittedly, being confined to the place on earth he loved above all others made the imprisonment as palatable as possible. But Peter was unaccustomed to constraint on his freedom, to constraint of any kind.

He had, of course, agreed to his present confinement—in fact, he had suggested it. And Peter's solemn word bound him more tightly than the heaviest of chains.

He was being a good citizen, a soldier for justice. It was a worthy endeavor—assuming the menace for which, *for whom*, he was waiting with such patient impatience was going to appear. With each passing day, the likelihood seemed increasingly remote.

Given the passage of time, perhaps the territory in which he roamed could be expanded—to the whole planet, ideally, especially its most lofty, lethal peaks. Even an occasional furlough to Seattle would be welcome, house arrest in the Emerald City, a tether that would allow him to wander from his penthouse overlooking the sound to his corporate offices on Fifth Avenue to the yacht club at Yarrow Bay.

Such expansion would not happen, nor would Peter suggest that it should. If, in fact, he *was* the seductress's next victim, Rhododendron Manor was the perfect place in which to seduce her. The estate was entirely contained—one road in, one road out. And given that everyone in his employ, both here and in town, had been *re*trained to reveal his whereabouts, no questions asked, there was no doubt that the usually reclusive—at least elusive—billionaire could be effortlessly found.

So come on, lady, whoever you are. Come and get me. *Now.*

The woods are lovely, dark, and deep.
Lauren's heart ached at the familiar verse, her mother's favorite, and as she walked ever deeper into the forest, she ignored the ominous quivers within. She should be wandering in the gardens, amid the brave blossoms, not journeying amid the shadowed pines.

But the woods beckoned, taunted. Indeed, perhaps it had been the promise of the woods—not of the flowers—that had lured her to Rhododendron Manor. The promise, the peril, the pain—Lauren felt all three as she surrendered to the emerald enchantment. She could remain here forever, embraced by the grandeur, intoxicated by the scents.

Here . . . where she felt so small, so insignificant, so safe.

But I have promises to keep.

And miles to go before I sleep.

Her mother had forsaken her promises, had chosen the lovely comfort of eternal sleep in the forest's leafy cradle. And now Lauren had the same choice. The gun, *the same gun,* was in her hand, and the wind fluttering through the pines was a most gentle serenade, a lullaby of peace, and Lauren *should* be permitted to sleep, for unlike her mother, Lauren had kept her promises.

You'll take good care of your sisters, won't you? her mother had asked on that Christmas Eve when she walked into the woods. And Daddy, too?

Yes, Lauren promised, as she always did. Her mother's request was familiar, a refrain that made Lauren feel needed, trusted—and which bound her in a special, private way to the mother she adored.

There was nothing alarming in the familiar question on that life-shattering day. But fourteen-year-old Lauren would wonder forever if there were clues she would have seen had she not been blinded by her own neediness, her fervent wish to be worthy of her mother's trust.

Lauren *had* taken care of her baby sisters, as promised, and of her father. Now the "girls" were fully grown, independent and strong, and her father had died two years ago, and . . . Lauren had kept her promises.

Now she could sleep.

She stared at the gun. Small, crafted for a lady, the weapon was oddly beautiful. Its pearl handle shimmered like a rainbow, its gleaming steel a shining mirror.

Lauren saw a face in that steel-bright mirror—her mother's face, *her* face.

The woods are lovely, dark, and deep.

Was that beloved verse dancing in her mother's mind when she pulled the trigger? Did she pull it urgently, unwilling to hear the rest, the reminder of promises? And was her private torment so unbearable that her daughter's heart was a small, and acceptable, sacrifice?

Or, in the end, had it been merely an impulse, whimsical yet irrevocable, urged by the embracing whispers of evergreens and the soft sighs of ferns?

Was she truly her mother's daughter? That was the question, *the* question, from which Lauren had been running for so long, and which now she must confront.

It was, she realized, the reason she was here. Suddenly, it all made perfect sense, at least to Lauren's sleep-starved mind.

This was the reason John had jilted her, evoking a despondency so extreme she could not sleep, and so desolate she turned to the radio for solace. Lauren had believed she was lured to the Manor by the promise of flowers. But that was wrong. The specter of the blossoms was merely a ruse.

She had come because of the woods. And her

room, the only vacancy in the lodge, was a conspirator, for it opened not to the gardens but to the forest, a dense wall of fragrant emerald through which she discovered a satiny ribbon of trail.

Her journey had brought her here, to this dark spot in the deep and lovely woods. Alone, *alone*, except for the peace of the forest . . . and the lethal weapon in her hand.

Is this my destiny? To be my mother's daughter in this most final and solitary way? Does it all end here . . . or is this where, at last, I truly begin to live?

The answer was in these woods, in the whispers of the towering pines. The mammoth evergreens were whispering to her now, so softly she could not hear their words. In time the chorus would grow louder, its song pure and clear. She would wait. She had to. And whatever the answer, whatever the verdict of the whispering trees, she would comply. . . .

"Hello." The voice was dark and deep, like the woods, and rich with lovely, astonishing, concern.

Lauren looked from the gleaming steel of her mother's gun to eyes the color of the forest—gleaming, too, and glinting with inner steel as they focused intently on her.

"Target practice?" he asked.

The wood nymph who had been startled to near paralysis by the appearance of a human in her leafy sanctuary managed a breathless reply. "What? Oh, no, I . . . No."

Because you don't need practice, Peter realized with a jolt. Because you *would not* miss. You would press the barrel against your temple with such fierce resolve that the missile would find its mark, straight, lethal, true.

Peter felt his own rush of fierceness, savage and intense. He wanted to protect her from the terrifying mandates of her despair. The urge was powerful and extraordinary. Such ferocious protectiveness was usually reserved for himself, for his privacy, his freedom.

The extraordinary urge to protect was swamped by other emotions as Peter gazed at the fragile vision amid the lacy ferns. Was she here at last, the lethal seductress who had kept him waiting, churning and restless, for so long? Had she chosen this particular guise, this heart-stopping distress, because she knew it was the only way to enchant the man who could not be enchanted?

If so, it was a truth that—until this moment—had been concealed even from him.

"Who are you?" he demanded.

Lauren did not answer at once, could not, for she was truly seeing him now, this man who had startled her.

He was like the woods to which she had journeyed for answers, for sanctuary, for peace. Powerful, majestic, possessed of secret wisdom, yet unreadable, impassive . . . except that now, as she remained silent, something deep and fearsome flickered in the molten depths of his dark green eyes.

Impatience—with her.

"Lauren," she murmured. "My name is Lauren."

Peter *was* impatient—now, still—and she was the cause.

Was she the sinister temptress? If so, she was

clever in the extreme. Not only had the crafty clairvoyant envisioned a secret passageway to his heart, she had made him wait, tormented him with the waiting.

She had needed some time, of course, in which to perfect her disguise—to become so thin she seemed more gossamer than real; and to deprive herself of so much sleep that her blue eyes became haloed by blackness; and to surround her entire being with an aura so haunted it appeared authentic even to him, the most skeptical of critics.

Finally, the *pièce de résistance*, the gifted actress had rehearsed this rendezvous in the woods, a dazzling performance that went far beyond surprise . . . for she stared at him with an apprehension so stark that, had he not known better, he would have believed she never intended that he find her, much less rescue her . . . as if the notion of his intervention was as horrific as her imaginary despair.

"Lauren who?" he pressed.

"Smith."

So compelling was she, so haunted and so wary, that she was beginning to convince even him. *And I need to pretend to* be *convinced*, Peter reminded himself. *I need to be as convincing as she.*

Peter banished the sharpness from his voice. "Well, Lauren, I'm Peter, and I need to take your gun. You can't wander in a forest, at least not in this forest"—*not in my forest*—"with a gun. The danger is simply too great, not only for you—"

"For me?"

"For you," Peter repeated. *The danger seems so great for you.* "You could stumble, the gun could fire, you might not be found in time. And there are hikers who enjoy the safe haven of these woods, as well as the creatures who live here."

"But I would never shoot anyone, or any*thing*."

"Accidents happen, Lauren. Tragic accidents, all the time. I'm afraid I'll have to confiscate your weapon."

"*No.* I mean, you can't."

"Actually, I can."

Lauren did not doubt the assertion. This black-haired, green-eyed stranger seemed a force of nature unto himself. His attire, however—well-worn denim, unadorned with emblems of any kind—was hardly a uniform, and his only weapon was the glinting steel of his unyielding gaze.

Still, his authority seemed absolute.

"You're a . . . ranger?"

"Something like that."

"The gun is a family heirloom."

"I'll guard it with my life. I promise. It will be locked in the safe at the lodge and will be returned to you when you leave."

But I need the gun, don't you see? I need to know if it's my destiny to sleep forever in these dark and lovely woods. I was so close to learning the answer. The whispers were becoming louder, and I was beginning to feel such hope, such peace.

Such hope, such peace . . . because the whispering pines were going to mandate that she pull the trigger, as her mother had—an end to all pain? Or were the wondrous feelings something else entirely, a quiet joy that even she, even Lauren, could begin again?

She didn't know. The whispers had been silenced

by his deep, dark voice. And now this man, this *man*, was presuming to give her the answer—you are not your mother—by demanding that she give him the gun.

Fine, she thought. I'll leave the Manor this instant, and the gun and I will find another leafy sanctuary, more private than this.

But Lauren believed in the whispers of *these* trees, and she wanted to stroll in the gardens. Seeing the flowers seemed so important now, and . . .

"Lauren, may I have the gun?" Peter heard the astonishing softness in his voice and felt the gentleness within. Gentleness, and worry, for he had just borne witness to a storm of sheer anguish on her pale, ravaged face. A bravura performance, he reminded himself, for which he should feel only disdain. But Peter Cain's voice had a will of its own. Gently, *even more gently*, he added, "Please."

Her answering shrug was a battle of thin shoulders against an immense, invisible heaviness. "I guess I don't have a choice."

"I guess not."

The weapon came to him as a weapon should, pearl handle first, a safe, expert transfer of death. Her delicate fingers, as cold as death, curled around the barrel, leaving perfect prints on the gleaming steel.

The prints were all that Peter needed, a criminologist's dream. So why, as he held the lady's pistol, did Peter embrace the lethal weapon as he wanted to embrace her, so ferociously protective that his steel-and-pearl caress destroyed every usable print?

"Why don't I escort you back to the lodge? The

woods can be confusing. The shadows play tricks, especially at twilight."

"I'm sure I can find my way." *My specialty, my only gift, is reading shadows . . . and maybe that's what the whispering trees were trying to tell me. That it's too soon to sleep forever. That I have promises to keep—to my patients.* "You probably need to finish your rounds."

"Rounds," Peter echoed. "That's a doctor term."

"I used to work in a hospital."

"And now?"

"I'm a gardener."

Lauren shrugged anew. But the gesture seemed less weighted, Peter thought, as if, without the gun, life was easier. *Of course it was easier—for she was succeeding brilliantly. He had captured her gun, and she had captured his attention.*

Peter searched for evidence of her triumph, the slightest curve of her lips, the faintest glimmer of satisfaction in her sapphire eyes. But he saw only apprehension, and the eagerness to flee—to leave him churning and restless . . . again.

"Well, I'd better go." A final politeness delayed her escape. "Thank you."

Then she was gone, a frightened fawn disappearing into the greenery, a near silent departure of ethereal grace.

Chapter Three

~

Peter removed from a locked file cabinet the confidential LAPD report. Written by Lieutenant Jack Shannon, it summarized the account given to LA's premier homicide detective by one of Beverly Hills's preeminent psychotherapists, a counseling session so alarming the therapist could not remain silent.

"Duty to warn," the mandate was called, a legal loophole that permitted those sworn to uphold the Hippocratic oath to violate the otherwise sacrosanct tenet of patient-physician confidentiality. When another life was in jeopardy, for example when a husband revealed his intent to murder his wife, it was not only permissible but *required* that the physician notify both the potential victim and the appropriate law-enforcement authority.

Which is why the psychotherapist came forward.

Her patient claimed to be a black widow, a woman who married well and murdered even better. She had killed four husbands to date, she said, an enterprise so simple it had become boring.

She murdered on her wedding night, within hours of becoming her rich, and elderly, husband's principal beneficiary. Her weapon was poison, a few drops sprinkled into a flute of champagne. The self-proclaimed killer declined to share with the therapist the precise identity of the poison, but she attributed its discovery to the wonders of cyberspace.

My very own World Wide Web, the elegant spider quipped. She crawled the net in blessed anonymity, lurking and learning as she journeyed from Websites for mystery buffs to those frequented by chemists, criminologists, and aficionados of all things morbid.

The black widow expressed deep admiration for the knowledge of her unwitting coconspirators, and praised as well the most appealing features of the poison they provided her: its colorless clarity, like a flawless diamond; the rapidity with which it caused death; its subsequent detection *only* if one was looking for it, which, of course, no one ever was.

In each instance, the local coroner had made a postmortem diagnosis of cardiac arrest—ventricular tachycardia followed by V fib, precipitated by too much champagne, too little sleep, and the adrenaline rush of being married to a young and beautiful wife.

The first three deaths had been witnessed only by her, in the nuptial privacy of luxurious bridal suites. To make life more interesting, to add even a whisper of risk, she decided to murder husband number four at the wedding reception itself. The five-tiered cake had been cut, and the bride and groom had danced the first dance, and while her octogenarian husband was chatting with his Main Line children, she dropped a few drops of poison into his champagne. It was proof of her great restraint, she told the therapist, that she didn't splash a few lethal drops in the children's honey gold bubbly as well.

Husbands one through four were old, and of old wealth, prominent within their rarefied circles but without far-reaching fame. Since her technique was perfected, and since elderly prey were a bore, husband number five would be young, vital, famous. And why not? she asked rhetorically as she reclined on the therapist's butter-soft couch. She *deserved* a reward, and the man she had in mind definitely qualified: gorgeous, devastatingly male, breathtakingly rich, and wedded to his bachelorhood.

Well, she purred contentedly, she would change his views on matrimony. And if you can't? the therapist queried. The patient frowned briefly, then smiled. It wasn't as though she *needed* his millions. But, with a pout, she remarked that she would be disappointed if deprived of the ultimate challenge— his death on their wedding night.

It would have to be more clever than the others. Any coroner worth his salt would not be so sanguine about a man of his age, and in his shape, succumbing to an arrhythmia, no matter how provocative the bride or terrific the sex. If cocaine was involved, however ... she smiled at the thought. *That* would be the greatest challenge of all, persuading this man to willingly taint his magnificent body with the illicit snowy powder.

All in all, she concluded, it would be easier if he wouldn't marry her. She could seduce him, enjoy him, and present him with a poisoned bottle of champagne as she left.

Him. Other than vague allusions to his looks, his virility, his bank account, and his aversion to marriage, the murderess provided few clues to the identity of her next victim. "A gardener who reached lofty heights," she said. And, something the therapist had forgotten until Jack Shannon teased it out of her, there had been a petulant remark about potential "coiffure chaos."

Veronique duBois had visited the therapist only once. She paid in cash, and her grand name, as well as her grand address on Bellagio in Bel Air, belonged to someone else. She wore Dior; and her jewels, the therapist decided, were quite real. Her hair color, by contrast, probably came from a Rodeo Drive salon. The tint was impeccable, an elaborate auburn laced with gold. But, the therapist thought, her natural color was quite dark. Her makeup was as impeccable as her dyed hair, and as elaborate. But she would be quite beautiful, quite striking, scrubbed bare; and without the green-tinted contact lenses, her eyes would be blue.

She was always in disguise, the murderess confessed. She *had* to be. But the masquerade was also part of her artistry. She made a study of the man she wanted, then became precisely the woman he wanted, his ideal courtesan.

Apology laced the therapist's voice as she recounted the session to Lieutenant Shannon. She had no qualms about her professional obligations. But this was Tinseltown, where facade and fiction reigned supreme. Veronique duBois might have been an actress, researching an upcoming made-for-TV role. In fact, she probably was.

Yet her utter absence of morality was so compelling, her sociopathy so convincing, that the therapist could not dismiss the encounter as a Hollywood prank. Either the woman had brilliantly mastered, or she truly possessed, the logic system of a human being without conscience, a scheme abhorrent to society at large, but which made perfect sense to a mind focused solely on itself.

Jack Shannon neither dismissed nor embraced the story. But he pursued it logically, and aggressively, beginning with an immediate attempt to get the mystery woman's prints. The auburn beauty had, the therapist recalled, longingly fingered the statue of Oscar, a gift from an Academy Award–winning client who had forsaken all glittering trophies in exchange for untarnished self-esteem.

The golden statue, the name of its recipient removed, was a favorite touchstone for many patrons of the therapist's plush office. But Jack Shannon was able to find an exact match to one of the sets. The allusion to Main Line children was the key. Main Line meant Philadelphia. Six months earlier, at the refurbished Bellevue Stratford, a multimillionaire patriarch had died at his own wedding reception.

The children had not suspected their father's young bride of foul play, only of transcendent greed. She had disappeared shortly after the funeral with their father's millions. The man's other heirs all lived in homes where daily dusting was de rigueur. However, his youngest daughter recalled that her future stepmother had feigned interest in a family photo album. On a sheet of plastic over a shot of the family villa in Cannes were preserved fingerprints identical to those curled covetously around the therapist's Oscar. And the bridegroom's exhumed body, when subjected to an array of tests, disclosed sky-high levels of a rare and lethal poison.

Jack Shannon's sworn duty to warn, yet not to alarm, required that he notify potential victims as soon as they were identified. Any number of onetime gardeners had achieved lofty heights. Jack spoke with them all. But the gardener who had, quite literally, scaled the planet's tallest peaks and whose home was the rain-renowned Pacific Northwest—certainly a culprit in coiffure chaos—was the one Jack notified first, and face-to-face.

Their meeting predated by weeks the post-mortem discovery of poison, the unequivocal proof of murder. At that point the homicide lieutenant had only the matching fingerprints and a hearsay story, which meant that—at that point—Peter's role would be fraught with peril. The black widow needed to be caught in flagrante delicto, so to speak, *after* she poisoned his champagne and *before* he took so much as a sip.

Jack would be nearby, of course, as would an army of undercover police. But the risk, the danger, the delicate balance between life and death would be entirely in Peter's control. Peter loved such moments on the edge. He thrived on them, physically, intellectually, at work, at play.

The physical challenge presented by Jack Shannon was as rigorous as it could get—life itself. And as for the intellectual one? It was almost as daunting—for the man who could not be seduced would have to become an actor in his own right, pretending to be wholly enthralled, hopelessly charmed.

Whatever drama might have unfolded was preempted entirely by the detection of poison in the hapless husband's lifeless tissues. The police had all the proof they needed for at least one count of murder one, and computers were whirring throughout the country, searching for other wealthy elderly men whose wedding and death certificates were issued in rapid sequence.

Although Peter remained the bait, his role was safe now, without risk, without challenge—a total bore. All he had to do was snare a set of her prints. The police would move in, and he would be free.

Assuming the murderess had indeed chosen him as her next victim, Peter imagined that the damning fingerprints would be captured on a crystal champagne flute, not a pearl-handled gun.

And now? Now Peter's frown glided from Jack Shannon's police report to the gun he had commandeered. It was a vintage Lady Smith, a collector's item, and possibly one of the first ever made. And she, the lady of the woods, called herself Lauren Smith. The name was bland compared to Veronique duBois, uninspired compared to Alexandra Chastain, the lethal Philadelphia bride.

Lauren Smith. Lady Smith. The black widow who had made him wait all this time? Or the phantom woman for whom he had been waiting, restless and churning, all his life?

Superficially, Lauren Smith conformed to what the Beverly Hills psychotherapist had described:

dark hair, blue eyes, and striking, captivating, without any makeup at all.

But where was the confidence of a sociopath—the abiding certainty that things were going to work out her way?

Peter had expected supreme confidence, the arrogance of madness. But this lady—*his* lady—was vulnerable, fragile, enchanting, *and a liar.*

Her lies, at first, had been magnificent—her startled surprise when he appeared in the woods; her unadorned candor when she spoke her unglamorous and improbable name; and her sheer innocence as she pretended not to know who he was.

Peter's assumption that she should recognize him was not an arrogant one. It was simply fact. The woman who, according to the information she had provided on registering, had lived in Seattle for almost a year would certainly have heard of him—and his stunningly successful assault of K-2.

Despite a sudden snowstorm Peter Cain had brought his entire party back alive, with only the faintest nips of frostbite, an accomplishment deemed so heroic by his fellow climbers that in their triumphant euphoria they had talked and talked and talked to the media. About him.

The *Seattle Times* featured the gardener-turned-entrepreneur on its business pages, in its travel section, and, one Sunday, devoted its weekly magazine entirely to Rhododendron Manor, his once-private estate that was now a gift of floral splendor to all who chose to visit.

The national press had similarly gone wild. *Fortune* did a cover story on the Pacific Northwest's latest self-made billionaire, and *People* proclaimed him one of the year's fifty most intriguing people. The magazine's mailbag bulged to overflowing following that issue. His photograph, taken by a fellow climber surely put him in contention—the absurdity of it made him laugh—for sexiest man alive.

Peter was not a participant in the publicity frenzy. Quite the opposite. He made a point of being out of the country. Indeed, it was a fluke that he happened to be in the States when Jack Shannon called, and then appeared to discuss the specter of the black widow.

If, indeed, Peter was the killer's intended victim, the media frenzy had come full circle. The murderess would not have known about him any other way. No one would have. Until the storm-ravaged assault of the Himalayan peak, Peter had managed to make his fortune, climb Mount Everest twice, and open to the public his elegant retreat with blessed anonymity.

But Peter Cain was anonymous no more, which meant that—unless his lady of the woods had spent the past year scaling faraway heights or dwelling in a shadowy cave—she had to know precisely who he was; and that the woods, which he insisted were to be weapon-free, belonged to him.

So her feigned innocence—"You're a . . . ranger?"—was a lie. And yet it was so magnificent that he had almost become a true believer, had almost decided it was sheer happenstance, glorious destiny, that she had journeyed on a trail known only to him and the deer: the slender ribbon amid the

ferns that was his favorite route from his penthouse suite in the lodge to the remote cabin that he
preferred.

Then came the truly glaring lie. It was a startling
falter for someone as expert as she—an actress whose
performance to that point had been quite flawless.

I'm a gardener, she had said. Her long, dark
lashes had fluttered as she spoke, delicate fans that
told the tale of her deceit.

She was a mirage, a fantasy created just for him,
his perfect courtesan, here at last.

And now all he needed to do, what he should do,
was call Jack Shannon. A private jet would have
the homicide lieutenant—and his team—here within
hours, and Peter could invite Lauren to midnight
supper in the Orchid Room. It didn't matter that he
had wiped the Lady Smith clean of prints because
there would be plenty more for Lieutenant Shannon's experts to peruse while Peter and Lauren
danced in the Camellia Lounge.

By two A.M. it would be all over. The black widow
would be in handcuffs, and one of the many assembled police officers would be placing a hand on
her head to guide her into the squad car, and Peter
would be free, caged no more.

Which was what he wanted, had wanted. And
now? Now he wanted her to be Lauren Smith, gardener from Seattle, who honestly didn't know who
he was, and who just happened upon his special
place in the woods, and whose gun *was* a family
heirloom, and whose thank-you came from a lovely,
wounded heart.

Peter wanted to know all about *that* Lauren Smith,

what haunted her, what could make her smile, what she was thinking when he found her, *where she gets her poison.*

The thought came with the fearsome power of an unforeseen storm. Peter felt the chill, weathered it, and a wry smile touched his face.

Call Lieutenant Shannon? Vanquish the challenge? Annihilate the risk?

Not a chance. Not before he learned everything he wanted to know about the lady of the woods—not before the two of them had slow-danced the dance of death . . . or waltzed the most wondrous dance of all.

Peter smiled as he dialed the five-digit extension to her room.

She answered on the second ring, an enchanting, uncertain *Hello.*

His smile faded. His jaw muscles rippled. "Lauren, it's Peter."

"Oh. Peter. Hello."

"Hello. I wanted you to know that your gun is safe." *Quite safe, wiped clean of all prints. But you, Lady Smith, you are not safe in the least.*

"Thank you."

"Sure. I also wondered if you'd like me to give you a tour of the gardens."

"Oh, well, I . . ."

"Tomorrow afternoon? About one?" Peter had work to do, an empire to run, overseas calls to make, E-mail to answer, an article he had promised to review. The article was a priority. It wasn't about him, but about the climb itself, how his team had survived, how other climbers could survive in similar circumstances. Peter liked everything about

the article, including the privacy of his own partici-
pation. He and the freelance journalist had commu-
nicated politely, efficiently, electronically. Now all
that Mike Gregory needed was his final approval,
which Peter would E-mail in the morning. Those
were the business reasons Peter couldn't meet with
Lauren until early afternoon. Then there was that
other reason, the one that should not have mattered, but seemed to matter most of all: the dark
black halos around her dark blue eyes. "How does
that sound?"

How did it sound to stroll amid the flowers with
Peter—the fierce and gentle force of nature? *Terrifying . . . wonderful.*

"Fine," she murmured. "One o'clock would be
fine."

Chapter Four

～

She was in the woods, and the trees were scream-ing, *Pull the trigger! Do it, do it, do it!*

And she was defying the impassioned screams. I won't. It's wrong. Please don't make me do this.

Then John appeared, as towering as the pines, and glowering, as he joined the deafening chorus that was commanding her to die.

This will prove your softness, John assured. Every-one will be surprised, impressed, that you're not made of ice after all. How *human* Lauren was, they will say. She had a heart, just like everyone else. *Do it, Lauren. Pull the trigger. Do it now.*

"No!" The scream was her own, a protest of such despair that it awakened her.

No. No. No. The mantra kept pace with her thun-dering heart, gaining strength with each racing beat—strength and determination and a feeling that felt oddly like joy.

No, I am not going to kill myself.

No, I never would, never could, no matter how I hurt, how lonely I feel.

No, I am not my mother.

When I hurt, when I ache, I need only to get outside myself, to marvel at the gifts of life, of living: the grandeur of starshine, the wonder of rose bloom, the splendor of my sisters.

You should have marveled at us, Mother. You should have treasured your daughters. We needed you so much.

At this midnight moment, in sheer darkness and awakened from frightening dreams, Lauren was choosing life. Was this, then, the answer? A bold assertion not from the whispers of trees, but from something deep within? Or was this boldness merely bravado—a necessary, yet fragile, antidote to the nightmare's terror?

I need to know. I must. *Now.*

She wore her nightgown still, and her feet were quite bare, and there were the darkest of shadows on this moonless night. But the shadow woman read the impenetrable darkness, saw the ribbon of trail as if it were glowing green satin.

Then she was there, in that place, *that place,* standing in the blackness beneath the towering trees, listening, listening . . . and when at last she heard the joyous whispers—choose life, choose life!—the chill night air turned balmy, the darkness bright.

I am not my mother, and this is where I truly begin. Tomorrow, tomorrow I will see the flowers . . . with Peter.

A cobalt sky shone above the indigo lake, and sun-caressed pines swayed emerald and gold. And between lake and forest were the gardens, a vast, bright, fragrant bouquet.

And there was Peter, waiting for her, ungentled by the sun's golden kiss, compelling, powerful, and still—save for the wind in his midnight black hair and the smoldering fire in his forest green eyes.

In sunlight, as at twilight, Lauren sensed that he wanted something from her—something terrifying . . . and wonderful.

But I have nothing to give you, Peter. Nothing you could possibly want. I am just born, you see, a shadow woman who this very day, this very moment, is beginning to journey from behind a murky shroud.

"Beautiful day," she murmured to the intense green eyes that wanted so much. Too much.

Beautiful woman, Peter thought. The dark circles beneath her eyes were a shade less exhausted, and something quite amazing trembled on her thin face—the delicate bud of a lovely smile.

Too quickly, the gentle curving shattered, devastated by a worried frown.

"I have a confession to make."

"Oh?"

"I'm not really a gardener."

"No?" *And you're not a murderess, either, are you? You can't be.* The silent query came unbidden, but quite welcome, as did the confident reply. The conclusion was precipitous, Peter knew, and, therefore, extremely foolish. So, he mused, he was facing a mutiny from deep within. It was a surprising mutiny, given the dispassionate logic, the rational calm, for which—from boardrooms to granite cliffs— Peter Cain was known. But the passionate rebellion was fine. Another challenge. Peter smiled. "What then, if not a gardener?"

"Someone who would *like* to be a gardener."

"A worthy ambition," Peter asserted softly. "Tell me why."

"Oh," she murmured, barely, momentarily ambushed by the softness of his voice. "Well . . . I suppose flowers have always seemed magical to me. I remember, as a girl, watching a neighbor planting bulbs. She was painting a picture, she said. The finished tableau wouldn't appear until spring, but she knew exactly how it would look, what color and fragrance and shape each of the bulbs would become."

"And she was right."

Lauren shrugged. "I've always imagined that she was. But I don't know. We moved to another neighborhood that winter."

"Haven't you ever planted your own garden?"

"No."

"Because?"

"I guess because I've always moved." *Beginning that winter, after our mother walked into the woods to sleep forever.* She had kept moving after that, kept running, as if the delicate roots that were Lauren would never survive being planted in one place. But now she had vowed to stop running, to appreciate the wonders of sisters, of starshine, of flowers. "So . . . these are the rhododendrons?"

"These are the rhododendrons," Peter affirmed, mesmerized by the palette of emotions, from stark hopelessness to defiant resolve. He wanted to know every tumultuous thought. But not now, not when the storm had passed, was in the past, and her sapphire eyes shimmered with hope. "This is Anna Rose Whitney."

"Anna Rose Whitney? They have names?"

"Sure. All flowers do. Anna, meet Lauren."

"Hello, Anna." Lauren extended a thin hand toward a deep pink cluster of blooms, but stopped just short of touching.

"It's perfectly all right to touch her. Anna's a very hardy sort."

Lauren's pale fingers caressed the pink velvet. "She seems happy here."

"She is. She thrives on the misting climate, as many rhodys do. It's in their genetic makeup, from their roots, as it were, in the Himalayan wilderness."

"Himalayan?" The word conjured uneasy images to the physician within—altitudes far higher than human beings were meant to endure, where one could suffocate from lack of oxygen and freeze from the bitter cold. "There are flowers—rhododendrons—in the Himalayas?"

"Absolutely. In fact, about two-thirds of the world's rhododendron species can be found in the misty valleys. There are forests of rhodys, hillsides of every imaginable color. Monkeys feast on their blossoms, birds guzzle their nectar, and bears hide in caves created by their foliage. The sight is truly breathtaking—rainbowed forests skirting the most treacherous mountains on earth."

"You've been there," Lauren whispered. "You've seen the rainbowed forests."

"Yes." *And you didn't know that, did you, Lauren Smith? You honestly don't know who I am.* The soaring thought came with a rush of desire. He wanted to take her to the Himalayas, not the death-defying peaks, but the forests of rainbows. *Her.* The clever murderess? No. This Lady Smith, *his* Lady Smith, was far more dangerous . . . an enchanting thief who was stealing his heart.

"Are there more Himalayan varieties in the gardens here?"

"Lots. Would you like to meet them?"

"Yes." *Every bold and brilliant bloom.* "Please."

They wandered the acres of rhodys, a leisurely sun-warmed stroll. Lauren felt as if she were at a festive garden party, a gala at which the guests, all save her, were glamorously dressed, haute couture of every imaginable shade and hue.

Peter was hosting the fragrant fête, and even in stone-washed denim he was utterly elegant, a sophisticate of grace, of power, of style—of glinting dark green eyes that told her she was the most honored guest of all.

At times Peter's forest green gaze was solemn, searching, and so fierce she had to look away—only to be compelled by something she could not name that commanded her to return. And when she did, he would smile, a slow, sexy, devastating smile, and he would introduce her to his glamorous, yet less important, guests. Mist Maiden and Windbeam. Jean-Marie de Montague. And Caroline, Cynthia, Purple Splendor, Pink Pearl.

Peter shared the floral pedigrees as well, and, because Lauren wished to be a gardener, he instructed her in their proper care.

"This is called dead-heading," he explained as, with strong and gentle hands, such talented hands, he pruned a cluster that was past its bloom. "You remove the spent flowers at the point where the brittle stem attaches to the main one. See?"

"Yes." Lauren frowned.

"What?"

"Dead flowers seem so sad, all that color, all that beauty, all that promise . . ."

"But the promise has been fulfilled, and will be renewed. In fact, if you look closely, you'll see there are already many new buds."

Babies, Lauren mused, daughters of the once bright blooms . . . daughters who, with proper nurturing, would have their day in the sun.

"If you don't want to do this, Lauren, you don't have to. No one dead-heads the rhodys of the Himalayas, and they bloom every year."

"But if I'm going to be a gardener . . ." Delicately, with great care not to damage the precious daughters, she removed a spent cluster from a spring-blooming varietal. "There. Did I do that correctly?"

"Perfectly."

Lauren smiled, tilted her head, and narrowed her intelligent blue eyes.

Peter laughed softly at the sudden scrutiny. "Yes?"

"You're really more gardener than ranger, aren't you? In fact, Peter, I do believe you're the head gardener."

It was an easy deduction. A small army was at work amid the blooms—an army, Lauren noted, whose enlisted personnel viewed Peter with all the respect of a five-star general.

"Guilty," Peter admitted.

"What a wonderful job."

"It is, and one with substantial perks, such as

meals from the Manor's gourmet kitchen. You must be famished."

"Oh, yes. I guess I am."

"You sound surprised. Did you have a big lunch? *Any* lunch?"

"I don't usually eat lunch."

"Or breakfast?"

"Or breakfast."

"Well, Lauren, gardeners must eat." *I must feed you.* "Follow me."

Chapter Five

~

"Another perk," Peter explained when they reached his rustic, yet luxurious, cliff-top cabin overlooking the lake.

The journey from the lodge to Peter's cabin had taken them past the place where he had first seen her, up and up the winding trail. Before beginning their heavenward trek, Peter had insisted they share one of the chef's famous Nanaimo bars. Carb-loading, he told her, essential quick energy for their rigorous climb.

Now, in the charming living room of his private retreat, Peter unpacked the contents of a wicker basket. He had carried the basket as if empty. But it was laden with food—high tea, Manor-style, elegant and nourishing.

"Eat," Peter commanded gently when the sumptuous banquet lay on the coffee table encircled by overstuffed chairs.

Lauren obeyed his command, sort of. Her thin fingers plucked a crustless wedge of cucumber sandwich from a mountain of delicacies. Peter arched a skeptical eyebrow at the meager serving she had taken, and was rewarded with a bountiful feast: amusement, aglow and sparkling in her bright blue eyes.

"Not enough?" she asked.

"Not nearly."

"Well," she murmured with amazement, "I really *am* hungry." *I am ravenous, for food, for life, for flowers . . . and for the way you are looking at me.*

"Good. You eat, and I'll talk—or not."

"I want you to talk."

"Then I'm all yours, Lauren. Ask me anything."

Anything. So many things. Why does it seem as if you can gaze into my soul, as if you want *to—and are untroubled by the shadows? And is that desire I see, desire for me, as if I were a woman of boundless passion? I feel like such a sensual creature when you look at me. I feel . . . alive.*

The thoughts swirled in Lauren's mind, a brief yet chaotic gust, which she summarily quelled. She was just born, newly awakened from a harsh winter that spanned decades. It was a wondrous awakening, and a precarious one. She needed to stay focused on her midnight vow to marvel at the treasures outside herself. Anything else, anything more, was premature . . . and far too dangerous.

Outside, outside. "Okay, well, you know the rhody beside the cabin door? The one that's dark blue? I don't remember seeing anything like it in the gardens."

"You didn't. It's Himalayan, very rare and extremely finicky. The only spot on the entire estate where it deigns to grow is up here. I'm not sure why. The slight altitude, perhaps, or the maritime mists that linger until noon, or the filtered sunlight through the pines. Whatever the reason, its choice of habitat is compounded by the pretension of the plant itself."

"Pretension?"

You know, like the ostentation of names such as Alexandra Chastain and Veronique duBois. Peter strangled the unbidden thought and smiled at the unpretentious woman who sat before him. "The blue beauty outside is a true blue blood—a pure bred, not a hybrid. A little mongrel blood would make her a whole lot hardier."

"Have you ever done that, Peter? Created a hybrid species?"

"No." Not yet, he mused. He knew the technique, of course, but he'd never had the patience. He could imagine creating a most extraordinary hybrid, a flower named Lauren, an exquisite blend of sapphire and cream. Now Peter Cain felt infinite patience . . . and a greater restlessness than he had ever known. "I've never had the patience. I've been restless for as long as I can remember, since my boyhood in Aloha."

"Aloha?" *Aloha, John; good riddance, good-bye. Aloha, Lauren; hello.* "You grew up in Hawaii?"

"No. In Aloha, Washington. It's a small town just a few miles from here. In fact, you drove through it on your way to the Manor. It was founded in the early 1900s by a man named Wilfred Dole. He was

born in the Hawaiian Islands, but came to the main-
land for college—Stanford—then moved to the
Pacific Northwest. His lumber company, was also
named Aloha."

Lauren heard the fondness in Peter's voice. "Was
he a relative? Your father? Grandfather?"

"No. He was just a very fine man, generous and
honest and kind. My father worked at Aloha Shake
and Shingle Mill, and when he died—a death that
had nothing to do with his job—Mr. Dole made certain our family was well cared for. That was the
kind of man he was." As a result of such kindness,
Peter Cain, employer of thousands around the
world, treated his employees with comparable loy-
alty, comparable care.

"Did you work at the lumber mill?"

"For a while."

"Until you became too restless."

Peter smiled. "Yes, until then. I left Aloha and
wandered for a while, quite a while, chasing rainbows. But now I'm back, like Dorothy."

"Dorothy? Oh, from *The Wizard of Oz*."

"You remember what she said? 'There's no place
like home.' " *No place like home.* "So, Lauren, that's
me, my life in a nutshell. Now tell me about you."

"Me?"

"Sure. Where's home for you?"

Nowhere. But it was time for the just-born flower
to plant gossamer tendrils in the rich, warm earth.
In Seattle, perhaps, the Emerald City . . . or maybe
here, in these woods, in this cabin, with him? Peter's voice had been so gentle when he'd said *home*,
and his green eyes had warmed with intimate mean-

ing, as if she had something to do with his coming home.

"Lauren?"

"Philadelphia—at least I lived there as a girl."

"Main Line?" Peter queried calmly.

"My mother was Main Line."

As was Alexandra Chastain's unfortunate husband.
Just a coincidence, the mutinous chorus within him
chimed. Peter had spent this magical afternoon siding with foolish, and ever more vocal, wishes over
mandates of logic. But now logic and wishes combined. For Peter knew, he *knew*, Lauren Smith was
not a killer. *Could not be.* "Tell me about the gun,
Lauren. A family heirloom, you said."

"Yes. My great grandfather—my mother's grandfather—had it custom-made for his bride. He wanted
her to be safe when he was away."

"A gift of love."

"Yes, and it's been an inheritance, a cherished
legacy, passed from mother to eldest daughter ever
since."

"You're the eldest daughter?"

Lauren nodded. "I have three younger sisters."

"And," Peter embellished gently, "since you have
the Lady Smith, the cherished inheritance, your
mother must no longer be alive."

"No. She's not." Lauren paused, then added quietly, "But she loved that gun. She was a crack shot,
would have been an Olympian had it not been
more important—to her family—that she become a
debutante and marry well."

"And did she?"

"The debutante part, yes, but not the marrying

well. My father's pedigree didn't begin to match hers. She was a blue blood, a pure bred, just like that Himalayan rhody." Maybe that's why she wasn't hardier. . . .

"Lauren?"

"Yes?"

"There's more, isn't there?"

Yes. *Yes.* And she had never told anyone.

You must tell Peter, a voice urged. It might have been the sage voice of the physician within, the doctor admonishing her that confession was good for her shadowed soul. *Physician, heal thyself.*

But the voice was more taunting than wise, the voice of experience. Tell him about your legacy of failure, of death.

She should, she knew. But she couldn't.

From her anguished silence, Lauren heard a voice, his voice, as deep as the woods, as gentle as the petals of a newborn rose. "She shot herself, didn't she? Your mother killed herself with the gun."

"Yes."

"I'm sorry," he whispered.

"So am I. She had so much to live for—my sisters, my father."

"You." *You.* "No wonder you're not long on trust."

Was it so obvious? Or was it that he was as clairvoyant as she? Lauren, radiologist extraordinaire, could read the shadows of illness, harbingers of death. But could this man, this elegant wizard of blossoms and blooms, read the shadowy secrets of the heart?

"I'm not?" she murmured.

"How could you be? What greater violation of

trust is there than abandonment by a parent?" Peter Cain had suffered no such betrayal. His wariness was instinctive, a consequence of smoldering restlessness and intense privacy. There were times, however, when Peter *had* to trust—on a cliff, linked to another human being by a slender rope. Then his trust was absolute. Then . . . in matters of life and death.

Trust me, Lauren. *Trust me.*

"What were you doing in the woods?"

Tell him. Tell Peter *everything.* The imploring voice was new, just born, a newborn whisper of courage . . . and hope. "I suppose I was trying to feel what she felt, to understand why she did what she did."

"And wondering if you could do it, too?"

"I realize that's something I've been wondering for a very long time—since her death."

"And? Do you know?" Or was the gun he locked in the safe beckoning to her still, tempting, taunting?

Lauren met his fierce and tender gaze. "I *do* know, Peter. I could never do what she did. Never. No matter what."

"Good," Peter whispered. He wanted to curl her in his arms, to protect her always. But this cream and sapphire wildflower was so contained, an island unto herself. So Peter touched instead her pale, cool cheek. Lauren's skin heated to his gentle caress, warmed to the light pink blush of perfect rose. "Why don't you get rid of the gun? You have your answer. You passed the test."

Lauren shook her head, a slight gesture that nonetheless dislodged his caress. She frowned at the chilling loss, then seemed to give herself a mental shake, as if his touch, his heat, had been merely a mirage. "I can't get rid of the gun, not without discussing it with my sisters."

"Which would resurrect their sadness about your mother's death."

"Which would *reveal* it to them. They don't know how she really died—at least the two youngest ones don't. It's possible that Ardath may have guessed."

"Would you really need to reveal the truth? The statistics are pretty clear, and pretty grim, about the dangers of handguns in the home."

"True. But the Lady Smith is being kept as a treasure, not as a weapon, and I'm the one who's keeping it . . ."

And you're the one who had it with you in the woods, testing yourself, tormenting yourself. Lauren was the gun's keeper, her sisters' keeper, the keeper of the family's darkest secret. It was an immense burden, Peter thought. But one that she was determined to bear, was bearing, on her own.

"Will you at least think about it?"

Her soft shrug tore at his heart.

"Well," he said finally, gently, "will you tell me about your sisters?"

Lauren greeted his request with gratitude, with relief, and as she spoke of Ardath, Dinah, and Yardley, her eyes glowed with love and pride.

Peter wanted to stop time, to preserve forever these moments when all shadows were vanquished. But even the most impassioned wishes of a passionate billionaire could not stop the world from spinning, and in due course his ringing telephone shattered the perfection. His guests had arrived, business colleagues with whom he would dine in the luxury of his penthouse suite.

"There's a staff get-together at the lodge," he lied. "It's a function I have to attend."

"Oh!" Lauren stood up. "Yes. Of course. I'd better go."

"We'd better go," Peter amended calmly. "I'm going to escort you, and the rest of this food, back to your room."

"I couldn't possibly eat another thing."

"Until the hearty breakfast you'll have in the morning?"

Lauren smiled. "Until long past that. Really. But it's so wonderful . . . maybe you could take what's left to your meeting?"

"Okay." He would drop the leftovers in the kitchen en route to his suite. The gourmet food wouldn't go to waste. The staff would happily consume the tasty morsels throughout the night.

In moments Peter had repacked the wicker basket, and they were on their way. It was an enchanted journey into a misting twilight, a lacy veil of silver and dew.

The shimmering silver enveloped them throughout their winding descent, and when they reached the cedar porch outside her modest room, silver blended with gold, as lamplight shone like a champagne moon.

Peter set the basket on the railing, freeing his restless hands—for her.

Restless hands, talented hands, so strong and gentle as he cupped her face.

"May I kiss you?"

"Yes."

"But?" he asked, as worry shadowed her lovely face.

"But I'm not very good at this."

"Really? I find that hard to believe."

But it's true. I'm ice.

At least, she always had been.

But now, as he kissed her, the most wondrous spirals of heat uncurled within, warm, confident tendrils of joy, gold and silver threads woven into a perfect dream.

Perfect . . . until Peter ended the kiss. But it was a perfect ending, for it promised more; it promised everything, a solemn vow embellished by a soft groan and glittering green eyes.

"I don't want to go," he whispered, hoarse and husky, against her lips. "But I have to. In the morning, if you like, I'll introduce you to the roses."

"Yes . . . please."

He touched her cheek, a farewell caress, before vanishing into the mist.

The soggy veil was dense now; opaque, ominous, foreboding, gray. The sinister adjectives traveled with Peter as if they were distinct beings, phantoms floating in the sodden air, taunting, haunting, watching.

Who could be watching him? Peter wondered. The lethal shadow of his enchanting thief?

Was it possible she could be both angel and killer, a splintered creature born of violent death and harsh betrayal?

Peter had not asked about Lauren's father. But, she had told him, her mother, her Main Line mother, had not married as well as her family had hoped. Had the mongrel husband driven his patrician wife to suicide, a trauma that, in turn, had driven his eldest daughter to seek revenge against her husbands?

If so, Lauren knew nothing—nothing—of her evil twin, the clever murderess who even now watched him in the shrouded darkness.

And if so, Peter would love the one . . . and protect the other.

Trust me, Lady Smith.

Trust me.

Chapter Six

~

It was after midnight when Peter's business meeting adjourned, after midnight when he searched anew for the menacing phantom in the opaque gray mist.

But the ethereal evil had vanished, floated away—if it, *she*, had never existed at all. As Peter roamed through lacy shadows, he felt only the nighttime splendor of the forest.

And Peter Cain felt as well the splendor of Lauren, whose lovely eyes clouded with sadness at the death of a flower.

No matter how wounded, or how grievous the wound, Lauren could not kill. Nor, he decided, could she harbor within her some hidden monster.

Was it wishful thinking—the consequence of misty magic, and the gauzy mist of his sleep-deprived brain?

Peter didn't sleep, didn't try. He roamed until dawn, a restless shepherd. At daybreak he showered, changed, and forsaking the hearty breakfast of gardeners—any breakfast at all—journeyed to the rose garden to wait.

Wishes were all the nourishment he needed. Wishes, and her. Or so he believed . . . until she approached. Then, and with a vengeance, his mind cleared and his powerful body went on full alert, watchful and wary. It was instinct, he knew, the survival instinct of a climber trained to function with clarity and logic at dizzying heights.

Now those finely honed instincts commanded him to look at her, really look at her . . . and as he did, the gray day glowed bright silver . . . as wishes wedded logic, a radiant marriage of luminous joy.

"Good morning," he greeted softly.

"Good morning."

"Did you sleep?"

"I dreamed," Lauren murmured. Wide-awake dreams—of him. Had their kiss kept him wakeful, too? Wakeful and restless and wanting? "Did you sleep?"

Peter smiled. "I dreamed."

Of you, his dark green eyes embellished. *You*.

They stood at the entrance of the rose garden, in full view of the veranda, the estate's glass-encased porch for casual dining. It was quite full at this moment with guests enjoying the rainbowed vista of roses as they savored the Manor's famous scone and honey buffet.

"Consider yourself kissed," Peter whispered.

She *was* kissed, by his eyes, his smile, his voice— an invisible caress that nonetheless evoked the brave and wondrous tendrils of happiness and heat.

"You, too."

"Thanks."

"You're welcome." She laughed softly, an escape valve for the euphoria bubbling deep within. She wanted to tell him about the effervescent joy, but this wasn't the place, and could she truly find the words? She found another word instead, and uttered it not with alarm but with celebration . . . as if each misting droplet were a kissing cousin of one of her very own giddy bubbles. "Drizzle. It's probably wonderful for the flowers."

"Absolutely. They don't mind getting their feet wet."

"Well, neither do I."

"But you don't have to. The equipment shack is fully stocked with boots and oilskins, which you will need, because this gentle drizzle is going to become a serious rain."

The rubber boots he found for her were brick red, and her oilskin jacket and coveralls glowed bright yellow. The jacket had a hood, which Lauren forsook, unconcerned about coiffure chaos.

It was coiffure magic, Peter decided. Her shining sable hair sparkled with a mist of diamonds, its curling tendrils dancing in the breeze. Her face became misted, too, dewdrops on a perfect rose, damp and fresh and lovely.

Then the rain came, just as he had forecast, an earnest downpour, drenching and cold. At last Lauren covered her rain-soaked hair. At last—and too late.

She was soaked, chilled to the bone.

"Time for hot chocolate," Peter announced.

Her smile wobbled, her lips faintly blue and trembling. "That sounds good."

"I'll have a pot ready for delivery to your room the moment you've taken a nice hot shower."

"Thank you. That sounds even better."

But not best, Peter mused. Best would be showering together, followed by an afternoon of making love before a roaring fire. But if, *when*, he took Lauren to bed, he wanted them to have forever; and he had conference calls beginning at two.

"I have an afternoon of paperwork. But could I interest you in dinner at eight in the Orchid Room?"

"You could. That would be lovely." And elegant, Lauren mused.

Far more elegant than the jeans and turtlenecks she had brought. But Rhododendron Manor was prepared for such contingencies, boasting a black-tie boutique, the perfect spot in which to find formal wear appropriate for dining in the five-star restaurant—the *expensive* five-star restaurant.

"You're frowning, Lauren."

Because she was wondering about offering to pay. Dr. Lauren Smith was a lavishly compensated shadow-gazer, after all, and he was a gardener. Would that truth, with its likely financial discrepancy, trouble him? No, of course not—not this strong, confident man.

He might be a little annoyed, however, at her deceit.

"Lauren?"

"There are some things I need to tell you about myself."

I have some confessions, too. "Okay."

"Tonight?" she asked as a shiver shimmied through her.

"Tonight," he agreed.

Then, because he couldn't resist, because he needed to reassure her that she need not fear confessions of any kind, Peter kissed the furrows of worry that shadowed her brow.

It was a private kiss, shielded from prying eyes by an arcade of roses and a wall of rain—a wandering kiss, from brow to eyelids to lips. She tasted of raindrops and roses and passion and joy.

But she trembled, from passion *and* raindrops.

"Hot chocolate," he whispered between kisses.

"Hot chocolate."

"And paperwork."

"And paperwork."

Peter drew away then, his eyes glittering with desire, yet so solemn. *So solemn.*

"Tonight," he told her.

It sounded like a promise.

It was a promise.

Tonight.

The dress was silk cream, adorned with a treasure trove of tiny pearls, and there was a beaded purse to match. She had never owned such a dress, Lauren realized as she studied her image in the three-way mirror outside the dressing room.

"He'll ravish you in that."

Lauren looked up. "I beg your pardon?"

The woman, who was strikingly beautiful, smiled with the secret knowledge of a pampered cat. "Peter will *devour* you in that."

"Peter," Lauren echoed quietly.

"I'm being presumptuous, aren't I? Don't answer, *of course* I am. And, since I intend to keep right on

presuming, I suppose I'd better introduce myself.
I'm Michelle, and you're . . . ?"

"Lauren."

"Well, Lauren, I've been watching you and Peter.
I've seen the grim truth with my own eyes."
Michelle sighed. "How I could let that man go?
How could I just *throw* him away, as if gorgeous bil-
lionaires were a dime a dozen?"

"There must be some mistake. Peter isn't a billionaire. He's a—"

"Let me guess, a gardener? That would explain
the time the two of you have spent wandering
among the blooms. My, my, hasn't Peter gotten devious? But speaking of devious, you *must* know
who he is. How could you not? You read newspapers, surely, and national magazines."

No, I don't. I read medical journals . . . and shadows.
"I don't know who he is."

"Which means you *can't* have known him very
long. The humble gardener pretense would be hard
to maintain. I mean, how does Peter explain his
E-mail, his faxes, his phone calls overseas? Not to
mention the business dinner, last night, in his penthouse suite?"

He *doesn't*, Lauren thought. He just pretends
there's a staff get-together or a little gardening-
related paperwork to do. "Who is he?"

"Peter Cain, gardener, entrepreneur, mountain-
climber, innkeeper. Rhododendron Manor is his, of
course—the lodge, the lake, the gardens."

*And the woods . . . the whispering pines, the sighing
ferns.*

"I want him back, Lauren. I'm letting you know

that, in the interest of fair play. And, in fairness, I should warn you that my chances are very good. Once, not so long ago, I was the love of Peter's life. It scared me. I mean, here was this sexy, gorgeous, passionate man, who could have any woman on earth, saying that he wanted *me*. I ran away from his love, but now I'm back."

"Watching him . . . us."

Michelle's reply was not repentant in the least, not a flicker of apology that she had invaded their privacy. Indeed, quite clearly, Michelle viewed herself as the injured party. "It's been torment—torment I *deserve*. I've even been tormenting myself with the idea of leaving as quietly as I arrived. Peter was so devastated when I broke up with him, and now I've seen the way he looks at you. But I *can't* leave, Lauren. The stakes are simply too high. I love Peter, and once, and quite *desperately*, he loved me, too. Besides, let's face it, your relationship with Peter seems tenuous at best, based on pretense and lies. Anyway, the die is cast. I just left a message on his voice mail, and any minute now he'll know that I've returned . . . and why. So."

Michelle's *so* was embellished by a dismissive wave of her left hand, as if she was powerless to prevent what would happen next, was merely surrendering to whatever destiny had in store. Hers would be a sparkling destiny if the gigantic diamond on her ring finger was any indication.

"It's an engagement ring," she explained. "A token *rock* from Peter. I tried to give it back, but he wouldn't accept it. He hoped to see me wearing it again, he told me, wearing it forever. . . ."

* * *

"Hello, Peter, this is Mike Gregory, aka Michelle Gregoire. I truly hadn't intended to keep my gender a secret, but since our only communication was in the sexually neutral ether of cyberspace, it never seemed relevant. I *have* to be Mike, of course, when I'm writing articles—for men—about the conquest of major mountains. But now all must be revealed, because here I am, at your glorious Manor. I was in the area and couldn't resist. I've made dinner reservations for eight o'clock in the Orchid Room, and I'm hoping you'll join me. If you can't, I'll be terribly disappointed, but I will understand. I know you're busy. And although I truly hope this isn't the case, I also realize you may be angry at my presumptuous, and impromptu, invasion of your privacy."

Angry? Hardly. Indeed, as Peter listened to the message—and the sultry voice that feigned uncertainty even as it seduced—he felt relief, elation . . . and icy shimmers of fear.

Fear was an unfamiliar sensation for Peter. Even at death-defying heights, he was accustomed to exhilaration, not fright.

But there wasn't a whisper of exhilaration now, for it wasn't Peter who teetered on a precarious ledge. It was Lauren.

Peter vanquished the fear, vanquished all emotion, and focused on what must be done. The man who had conquered the most treacherous mountains on the planet knew the necessity of caution. The slightest misstep could prove instantly fatal.

His first call was to the front desk, to Gertrude. She and Peter's mother had been friends since girlhood summers spent at Copalis Beach; and Gertrude worked at the Manor, ran the place in Peter's absence, because she loved it.

Gertrude felt quite free to offer certain maternal opinions, especially when Peter was in residence at the lake. She hoped to talk to him about Lauren, had already shared her observations with his mother. "It's *happened*," Gertrude had enthused to Elizabeth Cain. "Our Peter has fallen in love."

But Gertrude sensed that this was not the time for motherly inquiries about Peter's love life. The voice that asked her to take his call in the privacy of her office sounded more serious than she'd ever heard before. As did the request—it was a command—Peter issued as soon as she'd closed the door and returned to the line.

"Tell me about Michelle Gregoire."

"What about her, Peter?" *What about Lauren?*

"What does she look like?"

"Well, she's very beautiful. *Too* beautiful if you ask me. I prefer *interesting* to perfect, and beauty is as beauty—"

"What color is her hair?"

"Blond."

"Blond? Are you sure?"

"She's blond, Peter. Very, very blond."

"Do you think it's her real color?"

"Who knows? It doesn't look wrong for her, and I didn't notice any telltale roots. But in this day and age, it's difficult to be sure."

"Did you notice her eyes? Their color?"

"Green."

So she had dyed her hair—again—and was still wearing contact lenses. But it was her. It had to be. "When did she arrive?"

"Yesterday afternoon, while you and Lauren were in the gardens."

"Did you tell her where I was?" *Where Lauren was?*

Gertrude sighed. "I didn't want to, but I did. For the past few months you've made it abundantly clear that we were to tell whoever wanted to know precisely where to find you."

That's because I had no fear for myself . . . and never imagined there could be a Lauren.

"Peter, what's going on? And don't tell me nothing."

"I won't tell you that, Gertrude, and I promise to tell you everything, later. For the moment, I need you to work this evening. A man named Jack Shannon will be arriving, accompanied by several colleagues."

"We're full, Peter. Completely."

"That's okay. None of them needs a room. But would you show them to the private dining room as soon as they arrive, and page me right away?"

"Yes. Of course."

Peter's next call was to Lieutenant Jack Shannon in L.A. The homicide lieutenant would have made an excellent climbing partner, Peter decided. In tense situations, Jack Shannon, like Peter Cain, kept the dialogue focused and spare.

"She's here," Peter told him.

"I'm on my way," Jack replied.

The team of police officers, including the prints expert, would arrive by seven, to discuss specifics before Peter's eight o'clock dinner date with a killer.

Peter drew a breath before dialing Michelle Gregoire's lakefront suite, to accept her invitation to candlelit romance in the Orchid Room. There could be no edge in his voice, not while Lauren stood on the most precarious ledge of all.

But the black widow was not in her suite, and it scared the hell out of him.

What if she was with Lauren, sipping tea? What if she had dropped by Lauren's room to share—and poison—the hot chocolate he had sent?

Michelle Gregoire knew where Lauren was staying. Peter was sure of it. *Michelle* was the evil phantom who had haunted the silvery mist, a presence so ominous she had almost poisoned the lacy magic.

Peter wanted to run to Lauren, to pull her from the treacherous ledge, to form a human shield between her and all danger. But if the killer was watching, assessing the threat of Lauren to her plans, such impulsiveness would cause more harm than good.

He had to stay away from Lauren . . . to rescue her from afar.

Fear came back with icy vengeance as the phone went unanswered in Lauren's tiny room.

Answer, dammit, answer. *Please.*

"Hello?"

Relief flooded him, filled him. "Were you sleeping?"

"No." *I was just sitting, staring, waiting for your call.*

Her voice was so flat that fear shivered anew. "Lauren? Are you alone?"

"What? Oh, yes. Quite alone."

Of course she sounded flat, confused. His queries had been focused, harsh and intense, and she had absolutely no idea why.

"Hi," he whispered softly.

"Hi," she echoed, lifeless still, bewildered still. "Peter, is something—?"

"I have a favor to ask. Two favors, actually."

"Yes?"

"I need to ask you to trust me. I know that's not your strongest suit. But will you? Please?"

"And the other favor, Peter?"

"I want you to leave the Manor, right now."

"Because?"

Because it's dangerous for you here. He couldn't tell her that, of course. His lady of the woods did not run from danger. She confronted it. And if he happened to mention that he, too, was at risk? Peter's mind filled with lovely, and utterly terrifying, images of her deciding to protect *him*, rescue *him*.

"Because I'm asking you to," he said quietly. "I'll explain everything later—soon. I promise."

How? You don't even know where I live. Lauren intercepted her silent protest. Of course Peter knew. Rhododendron Manor was *his* five-star estate. He had full access to the guest register.

If Peter Cain wanted to find her again, he could.

But he won't.

"Okay."

"You'll leave?"

"Yes."

"And you'll trust me?"

"Sure."

Chapter Seven

~

It took her almost no time to pack, to toss her jeans and turtlenecks into the small suitcase. Lauren didn't toss the beaded silk dress. She folded it carefully, thoughtfully.

Still, the task took very little time. So easy to fold away a dream.

Lauren had purchased the magnificent dress, despite her encounter with Michelle. It was a symbol of the new Lauren, born that evening in the woods, the daughter who would not follow in her mother's footsteps, the shadow who was free.

The dress journeyed with her as she left the Manor, as did a rather remarkable confidence. She would wear the silken shimmer of pearls—someday.

Lauren bid a silent adieu to Rhododendron Manor, the indigo lake, the majestic pines, the fragrant blossoms ... him. It was a bittersweet farewell, but a grateful one. She had hoped merely to shake the shadows of depression, but she had shaken so much more, and even as she drove through pelting rain, a sunny chorus chimed within.

Aloha, Lauren. Aloha.

A few soggy miles from the Manor, the buoyant lyric suddenly appeared before her eyes. WELCOME TO ALOHA, the sign read, an inscription that glittered in the sodden gloom, a beacon that commanded her full attention.

You're running away! the golden letters admonished. And the new Lauren, the *aloha* Lauren, doesn't run away. Does she?

No, Lauren mused as she made a safe but decisive U-turn in front of the Aloha Shake and Shingle Mill. Not anymore.

The dress that would be worn someday would be worn tonight, at the Manor, as she dined amid the orchids—a private celebration amid the tropical blooms . . . Lauren celebrating Lauren. Peter would be nowhere in sight. But he would be celebrating, too, an intimate reunion with Michelle in the penthouse suite Lauren had never seen.

And would Lauren insinuate herself into that romantic rendezvous? Would she pound on the door until the lovers were compelled to answer, then confront Peter with his lies? Of course not. She felt no anger toward Peter, none at all.

Even so, she found herself wishing she could speak with him, just for a few moments. *Be honest with me, Peter. I can handle it. Tell me the truth.*

The truth. Lauren Smith might never know Peter Cain's truth about their time together. But she knew hers. *I've never felt this way, Peter. Never. Perhaps I couldn't until the new Lauren was born; or perhaps I couldn't . . . until you.*

That was her truth, and maybe after her solo dinner amid the orchids, and before beginning her late-night drive to the Emerald City, she would leave a confession on his voice mail—a confession, a thank-you, a good-bye.

The silken dress of shimmering pearls; the exotic orchids from paradise; the aloha to herself, and to Peter—each was reason enough to return to the Manor.

But there was something else, treasure and curse, which she had forgotten until now. The Lady Smith, with its very own shimmer of pearls, was locked still in the Manor's safe.

The Orchid Room was designed for lovers, a romantic venue of candlelit flowers. Their table, in a secluded alcove, had been hand picked by Peter, and the police.

A tuxedoed Lieutenant Shannon dined nearby, as did other comparably well-dressed members of his team, their elegant camouflage courtesy of the Manor's boutique.

The plan, formulated in the past hour, was methodical and precise, as meticulous as the preparations one made before assaulting the highest peaks on earth. Once finished with their gourmet meal, Peter would suggest dancing in the Camellia Lounge. While he and the murderess swayed beneath a crystal chandelier, the prints expert would go to work.

There would be a surplus of fingerprints by dinner's end—silhouettes of guilt on the china, silver, and crystal that were to be meticulously collected by their white-gloved *cop* waiter. The incriminating samples would be excessive, an abundance of evidence. But redundancy, like caution, was essential in matters of life and death.

And, unless fate intervened, there could be no deviation from the plans, no matter how restless one was.

No matter that this fraudulent evening of romance with a murderess felt like a betrayal of Lauren.

No matter that every fiber of his being churned with fury at Michelle Gregoire—who she was, what she had done, her utter self-absorption, her evil.

She *was* the killer. The woman whose goal was to seduce and to wed. Him. Peter had absolutely no doubt—despite the enormous diamond that glittered at him in candle glow.

Peter clamped down on his restlessness and his fury.

"That looks like an engagement ring," he observed mildly.

"It *is*."

Michelle's beautiful frown was an invitation Peter had to accept. "There's a problem with your engagement?"

Her sigh defined drama. "I'm afraid so, although he doesn't know it. Yet. I suppose that's part of why I came here—a minor reason, of course, compared with meeting you. I needed a little heart-to-heart time with myself. Oh, he's quite wonderful. Don't get me wrong. Rich, handsome, smart, funny—and totally devoted to me. But I feel the walls closing in, and every ounce of women's intuition I possess is screaming *don't do it.* Some women—and some men—are simply not suited to marriage. I'm afraid I'm one of them, in the female category." The provocative curve of her lips was designed to remind him just how female she was. "How about you, Peter? Are you the marrying type?"

Yes. "No. I'm a dedicated bachelor."

Her emerald-tinted eyes flirted shamelessly, flawlessly. "Then I'm safe with you."

"Absolutely."

Michelle's expression shifted then, subtly yet ominously—at least Peter Cain saw the new intensity as distinctly ominous. He was experienced at reading contrary signs; could see, when others could not, the deceptive innocence of a white cloud in an azure sky, the snowy destruction concealed within the billowy softness.

Peter sensed such impending menace now.

And he was right.

"Does *she* know your views on matrimony?" Michelle asked.

Peter shifted his focus, then. Fate had intervened. Plans would change. He would change them. The life-and-death battle had been joined, and he was resigned, resolved, supremely calm.

"She?" he echoed casually as he turned in the direction of the black widow's menacing gaze. *She* stood at the entrance of the Orchid Room, a vision of loveliness beneath a trellis of lilacs.

"Lauren," Michelle clarified. "I noticed the two of you in the gardens when I arrived, and I bumped into her this afternoon in the boutique. She was buying that dress. I got the impression she was buying it for you."

"I doubt it," Peter replied easily, evenly—a non-chalance that gave no clue whatsoever to the fierce destruction that raged within . . . the fearsome wish to destroy the woman who spoke Lauren's name as if she owned Lauren—as if Lauren were entangled in her sinister web.

"Really? Meaning she's not in love with you?"

"No. She's just a friend."

"A friend," Michelle echoed, "who seems to be dining alone. That seems so sad. Oh, wait a minute, we're not the only ones who've noticed her. In fact, unless my journalistic, and female, instincts are completely off, I do believe she has piqued the interest of that rather handsome man over there. They'd make a striking couple, don't you think? Never mind that he's wearing a wedding ring."

"He's very married."

"Oh, you know him, too?"

"He's a business associate." The business of murder, at which Lieutenant Jack Shannon excelled. Of course the homicide lieutenant had noticed the dark-haired, blue-eyed woman dressed like a bride. She, unlike Michelle Gregoire, matched perfectly the description provided by the Beverly Hills therapist.

"Who is dining alone because you're otherwise occupied? Just as Lauren is?"

"I don't think he minds, and, although I don't question your instincts, I think he's looking through her, not at her. My guess is he's plotting his next corporate takeover."

Michelle affected a lovely pout. "You're spoiling all my fun, Peter. So much for witnessing love at first sight in the Orchid Room." She tilted her impeccably dyed golden head. "Maybe we should ask both of them to join us. I have the distinct feeling that if it weren't for me, neither would be dining alone."

Peter feigned surprise. "You wouldn't mind?"

"Not at all."

"Well, I expect they'll say no, but maybe I should ask. I won't be long."

"Take your time, Peter. I'm quite content to sit here, sipping this magnificent champagne, surveying the dining room for other mini-dramas."

"Speaking of which—the champagne not the mini-dramas—I'm a little disappointed with this bottle. Have you tried Montagne Noir?"

"Not yet, but I'm eager to. Rumor has it that our very own Napa Valley is now producing the best champagne on the planet."

"Let's try it then. I ordered several cases for the Manor, which just arrived. Our wine buyer has flawless taste, but I'd been planning to sample it myself before offering it to my guests. But if you're game . . . ?"

"I'm definitely game."

"I'll have our waiter bring us a bottle. In fact, while we're at it, why don't we do a true comparison—Montagne Noir, Cristal, Tattinger, Dom Perignon?"

"Lovely. And, assuming Lauren and your married friend decline to join us, we can spend the evening toasting the single life."

Peter smiled with effort, an expression that faded to grim resolve the moment he turned away. Neither the homicide lieutenant nor the woman he loved would be joining them.

Peter needed to get to Lauren, to remove her

from harm's way. But before going to her, he instructed their cop-waiter to bring more champagne,
and more crystal flutes—and to remove the ones already used.

Then Peter Cain moved toward the trellis of white
lilacs, and the silken bride who stood beneath.

Lauren didn't see him until he was beside her.

Her greeting was an enchantment of happiness
and surprise. "Peter!"

"I thought you had left."

His glacial green gaze subdued her happiness,
froze it. *Oh, Peter, please don't be angry.* "I had,
but . . . I left in such a hurry I forgot the gun. I didn't
expect you to be here."

But Peter was here, no doubt furious with her for
breaking her promise, for tainting his evening of
celebration with the woman he loved. Lauren spotted Michelle in the alcove—Michelle, who lifted a
glass of champagne in salute, in triumph.

"I know all about Michelle, Peter, and I wish you
both the best. Truly. I'm not here to make a scene."

It was far too dangerous to speak his heart. He
couldn't permit either Michelle or Jack to witness
anything less than a harsh farewell. "Then leave,
Lauren. Please."

The roses in her cheeks died a sudden, anguished
death.

"Of course," she whispered. "I'm sorry, Peter.
Good-bye."

"Good-bye," he echoed to her stricken blue eyes.
Godspeed, my love. "Lauren?"

"Yes?"

"Drive safely."

She frowned, bewildered, then turned and walked

away, delicate yet strong, wounded yet proud. After a moment, Peter turned, too, and strode to Jack Shannon's candlelit table. He smiled as he approached, for Michelle was watching him. But when he reached the homicide lieutenant, Peter blocked her view of both their faces.

Lieutenant Shannon spoke first. "Who is she, Peter?"

The woman I love. You can't have her prints, Lieutenant. I won't permit it.

"I'm drinking champagne with your killer, Jack."

"You're sure?"

"Positive. So positive, in fact, that I've decided to step up the process. Your black widow and I will be doing a little champagne tasting, glass after glass, until you have all the prints you need. I want you to begin looking at them now, Jack. Now."

Like Peter, Lieutenant Shannon was accustomed to issuing commands, not receiving them. But, like Peter, Jack knew the necessity of adjusting to the unforeseen.

"All right."

"Thanks."

Then, as if he and his business associate had just exchanged an inside joke, Peter smiled, an easy grin that accompanied him to the romantic alcove and the lethal seductress awaiting him there.

"No takers?" she asked.

"No takers. One pleaded a feeling of awkwardness, and, as I suspected, the other was in the midst of a mental arbitrage. So, it's just us."

Michelle's green-tinted eyes flashed with pleasure. "Just us . . . and all this champagne."

"I'm afraid so."

"I guess I can live with that."

But could Lauren? Peter wondered. He had gotten her off the precarious ledge, only to leave her to descend the mountain alone. But he would be with her soon, *soon* . . . and until then there was nothing he could do but pour expensive bubbles of honeygold champagne into flute after flute of glittering crystal.

Chapter Eight

~

"Oh, Peter, here comes your business associate, looking a little grim. Maybe his mental greenmail didn't work out. Or maybe, married or not, he regrets having dined alone."

Or maybe, Peter mused, the prints *don't* match—at least not the perfectly manicured ones. But what if there *was* a match, from the delicate hands of the enchanting bride dressed in gleaming pearls? What if Lauren had been detained after all, because Jack Shannon was simply too compulsive to let such an obvious suspect go?

The request for her prints would have caught Lauren by surprise. But she would have willingly complied. She would have, after all, no consciousness of guilt.

"I wonder if I might have a word with you, Peter," Jack Shannon said. "In the lobby."

In the lobby, where perhaps she stood, in the

silk-and-pearl dream chosen just for him, stunned, bewildered, needing him. "Sure."

"Oh," the lieutenant added casually, "your dinner companion might be interested in coming along, too."

Might be interested. Jack's offhand, but not off-the-cuff, invitation brought Peter's thoughts into sharp euphoric focus. Jack wanted to lure the black widow away from the Orchid Room filled with innocent diners and into his own web, a snare that was completely in his control. . . .

Rhododendron Manor's lobby was, most definitely, in the homicide lieutenant's control. Neither hotel staff nor Manor guests were anywhere in sight—just an elite assembly of evening-clothed officers, a solemn yet elegant crescent-shaped wall.

"Ms. Gregoire," Jack began, "I'm Lieutenant Shannon, LAPD, and I'm arresting you for the murders of Miles Chandler—"

"*What?*"

"And Stuart Langstrom and Holden Worth. You have the right to remain silent."

"I don't *need* to remain silent."

"Well, humor me until I've finished reciting your rights."

She obeyed, at least was silent, while Jack completed the obligatory Miranda recitation. But her expression of haughty disdain blended with utter boredom sent the message that she was not truly listening, would not deign to listen.

Her facade remained impeccable. And yet, Peter decided, even in this muted light, she was profoundly changed. Was it, he wondered, because the light that shined on her was not the soft caress of a crystal chandelier, but instead the harsh glare of her incontrovertible guilt?

Whatever the reason, her golden hair suddenly looked quite tarnished, and he saw dark roots, hidden until now, and her beauty was a grotesque mask, crumbling before his eyes.

But the actress was still acting.

"Would someone please tell me what's going on?" she implored when Jack was through.

"What's going on," the lieutenant replied, "is that your fingerprints match those of the woman who murdered the three men I've mentioned."

"My fingerprints? You had no right to check my prints."

"I assure you, Ms. Gregoire, we had every right. We have a properly executed warrant, which, by the way, covers a search of your room."

"This is an outrage."

"Murder tends to be," Jack agreed. "Especially when it's cold-blooded, premeditated, with an abundance of malice and intent. For the record, we call that murder one."

The black widow opened her heavily lipsticked mouth, then snapped it shut, without uttering a word. Even now, even caught, she was careful, and confident.

"I *do* want an attorney. I'm going to sue every one of you—especially you, Peter."

The hotelier responded with quiet calm. "Be my guest."

"I will. Just you watch."

In fact, Michelle Gregoire's tenure as Peter Cain's guest came to a rapid end. Within moments she was escorted out of the lobby and into the rain, at which point, even during the short journey to one of the unmarked cars, her forecast of "coiffure chaos" became prophetic.

Peter watched their departure restlessly, impatient to be on his way, to drive like the wind until he overtook the car in which he'd watched Lauren drive away this afternoon.

But that car was still here. She was still here. Hurting, wounded, but safe . . . *safe.*

Or was she?

Peter ran through the pelting rain into the deep, dark woods. The sky didn't stop weeping when he entered the forest—he heard the desperate tears falling still—but the dense evergreen canopy shielded all dampness.

The woods were pitch black on this storm-ravaged night. Peter followed the trail by heart, *by heart.* His was the impeccably conditioned heart of a master athlete. But it pounded now, raced, a fury of fear, of hope, of thunder.

Then there was another thunder, shattering the night, a ferocious bellow of death. A scream of nature, or the anguished cry of a pearl-handled gun?

Nature, please, *please.*

Peter's prayers were answered by a flash of lightning, a bolt so brilliant its golden beams pierced the leafy dome. He saw her then, illuminated in the emerald sanctuary, standing there, alive there . . . a beacon that glowed even after the celestial flash was gone.

Lauren shimmered with her own heavenly light, the glitter of cream silk and gleaming pearls—and the luminous glimmer of her creamy silken skin.

Angel.

Bride.

Ghost. An ice-edged knife sliced through Peter as his gaze fell to her hand, the same hand that, with exquisite wonder, had touched a velvet rhododendron bloom.

That lovely hand was white, too white, the glow of skin and the glitter of pearls, and now it was moving, rising—

"*Lauren!*"

She froze, as if the voice belonged to a mirage of her mind, a phantom of her dreams.

"Lauren," he whispered.

She turned to him, a ballerina's twirl of breathtaking grace. "Peter."

"Hi."

"Hi."

Peter saw so clearly, so brilliantly, her faint and trembling smile. His eyes had adjusted, it seemed, to the darkness, or perhaps it was merely the inner brightness of her.

He moved toward her, close enough to touch; and his hand did touch, gently, urgently.

But it wasn't a pearl-handled Lady Smith he found in Lauren's grasp. It was a pearl-beaded purse. And was the lethal weapon housed in the elegant clutch?

No. *No.* He felt car keys, and a lipstick, and nothing else.

"You don't have the gun."

"No. It's in my suitcase, locked in the trunk of my car. Oh," she whispered, "you thought I might . . . Peter, I'm sorry."

"*Sorry?*"

"For worrying you . . . I'm *fine*. Truly. I'm not my mother. I could never do what she did."

"No matter how much you'd been hurt."

Lauren shrugged. "I should have left when you asked me to this afternoon, and not returned. And this evening, well, I was waiting for the rain to subside. Anyway, I should probably—"

"I am not in love with Michelle Gregoire."

"You're not?"

"Hardly. She has a rather unfortunate habit of murdering her husbands. I was her next target. I had to play along, to feign interest until the police could arrive and match her prints. In the meantime, I wanted you as far away as possible."

"But you didn't tell me."

"No," he said solemnly. "I didn't."

"Because," she murmured, "you thought I might be *her*. That's why you didn't tell me who you were—because you believed I already knew—and that's why you spent so much time with me."

Peter had asked this woman, who had so little reason to trust, to trust *him*. Which meant that now he must tell her the entire truth.

"You fit the description, physically. And here you were, in a place known only to me and the deer. And you pretended not to know who I was. But that wasn't pretense, was it? And you lied, in the beginning, about being a gardener. So yes, at first, I thought you might be her. But is that why I spent so much time with you? No."

"Because you checked my prints on the gun."

"I never checked your prints, Lauren. I knew you weren't a killer, *couldn't* be."

"But you barely know me."

"I know you well enough to have fallen in love
with you."

"Peter . . ." She frowned, but her sapphire eyes
glowed with hope.

Peter cradled her face and spoke gently to those
beautiful blue eyes. "Is there something I don't
know about you, Lauren, that you feel I should
know?"

"I'm a doctor, a radiologist."

Peter smiled. "Anything else to tell me? Anything *important*?"

She smiled, too. "No. Not really."

"And what about me? I take it you've discovered
I do things other than garden?"

"Yes." Like running a billion-dollar empire, which
didn't matter, was of no consequence at all. But
there was that other thing Peter Cain did, and it
was somehow terribly, and terrifyingly, important.
"You climb mountains."

"Not anymore."

"Really?"

"Really. I had to climb Everest, and K-2, because
how else would I have know about the rainbowed
forests of the Himalayas? And if not for those floral
forests, I would never have built Rhododendron
Manor, which means . . ." *I might never have met you.*
Peter didn't speak the words, stopped speaking
even before her petal-soft fingers touched his lips.
When he spoke again, his forest green eyes glittered
with fierce, brilliant fire. "I was searching for you,
Lauren, and now you are found . . . and you are
loved, Lady Smith, forever."

"So are you," she whispered. "So are you."

He kissed her then, at last, a deep, lingering

promise of always. And when they left their emerald paradise, the heavens wept no more, and the night sky glowed bright silver.

They made love throughout that silvery night, golden love, silken love, shimmering with pearls and fragrant with petals . . . and not tainted, never again tainted, by shadows.

PART TWO

Ardath

BY
ANNE STUART

Chapter Nine

❧

Fall 1997

Ardath Smith was driving recklessly. That was nothing new—she always did things at full-tilt. Driving, living, loving, hating. It had been a very long time since she'd allowed herself to love anyone, with the exception of her three sisters. But she was getting quite expert at the art of hating.

She slammed on the brakes as the car skidded around a sharp corner, wet leaves flying up around the windshield, then accelerated once more. The gun lay in her lap—small, delicate, lethal. It had killed once before. Twenty years ago her mother had taken that gun out into the woods on a snowy Christmas Eve, pressed it to her temple, and fired it.

Now, tonight, it would kill again. The same gun would kill the man responsible for her mother's death, and then maybe Ardath would find some peace in her tumultuous world.

It was raining heavily, the last leaves torn off the trees by the storm and wind. Winter was coming— Ardath could feel it in her bones—and the same dread was coming over her as well. Winter was when her mother died, and life had changed forever.

The road was narrow, steep, and twisty, and the days of rain had turned the packed dirt into slickly treacherous mud. Ardath's car, an aging MGB, wasn't made for that kind of terrain, but Ardath made no effort to adjust her breakneck driving. She turned into the skids with expert ease and simply plowed onward.

The radio yammered news bulletins about an escaped killer sandwiched in between braying car ads and syrupy Kenny G songs, but Ardath paid no attention to the noise, not even bothering to turn it off. She was intent, determined, armed and dangerous.

There was only one house at the end of this long road. One home, with one person in residence, and most of the people in Townall, New Hampshire, didn't even realize he was there. Ethan Jameson kept such a low profile that most of the hundreds of thousands of people who read his weekly column thought he lived somewhere in the Southwest. His darkly satiric writing gave nothing away, no hints of his own life. He chose other people as his victims.

Including Ardath's mother.

He'd been responsible for her death, she remembered that clearly now, after years of denial and silence and misdirection. Her mother's suicide was like the elephant in the living room: everyone knew it was there, but no one ever talked about it. Even now she had yet to discuss it with her sisters, and she had no idea whether they knew the truth or not. They hadn't been with Zoe in those last few hours, listening to her sobbing, drunken despair over her lover's desertion. They hadn't known of the times Zoe had crept away to meet with the young man who worshipped and then abandoned her.

Clayton had known. Her father had known everything, and his coldness had only made Zoe more desperate. Their mother had been a fairy-tale creature, too delicate for the harshness of this world, too delicate for a hardworking husband trying his damnedest to fit into the straightlaced upper echelons of Philadelphia society.

And Ardath was just like her.

She'd been told that all her life, by her father, her grandparents, her mother's ex-lovers and friends, and no one had been approving. Ardath was passionate, fiery, artistic, and impractical, just as Zoe had been. And if she didn't do something about the dubious legacy that haunted her, maybe she, too, would die by her own hand before her thirty-fifth birthday.

Personally, she'd decided killing Ethan Jameson was a much better idea. It would land her in jail, though there was always the chance she'd manage to plead temporary insanity. She'd considered asking her sister Dinah, the lawyer in the family, but decided against it. She remembered vaguely that there was some complication about premeditation that ruined an insanity defense, and besides, if Dinah knew what she had in mind, she'd undoubtedly try to stop her. Ardath's sisters were far too practical.

Her headlights speared through the heavy rain, reflecting off the fallen leaves as she sped up the curving mountain road. She'd tried to be practical about this entire endeavor, but practicality had never been one of her strong points. She'd planned it very carefully, down to having figured out how to get someone to load the small, cold gun that lay in her lap like a stone. She could picture the years spreading out ahead of her. They'd probably put her in some fairly pleasant prison farm, given her generally innocent nature and lack of a criminal record. Before long they'd let her work again, painting at least, and maybe even sculpting. As long as she had her work, she could be happy. There would be no men to flirt with her and make demands on her and eventually betray her.

Her sisters would weep, of course, but they'd get used to it. And Clayton was already dead, before she could ever make peace with him. He wouldn't have to worry about the embarrassment of having a child of his end up in prison. He'd already weathered the scandal of a faithless wife committing suicide, but he'd been old, weary by the time he died. For all that had been left unresolved between them, Ardath still didn't wish him ill.

The car skidded again, sliding dangerously close to the trees that lined the road before she was able to straighten the wheels, and Ardath took a deep breath, forcing herself to slow down. She wouldn't accomplish anything if she ended up wrapped around a tree. Ethan Jameson had no idea she was coming for him, and there was only one way to his mountaintop retreat. He'd have to pass her to escape, and she wasn't going to let that happen.

She knew what she had to do, as far-fetched and unlikely as it seemed. Too many signs had led her to this place on a stormy night in early November. Too many pieces had fallen together at the right time, and she wasn't about to ignore her destiny. She had no idea whether it was vengeance or justice. But killing Ethan Jameson was something she had to do.

She didn't usually bother with newspapers. She had no interest in columnists—they were usually right-wing ranters or cozy housewives or wry liberals, all of whom bored her. She had to have heard Jameson's name over the last ten years as his readership grew and his books hit best-seller lists, but for some reason she'd never made the connection—until a spiteful ex-lover had presented her with a copy of Jameson's latest collection of essays, a selection prominently marked.

"Sounds just like you, doesn't it?" he'd said in a smarmy tone of voice, making Ardath doubly disgusted with herself for ever thinking a smidgeon of artistic talent and a poet's face could make up for a small soul. But then, she'd never been a particularly good judge of character. She was much too prone to jump to conclusions about people, both good and bad.

"Zoe's Gift" was the name of the essay, written in what Ardath later discovered was Ethan Jameson's patented acerbic wit. It was funny, vicious, and horrifying familiar—the tale of Zoe and her besotted lover, an idealist who'd just had his terribly earnest first novel published. How he'd fallen under Zoe's dangerous enchantment, barely escaped with his life, only to have her commit suicide on Christmas Eve as final, melodramatic revenge.

Odd that he was able to make it sound funny in a macabre sort of way. Even odder that it all sounded so familiar to Ardath—the secret meetings between the mismatched lovers, the drug and alcohol-fueled scenes, the grandstanding and grandiosity that made a mockery of real emotions. The only thing missing was the silent witness, the daughter who heard her mother's drunken confidences and despairing confessions.

"Zoe's Gift" to the idealistic young writer was to keep him from ever writing earnest novels again. Instead of starving in a garret, he was cynical, wealthy, and immensely pleased with his life, or so the essay had suggested.

It didn't seem to matter that a woman had died for his comfortable life. It didn't seem to matter that he'd abandoned her, leaving her feeling she had no choice but to kill herself.

Ardath wondered if it would matter when she killed him.

The copyright of that particular essay was almost ten years old. He'd probably put all thought of Zoe long behind him. He carried no guilt; no ghosts remained to haunt him—until Ardath showed up at his doorstep with the gun that her sister had sent her.

Not that Lauren had the faintest idea what Ardath planned to do with it. Ardath had claimed to want to paint it, and Lauren had wanted it out of her hands, out of her life, so she'd sent it to her.

And Ardath had the gun, and the name of the

man who'd destroyed her childhood. The next step was obvious.

There were drawbacks, of course. Ardath had never fired a gun, and she hated killing things. Occasionally, she squashed a mosquito, but even then she felt a pang of guilt. She wore no leather or furs, she ate no meat, she did her best to live her life in a manner that endangered no other creatures. Murdering a man in cold blood would be a new experience for her, she thought grimly, speeding up again.

The narrow road veered to the left, posted NO TRESPASSING, and Ardath knew she'd found her quarry. She jerked the wheel, and the car slid sideways down the long, steep driveway. She tried to steer, but it was useless, and only when the car slammed to a stop against something painfully solid did she realize she had reached her destination. The car had stalled, but the lights still speared out into the darkness, and the newscaster on the radio continued at a hysterical pitch.

She climbed out in the soaking rain, pushing back the sleeves of her old flannel shirt, shoving the tiny gun in her pocket. She didn't bother reaching for her raincoat—a little rough weather would be a minor enough inconvenience.

The ancient sportscar sat flush against a huge maple, the fender curved around the tree trunk. She had no idea whether she'd be able to drive away, and she hadn't really expected to. Presumably, someone would call the police once they heard the gunshots, and running would be a waste of time. Besides, she was on a mission, wasn't she?

Her sneakers slid in the mud. The rain was cold, icy, stinging her face, soaking her tangled hair as she advanced on the darkened house. One light shone from a downstairs window, but she felt sudden worry that Ethan Jameson might not be there after all. She was in no mood to sit and wait for his appearance.

At least the back door had a porch to protect her from the rain. She shook herself like a drenched dog, pushed her hair back from her face, and took the gun out of her pocket, eyeing it critically. And then she reached out a fist and pounded on the door.

Ethan Jameson was in a foul mood. It had been raining for more than a week, his sister had informed him that she and her entire brood were coming for Thanksgiving, and he had a headache and the beginnings of a cold. All he wanted was a good night's sleep, listening to the rain pound on his metal roof. He didn't want to be wakened by some fool who'd taken a wrong turn and thought he was the kind of man who'd help.

He cursed, flicking on the light beside his bed. He never bothered to lock his house, and whoever it was would probably barge right in if he didn't come downstairs. It was bad enough being invaded by strangers. If worse came to worst and the idiot was stuck in the mud, Ethan could haul him out with his four-wheel-drive truck—probably ensuring he'd get pneumonia in the process, but his solitude was more important than his physical health. He wasn't in the mood for visitors.

He yanked on a pair of old jeans, grabbed his flannel bathrobe, and headed for the door. The pounding continued, echoing the pain in his head, and whoever was outside his door was going to be very sorry he'd bothered Ethan Jameson when he was coming down with a cold.

He took the narrow steps two at a time, stubbing his toe when he came to the bottom. The intruder stood outside the kitchen door, pounding, and Ethan flicked on the overhead light, crossed the room in a rage, and yanked the door open.

"What the hell do you mean by pounding . . . ?" He let the words trail off, struck silent for perhaps the first time in his eloquent life.

A woman stood there—a tall, glorious-looking creature, with a Pre-Raphaelite head of red wavy hair, a pale, beautiful face, a tall, curvy body, and a gun in her hand. She was pointing it straight at his genitals.

"Oh, Christ," he said in disgust, considering slamming the door again.

He didn't have the chance. She pushed into the room, the gun still steady on his privates, and kicked the door shut behind her.

"I'm not in the mood for this," he warned her in a caustic voice.

He'd managed to startle her. She had clear blue eyes with that mane of flaming hair, and she blinked in surprise. But the gun didn't waver.

"In the mood for what?" she asked. "Dying?"

She had a husky voice, oddly sexy given the circumstances. He took a careful step backward, wondering if he should try to run for it.

"Not in the mood for some loony showing up at my doorstep," he said. "It's usually right-wing radicals who want to shoot me, not pretty young women." He took another step back away from her.

"Don't!" she said sharply.

"Don't what?"

"Don't call me a pretty young woman or I'll . . ." she floundered.

"You'll drill me full of lead?" he suggested helpfully. "I thought you were planning on doing that anyway."

"Don't try to run. I'd rather not shoot you in the back, but I will if I have to."

"Why don't you want to shoot me in the back? If you don't mind my asking?" he added.

"Because I want to watch your eyes when I kill you," she replied, sounding very practical.

She didn't actually look crazy. Apart from her wild hair and the gun in her hand, she looked like a reasonable enough person. She even looked vaguely familiar.

"Do I know you?" he asked. "Did I do you some terrible wrong? Run over your dog, sleep with you and forget about it, cut you off on the interstate?"

"You sleep with a lot of women you've forgotten?" she said in a dangerous voice.

"Not anymore. But that doesn't mean I have everyone engraved in my memory. I was young and wild once." He tilted his head, getting a closer look at her. She must be somewhere between twenty-five and thirty, he thought, too young to have been a victim of his indiscriminate womanizing. Besides, he doubted he would have forgotten a woman like her. Just as he was certain he'd better not tell her that.

"And now you're old and staid? I don't buy it," she snapped.

"Older than you, sweetheart," he said.

"If you're in a hurry to die—"

"Not particularly. Are you in a hurry to kill me?"

He'd managed to startle her again. "I'm not sure."

"Well, why don't you think about it, and I'll pour us both a drink?" he said calmly.

"I don't drink."

"I do. And I need one, quite badly."

"A guilty conscience, Mr. Jameson?"

That answered the question as to whether she was a random maniac or had come for him in particular. "Name me one person who doesn't have a guilty conscience, and I'll show you a liar," he said. "I'm getting a drink. Shoot me if you get impatient, but I need something."

He'd given up heavy drinking around the same time he'd given up womanizing, more than eight years before, and the bottle of Irish whiskey was lost behind old tins of maple syrup and a gallon of windshield washer fluid. But somehow one of his occasional beers didn't seem to fill the bill.

He poured himself a glass, neat, and held the bottle in her direction.

"No," she said.

"It's Irish whiskey," he assured her. "Some of the best. You look Irish enough to appreciate it."

"No."

"It'll make killing me easier. You don't look like you're completely happy with this experience," he murmured, pouring another glass anyway and holding it out to her. If she reached for it, he could probably get the gun out of her hands. She hadn't cocked it. The safety was still on, and chances were she wouldn't have time to shoot him before he knocked her cold.

She wasn't coming any closer; she simply watched him out of her clear, troubled blue eyes. "What a thoughtful man you are, making things easier for me," she said in that ridiculously lush voice, mocking him. "I hadn't expected you to be nearly so cooperative."

He shrugged, taking a sip of the whiskey. It burned quite nicely, and he pulled out a straight-backed chair with his foot and sat down. "Everyone's got to go sometime," he said affably.

She looked at him, and just to increase the effect, he leaned back and crossed his ankles, for all the world as if he was used to entertaining deranged women in his kitchen. "Have a drink, lady, and tell me how I've done you wrong."

He wondered whether he'd pushed her too far. Apparently she decided he was relatively harmless, even if he was worth killing, and she reached for the glass of whiskey he'd poured her. He could have jumped her then, but for some mysterious reason he decided not to. He had this chance; he'd have other ones. In the meantime he could probably lull her into thinking he was no match for her.

There was a rocking chair next to the fireplace, and she sat down in it, daintily, the gun in one hand and the whiskey in the other. She had big, strong hands, and the gun looked absurdly small in them. He tried to search his errant memory for where he'd seen a gun like that before.

"Nice gun," he said. "Though you strike me as the type who'd prefer a forty-four magnum." The flicker of uncertainty in her eyes told him she knew absolutely nothing about guns. He wondered if she even knew how to cock the little lethal thing in her hand.

"I like this one," she said. "There's a certain poetic justice to it."

"Justice? What have I done . . ." He switched tacks. "Are you going to tell me your name before you blow me away? I'd like to know my executioner."

"Ardath Smith," she said.

"Ardath?" he echoed in disbelief.

She took another sip of whiskey, and he could see some of her tension beginning to ease. "Awful name, isn't it?" she said.

The name meant absolutely nothing to him—he was certain he'd never heard it in his life. "Guess you'll have to blame your parents for that one," he said.

It was the wrong thing to say. Her beautiful eyes narrowed, and the gun aimed for his chest. Better than his groin, though not much.

He was getting tired of this. The cold night air and the whiskey hadn't helped his head one tiny bit, and the charm of being held at gunpoint was wearing thin. "Look, Ardath Smith," he said irritably, "stop waving that damned gun at me. You may be doing a damned fine impression of a crazed stalker, but I don't think that's why you're here. Either tell me why you want to kill me, or get back in your car and drive away."

"I would have thought you'd recognize me."

"I've never seen you before in my life," he said flatly, certain of it. "You remind me of someone, I can't remember who, but it's only a passing resemblance."

"Wrong, Mr. Jameson. You've met me. Twenty years ago, when I was twelve years old, and you were screwing my mother."

He was unimpressed. "Lady, I screwed lots of mothers when I was in my twenties. Which one was yours?"

"Zoe."

"Oh, shit," Ethan Jameson said. And he drained his Irish whiskey.

Chapter Ten

~

He wasn't what she'd expected. She remembered him through the mists of childhood, as someone young, so handsome he was almost pretty, romantic and poetic and stone-hearted. She'd seen his grainy photos in the newspapers and had somehow come up with a mental amalgam of Byronic seducer and aging, cynical roué.

Which was both accurate and inaccurate. He was still astonishingly good-looking, and not nearly so old as she'd thought he'd be. His hair was long and black, liberally salted with gray, and his face had character as well as beauty. She wasn't going to allow herself to think about his body.

"How old are you?" she demanded abruptly.

He looked startled. Throughout the last few minutes he'd seemed more surprised and amused than actually threatened—until she'd mentioned her mother's name.

"Thirty-nine," he said. "Why?"

Ardath froze. "Then you were nineteen when my mother died?"

"Ah, the lady can do simple arithmetic," he murmured. "I was eighteen years old when I met Zoe. She was somewhere in her mid-thirties, I believe, though she never admitted it."

If he thought that would ameliorate her anger, he was mistaken. "You think that excuses your cruelty to her? She died because of you."

Ethan Jameson surged to his feet, slamming down his empty glass of whiskey and starting toward her. She kept the gun trained on him, hoping he couldn't tell that her hands were shaking, but he seemed to be beyond caring. He loomed over the rocking chair, leaning over her, ignoring the tiny gun.

"She died because of her own drunken vanity," he said in a cold, practical voice. "She killed herself in a maudlin fit because her third young lover in a row had finally had the sense to escape from her smothering possessiveness, and she knew her looks were fading, that she had no talent, and that her husband had finally had enough of her histrionics. She killed herself so that she could be the center of attention throughout eternity. And it looks like she succeeded just fine with you."

She lifted the gun and pressed it against his chest. He was shirtless, his flannel robe hanging open, but he didn't flinch when the barrel of the gun touched his skin. "Go ahead, Ardath," he taunted her. "Follow in Mummy's footsteps."

She couldn't move, frozen, looking up into his dark, dark eyes. He reached up and put his hands around hers, around the gun, and gently lowered it into her lap. He made no effort to take it from her. He probably knew he didn't need to.

He turned and went back to his chair, pouring himself another stiff shot. "Drink your whiskey, Ardath," he said in a rough voice. "And then maybe you can figure out why you're really here."

Ardath had made it a habit never to do what anyone ordered her to do. Not her father, her sisters, her teachers, her ex-lovers. She drained the glass of whiskey, shuddering, and glared at the man draped casually in the straight-backed chair. "You really are a bastard, aren't you."

"Have you ever considered therapy?" he countered sweetly.

"I figured killing you would be cheaper."

"Not really. You'll need a defense attorney, even if you plead guilty, and they don't come cheap."

"My sister's a lawyer. She'll handle the case."

"Not good form," Ethan said. "You'd be better off with a public defender. That won't cost you anything, but you'll probably wind up in jail."

"Don't you think I'd deserve a jail term?"

His grin was slow and wickedly seductive. "For killing me? There are any number of people who'd brand you a heroine. I've made a lot of enemies in my life, and I'm sure I deserve to die an early death. I'm guilty of a lot of things, but not the crime of breaking Zoe's heart. There was only room for one person in Zoe's obsessive love, and that was herself."

"She loved me."

His smile turned sour. "Did she? Or did she just think you were her little mirror image—a fashion accessory to parade around for everyone to admire, a work of art she couldn't screw up? You look a bit like her, you know. The same reckless beauty, the same full mouth and elegant bone structure. But your eyes are different. Hers were smaller, more calculating. I think you're dangerously unstable, but you still have warmer eyes."

Ardath didn't like where this conversation was going. She didn't like her reaction to his casual words. She didn't think of herself as a reckless beauty—more as a half-baked copy of the glorious Zoe, never as talented, never as pretty, never as lovable. Everyone had loved Zoe—everyone except the man she'd come to kill. "Did you ever care about my mother?" she asked curiously. "Did you ever love her?"

"I got over it," he said flatly. "Real fast." He sneezed three times, then glared at her. "Look, I'm coming down with a cold, I've got a killer headache, I'm cold and tired, and I want to go back to my nice warm bed. Either kill me or go away. I don't really care which it is, as long as you do it now."

"I haven't made up my mind whether I'm going to kill you," she said coolly.

"Well, come back when you decide."

"My car's wrapped around a tree out there."

"I'll call you a taxi."

"They have taxis up here?"

He sighed, exasperated. "No." He rose, and she could have wished he were a little shorter, that his flat stomach had grown paunchy with advancing age, that he had masses of hair all over his chest and shoulders and knuckles. She could have wished he weren't still a mesmerizingly beautiful man closer to her age than she'd ever suspected. "Look, give me a minute to get some warm clothes on, and I'll drive you back into town. Someone can come out and look at the car tomorrow and—"

"Don't bother," she said. "I have no intention of going anywhere."

He eyed the gun that she'd pointed toward him once more. "Hell," he said.

"I'm holding you hostage until I decide what to do with you," she said. "Maybe I'll kill you, maybe I'll just maim you a bit. Maybe I'll decide to forgive you."

"Big of you," he muttered.

"But in the meantime, neither of us is going anywhere."

"Don't you think this has gone far enough?" he said.

"No, not at all. Look at it this way, if I let you live, you'll have material for any number of columns. You can mock me as you mocked my mother."

He had the grace to look uncomfortable. "I didn't mock your mother."

"How do you think I finally remembered you? I read 'Zoe's Gift' and finally discovered the name of the man who'd broken my mother's heart."

"Give me a break," he muttered, rolling his eyes.

"Don't annoy me. You wouldn't want me to rush into anything too hastily, now would you?"

"Yes," he said flatly.

"You can go up to bed if you want," she said. "As long as you don't get any bright ideas about calling for help. As long as things stay peaceful around here, I'll consider letting you live. The moment someone turns up looking for trouble, I'll be more than happy to give it to him." She wished she smoked. A cigarette would have gone beautifully with that last little speech. She had to make do with a curt gesture with the small gun.

Ethan Jameson did not look impressed. "There's no telephone upstairs. Only one in my office, and I seldom answer it. That should make things easier for you." He rose, but she stayed put. He towered over her anyway, and his height, his lean, semi-clothed body made her uncomfortable. Standing next to him made it even worse—she was better off rocking back and forth in front of the banked fire and clutching her gun.

"Where are you going to sleep?" he asked.

"Right here. Though I don't expect to do much sleeping. I have some decisions to make. Whether I'm going to kill you or not. Or whether I'll be satisfied with having you write a proper portrait of my mother—one that is loving, appreciative, respectful."

"I don't write fiction," he said. He started for the door and the narrow stairway leading up.

"You're making a mistake if you don't take me seriously," she called after him.

He paused, looking over his shoulder. "I take you very seriously, Ardath. You have a gun, you hate me, and you're a woman. Add to that you're Zoe's daughter, and it means I'm in deep shit. I'm also tired. Shoot me in the back if you want, otherwise I'm going to bed. Good night."

He didn't wait for her to respond, which was just as well. He closed the door behind him, and she heard him going up the stairs.

She shivered. A thick cotton throw lay on the wooden bench by the fire, and she pulled the warmth around her, edging closer to the dim coals. She wasn't used to this damp, bone-chilling cold. She was exhausted, more by the tumult of her emotions than the long drive northward through the spitting rain.

He wasn't what she'd expected—he was far more disturbing, and her choices no longer seemed so clear-cut. If she had any sense at all, she would kill him, find his office and telephone, and call for the police to come and take her away.

But she was no longer sure she really wanted to kill him. She wanted him to suffer, as her mother had suffered, as her family had suffered. But she didn't actually want to shoot him. At least, not much.

She leaned back in the rocker and closed her eyes, just for a moment. She was so tired. There'd be no rest for her until she decided exactly what it was she wanted to do with him. In the meantime she could find a brief, temporary peace, just for a short, blissful moment.

Couldn't she?

Ethan put the phone back silently in its cradle without dialing, then stretched out on his bed. His crazed stalker was far too trusting. He had a total of four telephones in his rambling old farmhouse, as well as a cellular phone in his pickup. He might prefer his solitude, but he had no choice but to stay connected.

He really thought he'd call Zeke down at the Townall Police station and get someone up here with a SWAT team. If they even had SWAT teams in New Hampshire, which he doubted.

He changed his mind. He didn't want a group of armed men storming the house, particularly when there wasn't any real need for them. Ardath Smith wasn't going to shoot him—he was willing to bet his life on it.

She wouldn't shoot a SWAT team that showed up either, and calling them in would be a good way to get rid of her, fast. It would also entail just the kind of publicity he hated. He could see the tabloids now. They usually didn't bother with him, but this whole episode would be just too juicy to resist.

No, he didn't want the publicity, he didn't want an invading army, and the grim, unacceptable fact was that he wanted Ardath Smith—Zoe's daughter.

It gave him the creeps. She was nearly a decade younger than he was, the daughter of a woman who'd seduced him and managed to do a fairly thorough job of screwing him up completely. She even looked a little like her mother, and Ethan wasn't a man who liked to repeat his mistakes, relive ancient history, or get involved in something that felt uncomfortably close to emotional incest.

All that was completely sensible, but didn't make the slightest bit of difference. She sat in his kitchen, dressed in jeans and flannel, her damp hair a mess, a gun in her hands, and he wanted her.

He stretched out on the bed, tucking his hands behind his head, and tried to remember Zoe. It had been years since he'd even thought about her—writing "Zoe's Gift" had finally given him some much needed resolution about the whole thing. He'd let go of Zoe—fascinating, bewitching, demented Zoe—only to have her gun-toting daughter show up, ready to finish the job her mother had started on him.

Odd, she might look like Zoe, but she didn't really remind him of her. Zoe had always worn wispy things that showed off her willowy body, clanking jewelry and artful makeup that hid the beginning ravages of age and alcohol. Her daughter's face was scrubbed clean. She wore a man's flannel shirt and faded, loose jeans, not a piece of jewelry anywhere on her. Zoe had had small hands, delicate. Ardath had strong hands.

He wondered what she'd do if he went downstairs and kissed her. He wanted to. Her mouth was full and generous, and he wanted to see how her strong body felt up against his.

She'd probably shoot him if he tried. Either that, or she'd run away. And since he decided she really wasn't going to shoot him, going back downstairs and putting moves on her was probably the smartest thing he could do. If she ended up walking down the mountain to the main road, she'd get a hell of a cold but she'd survive. It wasn't cold enough to snow, and maybe he could call Zeke after all and have him give her a ride to the airport in Manchester.

He didn't make any effort to descend the back stairs quietly. The narrow steps creaked beneath his bare feet, and there was no way he could avoid the noise. He pushed the door open into the kitchen, prepared to duck in case he'd underestimated her homicidal tendencies.

The room was still and silent, and for a moment he thought she might have left. Either that, or she was searching his house for God knew what. It took him a moment to see her curled up in the rocking chair where he'd left her, sound asleep.

The gun lay on the table beside her. He walked across the room, but she didn't wake. It was cold down there—the fire had died out, and he hadn't put the wood stove back in for the winter yet. She looked pale in the dim light, with purple shadows beneath her eyelashes. She had freckles.

He'd always been a sucker for freckles. If Zoe had had freckles, he might not have been able to escape from her. Her daughter had them—a sprinkling of gold flecks across her nose and cheekbones—and like an idiot he stared down at her.

She wasn't about to wake up, even with him watching her, so he finally came to his senses and reached for the gun. It was loaded, which surprised him. She didn't hold the gun as if she knew anything about it, much less was able to load and fire it. Ethan knew a great deal about guns, and he emptied the five bullets from the chamber and tucked them into his jeans before returning the gun to the table. An expert might be able to feel the difference in weight. Ardath was no expert.

She was tall, maybe five foot eight or nine, but no match for his six foot three. And now she had no weapon—it would be a simple matter to wake her up and dump her outside in the pouring rain.

Except the rain was noisier now, making a nasty clacking sound that signaled it was freezing solid on every available surface, including the roads.

There'd be no way he could get her out of there if they had a full-fledged ice storm.

Besides, he might have a hard time if she were defenseless. Ethan had a romantic streak when it came to helpless women. Though probably a despicable remnant of his upbringing, it was impossible to resist. Show him a helpless, needy woman, and he caved in.

He didn't want to think Ardath was needy. She was dangerous enough already, not because of the gun or her formidable rage, but because of the powerful feelings she stirred deep within him. He didn't need to feel tenderness as well as lust—the combination of the two could be lethal.

The room was cold, and she had only a light blanket around her. He could still see rain sparkling in her hair, and he considered building up the fire, then thought better of it. She slept heavily, but dumping logs would be enough to jar anyone.

He fetched a down throw from the living room sofa and tucked it around her with gentle hands. She murmured something sleepy, and for a moment her cheek brushed against his hand. He froze. He wanted to cup her cheek and move her mouth toward his.

Big mistake, and he'd already made too many mistakes in his life. With luck she'd be gone by morning. She'd wake up, the rain would have stopped, and she would have come to her senses. If her car was really immobilized, she could walk, or steal his truck. He ought to leave the keys out as a helpful suggestion.

With luck. He'd lived too long to put much faith

in a changeable creature like luck. Good things happened when you needed them least; disasters always tended to be compounded. This current situation was difficult enough; he wasn't sure how it could be made worse.

He looked down at her, and had the gloomy suspicion he might be about to find out.

Physical cowardice had never been one of his failings. On the rare, unlikely chance she'd be gone and he'd never see her again, he leaned over and brushed his mouth against hers. Her breath was warm, sweet, tasting like the whiskey he'd forced on her, and he wanted to tip the chair back and kiss her more fully.

He had enough sense not to. He'd learned his lesson with Zoe, and he wasn't going to repeat his mistakes with her daughter, no matter how tempting she might be. If she were anyone else in the world, he would have done it, would have kissed her into sleepy wakefulness and then into drowsy seductiveness.

But his sense of self-preservation stopped him, and he moved away before he could make another mistake.

If she wasn't gone by morning, he'd tie her up, toss her in the back of his four-wheel drive pickup, and take her to town himself. He needed his solitude back, and he needed Zoe's daughter long gone.

And he had every intention of seeing to it.

She woke up cramped, stiff, cold. The covers lay in a pile on the floor—she must have pushed them off at some point. She didn't remember where the

soft down cover came from—had she gone in
search of it while she was half asleep?—but she
didn't care. She reached for the gun in sudden
panic, breathing a sigh of relief as she clutched the
cold, smooth steel.

She'd been a fool to let herself fall asleep. Ethan
Jameson could have taken the gun, called the police, and ruined all her plans.

But he hadn't, and right now she wasn't certain
what her plans were. Everything seemed to have
changed almost the moment she'd looked at him.
Theory was all well and good, but reality was dis-
tressingly . . . real. If she shot him, he would bleed.
If she shot him, he might die.

She found the bathroom, aspirin, toothpaste, and
an extra toothbrush. By the time she emerged, she
was no longer hobbling stiffly, and she headed for
the sink, in dire need of coffee, when she noticed
the eerie blue light coming in the bank of multi-
paned windows.

She opened the door to get a better look, staring
in absolute wonder at the landscape. Everything
was coated with a thick film of ice, each delicate
tree branch, her banged-up car, the evergreens, and
the split rail fence. She took a step out onto the
porch, her feet went flying, and she landed hard on
her butt on the ice-covered steps.

Ethan Jameson stood in the doorway behind her,
and for half a second she expected him to slam the
door shut. He didn't, nor did he make any effort to
help her up from her ignominious position on the
ground.

He simply looked past her, staring out over the

ice-glazed landscape with an expression of defeat and disgust.

"Looks like you're not going anywhere today," he said grimly. He turned and left her sitting on the ice as he headed for the kitchen sink.

Her jeans were getting wet, her back hurt, and she'd left her gun on the table. She scrambled to her feet, barely able to keep upright as she clutched the doorknob and stumbled back into the kitchen. He didn't even look up as she raced for the table where she'd left her gun.

"I like my coffee strong and black," he said, keeping his back to her. "If you've got any objections, you can make your own."

She clutched the gun tightly in her fist. "You missed your chance," she said.

"Did I?" He seemed unconcerned. "You're not going to shoot me, Ardath, and we both know it."

"I haven't made up my mind yet."

"Well, until you do, put the damned gun down. I don't like drinking coffee while staring at a weapon."

She considered several choice responses, none of them particularly mature. "We'll compromise. I won't point it at you. Unless I don't like your coffee."

He turned to look at her then, and she was struck again by how dangerously good-looking he was. It should have come as no surprise—Zoe insisted on being surrounded by beauty. What shocked Ardath was her own reaction to him. She would have thought that she, of all people, would be impervious.

She glared at him. "Don't push me."

"Push you?" He smiled then, a slow, mocking smile that was somehow shockingly seductive. "I hate to tell you, Ardath, but I'm a very pushy guy."

And he started toward her.

Chapter Eleven

~

"You think I won't shoot you? Think again," she said, pointing the gun at him.

He stopped his advance. The bullets to the small gun were upstairs hidden in his dresser drawer, no threat to anyone. "Yeah, right," he said. If she knew her gun was empty, it might push her over the edge. Not that he thought she was particularly close to it, but he wasn't in any mood to find out—at least, not before coffee.

He went back to the sink, making the coffee while she watched him, her useless little gun still trained on him. "Your kitchen is spotless," she said. "So's the rest of your house."

"Yeah," he said. "So what?"

"I don't trust a neat man."

He hooted with laughter. "I don't think trust is much of an issue in our relationship."

"We don't have a relationship!" she shot back.

"I think we do. If it makes you feel any better, I

have a local woman comes in three times a week to pick up after me and do some of the cooking. I'd appreciate it if you didn't shoot her."

"Working for you is probably torment enough. When do you expect her?"

"Not till tomorrow, and that depends on how long it takes the ice to melt. Roanne won't be attempting the hill road until it's well sanded."

"Won't they use salt to melt it?"

"Can't use salt on a dirt road," he said. "Flatlander," he added genially, watching the coffee drip into the pot with agonizing slowness. "Where exactly did you come from?"

"You don't need to know anything more about me," she said in a repressive little voice.

"Just making conversation. Considering we're trapped together for the time being, I thought it might help pass the time. Make things more interesting for you as well, until you decide to shut me up with a bullet."

"I told you, I haven't made up my mind."

He gave her a wicked smile. "Tell you what. Why don't you tell me the story of your life over coffee, and I'll come up with some healthy alternatives to cold-blooded murder."

"I don't need career advice from you, Ethan Jameson."

"I can't say much for your current avenue of endeavor." It was dark in the eerie blue light of the ice storm, and he leaned over and flicked on the bank of recessed lights in the ceiling. His unwanted guest blinked at the brightness, shaking her head, and her red hair billowed out around her. He wondered what it felt like—if it would be soft and silky, or wiry.

"Revenge is an old and honored tradition," she said. "Don't try to tell me you've never succumbed to the temptation to avenge yourself for wrongs done you. I won't believe it."

"What do you think 'Zoe's Gift' was?" he shot back.

"A way to cash in on my mother's death."

She was beginning to piss him off. He yanked the coffeepot from under the filter, ignoring the splatters that hissed onto the warmer as he poured himself a mugful. "One column doesn't make me a millionaire."

"I read that column. You said if it wasn't for Zoe you'd be writing earnest little novels that no one ever read. Instead you're rich and successful and happy."

"I said that?" The notion amused him. "I don't believe it. I've never admitted to being happy in my life."

"Maybe that's because of the life you've lived."

"Sounds good to me," he said in a careless voice. "Let's just figure that God is punishing me by making me cold and lonely and miserable and leave it at that. You can go on your way, secure in the knowledge that I'm suffering, and I can live out my life in solitude and repentance."

"I don't think so. Are you going to give me any of that coffee?"

"Help yourself." He moved out of the way, but not very far. He knew his proximity made her nervous, and he wasn't quite sure why. It wasn't as simple as the fear of being overpowered by someone a hell of a lot larger. She had the gun, and she mistakenly thought she could shoot him if he jumped her.

No, there was some other reason she didn't like him standing too close to her. Which, of course, made him absolutely determined to loom over her every chance he got.

She managed not to touch him as she poured herself a mug of the strong dark coffee he'd made, but only barely. She slopped some on her hand as she scuttled back to her spot by the table, and he leaned against the counter, watching her with reluctant fascination. He wouldn't have thought someone could scuttle gracefully, but Ardath Smith managed that feat. She seemed totally oblivious to her beauty, to her sheer femininity, and her passing resemblance to her late mother made that obliviousness even more interesting. Zoe had been totally obsessed with herself—with her looks, her emotions, the soap opera she constructed around her. Ardath moved through life with a total disregard for all the clever little gestures and expressions Zoe had excelled in. And that lack of self-consciousness was making Ardath completely irresistible—at least, to Ethan.

And he didn't like it, he reminded himself. He wasn't about to get involved with a pistol-packing redhead of dubious ancestry. He needed to kick her ass out of his house, out of his life, and then he needed to go someplace warmer, sunnier, and get himself royally laid.

He suspected that particular cure wouldn't work, though. He'd grown up in the last decade, and casual sex had lost its appeal. It was too easy, too empty, and if he needed a quick release, he could take care of it himself with no complications and no danger of nasty diseases. He'd gotten past the point of letting hormones rule his life.

Except that they seemed to be doing that very thing. He was stupidly, idiotically in lust with Zoe Smith's daughter, and the thought of anyone else failed to arouse even the slightest bit of interest in his usually cooperative libido.

He had to get her out of his house. And then he could control his life and his lust with his usual measured calm.

She peered at him over her mug of coffee, an odd, vulnerable look in her blue eyes. When he looked into those eyes, he forgot about everything except the need to . . .

He stopped himself, cold. It might be his imagination or wishful thinking, but there could be a very simple reason why she would keep her distance, why she would look at him with such an odd mixture of wariness and longing. He wasn't a vain man, but he'd lived with his body and face long enough to know that women generally found him attractive. And he suspected, illogical as it seemed, that Ardath Smith might possibly suffer from the same problem.

If he found the idea of sleeping with her faintly incestuous, she must have an even stronger reaction. After all, she was the one who came looking for him with a gun. She probably considered him the Antichrist.

But that was the interesting thing about Satan. He was very tempting.

He set his coffee down slowly, considering his options. It was a danger, of course. She would most likely go screaming into the countryside once he put his hands on her, and then he'd be well rid of her.

But what if he found he didn't want to let her go?

He had to be out of his mind for even considering such a possibility. She was still looking at him as if he were a cross between Adolf Hitler and Brad Pitt, and the answer to his little problem was obvious. All he had to do was go for it.

He started toward her again. She held her ground, her soft mouth tightening as she instinctively recognized the threat, and she drained her coffee before setting it down with a thunk on the hardwood table.

"Dutch courage, Ardath?" he murmured. He was taking his time. To make the threat more effective he had to move slowly and let the full impact of the danger take control of her.

"Your coffee's too weak," she said, but there was a faint waver in her voice.

"My coffee is strong enough to dissolve paint," he said, moving closer.

She pointed the gun at him, and her hands were shaking. "I don't know what you think you're doing, but if you come one step closer, I'll shoot you," she said.

"I'm going to kiss you," he said lazily. "And then maybe I'll take you up to bed and see if we can't work some of this anger out of your system."

She turned pale. "You smug bastard," she said. "If you even touch me, I'll blow your head off."

"You can't shoot me, Ardath." He stopped. He

was so close their clothes brushed, so close that he could feel the warmth of her body, so close he could feel her fear, and her longing.

"You don't think I'm strong enough, is that it?" she said dangerously. "You don't think I could do it?"

"Of course you could," he said gently. "But the fact is, I took your bullets." He put his hand over the gun and took it from her, and she let it go, staring up at him.

"Don't," she said in a quiet, desperate little voice.

"I have to," he said regretfully. And he cupped her face with his hands, feeling the softness of her skin beneath his fingers. She let her eyelids drift closed to hide the panic in their blue depths, and she held herself very still.

He wanted to laugh at her martyred expression. He wanted to laugh at himself. Instead, he brushed his mouth against hers, tasting the coffee, tasting her fear.

Her lips were soft, beguiling, and he kissed her again, just as carefully. Tension was running through her body like a strong current, and he wanted to warm her, ease her, pull her up tight against him, and see how well her tall, strong body fit.

She moved with little prompting, pressing up against him, and she fit just fine—perfectly, in fact. Her breasts were full and soft beneath the flannel, her hips cradled his erection, her arms moved around him, clinging to him, as her mouth tilted beneath his, opening for him, and he wondered if he could take her on the table.

Probably not. "Come upstairs with me," he whispered against her mouth.

She made no effort to pull away. "You're sick," she said.

"Actually, I'm feeling very healthy at the moment," he answered, rubbing against her. "Come upstairs, and I'll show you."

"I make it a habit never to sleep with my mother's ex-lovers." She was trying to sound cold and icy, but her fingers were absently caressing the loose cotton of his shirt.

"Good," he said. "The rest of them are too old for you." He kissed the side of her neck, moving his mouth up to the sensitive spot behind her ear. Her thick red hair was soft and silky to the touch, and it smelled like autumn rain. It shouldn't have been an aphrodisiac, but it was. Everything about her, including the fact that she'd tried to kill him, was erotic. He must be sicker than he realized.

And he didn't care. She'd moved her arms up around his neck now, and she was starting to kiss him back, just slightly, her lips clinging for a moment, reaching for his, and he was thinking the table would do just fine after all when the door to the kitchen suddenly slammed open, letting in a blast of numbing icy wind, and something even worse.

"Well, now, ain't this sweet," said a rough male voice.

Ethan froze. He looked down at Ardath, who was staring past him in shock, and his sense of foreboding increased. "Don't tell me you have a jealous husband," he said.

"Oh, I'm a jealous husband all right," the stranger said. "I'm just not *her* husband."

Slowly, Ethan released her to turn and look at his

newest intruder. This one wasn't nearly so pretty as Ardath Smith. He was a stranger, a man in his late twenties, with lank, greasy hair, an acne-pitted face, and the soul-dead eyes of a killer. The gun in his hand was a .44 magnum, much bigger and more efficient than the little gun Ardath had turned on him, and the man held it with the ease of someone used to weapons.

"Shit," Ethan said flatly, turning back to Ardath. "Do you know him?"

She shook her head, obviously stunned. He let go of her, turning to face the man, keeping his body between the gun and Ardath. He didn't know why he bothered—gentlemanly self-sacrifice wasn't usually his style, particularly since Ardath had been the one holding a gun on him just a few minutes before. But he went with his instincts rather than his common sense.

"Who the hell are you?" he demanded irritably.

"Roanne Wilmer's husband, Tom."

"Shit," Ethan said again, a feeling of dread wiping out almost the last trace of his lust for the woman behind him. "She divorced you."

"I don't hold with divorce," the man said. " 'What God has joined together let no man put asunder.' "

"I thought you did a pretty good job of putting your first wife asunder," Ethan said, perhaps unwisely. "Even if they couldn't prove you shot her."

"That won't be a problem this time around."

Ardath moved from behind him, ignoring Ethan's efforts to keep her shielded. "This time?" she echoed in horror.

"Roanne oughtn't to have left me," Tom Wilmer said in a flat, emotionless voice. "I told her so, but she didn't listen. She had no right pressing charges, either. I lose my temper sometimes. A man's got a right to lose his temper, doesn't he?"

"Not if he breaks his wife's bones when he does it," Ethan said.

"Sure, she comes crying to you," Tom scoffed. "She comes crawling into your bed, thinking you can take care of her, and she doesn't have to dirty her hands with the likes of me. But she's gonna learn otherwise. She belongs to me. Forever, and I aim to see to it."

Ethan took a deep breath. "Look, Tom, you don't really want to hurt anyone . . ."

" 'Course I do," Tom Wilmer said. "I don't give a shit how many people I do hurt. The fact is, Roanne's coming with me. We belong together, and she knows it, even if you put ideas into her head. Women don't have any brains; they just need a strong man to look out for them. If Roanne hadn't lost her temper and had me thrown in jail, you wouldn't have been able to come sniffing around her, getting her all confused."

"But they let you out, didn't they? She must have dropped the charges."

"Hell, they put me away for five years. Five years for getting a little physical sometimes with my wife. The law's crazy, I tell you. And I wasn't about to spend no five years in jail. Killed a guard, but that don't matter."

Ethan felt Ardath's sudden jerk of horror. "They'll come after you," he said in a measured voice. "If you have any sense, you'd get the hell away from here while you still have a chance."

"I don't need a chance, mister," Tom Wilmer said, his voice rich with contempt. "I'm not going anywhere until Roanne shows up, and then we're not going far. We're going to a place where no one can bother us, no one can interfere between a man and a wife. A better place than this world."

Ardath pushed past Ethan. "You can't," she said in a hushed voice. "You can't kill your wife."

"Oh, yes, I can. And I'll kill the pair of you if you try to stop me," he said, then glanced around the kitchen. "Got any more of that coffee?"

The wind was whipping through the kitchen door, and Ethan sneezed. "You think you might close the door, Tom?" he asked in a deceptively affable tone of voice.

"Oh, yeah, sure," the man said, looking suddenly like a little boy chastised by his grandmother. "Sorry, I wasn't thinking." And he turned to reach for the open door.

Ethan didn't hesitate, didn't even stop long enough to think about what a damned fool thing he was doing. He dove for Wilmer, tackling him and knocking him out onto the ice-coated porch.

Ethan saw it coming, almost in slow motion, the huge gun coming up toward his head as he tried to wrestle it out of Tom Wilmer's brawny hand. He heard Ardath scream, and the sound seemed to come from far away, and he had the sudden, random thought that he was going to die without getting her in bed.

Then everything went black.

* * *

Ardath hurtled herself across the room in a mindless rage, but Tom Wilmer was already up, kicking Ethan Jameson's unconscious body out of the way, and he knocked her sideways with a casual swipe that left her breathless, collapsed against the kitchen cupboards. Ringing filled her ears, and she shook her head, trying to clear her vision. Wilmer kicked the door shut, dumping Ethan in the middle of the pine floorboards. Blood poured from Ethan's forehead in sickening amounts as he lay, cold and pale and still.

She managed to scramble to her knees, starting toward Ethan after a wary glance at Wilmer. He had moved over to the counter, calmly pouring himself a mug of coffee.

"He oughtn't to have done that," he said in his eerily polite voice. "I don't have no quarrel with you, little lady. You behave yourself, and we'll get along just fine."

He was skinny, not too tall, and despite the gun in one ham-handed fist, he looked deceptively harmless. Ardath hadn't been called "little lady" by anyone in her entire life, and she didn't like it.

She grabbed a clean dishcloth, knelt beside Ethan, and pulled him into her arms, mopping up the blood. The cut on his forehead was shallow, and she remembered from somewhere that head wounds always bled dramatically, but he still didn't move as she curled up beneath him and cradled his head in her lap. "Don't be dead," she whispered, a combination of prayer and threat. "Please God don't be dead."

"He ain't dead," Wilmer said irritably, sitting down in the rocker and setting the huge gun in front of him. "He's got a hard head. It takes more than that to kill a person."

She kept mopping the blood, trying to calm the panic and rage that filled her. "I guess you'd know," she said bitterly.

"I guess I would."

It wasn't a reassuring response. Ardath ignored him, concentrating on the man lying in her lap. He was pale and still as she leaned over, trying to see if he was breathing. "Ethan," she said urgently. "Ethan . . ."

"He's right, I'm not dead." He opened his eyes, looking at her with a mixture of surprise and wariness.

"Thank God," she breathed, fighting back the sudden tears.

"Why? I thought you wanted me dead."

"She wants to kill you, too?" Wilmer said from his spot by the fire. "You must make a lot of enemies."

"More than my share today," Ethan said. He tried to sit up, cursed, then sank back in her lap again with a groan.

"Lie still," Ardath said. "You just stopped bleeding, and I don't want you to start again."

"In case you haven't noticed, the floor is hard and cold," he said sharply.

"In case you haven't noticed, my lap is soft and warm."

He glanced up at her. "True. But I can't rid myself of the feeling that you're going to dump me."

"You'd deserve it," she said, then realized she'd been absently stroking his hair. She started to take her hand away, but he reached up and caught it, holding it with his as he looked up at her. She let her hand rest in his, foolishly.

"Ain't this sweet?" Tom Wilmer snorted. "Better not get too fond of him, lady. He ain't gonna be around long enough for you to get too cozy."

"What do you mean?"

He picked up the gun, fondling it lovingly. "Just that I'm gonna wait till my Roanne gets here, and then I'm probably gonna blow his goddamned head off. Then I'm gonna take Roanne up to the top of Sugar Mountain and finish the job. I expect they won't find our bodies till the spring." He sighed gustily. "Sounds real romantic, don't it?"

"Charming," Ardath said in an icy voice. "But why would you want to kill Ethan?"

"Because he's been sleeping with my wife."

"The hell I have . . ." Ethan tried to sit up, but Tom Wilmer quickly pointed the gun at him. "I haven't touched your wife," he finished more calmly.

"I can't say as I blame you. Roanne's more woman than most men ever see, but she's mine. My property, and you had no right to interfere. Just be glad I'm leaving your little lady friend behind."

"I'm not his friend, I'm not little, and I'm no lady," Ardath said.

"You're little compared to Roanne," Ethan murmured dryly.

She glanced down at him. For a man with a gash in his forehead, facing imminent death for the second time in twenty-four hours, he seemed much too amused by the entire situation. "That man is planning to kill you," she said. "Why are you so damned lighthearted?"

He reached up and touched her cheek. "Because, dear heart, there are things worse than death. And I suspect falling in love with you might be one of those things."

His head bounced when she dumped it on the hardwood floor.

Chapter Twelve

~

Ardath Smith wasn't taking his declaration of love too well, Ethan thought as his head smashed against the floor. He supposed he could have phrased it better, but frankly, he wasn't in any mood to worry about semantics. He meant what he said. He didn't want to fall in love with the deranged daughter of a former lover who'd almost ruined his life. He didn't want his safe, secluded life disrupted, nor did he want to rearrange his emotions, his space, and his comfortable life. If he let down his guard, he'd probably end up writing earnest little novels once more, and die a pauper.

It looked as if he was going to die a relatively wealthy man at the blood-stained hands of Tom Wilmer. He remembered far too much about Roanne Wilmer's crazed husband. He'd killed his first wife and gotten off on a technicality. He'd done time for assault on a number of women too smart to marry him, but Roanne had at least had the sense to press charges. This time they kept him locked up, away from the woman he'd sworn to kill.

Until he'd managed to escape.

The local police force in Townall, New Hampshire, wasn't particularly sophisticated, but the state police would probably be called in as well, and Roanne would have been warned, maybe even whisked off to some safe place where they stashed abused and endangered wives. Common sense told him that she wouldn't come in and precipitate a bloodbath.

But what would happen when Tom Wilmer grew tired of waiting? He was edgy, nervous, and his pale, almost colorless eyes had the glassy sheen of someone so far gone there might be no coming back. Would he kill them both? Ethan was totally unimpressed with the notion of dying young.

"When does Roanne usually get here?" Wilmer demanded suddenly.

"About ten. But she's not coming today. Why don't you go out looking for her?" Ethan suggested helpfully, earning Ardath's horrified condemnation.

"Don't lie to me. She comes every Monday, Wednesday, and Friday. She can't wait to get up here, and I know why."

"But today's ..." Ardath's voice trailed off at Ethan's abrupt, silencing gesture. It was Thursday, Roanne's day off, but Tom Wilmer was unlikely to go along with that helpful information.

"Today's what?" Wilmer said, his eyes narrowed suspiciously.

"Icy," Ardath supplied brightly.

"Yeah, well Roanne's a country woman. She ain't gonna let a little ice get in her way." He rose, swaying slightly, and Ethan realized he was at the edge of exhaustion. If they were lucky, he'd fall asleep, just as Ardath had done. Ethan didn't think they were going to be that lucky.

"Listen, little lady," Wilmer said, "how about rustling me up something to eat? I haven't had anything but a Big Mac in the last twenty-four hours."

"I don't cook," Ardath said icily. "And I told you, I'm neither little nor a lady."

Wilmer pointed the gun over her head and fired it.

The explosion was deafening in the enclosed kitchen. The bullet slammed past them and embedded itself in the wall. Ardath screamed, then slapped a hand over her mouth, as if ashamed at such a logical reaction.

"Time to learn," Wilmer said affably.

Ardath scrambled to her feet, clutching the wooden counter for support. "Never seen a gun fired, Ardath?" Ethan taunted her. He was in no mood to rise and help her, nor to put himself in the line of fire.

"There's a first time for everything," she said. She glanced at Wilmer. "I can boil you some eggs," she said. "That's about the limit of my cuisine."

"It'll do."

She glanced down at Ethan sitting at her feet. He would have one hell of a headache, but at least the blood had stopped.

He leaned back and watched her as she rummaged through his refrigerator. "I'll take a couple of eggs as well," he said affably.

One went whizzing past his head. It missed, smashing against the cupboard next to his head and running down onto the floor in a slimy mess.

"You oughtn't to let her get away with that shit," Tom Wilmer advised him. "A slap upside the head would set her straight soon enough."

"She's likely to hit me back," Ethan said lazily. "I'm a real coward when it comes to physical violence."

Wilmer's slow grin revealed a set of stained, uneven teeth. "You keep that in mind, and maybe we'll get along real well. As long as you don't come between me and Roanne, maybe I'll let you live. Maybe."

Ethan wasn't going to place any bets on it. He glanced up at Ardath, wondering if she had any idea just how dangerous their situation was. She was a ridiculously fearless creature, and if she made the mistake of throwing an egg at Wilmer, he'd probably shoot her instead of the wall.

She was fearless, but she wasn't stupid. She cooked in silence, setting the bowl of boiled eggs in front of Wilmer, then sank down on the kitchen floor a few feet away from Ethan. Close enough to touch if she really wanted to. He suspected she did. Escaped killers made strange bedfellows out of the oddest couples.

"How's your head?" she asked quietly.

"Lousy." He sneezed twice and groaned. "I need my life back."

"I think I'd be happy to give it to you," Ardath said, glancing toward Wilmer.

"Yeah, well, don't hold your breath," Wilmer called to them from the table. "I'm running things around here, and you'll do like I say."

"She's not coming, Wilmer," Ethan said evenly. "By now you should realize that. They've probably got police out looking for you, she's off someplace safe, and you're just wasting your time. Why don't you take off before the police find out where you are?"

"I figure it won't take even a dumb cop that long to put two and two together and figure out where I am. If Roanne doesn't show up here like she's supposed to, then I've got nothing to lose. And you're beginning to annoy me."

"Why don't you leave, then? You could rip out the telephone cord so we can't call for help. That would give you plenty of time to get away from here, lie low for a bit. If you're so determined to kill Roanne, you'll have to find a time when she isn't on guard."

"Oh, great." Ardath kicked him. "Give him advice on how to kill his wife just to save your own sorry butt."

"I don't need no advice!" Wilmer thundered. "I done it before, I can do it again. Killing's one thing I know about."

"You screwed up this time. Your wife's not coming anywhere near you."

Wilmer pushed back his plate and rose, a look of serenity on his still features. "Then I guess I'm gonna have to make do with killing the two of you. That'll send her a little message, don't you think? Make her feel guilty as hell, not to mention scared shitless. She'll know she can't hide from me forever. When she least expects it, I'll be there, waiting for her."

"You're crazy, aren't you?" Ardath said with a noticeable lack of tact.

Ethan sighed. "Did you just figure that out?"

"Shut up, the two of you! I'm sick of yer yammering at me. If Roanne knows I've escaped, then she'll probably know where I'm headed, and she'll tell the police. They'll come up here, sooner or later, and then I can use the two of you for bargaining power."

"They're not going to hand Roanne over to you, Wilmer."

"They're not going to let me kill you without doing something."

"Great," Ethan said. "They'll import some SWAT team and storm the place, and then we'll all end up dead." He glanced at Ardath. She was paler than she had been, the soft sprinkling of golden freckles standing out across her cheekbones, reality beginning to sink in.

"No more talking," Wilmer said. He moved toward them on unsteady feet, his eyes glittering. "I think I'm gonna need to do something about you two. I'm tired of looking at you, tired of listening to you. Hell, I'm just plain tired."

"Why don't you take a little nap, then?" Ethan suggested helpfully.

"I'll do that—after I take care of you two." And he pointed his gun in the middle of Ethan's forehead.

This wasn't precisely what Ardath had had in mind when she'd set off from her apartment three days before, she thought, scrunching down in Ethan's huge old bed. It had all seemed so ridiculously simple—she'd drive to northern New Hampshire and kill someone.

She'd seen too many movies, read too many

thrillers and mysteries. What had seemed a simple, straightforward act of dramatic justice now appeared both horrifying and childish.

"I should never have come here," she said.

"You just figure that out?" Ethan countered in an irritated voice. "You're not too bright, are you?"

"Don't push me," she warned. "It won't take much to stir up my decision to kill you."

"I don't think it's going to be up to you. Tom Wilmer seems determined to take that honor for himself. Of course, I imagine he's going to blow you away as well, which, if you'll pardon my saying so, serves you damned right."

She ignored him. "If I had just stayed where I was, Wilmer would have come up here, blasted you, and justice would have been served."

"I hate to tell you this, Ardath, but I don't deserve to die any more than you do."

"A matter of opinion," she said with a great deal of dignity. Considering that the two of them were lying in his big bed, tied together by a cord of nylon rope, dignity was a hard-won commodity.

"Personally, I think if anyone gets killed, it ought to be you. After all, she who lives by the sword dies by the sword and all that."

"Generous of you." Her body was plastered up against his, the thin nylon cord encircling their ankles, knees, and waists, binding them together, face-to-face. Wilmer had tied their hands around each other's bodies and then shoved them down on the bed with a coarse laugh and the suggestion that they find some way to enjoy themselves. Ardath was not having a good time at all.

The bed was soft beneath them, but the room was

cold. At some point the power had gone off, plung-
ing the room into a blue-lit gloom, and even Ethan's
prodigious body heat couldn't quite penetrate to
her bones. She was shivering, determined not to let
him feel it. All her life she'd done her best to protect
herself from feelings of inadequacy, need, longing.
She didn't want help from anyone or anything,
even the simple help of someone's body heat in a
desperate situation. If you counted on someone,
loved someone, that person abandoned you. She'd
learned that one Christmas Eve twenty years ago,
and no one, not even her sisters, had managed to
convince her life could be any other way.

Ethan tried to shift away from her, but they were
bound too tightly, and he merely succeeded in
yanking her toward him.

Her hair was in her face, her wrists hurt, and she
was so damned cold. "I don't want to die," she said
in a small, soft voice, half expecting some cynical
response from him.

He was silent for a moment, and his response
was surprisingly gentle. "You won't," he said.
"Neither of us will."

"I wish I could be so sure of that," she said. A
faint shiver ran over her body, and she tried to
stiffen her muscles.

"I'm sure," he said, and he sounded so definite,
so annoyingly confident, that she believed him.
"You're cold, aren't you?"

"I'm fine," she lied as another traitorous shiver
shook her body.

She was unprepared for his response. He rolled,
flipping her body beneath him so that she sank into
the soft feather bed and his bound body covered

hers. He was heavy, but he was warm, and after a few strange hunching motions he'd managed to pull a duvet over them as well. She was wrapped in a cocoon of feathers, with his hard, hot body plastered against hers, and it was deliciously, deliriously fine.

"How's that?" he murmured in her ear.

It was heaven, even if she was having a little trouble catching her breath. She wasn't sure if it was his weight pressing down on her or the strange catch in her heart, but she did her best to summon her defenses. "You're smothering me," she said dryly.

He rolled onto his side, taking her with him, and there was nothing she could do but try to find a comfortable way to drape herself against him. His shoulder was bony beneath his soft, worn flannel shirt, but there was an odd comfort in it, the feel of flesh and muscle encasing bone, and she pushed her face against him like a sleepy kitten, letting out a reluctant sigh of contentment.

"That's better," he whispered. "Now go to sleep."

She made one last effort. "How can I sleep?" she demanded in a tired, cranky voice. "He'll probably come up and put a bullet in my head."

"Being awake won't stop him, and if he does decide to do that, you'd be better off asleep. There are worse ways to die. But don't worry—Tom Wilmer isn't going to do that. He won't cheat himself out of the pleasure of terrorizing another woman if he's got the chance."

"What do you mean?"

"I mean he's spent most of his life beating and

hurting and frightening women. It would ruin the sport if he just flat out killed you."

"You're so reassuring, Ethan." She was too comfortable to sound suitably outraged.

"Go to sleep, Ardath. I'll think of something to save us."

"Oh, my heart's a-quiver."

"Yes," he said. "It is."

She was tired of arguing with such a conceited, obnoxious creature, especially since she was roped tight against him. Her body was betraying her mind, making her muscles relax against him, making her skin warm to him. She was trapped for the time being, and all the fighting in the world would only make it worse.

"I hope he shoots you," she said sleepily, closing her eyes and letting out a deep breath.

"No, you don't."

But she was too far gone to argue.

He woke up before she did, and the room was cool, pitch-dark, and utterly silent. At some point he'd rolled over onto his back, and she was draped across him like a sleeping cat, relaxed and trusting of her ownership. He'd always liked cats—their queenly self-sufficiency, their boneless grace. Ardath was sleek and soft and gloriously feline, up to and including her murderous streak. In another lifetime she'd probably been a very effective mouser.

She stirred against him, making a soft, whimpering sound that was unaccountably erotic, and her body jerked lightly. He wondered if she was having a hot dream. Was she dreaming about him? Her nipples were hard through the layers of clothing, beneath the heat of the duvet, and he figured it was just as well she was asleep. Even if she was as turned on as he was, she'd probably object to the hard ridge of flesh pressing against her belly.

She jerked again, and her eyes fluttered open in the darkness. He could see her face in the eerie half-light. She looked sleepy, confused, and completely desirable.

"Where . . . ?" she whispered in a daze, tugging at her trapped arms. "Oh," she said, as she began to wake up more thoroughly.

"Oh, indeed." He kept his voice low and cool. His erection hadn't lessened one bit, and as long as she kept rubbing up against him, he doubted it would, but maybe she wouldn't notice. "We're in my bed, tied up by a murderous madman, and the power's still off."

She tugged again, which only made his body rub up against hers even more. "My hands are asleep."

He rolled onto his side, so that her hands were loose behind his back. It may have made her feel better, but it made him a hell of a lot worse. He was nestled against the cradle of her thighs, and there wasn't a damned thing he could do about it.

"Is that better?" he whispered in a deceptively even voice.

"A little." He could feel her hands flexing behind his back. "It's very quiet. Do you think Wilmer gave up and left?"

"Not a chance. I've been awake long enough to hear him moving about. I don't think he's going anywhere until he gets what he came for."

"But you said the police probably warned Roanne."

"Yeah. But they may not figure he'd come up here looking for her, and they could be looking anywhere for him. If there was some way I could get to the phone, maybe we could call them."

"What phone?"

"The one right behind you, on the bedside table."

She froze, and it took him a moment to realize he'd made a tactical error. "You told me you had only one telephone in the house and it was in your office," she said in a cool, dangerous voice.

"So I lied. You can't expect truth from a man you're holding a gun on. I have four telephones in the house."

"So where are the police? You must have called them last night after I left you alone. Why haven't they shown up? The ice storm?"

"Icy roads aren't going to stop the local police. They're used to bad weather," Ethan said.

"Then why aren't they here?"

"I didn't call them."

He could practically feel her turning that information over in her clever, bloodthirsty brain. "Why not?" she said finally. "Did you think I wouldn't really kill you? Did you think I was too weak to do it?"

"I think you're not really someone who goes around killing people. And I could tell by the way you held the gun that you knew absolutely nothing about firearms. You might have shot me by accident, but that was about the only way you were going to manage."

"What makes you such an expert on guns?" she snapped. "Some dark, romantic past in the CIA?"

"I don't think the CIA would be that romantic. Bureaucracies seldom are. My father's a survivalist."

He'd manage to shock her. "He's what?"

"One of those loonies who lives in Idaho and stockpiles weapons for the coming Armageddon. He's basically harmless—a vegetarian who wouldn't even shoot a rabid dog—but he's convinced the end of the world is coming, and he wants to be ready. And you can't grow up around a gun nut without absorbing some information, whether you want to or not."

"So you know about guns? Enough to shoot Wilmer before he shoots us."

"For that we'd need a gun."

"We have one. Somewhere. What did you do with it?"

He couldn't believe he'd forgotten about the Lady Smith. He'd been incensed enough when she first pulled it on him, but in the meantime other considerations had taken precedence. "I don't know," he said simply. "I don't remember what I did with the goddamn gun."

"Some help you are," she said.

"I had other things on my mind."

She snorted.

"Listen, while you've been sleeping like a baby, draped all over me like Cleopatra on a barge, I've been busy thinking," he shot back.

"About what? What a good column this will make if you survive?"

"Actually, that never entered my mind," he said in surprise. "Though now that you mention it—"

"What were you thinking?" she demanded.

"Two things. One, how the hell are we going to get out of this mess?"

"Logical enough. Did you come up with any answers?"

"Not yet," he admitted, rocking against her lightly. She felt soft and pliant against him, and he wanted to curse.

"What else were you thinking of? You said two things."

"Oh. The other one's no big deal."

"What?"

"I was just wondering how the hell we were going to have sex when we're tied together fully clothed like this."

Chapter Thirteen

~

For a moment Ardath wasn't certain she'd understood him. Plastered up against him, there was no way she could have missed the fact that he was either spectacularly well-endowed, or he was reacting to her. Considering that she'd arrived in New Hampshire with the express purpose of killing him, the realization that he might be turned on by her seemed both far-fetched and unhealthy.

"You're perverse," she said, but there was nothing she wanted to do more than melt against his warm, strong body.

"Maybe," he said.

"Making love to me would be like trying to make love to my mother. You can't bring her back."

"I don't want to bring her back," he said with a shudder. "I like you better."

"How flattering."

"You're honest. You don't lie about wanting to kill me."

"And you find that irresistible? Tom Wilmer wants to kill you, too."

"Yeah, but he's not my type."

She'd ducked her head, trying to keep her face away from his too discerning eyes. He told her she didn't lie, and he was right about that. She hated lies, trickery, and deceit. No matter how difficult it was to face, the truth was always better in the long run.

But what if he asked her the truth about him? About whether she wanted him? Would she lie this time? Would she deny the irrational, overwhelming attraction that was practically melting her brain?

Given the bound condition they were in, she was reasonably safe in admitting to anything—if she had to. There was nothing he could do about it.

"Look at me, Ardath," he said.

She lifted her head defiantly, staring up at him in the blue-lit darkness. He needed a shave, his hair was too long, and his eyes dark and unreadable. He was the architect of the disaster that had ruined her life, and if she had any sense at all, she'd spit at him.

She had no sense. Emotion was ruling her life, and she couldn't fight it. "What do you want from me?" she asked, knowing there was surrender in her voice.

He leaned his forehead against hers, and his mouth was tantalizingly close. "Everything," he whispered.

She kissed him. Fool that she was, she crossed the few inches between their mouths and kissed him, a harsh kiss, full of despair.

She was unprepared for the speed and intensity

of his response. With his hands tied he couldn't hold her, but he rolled her underneath him, his body touching her everywhere, pressing against her, as his mouth slanted across hers with a deep hunger that shook her. She didn't want to fight him; she didn't want to think. She wanted to lie beneath him, sandwiched between his hard, dangerous body and the soft feather bed. She wanted to touch his face, his body. She wanted to open her legs and pull him deep inside her until she cried out with the joy of it.

He kissed her eyelids, her nose, her cheekbones, the soft spot behind her ear. He bit her earlobe, and she nearly climaxed, arching up against him with a strong shudder. And then she froze.

"Ethan?" she said in a calm voice.

He was trying to unbutton her shirt with his teeth, but he lifted his head to look at her questioningly.

"I hate to ask this, but is that a gun in your pocket or are you just glad to see me?"

He stared at her blankly for a moment. "The gun," she repeated calmly.

"Jesus," he said. "I must have shoved it in my pocket. The damned thing's so small I didn't even notice it."

"Okay," Ardath said calmly. "We know where the gun is, we know where the bullets are. How do we get to them?"

"How tightly did he tie your hands? Is there any chance you could get loose?"

"If I could, I would have long ago. I don't find you that irresistible."

He was lucky her hands were tied. His slow grin

made her long to slap him. He didn't dispute her claim, however. "Well, then, we'll just have to get the gun some other way. Hold still, and let me see what I can do."

The ropes didn't allow for much give. He slid down a few inches, then pushed up against her with his hips, trying to dislodge the gun from his pocket. The effect was profoundly stimulating.

"Don't!" she gasped.

She expected him to leer at her. Instead, he looked grim. "Trust me, my sweet, this is worse for me than it is for you." He thrust at her again, and she trembled uncontrollably, struggling at her ropes.

She took a deep breath, closing her eyes as she tried to compose herself. "What if it goes off?" she asked in a strangled voice.

"Are you talking about the gun, or me?" He thrust against her again, and she wanted to scream. "The gun isn't loaded. I am, but I'll do my damnedest to control myself." Again, and she bit her lip, so hard she could taste the blood.

Maybe if she kept talking, she could negate the effect he was having on her—the hot, inexorable rise of desire that spread throughout her body, building, burning. "Is this . . . oh, God . . . really necessary? What are we . . . going to do with the gun once we get it?"

The old bed rocked lightly beneath them. "Damned if I know." His voice was showing the strain as well. She had no idea whether he was making any progress with the gun; she was far more concerned with the solid ridge of flesh thrusting, teasing, pushing against her tightly closed thighs. "I figure it can't hurt."

"It might kill me," she whispered. "How in God's name can people *like* bondage?"

He thrust against her again, and the room grew darker, warmer. Her skin tingled painfully, but she knew there was no way she could climax like this, with this wickedly frustrating tease. She needed him to touch her, and he couldn't. She needed him to take her, and he couldn't. All he could do was thrust himself against her and drive her out of her mind.

"Actually, it can be fun," he said in a strained voice.

"What can?"

"A little light bondage. You know what I mean—I tie your wrists to the bed and make you come. That sort of thing."

"Sounds like utter hell," she gasped.

"Don't be Victorian, darling. You'll enjoy it. I promise you."

"Don't . . . call me darling. And I am not going to bed with you."

"Sweetheart, you're already there."

"No, I'm not," she said between her teeth, struggling with the ropes that bounds her wrists. Her hands were numb, slippery with sweat, but there seemed to be some give in the thin nylon cord, and she fought harder, growing desperate.

"Please," she whispered, unable to catch her breath. "Stop. Just for a moment. I can't . . . stand . . . I can't . . . don't . . ." She could feel tears of frustration running down her cheeks. There was no way she could even reach for what she needed; she was trapped, lost, desperate for reprieve or completion, she didn't know what.

"Stop fighting, Ardath," he said in a rough voice, and she knew the gun was forgotten. "Let go."

"I can't," she gasped, struggling against the black cocoon that smothered her. "I won't—"

He covered her mouth with his, silencing her, making certain this had nothing to do with escape and survival and everything to do with sex. She couldn't stop him, and she no longer wanted to. All she could do was lie beneath him, suffering, dying. . . .

The bastard knew her body better than she did. The climax slammed through her, and his mouth silenced her scream as wave after wave of fierce, hot pleasure shook her body, tossing her down a dark, slick tunnel of endless fire.

It took her forever to catch her breath, to let the fury ease in her body. He was lying very still against her, not moving, his face buried in her neck, and she shuddered, drawing in a deep breath.

"I'm going to kill you," she said.

It took him a moment to move. He lifted his head to look at her, and the expression in his dark eyes gave her pause. "So what else is new? Trust me, Ardath," he said in a tight voice, "I'm suffering for my sins."

She stared into the dark, fathomless eyes of the man who'd destroyed her life—the man she would most likely die with in the next few hours. And none of it mattered. Out of nowhere a bubble of strange happiness filled her, and she smiled at him, a dazzlingly bright smile. "Serves you right," she said.

There was no mistaking the stunned expression

on his face, even in the darkness. "I didn't know you could smile," he said.

"I can laugh, too."

"And how are you at loving someone?"

She stared at him in the darkness. It was strange, surreal, and yet somehow completely right and natural to be having this conversation with her worst enemy. "I'm out of practice," she said.

"Me, too. I hear it's like riding a bicycle or having sex—it's easy to do once you've learned how."

"I'm not sure I ever learned."

"Maybe I can be patient," he said, and she doubted he'd ever been patient in his life. "I want you, Ardath. It makes no sense at all, but I want you here, with me. For as long as you can put up with me."

"You're crazy."

"Yes."

She looked at him. "So am I," she said finally.

"I know." His voice was gentle.

She shifted against him, rubbing slightly, like a hungry kitten. He groaned deep in the back of his throat, and she realized that his cock was the only hard thing pressing against her. "Where's the gun?"

"At our feet, I think," he said casually. "Be careful not to kick it on the floor."

"I'm more interested in kicking you. Why didn't you tell me you'd gotten it?"

"I had other things on my mind. Still do, in fact."

She yanked at her wrists again. "I think I can untie my hands if I work at it," she said. "The ropes loosened a bit when we were . . . when we . . ."

"I get the idea," he said dryly. She pulled at them

again, pulling his body up against hers as she did so, and he groaned.

"Watch it," he warned her. "I'm at about the limit of my endurance."

"Then hold still."

"I'm holding." He lay on his side, completely still, while she worked at the tight knot that bound her wrists around his body. She could feel pain, almost from a distance, a deep, aching pain through the numb flesh of her hands, but she ignored it, tugging, pulling, feeling the rope, then her hands gave a bit.

Finally, one hand was free, but the pain was so blinding that she slammed her face against his shoulder, muffling her cry as she cradled her wounded hand between them. The pain was raw, raging, and she tried to take deep, calming breaths to control the agony.

He held her, but only briefly. The ropes were intertwined between the two of them, and within moments he'd managed to release them, scooping up the gun that lay at their feet.

The floor of the bedroom squeaked slightly when he set his feet down, then was mercifully silent as he crossed to the dresser. He was only a shadow in the darkness, but she could tell by the sound of the drawer, the metallic click, and snap, that he was loading the gun.

Her gun, her mother's gun. He was going to face that crazy man, and he was going to die, Ardath knew with sudden desperate certainty. And she knew she wasn't going to let him.

She found him in the darkness, reaching for him.

"No," she whispered, trying to catch hold of the gun. She was unprepared for his sudden reaction.

He caught her in his arms, hauling her against him, and in the now pitch darkness she lost all sense of where she was, where he was. His hands were on her waistband, yanking it open with silent desperation, shoving her jeans down her long legs, taking her underwear with them. She helped him, kicking the jeans away from her, and he lifted her up onto the dresser as he fumbled with his own zipper.

She made no sound when he entered her, only a deep catch of indrawn breath as he filled her. He caught her hips in his hands, pulling her legs tight around him and lifting her off the dresser, and she clung to him, her face buried in his neck, trying to silence her choking sighs.

He made no sound at all when he came, utterly still as he climaxed deep inside her, and it was all she could do to keep her reaction silent as she con-vulsed around him, her fingers digging into his shoulders, clenching the soft flannel of his shirt.

He set her back on the dresser, and she realized absently that he was shaking. She wanted nothing more than to go back to that bed that had been their prison, but she couldn't move. She could only sit there, half naked, dazed, helpless.

His hands cupped her face, stroking her skin with such tenderness that she wanted to cry. He kissed her—soft, hurried kisses on her mouth and eyelids—and she felt something dark and hateful leave her, draining away with the suddenness of a January thaw. She kissed him back.

She pulled her clothes on in the darkness as he

moved silently away from her, heading over to the door. There was no light—darkness had fallen completely, and either the power was still out or Tom Wilmer had left hours ago. She doubted they would be so lucky.

She bumped into Ethan's tall body, but resisted the impulse to lean against him. "Do you smell something?" His words were barely audible.

"Like what?"

"Like gasoline."

"Oh, shit," Ardath said.

He turned, and even though she couldn't see him, she could feel his intensity. He caught her arms tightly, and she could feel the gun in one of his hands. "Listen, you stay here. If he sets the place on fire, go out the window onto the porch roof. From there it's not that big a drop to the ground."

"Why don't we both just go?" she asked reasonably. "Get the hell out of here before he realizes we broke free."

She didn't have to see him to know that he shook his head. "I'm not leaving this place in his hands," he said.

"I don't want you to die."

"Unless you get to kill me?" he said with a thread of humor in his voice.

She knocked free of his grip and reached up to catch his face in her hands, drawing him down to her. "Don't do anything macho and stupid," she warned him. "Or you'll have me to deal with."

"Yes, ma'am," he said. "Now stay put while I sneak downstairs. At least I've got darkness on my side. I know this house, and he doesn't."

He left her standing in the doorway to the bedroom, and she didn't hear a sound as he moved down the hallway. She counted to ten, then followed him, blessing the unexpected silence of the old farmhouse floors.

A faint light shone at the bottom of the steps, and Ardath figured Wilmer must have left the door open. Ethan's large shadow darkened it for a moment, and she held back, determined not to distract him. By the time she reached the bottom of the stairs, the door closed silently against her face.

She didn't make a sound as she fell back against the steps, both hands clutching her wounded nose. There wasn't a sound beyond the door, and she held her breath. Maybe they'd been wrong; maybe Wilmer had left hours ago, maybe—

The lights came back on with a sudden, glaring brilliance, and all hell broke loose. She stayed where she was, frozen, fighting against the desperate need to rush in and join the fray. If she distracted him at the wrong moment, she could be his death. He was a big man, taller than the scrawny Tom Wilmer, and he was armed, though the little Lady Smith was pitiful compared to Wilmer's cannon. She would only get in the way.

She heard glass shattering, and a gunshot echoed through the house like thunder, followed by thumps, groans, and curses. Then everything was ominously still.

Footsteps approached the closed door, and she readied herself to launch her body into her savior's arms.

The door opened, and Tom Wilmer stood there, a crafty expression in his pale, mad eyes. "Come on out, little lady," he crooned.

It was too late to turn and run, and Ardath had no interest in escape. He caught her wrist in his grimy hand, and the sudden, searing pain made her dizzy as he hauled her into the brightly lit kitchen.

It took a moment for her eyes to adjust. Ethan lay in a heap on the floor, unmoving, but at least this time there was no sign of blood. One of the kitchen windows had shattered, letting in great gusts of wet, cold air, and the curtain flapped heavily in the breeze.

"Did you shoot him?" she asked in a deceptively calm voice. "Is he dead?"

"Not yet, little lady. I just wanged him on the side of that hard head of his. That boy don't learn, does he? And what the hell is this?" He held up the Lady Smith with casual disdain. "What kind of real man uses a pussy weapon like this?"

"It's mine."

"You don't say so?" Wilmer chortled. "Can't do a whole lotta damage with a little bitty gun like that."

"It can kill," Ardath said fiercely. "It killed my mother."

"Well, shee-it," said Wilmer with an admiring whistle. "You didn't strike me as the kind of lady who'd shoot her own mama."

"She killed herself," Ardath said hotly.

"Girly, it's gonna kill her daughter, too, if she doesn't sit down and shut her trap. I gotta tie up this fool boyfriend of yours, and I don't fancy arguing with you while I do it."

She didn't even bother denying the boyfriend part. "Then what are you going to do?"

"Tie you up next to him, set the place on fire, and get the hell out of here," he said sweetly. "I figure

Roanne ain't gonna show, but if this place goes up in flames, everyone in town will be busy trying to put it out, and they might just forget about watching my wife."

"You're going to let us burn to death?"

He grinned at her. "Why, sure. Unless you'd rather I put a bullet in your brain to spare you the pain. That could be real unfortunate if the fire department gets here in time, though. If I were you, I'd take my chances." He tossed the tiny gun onto the table and reached down to haul Ethan upward.

There was no sign of a gunshot wound, though the cut in Ethan's forehead had opened again and was oozing blood, matting his long dark hair. Wilmer dumped him in one of the ladder-back chairs, turning his back for a moment to reach for the rope.

Ethan moved with the suddenness of a striking serpent, jerking upward, but Wilmer was too fast for him. He lunged for his gun, spinning around and pointing it at Ethan, and Ardath made her move with pure instinct, reaching for the gun on the table.

It went off, jerking upward, and Wilmer let out an agonized howl, falling facedown, his own huge gun skittering across the shiny wood floor of the old kitchen.

Ardath dropped the Lady Smith in horror. Her hand was numb with the vibrations, and she could smell metal and blood. Wilmer lay absolutely still, a pool of blood beneath him.

"Did I kill him?" she whispered, sinking back into the chair and clutching her stomach.

"I don't know, and I don't care," Ethan said.

"We'll let the medics figure it out. I'm going to get my cell phone and call them." He paused in the doorway, staring at her. "Are you all right?"

"Perfectly fine," she said—and slid off the chair in a classic Victorian faint.

Chapter Fourteen

~

Ardath was lying on an oversized, shabby, wickedly comfortable sofa in a room she'd never seen before. She'd been awake for a while, keeping her eyes half closed and drifting as she listened to the noise beyond the closed door to the kitchen. The sirens had first alerted her, and they seemed to have started almost the moment she hit the kitchen floor, but time had gotten mercifully vague, and she had no idea if it had been five minutes or five hours since she'd shot and probably killed Tom Wilmer.

She wondered whether she should feel some regret. At that moment she was too numb, physically and emotionally, to worry about it. Maybe later she'd suffer. For now she knew only that he was no longer a threat to anyone.

Someone was messing with her hand, and she opened her eyes a fraction of an inch to squint at Ethan Jameson. He was holding one of her hands while he bound her wrist. "You sure made a mess of yourself," he said in a calm voice. "Rope burns, raw skin, bruising. Though that's better than a gunshot wound. How's your head?"

Ardath opened her eyes wider. "Screw my head; is Wilmer dead? Did I kill him?"

Ethan gave a slow, wicked smile. "He'll survive, though he might very well wish he didn't. I don't think he's going to be bothering Roanne or any other woman again. Not ever."

"What do you mean?"

"From now on the man is going to have a singular lack of testosterone."

"Ethan," she said dangerously, "stop being so cryptic!"

"You shot his balls off, darling. Remind me to make sure I keep all firearms away from you. You're more dangerous than I realized."

"I did what?"

"Well, I assume it was an accident, though Zeke is going to want a full statement. I don't suppose you had a license for that gun?"

"Of course I had a license," she snapped. "I'm a responsible woman; I planned to use it."

"Such a law-abiding creature," he murmured. "Do all your killing with a licensed gun. At least that'll make things simpler."

She tried to sit up, but he put one hand against her shoulder and pushed her back down again. "Stay put. You've been through a lot. I don't want you keeling over in a dead faint again. It doesn't suit you."

"I didn't faint."

"All right, your blood pressure dropped and you became dizzy. Looked to me like a swoon." He finished binding her wrist and set it back on the sofa. "Are you ready to give Zeke a statement?"

"Give me a minute, will you?" she snapped, trying to shove her tangled hair out of her face. Ethan looked remote, distant, a total stranger, and the reality of the last few hours just came crashing down.

This time when she sat up he didn't push her back down again. He rose, standing over her, a wary look in his dark eyes. "They've already stabilized your victim and taken him to the hospital," he said lightly. "And they've towed your car down to town—"

"You think this is pretty funny, don't you?" she demanded.

"That you shot Tom Wilmer in the balls? It has its moments," he said. "At least you got to shoot someone, and he deserved it a hell of a lot more than I did."

"Yes," she said. She took a deep breath. "I'm sorry."

He stared at her in mock disbelief. "You're sorry? For what?"

"For trying to kill you."

He shook his head. "Will wonders never cease? Have you figured out I'm not a wicked, heartless seducer who ruined your life?"

She looked up at him, utterly fearless. "As a matter of fact, you are."

He made a sharp gesture. "Look, your mother was the one who—"

"I'm not talking about my mother. I'm talking about me."

He didn't move. "I ruined your life, did I?"

"Yes," she said flatly. "Not that there was much to ruin," she added with complete honesty. "I haven't been very happy."

"I hope you don't think I'm about to make you happy?" he demanded in a horrified voice.

"I don't believe in fairy tales, Ethan." She was pleased with the dignity she had mustered, considering how recently she'd been wrapped around his body, shivering in ecstasy.

"But I am a wicked seducer?"

"Very wicked," she said in a small voice. "Very seductive." She took a deep breath, determined to say it all, before the police took her away. It wouldn't make any difference to him, but it would to her. "You're a dangerous man, Ethan Jameson—dangerous to my heart and soul and whatever well-being I had. If I were a total idiot, I'd tell you I was in love with you, but I'm not a total idiot—only a partial one." Her voice trailed off.

He didn't say a word, just looked at her, and she was afraid to look back. He'd vanquished her, when she'd never realized how well armed he was. Everything that she'd ever believed was shattered at her feet, including her pride.

Zoe had been no abused saint, betrayed by a cruel lover. And Ardath wasn't Zoe reborn, and never had been. She was her own woman—strong, smart, stupid beyond belief sometimes. But she wasn't Zoe. She was simply a woman who'd fallen in love for the first time in her life, at the worst time in her life.

She looked up at him, willing him to say something, anything, when the door opened and a burly, uniformed man barged in. "Hell, Ethan, I can't wait any longer," he said, scratching his balding head. "I gotta get down to the hospital myself and take care of paperwork. Just let me talk to the little lady myself and get a preliminary statement, and then I'll make myself scarce."

"She's not a little lady, Zeke," Ethan said with a trace of humor in his voice. "Tom Wilmer called her that and look what happened to him."

Zeke made an instinctive move to cover his crotch, then laughed uneasily. "You're a joker, Ethan," he wheezed.

"A barrel of laughs," Ethan murmured— watching her.

"So how come Miss Smith shows up here with a gun? You didn't tell me you were expecting anyone, Ethan," Zeke said, eyeing them both suspiciously.

Jail probably wouldn't be so bad, Ardath thought. After all, that was where she'd been planning to end up, anyway. And since she didn't actually shoot anyone, except in self-defense, her sister Dinah would have no trouble getting her out on bail.

"I don't usually make a habit of clearing my romantic engagements with you, do I, Zeke?" Ethan said lightly.

Ardath looked at him in shock, but Zeke was too busy to notice. "Now, Ethan, you usually tell me about who you're . . . that is . . ." He blushed. "Well, you know. It's just man talk."

"Ardath is different," Ethan said coolly.

"Well, sure," Zeke said hastily. "Of course. That is, if you . . ." He stumbled to a halt. "You mind if I take her down to town and get a statement from her? Or would you be wanting to drive her down later?"

Ardath rose, not waiting for his answer. "I'll be ready in a few—"

"Days," Ethan broke in.

"Now, Ethan, days won't do!" Zeke protested.

Ardath was staring up at Ethan in shock, uncertain what she expected to see in his dark, distant eyes. "She's not going anywhere but upstairs. She needs bed rest, Zeke—days and days of it. We'll come down to town eventually and help you clear things up."

"But, Ethan . . ." Ethan walked past Ardath, not looking at her, not touching her, instead taking Zeke's arm and efficiently escorting him out of the room and the house. Moments later, she heard the kitchen door slam and the engine of what must have been the police cruiser rumble to life. By the time Ethan walked back into the living room, Zeke was already gone.

"So," he said, looking at her.

"So," she said, wary.

"Zeke's got the gun—just in case you get tempted again," he said.

"I don't ever want to see another gun in my lifetime."

"Good. I'd hate to spend the rest of my life on my best behavior."

"The rest of your life?"

He came up to her. She was a tall woman, a strong woman. He was a tall man, a strong man. "I think I like you better as a total idiot," he murmured.

"What do you mean?"

He cupped her face with his elegant hands. "Stay with me, Ardath. Love me like a total idiot. Redeem me from my wicked past."

She reached up to pull his treacherous hands away, but instead she covered them with her own. "Why? Because I remind you of my mother, and this time you want to do it right?"

Hurtful words, but he didn't even blink. "No," he said. "I think I fell in love with your mother because she was the closest thing to you. This time I want the real thing."

She didn't move. "You realize this is both irrational and unhealthy?"

He managed a crooked grin. "Probably," he agreed.

"Will you love me?"

"Definitely."

She looked up at him and smiled dizzily. "All right," she said, "I guess I won't have to kill you."

PART THREE

~

Dinah

BY
DONNA JULIAN

Chapter Fifteen

❦

Winter 1997

It was the Christmas season, December 23rd. Jingle bells, ho ho ho, and deck the halls with boughs of holly. Two shopping days remaining; today the last on the court docket until after the New Year. Hallelujah!

Dinah Clayton Smith wore red—bright red. Red dress, red coat, red lipstick. It had nothing to do with holiday spirit and making merry. It was simply a significant part of a very carefully devised strategy to win a megabucks divorce settlement for her client, Melanie Warren.

"Wow," Stan Rosenthal said as he approached from the elevator banks on the opposite side of the hall. "You look like a million bucks, which is almost exactly the fee you're charging my client's wife, if my sources are correct."

Dinah rolled her eyes. Stan was counsel for Paul

Warren, Melanie's soon-to-be ex. Stan was also a slick little worm with a python-size ego. "Nice suit, Stan. JCPenney?"

He was, in fact, wearing a Valentino original that had set him back a couple K. He laughed, easily catching the implication. "Cute, Smith. Real fucking cute."

"We aim to please," she said, treating him to one of her dazzling smiles.

"Yeah, well, I'm afraid you're not going to be pleasing the lovely and faithless Mrs. Warren. You've got a loser this time, sweetheart. Should have accepted Paul's generous offer. A two-mill-above-the-prenup bonus would have kept her in boy toys for a helluva long time."

They had arrived at the courtroom door. Dinah came to a sudden stop, flicking her wrist and giving her watch a cursory glance. Five minutes till show time. She shrugged from her coat, revealing a smart, sleeveless A-line dress that emphasized her diminutive and ultrafeminine figure. She dropped the coat along with her briefcase and handbag onto a bench and turned back to her colleague. She stepped closer to him, then set about straightening his tie. She took her time, keeping her gray eyes lowered, focused on her artwork. When she finished, she looked up, meeting his gaze. "There. Now you look perfect. A real dragonslayer. Too bad we're going before Thomas Fowler. Leah Quick would no doubt have been squirming in her honorable panties."

He grinned. "You're a bitch, Smith, but so goddamned gorgeous I really hate what I'm going to do to you in there."

"Oh, don't be silly. A guy's gotta do what a guy's gotta do. Besides, I'll tell you a little secret." She laid a hand on his shoulder as she took a step closer to confide in him. "Yesterday evening I stopped by the Galleria for some last-minute shopping. While I was there, I paid Santa a visit." She reached up to whisper the last in his ear: "I sat on his lap, Stan."

The natty little man arched a thick brow and folded his arms across his chest. He chuckled. "I swear, sparring with you is better than sex. So, go on. What happened next?"

"Why, Santa asked me what I wanted for Christmas, silly."

"Oh, right. Sorry. Me being Jewish and all, I forget. So, what did you tell him?"

Dinah held up her first two fingers, wagging them in front of him. "Just two things, Stan. I said, 'Santa, sweetie, I'm a very lucky girl, and I feel positively wicked asking for anything at all.' But he asked if I'd been good all year, and of course, I had to tell him how very, very good I've been, so he said I deserve whatever my little heart desires, and he promised to deliver whatever it is."

"So all right, already. I can't stand the suspense. Tell me."

Dinah shook her head, pouting prettily, and pretending disappointment. "Oh, Stan, it's so easy, I can't believe you can't figure it out. All I want for Christmas are your client's balls hanging from my tree."

The attorney threw his head back as he howled his delight, and Dinah turned back to the bench where she'd laid her belongings.

A man sat there now. He grinned as their gazes

met. "That was good," he said, handing her the coat and handbag as she picked up her briefcase.

Dinah offered a tentative smile in return. "Thanks."

"Sure," he said. "Good luck ... with nailing his client in there," he added as her fine, dark brows came together in question.

Dinah smiled once more, then turned away and stepped through the door Stan was holding open for her. Melanie was already seated in the room, looking jittery and unsure. Dinah quickened her pace, but her thoughts lagged behind with the stranger in the foyer. He was handsome—exceptionally so with the sharply contrasted tanned face against deep-set green eyes and premature iron gray hair. She'd been immediately attracted, but the sensation that lingered now was more a gnawing twinge of unease. She had the odd feeling that they'd met before, though of course that was ludicrous. A woman didn't forget a man as good-looking as that. Not in a lifetime.

Dinah's gaze dipped to her hands folded on the table in front of her as Judge Fowler rendered his decision. She allowed herself only the slightest smile as a sign of her pleasure at their victory. At her side, a soft almost imperceptive chirp of surprise escaped Melanie Warren's lips. Dinah glanced over at her, winking her approval. The former cocktail waitress had comported herself exceptionally well throughout the hearing. Behaved like a true lady, a real through and through blue blood. But then, Dinah had coached her long and hard, and of course, Melanie had been accomplished enough as an actress to snag the hotel tycoon in the first place.

Dinah looked over at opposing counsel's table a few feet away, a slight frown quickly forming beneath her heavy bangs. Her client's now official ex-husband was throwing quite a fit.

Dinah turned her attention back to Melanie, a wide smile replacing the momentary frown. "Congratulations."

"Thank you," her client said, her eyes filling with genuine tears, which she dabbed at carefully with a corner of her lace handkerchief. Suddenly, she laughed. "Wow, Dinah, I knew you were good, but honey, you pulverized him!" She laughed again.

Dinah allowed herself a soft chuckle, but she sobered quickly. "Which is exactly what we planned to do, but you listen to me, Mel. As happy as you are right this minute, that man is just as angry. It's obvious he doesn't enjoy losing. It's going to take him a while to cool off, and until he does, I want you to stay away from him. When you leave here, I want you to go straight home. Turn on your security system. If you want to celebrate your new single status or even the holiday season, for that matter, invite friends in. Don't go out."

Melanie's dark eyes widened. "Oh, come on, Dinah, Paul might be showing his ass right now, but he's as harmless as a stuffed teddy. Besides, he's only mad because he still loves me." She giggled. "And the truth is, I still love him, too. It's just that monogamy is unnatural, especially for hot-blooded people like Paul and me."

"Whatever," Dinah said, opening her briefcase

and beginning the process of packing up with the resolution of her last case of the year. "Just be careful and trust me on this one: The fury of a woman scorned can't begin to compare to the anger of a man fleeced."

Melanie shrugged. "Okay, you darling little worrywart, I promise not to invite poor Paul over for eggnog tomorrow night. Now, you promise me something."

"What?"

"Enjoy the holiday. You've worked your butt off on my behalf these past few weeks. Now it's time for you to relax and make some merry."

"Relaxation is precisely what I intend to treat myself to"—Dinah paused, glancing at her watch—"beginning in approximately fifteen minutes."

"Good, so why don't I wait for you and treat you to lunch, kind of our own private girlfriend celebration."

Dinah squeezed the other woman's hand. "Thanks, but I'm on my way out of town. I have one last little item to take up with my esteemed colleague over there, and then I'm outta here."

The two women embraced, and Dinah watched as Melanie rushed after her former spouse, stopping him at the door to give him a warm hug.

Dinah rolled her eyes as she snapped her briefcase shut.

"Go figure, huh?" Stan Rosenthal said over her shoulder, just inches from her ear.

"Damn it, Rosenthal, you startled me."

"Sorry. Just came over to congratulate you." He ran a hand over his sleek, salon-cut hair. "I swear, Smith, I don't know how you do it. I would have

bet my entire fee in this case that Judge Fowler was
going to laugh you right out of his court. I mean,
hell, that lady was doing her old man's competitors regular as other wives do the laundry." He
chuckled. " 'Course it didn't hurt that you dressed
her up in that little checked number like a fucking
parochial schoolgirl, then came in here yourself
looking like the gift-wrapped package of every bad
boy's dreams."

"Truth is, Stan, my man, you blew it. My client
simply chose to take a proactive role in Paul's hotel
business. One could say she was really doing some
hands-on test marketing for him as a guest in
his competitors' luxury hotel suites. And as you
learned today, your client's rivals weren't merely
whispering sweet nothings in the enterprising
Mrs. Warren's ear. With the significant information
she gathered in her, um, research, she more than
quadrupled her husband's net worth. According to
his honor, she more than earned the settlement we
requested."

"Yeah, yeah, I heard the ruling. My guy got
stung, while your client walked away with the
honey pot. But that's over and done with; case
closed." He rubbed his jaw and shook his head.
"So, forget the Warrens, and let's talk about the
Lady Di."

Dinah hated the sobriquet her colleague had
tagged her with, and though she tried to disguise
her pique, she was confident her eyes were suddenly more silver than gray. On the other hand,
what difference did it make? It didn't take much
imagination to figure out where this was going, and
she didn't intend to listen to a lecture on the end not

always justifying the means from one of the guys just because she'd whipped him again. She sighed and folded her arms across her chest as she leaned against the gallery railing, buying a few seconds to regain her cool. "Look, Stan, I respect you, and I'm sorry if your ego got a bit bruised today. But as you said, it's a done deal. Over. Finito. Now, it's time to start celebrating the holiday season, and I have a long drive ahead of me before I can do that. So—"

"Where you going?" he asked so abruptly, Dinah blinked with surprise.

"To the lake," she mumbled as she stepped away from the railing and started gathering and straightening papers. She glanced around the room. The bailiff was still busy changing the calendar to the first court date after the New Year. One man, the good-looking guy she'd met in the foyer, sat in the back near the door. Neither of them was close enough to have overheard the careless slip, she decided. Still, her hands shook and her heart was hammering a pretty good tattoo. "I . . . I'm sorry, Stan. I can't be more specific. I shouldn't have even said that much. The police . . . well, you know."

"Yes, I do know. This jerk Jacobs has you on a very short hit list. One woman is already dead. That only leaves Tori Jacobs, Judge Bianci, and you, which is exactly the point I'm trying to make here, Counselor.

"You're a damned fine attorney, but you've changed. I don't know exactly what it is. Maybe success came too soon or too easily. Or maybe you're so impressed by your rich and famous clientele, you been blinded by the stars in your eyes. Whatever, you've turned the practice of law into some sort of game where anything goes. Doesn't matter who gets hurt, how dirty the tricks you pull out of that little bag of yours—"

"Damn it! I knew this was where you were headed. But couldn't it actually be that the mighty Rosenthal is simply indulging himself in a hissy fit because I've encroached on territory that was always the exclusive property of a few good ol' boys?"

"Yeah, could be, I suppose," Stan said, his swarthy complexion suddenly a couple of shades darker. "Or could be I'm a pal who's genuinely worried. And not just about that nutcase Jacobs. The police have their dragnet in place, and I'm sure they'll pick him up before he can get to the rest of you."

Dinah gave a sharp, humorless laugh. "You're worried about me, about my soul. Is that what you're trying to say?"

Stan shifted his weight from one foot to the other, looking uncomfortable, though he didn't back down. "Yeah, Dinah, that's exactly what I'm worried about."

"Then you can stop. The name's Smith, not Faust. My soul's safe, Stan. I haven't bargained it away to the devil or anyone else."

"You sure?"

"Why can't you simply admit that I'm a very good attorney? You know what your problem is? Three years ago, when I walked into this courthouse for the first time, you boys took one look and saw this—you'll pardon my immodesty—attractive young woman and decided she might be taken to dinner, bed, or anywhere else as long as she wasn't taken seriously in court."

Stan's gaze moved to the floor, and Dinah laughed. She laid a hand on his arm. "Oh, come on. Don't be embarrassed, and don't be mad. I'm not. As a matter of fact, I'll tell you a little secret. I love being underestimated, and I adore being flirted with even while we're arguing before the bench. And I don't blame you for being irritated. My win record may be short, but it's perfect." She picked up a small, gift-wrapped box from the table beside her briefcase and handed it to him. "As a matter of fact, I was so confident about the way this one would go, I even bought you a little consolation gift. So, happy Hannukkah, Stan."

Annoyed as he was, he couldn't resist a grin. "Really, Smith, you shouldn't have."

She chuckled as she stretched a couple of inches on her toes to kiss his cheek. "Oh, yeah, I definitely should have. Besides, you're so damned cute I couldn't resist," she said as she picked up her purse. Her wide smile immediately wilted, replaced by a grimace as she glanced at her watch and realized how late it was. She needed to hustle if she wanted to get to the lake before sunset.

"Something wrong?" Stan asked.

"Hmm? Oh, no." The corners of her lips tipped upward just a little. "Go on, open your gift. I've got to run. Have a good holiday, Stan. I'll see you next year."

As she approached the courtroom door, suddenly the handsome, vaguely familiar stranger was standing there in her path. "Excuse me," she said, her tone reflecting her impatience.

He opened the door, stepping aside. "You forgot your coat and briefcase," he said.

Dinah froze, and her bare arms dimpled with gooseflesh. All at once she knew. She remembered. She'd heard that voice before. Once, several months ago. But there wasn't any doubt. A woman didn't forget a man who could make a simple, innocent sentence sound like an invitation to make love . . . especially when the same man had promised to kill her.

Chapter Sixteen

～

It was the same voice. Adam Jacobs's voice.

And the eyes, too. She remembered the eyes. How could she not? Deep-set, green, sharp and lethal as broken bottle glass that had cut right through her that day in court when he'd been granted his freedom at a staggering cost.

But the rest—the face, hair, even his build—was off. Different. Wrong.

Dinah's thoughts raced out of control, crashing helter-skelter into one another like bumper cars.

A crooked smile flashed out of nowhere across his deeply tanned face, and damn her for the fool she was, Dinah smiled back.

"I'm, uh, just going to the ladies room. I'll . . . I'll be right back."

She smiled once again, then spun away, struggling against the urge to run. *Don't panic, girl. Walk. Slow. Slower.*

But once inside the bathroom, she gave up all

pretence of calm and went with her fear, leaning against one of the sinks and gasping for air. She trembled from the top of her head to the soles of her feet, and her heart pounded a frantic mambo in her chest.

Dinah gasped as she met her reflection in the mirror. Her chin-length black hair shimmied like strands of silk fringe. Her eyes, normally pearl gray, were dark as slate, and her face, even under meticulously applied makeup, looked pale and drawn.

"Lipstick," she said, pulling the purse strap from her shoulder and fumbling with the intricate clasp some moron designer had crafted just to drive her crazy. "I just need some lipstick. Lipstick and some powder."

She reached inside her handbag for the cosmetics. Her hand closed around the smooth, cool handle of a gun instead. "Oh, my God," she groaned. She'd forgotten all about the gun Ardath, had insisted she carry.

Dinah had laughed when she related the death threat she'd received from a disgruntled ex-husband of a former client and the police detective's suggestion that she buy a gun and learn to use it. Ardath, on the other hand, had taken it to heart, lecturing her relentlessly until Dinah had sworn to listen to the police, get the permit to keep a concealed weapon that was issued in special cases of "extreme and dire circumstances," and carry the gun with her everywhere. And then to make sure Dinah did as told, Ardath had sicced Lauren on her, knowing full well that if their revered eldest sister asked for the promise, it was a done deal. Only Di hadn't realized how much she hated guns and how hard it would be to keep her word until she'd actually held the gun in her hand.

It was a .22—a Lady Smith. Very compact, light, even pretty with its short, two-inch barrel and uncommon mother-of-pearl handle. Looked more like a cute toy than a lethal weapon. She'd actually laughed at the prospect of loading it, putting five little bullets into their tiny chambers.

Once she was finished, though, she wasn't laughing anymore. She set the gun on the table and sat staring at it, rocking back and forth and hugging herself. A memory of tragedy so great she had never been able to confront it, had been stirred by the weapon, and it had taken several tries before she could pick the Lady Smith up again and put it back in her purse. And then she'd buried the purse under the cushions of her sofa, unable to look at it without thinking about the implication of the loaded weapon inside.

It had taken her several days to grow accustomed to carrying it, and she even succeeded in convincing herself it was nothing more than a pacifier for the police and her overanxious siblings. By this morning, she'd almost forgotten it all together. But now, here she was holding it, her finger curling around the trigger with the prospect of having to use it to protect herself.

No! That was ridiculous. She would never shoot another human being. Couldn't. She could bring a man to his knees in the courtroom, castrate him even, as was often necessary. But divorce court was not life and death.

Sanity returned along with a measure of calm.

The man out there couldn't possibly be Adam Jacobs. It was absurd to think he would waltz right into the courthouse to kill her. He might be crazy, but no one had accused him of being stupid.

So why was she hiding in the rest room, shaking like a cat in a room full of rocking chairs?

Because the police, her sisters, and everyone else had made her a nervous wreck.

Because the poor, handsome schmuck had a bedroom-soft voice that sounded as much like Michael Bolton as Adam Jacobs.

Because he had the temerity to possess very similar, very sexy green eyes.

And what about the unmitigated gall he'd demonstrated by smiling at her and opening the door for her? Worst of all, she couldn't forget how he had played the good Samaritan by pointing out the briefcase and coat she'd left behind. Good grief, no wonder she'd gone running for cover. The man was obviously a fiendish devil!

"You're an idiot," she told her reflection as her fingers moved from the handle of the .22 and closed around a slender tube of lipstick. "And that very gorgeous man out there is not Adam Jacobs."

Her hand still trembled slightly as she applied Berry, Berry Red to her lips, but her heart had quieted, and she was able to catch a deep breath once again.

So maybe if she hurried, he would still be around, and she could redeem herself by demonstrating a semblance of normalcy. She blotted her lips, finger-combed her hair, and fluffed her bangs.

She adjusted the silk scarf at her throat, made the

best-flirtateous-smile-in-the-mirror test, and stepped out of the powder room.

The stranger was standing only a few feet away, leaning against a wall. Her briefcase rested beside his leg on the floor, and her coat was draped over his arm. "Hey, there you are," he said, picking up the case and holding it out to her. "Here. Everyone's gone, so I thought I'd better get these out of the courtroom before the janitor locked up.

"Thanks," she said, tucking a strand of hair behind her ear as butterflies started up in her stomach again. She looked around the empty foyer. "Everyone's already gone?"

"Just about. Except for a couple security guards and the cleaning crew," he said, stepping away from her and crossing the hall to jab the down button beside the elevator banks. "Can't blame them. Lots to do this time of year. Last-minute shopping. Parties to get to."

The elevator arrived, and the doors opened. Dinah hesitated. *So, why are you still hanging around?* she wanted to ask. *And why are you still carrying my coat?*

He motioned with his hand for her to enter before him, a pleasant smile helping to smooth a bit of the edge from her jagged nerves.

"By the way, your friend got a kick out of your gift. Showed it to the bailiff."

Dinah frowned and shook her head as the doors closed behind him, and he punched the button marked G.

"The sucker," he explained.

Ah, the oversized lollipop she'd bought in anticipation of her big win. Dinah laughed, then looked up at him and grimaced. "Pretty mean, gloating like that, huh?"

"Hey, I thought it was great," he said. "And he was a pretty good sport about it, considering you took his client to the cleaners." He laughed, shaking his head. "I'd watch my back if I were you, though."

"Oh, I have no doubt he'll come up with something clever," she said, suddenly completely at ease as the elevator doors parted, and she stepped out into the cold parking garage. "Brrr," she said, shivering and turning to reach for her coat. "Well, happy holidays, and thanks for getting my things, Mr. . . ."

"Jacobs," he said, handing her the coat and revealing the gun he held pointed directly at her chest. "And you're very welcome, Ms. Smith."

Chapter Seventeen

~

A shriek as involuntary as a hiccup slipped through Dinah's lips, and the man's gloved hand closed over her mouth in the next instant. Dinah shook her head vigorously. She wasn't trying to escape. She merely wanted to beg him not to hurt her. But that was crazy, wasn't it? Of course he was going to hurt her. He was going to kill her, just as he'd promised in the letter he had sent two weeks before. Just as he had killed Rhonda Harker, his mistress, who'd been named as corespondent in the divorce suit.

An arm tightened around her waist, and she was lifted from the ground. Maybe if she could swing the briefcase, wield it like a club, she could—

"Don't fight me," he whispered against her ear. "Cooperate, and I won't hurt you."

She managed a couple of puny jerks she hoped he would take as nods of agreement.

He must have understood, because he set her down and slowly moved his hand from her mouth, though it dropped only as far as her shoulder. She could feel the gun's muzzle pressing against the small of her back. "Get your keys out of your purse," he said, his tone still hushed.

Her purse! Her gun was in there. If she could just get it without him noticing, she would ... what? She was shaking so badly she couldn't manage the latch. Even if she succeeded in retrieving it, she'd probably end up shooting herself.

"Hurry," he whispered, his fingers biting into her shoulder.

"Ow," she complained as she finally freed the clasp and yanked out the keys. "I'm freezing, and my hands are practically numb. Can I put my coat on and get the gloves out of my pocket?"

He snatched the keys out of her hand, pressing a button and shutting off the alarm on the high-priced late-model sedan. "You'll warm up in the car."

"Where are we going?" she asked.

Instead of answering, he opened the door on the passenger side. He tossed her coat into the backseat and motioned with the pistol for her to do the same with the briefcase and purse. "Get in," he said. "Slide over behind the wheel."

He climbed in after her, pressed the automatic door lock, and handed her the keys. "You're turning blue. Start the car and then put on your seat belt."

"Worried I might have an accident and get hurt?" she asked bitterly.

Jacobs grinned. "Not at all. You're a very good driver. I know, I've followed you. But I also know you're a lady of habit, and you always buckle up.

The old guy at the exit might notice if you aren't wearing it."

He shrugged out of his heavy, black jacket, rolled it up, and laid it between them on the seat. He nodded at the digital temperature gauge. "Already sixty degrees. Can't beat the climate control systems in these high-priced babies."

He was right, of course. The car would soon be a comfortable seventy-five degrees, while the chill index was minus fourteen outside.

"So, will you tell me where we're going?" Dinah asked with a defeated sigh as the arm at the garage exit rose, allowing them passage.

Her abductor cast her a sidelong glance, then leaned forward to open the glove compartment. He pulled out a map that was marked with a heavy red line indicating a preplanned route. He tossed it in her lap. "Looks like we're headed to your cabin in Osage Beach. I'm sure you could make the drive blindfolded, but I took a few minutes to familiarize myself with the map before I came into the courthouse to watch you in action."

"You . . . you were in my car?" she asked, incredulous.

"Yeah, well, like I said, I wanted to memorize the way to our little hideaway." He jerked his head toward the backseat and added, "Besides, why lug my duffel bag inside when I could leave it here."

Tears filled Dinah's eyes, and her throat ached with the effort of repressing a ragged sob. Her knuckles were bleached white with her tight grip on the steering wheel, and her fingertips were beginning to numb. She was terrified, but she was suddenly mad as hell, too. How dare he break into her car? Invade her space? But what was a minor infraction like breaking and entering compared to kidnapping? And . . . and murder. Oh, God, that was what he was planning, wasn't it?

She clamped her teeth together and straightened in the seat. She was barely keeping it together. Just one teensy eensy slip and she'd lose it.

Suddenly, she wanted to laugh. Okay, so she'd lose it. So what? What would happen if she fell apart, started shaking head to toe and got so hysterical she couldn't drive? Would she wreck the car? Get hurt? Maybe even killed? And if she kept her cool, she wouldn't die until she got to the remote lake area. Then she would be cut to ribbons, like poor Rhonda Harker. Only, her body would most likely be buried in a shallow grave in the woods and not found for months . . . maybe even years.

No, she wasn't going meekly like a lamb to the slaughter. She exhaled slowly, forcing her body to a more relaxed posture. Her spine bowed slightly, her shoulders slumped, and she loosened her grip on the steering wheel. She ruffled her bangs, then let her hand drop with seeming nonchalance to her leg. She'd made a decision. She knew what she had to do, but she couldn't act just yet—not in the congested city roadways. But once they were on I-44, somewhere near Pacific where traffic tended to thin, then, by God, she was going to disrupt Mr. Jacobs's plans.

The gun that he'd held hidden beneath the parka appeared suddenly, aimed right at her chest. "What . . . what are you doing?" she stammered, her ice-hard decisiveness reduced at once to slush.

"See that church? Pull into the parking lot."

"But—ouch."

He jabbed the muzzle against her rib cage, causing it to bite painfully into her tender flesh, effectively cutting off any protest. She switched on the right turn signal and eased the car into the church lot as he'd directed.

"Pull around to the back," he said.

Oh, God, he'd changed his mind. He wasn't going to wait. He was going to kill her right then and there. *No, no, no.* She wasn't ready to die. She slammed on the brakes, jammed the gearshift into park, and turned in the seat to face him. "Okay, that's it! If you're going to commit murder, Adam, you're going to have to do it right here in view of the street and all those people driving past in their cars. I'm not going to make it easy for you by going around back where you can kill me, dump my body, and then drive out of here like nothing ever happened."

"First of all, my name's not Adam. I'm Evan Jacobs, A.J.'s brother. You can call me Jake. Everyone does."

"Well, then, I guess that should make me feel better. I wasn't completely crazy, wondering how I'd failed to recognize you." She folded her arms across her chest, feeling somewhat encouraged by the modicum of spunk she'd recovered. "However, you'll forgive me for pointing out that I don't really give a rat's behind what anyone calls you. Your last name's Jacobs, you're obviously part of a sick revenge scheme that's already cost one woman her life, and now you're going to shoot me, for God's sake!"

Jacobs grinned. "Amazing," he said.

Dinah turned her head, refusing to give him the satisfaction of asking what the hell he was talking about. She sighed deeply.

"Your eyes. They turn to silver whenever you get angry. It's how I knew we weren't going to make it all the way to your cabin at the lake without you trying something stupid. Maybe somebody should have warned you that those gray eyes of yours are as good as a barometer."

Someone had warned her—Lauren, her wonderful, wise sister—countless times. *You're going to have to learn to control that temper of yours, my little love. You can't hide it. It flashes in your eyes like quicksilver and gives you away every time.*

Tears washed to the surface as unexpected as the shiver that suddenly rocked her body when she thought of the beloved sister she would probably never see again. She cried out and clamped a hand over her mouth.

"Okay, don't go ballistic on me," the man called Jake said, his tone gruff. "As you pointed out, I don't want to have to shoot you right here with the potential for a couple hundred witnesses. So, you calm down, do as I tell you, and we might make it to the lake, after all."

Dinah dashed the tears from her eyes and snapped her head around to pierce him with another hard glare. "Oh, well, if you put it that way, how can I refuse? I mean I get to live for another terrifying two hours, and you get to kill me in the privacy of a winter wilderness."

"Hey, my brother tells me you're the best lawyer he's ever met. I watched you in action today, and I agree. So, don't tell me you'd trade all the possibilities that even a couple of hours could provide for certain death right here and now?"

Dinah met his gaze, holding it for a long moment.

Who are you? she wondered. *Are you so devoted to your brother, you'd commit murder for him? Are you so dedicated to his vendetta, you'd sacrifice yourself by killing me right here and now on a crowded street? And when we get to the lake, what then? Are you really going to do his dirty work for him, or will you then signal our location so he can come attend to me personally?*

Her eyes burned with the intensity of her stare as she searched for answers, but it was a futile quest. His eyes held the secrets of his heart much better than her own. Still, she knew he was right. She had no choice but to cooperate. She drew in a long, trembling breath and nodded. "Okay," she said. "You're right. I don't want to die." She managed a thin smile. "Who knows, maybe you'll even listen to me; give me a chance to convince you how wrong this all is."

He surprised her by returning her smile, and though his eyes remained as hard and opaque as jade, her heart fluttered with hope.

"Pull around back," he said.

Oh, God. "Why?"

He waved the pistol in front of her eyes. "That steel I saw in there, remember? You were planning something, and I don't want you trying some crazy stunt that will get either one of us hurt. I'm going to drive."

She almost giggled with mingling relief and amazement. He really had read her thoughts, and now he wanted to drive. *Good.* No, make that better than good. Make that fabulous! Now, she didn't have to worry about working up the nerve to wreck the car, which might or might not have accomplished a darned thing. With him behind the wheel, she could concentrate on thinking of a way to escape or signal for help. Her heart quickened with hope.

She shifted into drive, and pulled around the long white brick building to a dead-end alley.

"Just park it beside the Dumpster," he told her.

Dinah did as instructed, stopped the car, unbuckled her seat belt, and graced him with a dazzling smile. "Okay. Want me to just slide over while you go around?"

"No, ma'am. I want you to take off that pretty silk scarf, get out of the car, and walk around to the back."

"You lied," she said flatly.

"About killing you now instead of later? No, I just don't want any more delays."

"But . . . but what are you going to do with the scarf?"

"Tie it around your mouth so you can't cry out for help." He waved the pistol in a firm, unspoken directive for her to get out.

She wasn't sure she believed him, but what choice did she have? She opened her door and climbed out, pausing only long enough to cast a wistful glance at her purse lying in the backseat, and walked resolutely to the back of the car.

"Aren't you afraid a scarf tied around my face might just attract a wee bit of attention from other drivers on the road?" she asked, even as she turned her back to him.

He didn't answer as he fitted the gag and knotted it in place. He didn't have to. He'd pulled the keys from the ignition even as she was climbing out of the car, and she heard the trunk lock click.

Well, he was right. He hadn't lied, she thought ridiculously, as he pinned her arms in a viselike grip, then scooped her up and dropped her easily inside the trunk. He wasn't going to kill her here. He wasn't going to have to kill her at all. She would freeze to death before they ever got to the lake.

Chapter Eighteen

~

She didn't freeze. In fact, except for the rough way he'd trussed her up like a Christmas goose after depositing her in the trunk, she'd been quite comfortable with his warm down-filled jacket covering her and her own soft wool coat balled up under her head as a pillow. It seemed Evan Jacobs was a killer of the chivalrous variety. Probably wouldn't even shoot her until he was certain she was nice and comfy.

She'd considered struggling to reposition herself so she could try to kick the trunk lid and attract attention with the noise. It was a ludicrous idea that she gave up almost at once. The chance of anyone hearing her was practically nil, and besides, she didn't dare risk losing the warm cover of his jacket.

She'd spent the next two hours raking her mind for a way to escape once they arrived at the cabin, and had come up with a half dozen harebrained schemes. Unfortunately, every scenario involved some daredevil stunt her five-foot-two-inch, one-hundred-five-pound frame could never accomplish. Such as wrestling him for his gun. Or racing him down the frozen mountain terrain toward Highway 54, the main thoroughfare. Or persuading him to let her build a fire so she could gain access to the poker and split his skull the moment he turned his back. Of course, that was assuming she could even successfully strike his head, given his considerable height. There'd been others. Wilder, crazier, but in the end, she knew the only realistic hope she had was of getting her purse and, somehow, shooting him with her Lady Smith before he realized what was happening.

But as she felt the tires leave blacktop and start up the steep gravel drive to their destination, she felt her stomach knot in fear, and faced what she'd been subconsciously acknowledging ever since he'd revealed his weapon: It was too late. The time to save herself had long come and gone. She'd refused the offer of police protection. Turned down Ardath's invitation to come to Vermont until Adam Jacobs was apprehended. Even refused to discuss her plans for the holidays, except for the casual mention to Stan Rosenthal. Well, at least when she turned up missing after the New Year, good old Stan could tell them where to look for her body.

As the car slowed, rolling toward a stop, she thought of her sisters. Dear, devoted Lauren, who had always felt so responsible for the others. How she would berate herself for being so happy in her newfound relationship that she'd neglected Dinah in her time of crisis!

And passionate, ardent Ardath—how angry she would be that Dinah hadn't heeded her warnings and taken her situation seriously. As always, Ardath would turn her wrath on her art . . . or maybe not this time. Maybe love had tempered some of her fire.

A tear leaked from the corner of her eye as she thought of Yardley, the baby. Of course, not really a baby for a long, long time now. All grown up into a beautiful, sweet young woman. The sentimental one of the four ladies Smith. What, Dinah wondered, would Yardley select from her belongings to cherish her memory by? There would be something—some special little treasure Yardley would most associate with her. Of that Dinah had no doubt. And then she realized what it was—the emerald ring she always wore. Her father had given it to her on the day of her graduation from high school, and she remembered, now, that Yardley had been thrilled that Dinah had loved it so much, because she'd helped him pick it out. If only she could work it off her finger so it could be found here in the trunk instead of being buried—

The lid was raised suddenly, letting in light, even though the day was darkened by a heavy winter cloud cover. Something cold and wet fell on her cheek, and she realized at once that it was snowing.

She'd closed her eyes against the assault of the unexpected light, but she opened them now, refusing to miss the beauty of her own private winter wonderland.

Jacobs leaned inside under the lid, a pocket knife in his right hand.

Dinah shook her head back and forth and managed a few panicked squeaks behind the gag.

"Hey, calm down. I'm only cutting the ropes so I can get you out of there."

Adrenaline coursed through her, making her weak and dizzy, but she stopped struggling, and in the next instant she was being lifted out of the trunk and carried toward the cabin.

With her hands freed, Dinah pulled the scarf from her mouth. "You don't have to carry me. I can walk," she said.

He shook his head and kept on going. "You've been tied up for a long time. Your feet and legs are probably numb."

She started to argue, then realized he was right. She could feel little needle pricks in her toes as blood began to stir again.

At the door he held up the keys. "Which one to open the door?"

"The second one. That one with the green plastic hook."

The door creaked loudly as he turned the handle and pushed it open, and she recalled how she'd always thought of it as a warm, hearty welcome and responded with a chipper greeting of her own. Was it her imagination, or had it sounded more like a long, sad groan today instead?

"Got a preference about where you sit?" he asked.

The unexpected intrusion of his voice startled her, and her gaze must have reflected the jolt, because he laughed. "Damn, those eyes of yours are really something. Do you know they turn almost blue when you're surprised?"

And his were as bright as emeralds when he laughed, she thought, but she would never give him the satisfaction of knowing she even noticed. "Just put me on the sofa," she said, irritation sharpening her tone.

He set her down, then pulled the gun from where he'd tucked it in his waistband. "Okay, you just sit there while I take a quick peek past the doors of these other rooms and check the lock on the back."

Dinah laughed derisively. "Don't worry. I'm not going to try and escape. I thought about it, but realized I couldn't outdistance you even if I were in sensible clothing and had a good five-minute start."

He winked. "Knew you were smart, but my esteem is growing by leaps and bounds."

He went from the bedroom doorway to the bathroom, then cut a path through the living room to the back door beside the kitchen table. He made one more stop at the kitchen cabinets, and she watched him collect the butcher knives and a long two-pronged fork. He dropped them into a plastic sack he pulled from beneath the sink, then came back to stand in front of her. "Everything's locked up good and tight. You can't get out the back without the key to the dead bolt, and I don't think you could get those windows open without them hollering loud as that door did when we came in. It's colder than a witch's tit in here, and I want to get a fire going, but I need to carry in more wood before it gets too snow covered and wet." He held up the bag with the knives and fork. "I got the most lethal-looking stuff, but I don't have time to go through every cabinet and closet and drawer, looking for potential weapons. So, the question is, do I tie you up in the chair, drag you back and forth with me in that dress and those slippery little shoes, or trust you to sit here while I get the job done?"

She started to answer, but he held up a finger, stalling her. "One more thing you should know before you commit yourself." He raised the gun, turning it this way and that, showing it off. "This is a Glock semiautomatic pistol, police issue in a lot of departments. Know why?"

Dinah raised a sarcastically quizzical brow.

"One, it's fast. Two, it's powerful, so it stops its man. Three, and most important, its aim is sure and its range is long, so it's almost impossible to miss even a fast-moving target. In other words, if I can line it in my sight, I can kill it with this honey."

"Okay, Dirty Harry, I'm sufficiently impressed. I won't move."

"Good girl," he said with a tight, sardonic grin.

She kept her word, not moving except to slip her heels off, and tuck her feet under her as she waited for the fire he soon had going to spread its warmth through the small, cozy cottage.

A large pile of wood stacked high, and the fire blazing fully, Jake brushed off his gloved hands, then went outside one last time. He returned only a couple of minutes later with his duffel bag slung over his shoulder, her two-piece set of luggage tucked under his arms, and her purse and briefcase in his hands. He dropped everything but her twin suitcases on the floor near the door, then deposited the luggage in the bedroom.

"Go on in there and get changed into some jeans or something. Might as well be comfortable; we're going to be here for a while."

"Then you're not going to kill me?" she asked.

"Not unless I have to," he said, his tone as bland as tap water.

"So, you're just the delivery boy?"

A muscle ticked in his jaw, but his green eyes were once again as murky and unyielding as pond scum. "Go get changed."

She stood up, her gaze moving to the floor beside the door. "I . . . uh, could I get my purse?"

"What for?"

"I, um, have a slight headache. I thought maybe I'd take a couple of aspirin with some water in the bathroom before I change."

He patted the sides of his jacket, then reached into one of the many pockets and pulled out a small pill bottle. "Tylenol work for you?"

Damn it! She smiled. "Sure, even better than aspirin, as a matter of fact." She took the bottle as she passed him, keeping the smile in place and repeating a silent mantra all the while: *Please don't let him look in my purse.*

He turned toward the front door just as she reached her bedroom, and her heart made a valiant effort to climb right out of her throat. She almost crumpled to the floor with relief when he gazed out the window instead of reaching for the handbag.

"Someone plowed the road before we got here."

"Gus Abbot. Lives about two miles up Highway H. He and his wife, Dolly, look after the place for me. He cleans out the chimney, cuts the wood, plows the road—generally winterizes it. Keeps the lawn mowed and the garden weeded in the summer. She keeps it dusted year round, and stocks groceries and supplies whenever I let them know I'm coming."

"And do they come up to check on you?"

Oh, God, they did! In fact, they should be by in the next hour or so!

She'd taken too long to answer, and he turned to look at her.

"Do they stay long?" he asked.

"No," she said truthfully, shaking her head for added emphasis. "It's usually just Gus, anyway. Especially when it's cold out. He'll just come to the door to make sure I'm settled in safe and sound."

"How often does he come back to check on you while you're here?" His gaze was locked on her eyes, preventing any telltale lie that would be detected in their color that changed as predictably as the stone in a mood ring.

"Depends on the weather and how long I'm staying. He might come back the day after Christmas this time if the snow keeps up, to check on supplies since I was planning on staying until the New Year."

His brows came together as he thought about her answer. After a moment he looked up. "Maybe you'd better tell him you've had a change of plans. Explain that you've decided to go on home the twenty-sixth instead of staying on."

So he doesn't wonder where I've disappeared to after your brother kills me, she thought.

He'd been looking at her, his gaze intense, but he lowered his eyes suddenly, and she knew he'd successfully read her thoughts again. Yet what could he say? He couldn't very well argue with the truth.

Chapter Nineteen

❧

Jake was keeping a vigil at the window when Dinah emerged from the bedroom. He half turned, gave her a slow once-over, then turned away again. "You look good in jeans," he said softly, as if to himself.

"Thanks," Dinah said, glancing at the floor a few feet away from him and wondering what had become of her purse and briefcase. Ah, well, she'd find out later. Right now she had other plans. Like lessening some of the tension that stood between them. She'd made up her mind while she changed. If Jake was going to wait for A.J., she might have a chance. If she could get to know him. Find out what he stood to gain. Why he'd commit a felony to help his brother. And was there anything or anyone he stood to lose?

"No sign of Gus, huh?" He didn't answer, and she went on as if she hadn't expected him to. "Won't be long. He'll be around before nightfall.

Why don't you keep watching and I'll brew us some coffee."

"There's a couple of six packs of beer in the fridge," he said. "I wouldn't have figured you for a beer drinker."

She'd already gone to the tiny kitchen, which was separated from the large room only by a row of cabinets. She pulled a filter from a cabinet, placed it in the coffeemaker, and opened a can of Folgers. "I enjoy a good cold beer every now and then, but the truth is I always have a couple of six packs on hand for Gus. He likes to drink one or two while he's piddling around the place. Those may have been in there for weeks."

She turned on the water, filled the carafe, and missed what he said in return. She emptied the water into the top of the coffeemaker and flipped the switch. "I'm sorry, what did you say?"

"Forget it. Coffee sounds good. I'll have a cup with you soon as your caretaker comes and goes."

"What are you going to say to him?" Dinah asked.

He turned to look at her, and she was struck by how handsome he looked standing there in the dusk of day with only the flickering light from the fireplace to highlight his sharply chiseled features. He was utterly male, even with his long-lashed, deep-set green eyes, and his powerful, masculine physique was delineated by the fit of his worn jeans and faded flannel shirt. He wasn't overly tall. Five foot eleven, maybe, yet in very good shape and powerfully built. A man who worked outdoors judging from the deep tan he'd retained despite the winter months, the strong, corded neck, and biceps that strained against his shirtsleeves.

A smile crept across his face, and she suspected he'd successfully followed her train of thought again. She decided to fuel his ego a bit.

Grabbing a dishcloth from the counter, she wiped her hands and came as close as the fireplace. "You look like one of the guys on TV in those 'come see Alaska' tourist ads."

He grinned again, flashing even white teeth and looking almost like a boy with the earnestness of his expression. "Feels like I'm working in Alaska sometimes when it's this cold out."

"What do you do?"

The smile fell away, and he turned away as he answered. "I build houses. J & J Construction. A.J. runs the company from the business side. I handle the physical stuff."

Dinah sighed. She'd almost succeeded in easing the pressure between them. Well, she'd try again later. Right now, the intuition she'd honed as an attorney was telling her to back off. "I haven't eaten since breakfast. I think I'll get out some cheese and hard salami, crackers and fruit. As soon as Gus leaves, we can eat. How does that sound?"

He didn't answer, but stepped quickly away from the window, and in the next instant lights washed over the front of the house. Dinah recognized the loud rumble of Gus Abbot's truck.

"Where are you—"

"In the bathroom," he said, cutting her off. "Go to the door. Act normal. Hell, invite him in if that's what you usually do, but don't let him stay too long."

"I know," Dinah said, still afraid, yet wearying of the constant reminders about his big bad gun and what he'd do with it if she forced him to, "you'll kill us both if I let on you're here. I get it." With a resigned sigh she opened the door.

"Hey, missy," the old man called as he stepped stiffly from the cab of the battered truck. "See you made it fine. The missus and me was worried. 'Fraid the snow might get in too far ahead of ya."

Despite her predicament, Dinah was at once warmed by the familiar sense of welcome at the sound of the old mountain man's words. "I made it just fine, Gus. But it always makes me feel a little safer knowing there's someone waiting for me in case I ever do have trouble."

"Well, you have that, all right. You surely do have that," he said as he came up the steps to the front door, dusting snow from his pants with one hand and carrying a brightly wrapped package in the other. He handed it to her at the door. "Merry Christmas, missy," he said. "From Dolly and me both."

"Oh, I have something for you, too. Come on in, Gus. It's in the bedroom, still packed in my suitcase. It'll just take me a minute to get it."

"Naw, now I'm fine right where I am. Ain't gonna track snow all over them floors Dolly jes' got done cleaning yesterday, and ain't gonna give folks any excuse to speculate on what I was doing inside my pretty young neighbor's house when she was here alone."

Dinah smiled at that as she hurried to her bedroom for the gift she'd packed in one of her bags. She sobered as she passed the bathroom and saw only the ugly mouth of the gun barrel in the cracked door.

"Here you go, Gus," she said, handing him the gift. "Merry Christmas."

"Well, it ain't necessary you buying us presents, but we do thank ya." He scratched the white stubble on his jaw, uncomfortable with the next part in his requisite visit. "Uh, we know how ya feel about the holiday, young lady, and we respect your feelings. We surely do. But the missus insists I invite ya for Christmas dinner. The kids is in—all seventeen grandchildren and the eight grown-ups—so it's real crowded. Loud and pretty wild, too, I ain't gonna lie to you. Still, you're welcome same as always."

Dinah felt the needle-sharp prick of tears behind her eyes. "Thank you, Gus," she said, pushing the door wider as she stepped forward to hug his neck tightly though briefly so as not to embarrass him or risk upsetting the man spying on them from her bathroom. "I appreciate the invitation as always, but you know—"

"Yeah, I know. I don't like it. Sure don't understand it, and don't think it's good for you to come down here and shut yourself up every year till the holiday's over." He shrugged. "But then, I don't reckon it's any of my business."

The snow was coming down in huge, wet flakes, and the wind was blowing them inside the open doorway. Dinah laughed as she wiped one from her eye. "It's getting pretty hairy out here. You better get on home, Gus. As you can see, I'm all tucked in nice and warm."

"Yep. See ya got yourself a good fire going, too. Jes' don't go off to bed till you've let it die down."

"Hey, this is my third Christmas here. You've taught me better than that by now."

"Well, then, I'm off." He turned away and tucked his head against the wind as he made his way to the truck. But as he opened the door, he stopped and, cupping his hand around his mouth, shouted a question up to her. "You got that cellular phone of yours with you, 'case you need anything, missy?"

Dinah caught only a couple of words, but enough to understand and nod in the affirmative. "Yes!" She hollered back. "Thanks!"

She watched until he'd maneuvered the old truck in a tight circle and headed off down the long, steep drive. She didn't close the door until the red glare of his taillights blinked out of sight. She wasn't worrying about the old man's safety. He could make the two-mile drive home blindfolded in a blizzard. She was fighting to contain her elation, giving it time to mellow and fade before she turned back into the room and took the chance of it showing in her damned revealing eyes. But it was no use. Hope continued to well like a bubbling spring just breaking ground and refusing to be restrained.

The phone! What an idiot she was. She'd forgotten all about the compact, wallet-sized lifeline she carried in her briefcase. All the while, her thoughts had been trained on the Lady Smith hidden away in her purse. But the little cell phone was the perfect solution to end this nightmare! Dinah giggled at the realization.

"What's so funny?" Jake asked just inches behind her, causing her to jump.

She spun around and stepped past him. "Excuse me," she said, keeping her head bowed, her gaze focused on the box in her arms. She carried it to the coffee table and sat down on the sofa. Tucking her hair behind one ear, she started working the ribbon from the package. "Don't pay any attention to me," she said, finally allowing herself a glance at his face. "I'm just like a little girl when it comes to presents."

"I see that," he said, his tone quiet . . . wary?

She nodded, forcing herself to give him a smile she hoped was convincing. Then she went back to work on the unwrapping.

She could feel his gaze on her, burning in its intensity.

A moment later, she pulled an ivory hand-crocheted blanket from its bed of tissue and held it up for him. "It's lovely, isn't it?"

"Yeah. Looks like somebody went to a lot of trouble. I'd say those folks are very fond of you. Hope they won't be a problem."

Dinah felt her temper flare and busied herself with refolding the blanket and stuffing it into its box once again. "You were listening. I'm sure you heard Gus say they have a houseful. I doubt they'll give me more than a 'poor Dinah up there all alone' thought for the next several days. By then, your brother will have come and gone. Nothing for you or him to worry about, after that. Right?"

"Right," he muttered, going once again to his earlier post by the window.

Dinah watched him clear a circle in the fogged-up glass with his shirtsleeve, then pushed herself from the sofa and headed for the kitchen. She was still excited about the phone, yet her heart was fluttering nervously. Why the determined vigil at the window? Was Jake really just worried about neighbors and unexpected visitors, or was he already expecting A.J.? And if so, would there be time to find her phone and sneak a call to the police?

"After I make something to eat, do you mind if I work for a while . . . Jake?" she asked, trying for a casual tone as she pulled food from the refrigerator.

He shrugged.

She frowned.

"What does that mean? You don't care if I work? Or it's stupid for me to work when I'll be dead soon, anyway? Or A.J.'s already on his way up here, so there won't be time? What?"

He looked at her then, his eyes meeting hers for a long moment before moving away in the direction of the hallway. "It was just a shrug. Didn't mean anything. I put your briefcase in the hall closet. I'll get it for you after we eat."

Hope sparked. He hadn't exactly cleared up the question of A.J.'s estimated time of arrival, but if he was going to let her work that must mean she had tonight at least. "Okay, then," she said, "if you'll give me back one of my knives, I'll get the cheese and salami sliced so we can eat." *And I can get into the bedroom and make my call for help.*

"I'll slice the salami and cheese," he said

"Whatever. I'll wash the fruit and lay out the condiments and crackers."

"Sounds like a plan to me," he said, coming toward the kitchen.

Dinah lowered her gaze to the grapes she was rinsing in the sink as she bit her lip, checking a victory grin. She looked up again in time to see him pull something from his pocket. She whirled around, crying out in frustration as she recognized what it was.

"I hope you weren't counting on using this." He held her cell phone in his hand for a moment before stuffing it back into his pocket.

"You went through my things?" she asked, amazed at the incredulity she heard in her own voice. Why was she so shocked? He'd kidnapped her, was holding her hostage until his brother got here to kill her, and she was surprised he'd snoop through her briefcase? She clamped a hand over her mouth as a sharp, bitter sound that was part sob, part laugh slipped from between her lips.

"You left your briefcase open on the table in the courtroom, remember? I took it out then."

"Oh, well, excuse me all to hell and back for accusing you of prying. How utterly unfair of me!" She dropped the grapes, dried her hands and started past him. "After all, besides aiding and abetting a murder, you're probably a very decent guy who would never snoop through someone else's property without his or her permission."

"Where are you going?"

She stopped in the middle of the living room and ran a trembling hand through her hair as she considered his question. Where the hell *was* she going? She spun around on her heel to glare at him. "To bed. I'm suddenly not hungry. Nor do I any longer feel like working. And most of all, I want to be away from you, so I'm going to get in my bed and pretend this is all just a horrible nightmare." She threw up her hands. "And who knows? Maybe when I wake up, you'll be gone, and I'll realize this was all just the beginning of another miserable Christmas, complete with my own monster."

Chapter Twenty

❧

Dinah hadn't slept even two hours all night long. She'd lain awake, alternately conjuring possible methods of escape and dreaming up horrific means of torture and revenge to exact on her handsome and enigmatic kidnapper and his evil twin—figuratively if not literally speaking. Mostly, though, she'd been tossing and turning, frustrated and desperately afraid.

She came out of her bedroom three times in the night, twice to use the bathroom, and once to get a glass of juice from the kitchen.

Jake sat in a chair he'd repositioned to face the hallway, making it impossible to ignore him, but each time she kept her gaze lowered to the floor. She might not be able to forget him, but she could damned sure refuse to acknowledge him.

By morning, her stomach was aching. She dressed at daybreak, yet refused to give in to her growing hunger. For more than three hours after a glorious

fuchsia sunrise, she staved it off by pacing the room
from time to time, passing long minutes staring out
the window at the sparkling white landscape, then
sitting on the side of the bed, fists clenched and
teeth clamped. She gave up the fight just after ten.

Her entrance was heralded by the crash of her
bedroom door as she swung it wide, allowing it to
slam against the wall.

She stalked past Jake's post in the easy chair,
slowing only enough to grace him with a dark glare.
Her hand on the refrigerator door, she stopped, turning to face him as she heard the chair groan. He was
getting up. "Look, Jake, I'm tired. It's Christmas
Eve, which is a bad time for me under the best of
circumstances, and I'm sick and tired of worrying
when your damned brother is going to show up."
She paused and took a deep breath. "Please just
stay away from me, and let me make breakfast.
Much as it galls me, I'll even play Little Suzy Home-
maker and fix you some eggs and bacon if you'll
just leave me alone."

"Why?" he asked, setting the pistol on the counter
and bending over to rest his arms beside it.

"Why, what?" she asked with an exasperated sigh.

"Why do you hate Christmas?"

Dinah already had a carton of eggs and a package
of bacon in her hands. She slammed both on the
counter beside the sink. Several shells cracked, provoking a muttered expletive under her breath. "You
know what, Jake?" she asked as she began scooping
ruined eggs from the carton and dropping them
into the sink. "You can hold me here against my
will. You can scare me so bad I don't sleep. You can
even kill me yourself instead of waiting for your

brother. The one thing you cannot do is make me tell you anything about my personal life." She turned then, egg yolk dripping from her hands and tears standing in her eyes. "Please. I don't want to talk to you. Last night I tried to pretend this wasn't happening. When that didn't work, I tried to convince myself I'd find a way out of here alive. Well, I give up."

Thirty minutes later, they sat at the table and ate in silence. When they were finished, he helped her carry the dishes to the sink. Then he went back into the living room, stopping at the table long enough to pick up a chair, which he carried to the window. He sat looking out at the frozen countryside until midafternoon, when the sound of voices suddenly carried into the house. Then he stood up for a better look.

Dinah came to stand by him at the window. "Who is it?" she asked in a hoarse whisper.

Jake didn't answer for a long, tension-filled moment. Then he pointed to a ridge just south of the driveway and three kids slowly mounting a hill on horseback. "Relax," Jake said. "Looks like some of your caretaker's grandchildren are taking advantage of the clear morning for a ride."

Dinah couldn't speak. She was shaking so hard, her teeth were clattering, and her throat seemed almost incapable of taking in even a shallow breath.

Jake looked down at her and grinned. "Guess that scared you nearly as much as it did me. You thought it was A.J., and I was convinced . . ." He cast her another of his hooded, indecipherable glances and shook his head. "Never mind. I forgot you don't want to talk. Go on back to what you were doing."

I wasn't doing anything except waiting to die, she thought. But of course she wouldn't say that. What difference would it make? He knew.

Chapter Twenty-one

～

Jake knew she was scared. Hell, *he* was scared. But what could he do about it? A.J. was his brother, and he'd promised to help. Blood was thicker than water.

But he was going crazy holed up inside the cabin. He was tired, too, and struggling with the need for a couple hours of sleep—sleep that he wasn't going to get until this whole mess was over.

He glanced over his shoulder at the woman standing at the kitchen sink, washing dishes. She was something else. Special. Petite and fragile as a china doll. Exceptionally beautiful with that translucent fair skin and silky blue-black hair. She had a wide, generous mouth, a perfect nose, and big, gray eyes—now, *they* were wild! The way they could pierce a guy's heart with their honesty and intimidate the hell out of him when they gleamed the exact same ominous silver as razor wire. But more than her exotic beauty, he admired the woman's courage.

Initially, in the first few moments of the abduction, she'd been frightened. But she hadn't fallen apart. Instead, she'd immediately started looking for a means of escape. And later, when he'd dashed her hopes with his revelation about finding the phone, she'd been daunted, set back. But not for a single moment had she given up or given in to the terror he'd seen in those spectacular eyes.

Oh, yeah, she was something.

"Hey," he said, louder than he'd intended. Then, in a more moderate tone, "Dinah."

She twisted around from the waist.

"I noticed you keep a heavy jacket and boots in the closet."

She arched a brow.

"Come on," he said. "Get 'em on, and let's get out of here. I'm getting cabin fever, and you have to be going stir crazy as well."

"I'm fine," she said, turning back to the last of the breakfast dishes she was now drying and putting away. "But you go on without me if you like."

He laughed. She was funny, too, in a sharp, acerbic way he doubted many men appreciated. "No can do, I'm afraid. I'm a city boy. I'd get lost out there in the wilderness by myself."

"Now that would be a pity."

He grinned again. "Come on," he said, his tone more assertive this time. He hated it that he had to force her, but she wasn't giving him any choice. He walked to the kitchen, stopping just behind her. He pressed the muzzle of the Glock into the small of her back. "I insist."

Several minutes later, they exited the rear door of the cabin. "Okay," she said, tipping her head back to peer at him from under the fur-edged hood of her parka. "Where to?"

"Well, Highway H is back that way, west. The Abbots live to the south, and Osage Beach is to the north, right?" At her nod, he pointed east. "What's up this way?"

"Mostly just wild, untamed land. There's a meadow over that ridge, and a half mile or so past that there's a creek that borders the edge of my property."

"No more cabins?"

She shook her head. "Not for another mile past the creek. Brinkleys own two hundred acres, but their house is at the far end of the property."

"Feel like walking?"

Dinah canted her head and shielded her eyes with her hand as she stared up at his face. "Sure. I love it. But tell me something first."

"Shoot."

"Why are we doing this?"

"I already told you," he said. "I was getting restless, and it was pretty evident you were about to explode. Thought the exercise might do us both some good."

She opened her mouth, as if to ask another question, then shook her head, apparently with a change of heart.

"What?" he pressed.

"Nothing," she said firmly, and started off into the wild, and away from likely encounters with neighbors.

He caught up with her after only a couple of

steps, grabbing her shoulder and bringing her to an abrupt halt.

"I'm not taking you out here to kill you, if that's what you were thinking."

She hunched her shoulders, tucking into the collar of her parka, her face lowered. Damn her eyes for giving away her thoughts again. "Whatever you say."

"Oh, hell," he said, reaching out to catch her face between his big, gloved hands. He tilted her head back so that she had no choice but to meet his gaze. "What would you be doing right now if I hadn't—"

"Kidnapped me at gunpoint?" she snapped.

He clenched his teeth, and a muscle ticked in his jaw. "Yeah, okay. If I hadn't come with you, what would you have done this morning after breakfast?"

He still held her head pinned between his hands, but Dinah managed to find a patch of sky just past his shoulder to stare at instead of his face.

"What?" he demanded.

"I would have come out here for a walk," she finally admitted.

He sighed, satisfied with the hard-gotten admission. "So, nothing's different, except that you have company. Okay?"

Dinah's eyes darkened to the gray-black of a stormy sky. She reached up to shove his hands away from her face. "No, Jake, not company. Company is invited. You're the bastard who has kept me imprisoned and terrified for the past twenty-four hours. No matter how much you'd like me to pretend otherwise, I'm your hostage out here the same as I was inside the cabin." Her bitter laugh sounded as hollow and flat to Jake's ears as the expression he saw suddenly in her eyes. He recognized defeat and hated it.

"I'm sorry," he offered, his voice hoarse against the lump that had formed in his throat.

Dinah waved her hand, dismissing his apology. "Hey, forget it. It's not just you. Today's Christmas Eve. . . ." Her voice trailed off, her eyes infinitely sad.

Jake stared at her for a long moment before clutching her elbow and steering her back around toward the path they were going to take. "Come on. The walk will do us both good, no matter how undesirable the circumstances."

She tilted her head to toss him a sidelong smirk. "I read an article somewhere about how death row inmates are exercised daily. Some prison psychiatrist's brilliant remedy for despair. Sounded pretty stupid to me then. Seems even more ridiculous now that I'm experiencing it firsthand."

Jake laughed as he took her hand in his and guided her along the ice-slick path at a careful pace. "Maybe the guy was a staunch opponent of the death penalty."

"Uh huh," Dinah huffed. "And the Pope's Protestant. Or better still, maybe you're actually some sort of undercover agent assigned to kidnap me and keep me safe until your buddies round up the real bad guy."

Jake didn't answer. What could he say? He'd started it, egging her on because he wanted to inspire a spark of fire that had dwindled inside her. Now that he'd succeeded . . . shit, why did women always go too far?

He tightened his grip on her hand and quickened his step.

Dinah was practically lifted off her feet as she was tugged along. "Hey, slow—"

Jake didn't answer. Instead, he walked faster. He could feel the strain against his arm as she struggled to keep up and retain her balance at the same time, but she didn't protest again. Guilt gnawed at his gut, but Jake ignored it.

By the time they crested the top of the steep hillside, his lungs burned and wind-stirred tears swam in his eyes. He let go of Dinah's hand to fall to his knees before rolling over and dropping onto his backside. "Woo!" he gasped as he drew his knees up and hung his head. "I feel like I just ran a twenty-six K. How about you, Dinah? You okay?"

There was no answer, and all at once he knew why. He heard it in the crunch of snow several yards away and in the harsh gasps of her breath as she ran down the other side of the mountain. "Shit," he muttered, pushing himself stiffly to his feet. He kicked angrily at a snowdrift and cursed again. Didn't she know he'd catch her? And that then she was going to have twice as far to walk back. And, damn it, so was he.

Chapter Twenty-two

~

Jake carried Dinah over his shoulder all the way to the cabin from the meadow on the far side of the mountain, where he'd caught up with her after her futile attempt at flight. This time, though, she hadn't been taken without a struggle. And neither was she making any further pretense at cooperation.

She glared at him when he dropped her unceremoniously onto the thinly cushioned sofa, fighting even his attempts to free her of her snow-covered coat and boots. The moment he reached for the zipper on her parka, she screamed and shrank away from him, while scratching at his face and swatting at his hands at the same time. She aimed a kick at his groin, though she connected with a rock-hard thigh instead, which she was certain hurt her far more than him.

The scuffle was brought to an abrupt end when the barrel of the pistol bit into her ribs.

"Ow," she complained with a measly little squeak.

The gun was big and mean, but it was the menace she found in his gaze that provoked true terror for the first time since the initial moments of her kidnapping.

"Don't move," he whispered between harsh, hard-gotten breaths. "Don't wiggle so much as a toe, and don't make another sound. You got that?"

Oh, yeah, she had it now, and she hoped he read her answer in her eyes 'cause she wasn't even batting an eyelash.

An eternity seemed to pass before he finally moved away from her. Even then, she didn't take her eyes off him. She watched him tuck the scary-looking weapon into the waistband of his jeans once again, take off his jacket, and sit down across from her while he pulled off his boots.

Her eyes followed him as he built a fire and padded outside in his stocking feet to carry more wood in from the stack on the porch.

Her eyes widened when he pulled the handmade afghan from the box and silently covered her with it, then disappeared around the corner into the kitchen.

She tried to make out what he was doing, but the sofa was backed against the counter dividing the two rooms. So, unless she stood up, which, of course, she wasn't about to do, it was impossible to make out more than his shoulders and head from time to time when he came into view.

A brow lifted with surprise as she recognized the whistle of the kettle moments later, then captured a whiff of richly scented tea.

She was shivering, even under the warmth of the afghan, which she'd drawn up to her chin, and almost cried out with gratitude when he appeared around the corner and set a tray on the table in front of her. "Thank you," she muttered, unsure if he even heard as he went to the fireplace to throw on another log, then left the room again without a word.

Well, screw him, she thought, as she squeezed lemon into the steaming cup of her favorite tea blend. Anyway, why should she worry about being polite? The man was holding her prisoner!

She picked up the cup, holding it in both hands as she sipped and savored the warmth as much as the delicious flavor.

Jake had sliced some of Dolly's home-baked pumpkin bread, too, and Dinah nibbled on a piece as her thoughts continued along the same train about her captor.

Somehow, she'd undermined Evan Jacobs's part in all of this. Discounted the danger because of a sexy grin and deep-set green eyes. Because of a damned chamois-smooth voice and a gentle touch in such a powerful man. How could she have been so stupid? Dinah Clayton Smith, celeb divorce attorney, who wielded legal prowess like a surgical scalpel to emasculate her clients' husbands.

But wasn't she forgetting the other Dinah? The soft, playful kitten who had nothing in common with the she-tiger of courtroom notoriety? The girl who refused to see ugliness if there was so much as a glimmer of brightness to focus on? Wasn't that why she'd refused to believe that the mild-mannered corporate CEO she'd met in a single brief encounter in a divorce hearing was truly behind the death threats, even after the body of

Rhonda Harker had been found in her Webster Groves condo?

Regret washed over her as she accepted responsibility for her present circumstances. It was that twin thing again—her damned Gemini birth sign.

Dinah squeezed her eyes shut briefly, then set the teacup on the tray. Lying down, she curled up on her side, hardly noticing as the blanket slipped to the floor.

"Oh, God," she groaned as a fierce ache swelled in her chest. Ever since the accident twenty years before—this very day—she pretended to understand that Mama was really, truly gone; wasn't ever coming back. She let Lauren console her, holding her close and wiping away her tears, even though Dinah knew she would never stop crying deep down inside. And later, she proved how unfazed she was by her motherless status by excelling at everything she attempted. No one caught on. Not once. And no one ever guessed that the other one—sweet, trusting Di—was always searching for that love that would pull both parts together again and make her whole.

Dinah fell asleep with the first tears she'd shed in years just starting to trickle from the corners of her eyes. And dimly, from somewhere far away from her dreams, she snuggled under the warmth of the afghan as it was draped over her, and smiled as she heard a deep male voice talking to her.

"Wake up, Dinah."

She sat up with a start, rubbing her eyes in an effort to push away the residual grogginess of sleep. Her heart was hammering and her body ached, though for a moment she couldn't recall what had caused either. And then she saw him hunkering in front of her, his face level with hers.

"I, uh, I didn't mean to fall asleep," she mumbled as everything came back to her in a sickening rush. She looked at the window and realized with some amazement that it was dark outside. She'd slept the entire afternoon away.

"It's all right. I'm glad you were able to rest."

"Then why did you wake me up?" she asked. "What's wrong?"

Jake smiled and something new shone in his eyes. Kindness? Regret? Dinah couldn't identify it. "What is it?"

He laid a hand on hers, giving it a brief squeeze, and she felt her heartbeat quicken with dread. Something *was* different. But what? And then she knew!

"They caught him! Adam!" She gripped his shirt in her hand as she probed his gaze for the answer. "That's it, isn't it?"

He pulled free of her grasp and stood up, looking away as he dashed her hopes. "No, Dinah. They haven't caught Adam. But you're right, something has happened, and we need to talk." He hooked his thumbs in his jeans pockets and averted his gaze. "I've made a pot of stew. I'll go check on it while you get yourself awake. Then I'll, uh, tell you what's going on."

Dinah struggled to untangle her legs and feet from the afghan as he disappeared around the corner. "Jake, wait." She hurried after him, almost colliding with him when he started back toward her. "Sorry," she muttered.

A corner of his mouth tipped upward in a poor

imitation of a smile. "How about a glass of wine or a beer?" he asked, turning toward the refrigerator.

Dinah opened her mouth to answer, but her attention was caught by the gun still tucked in his waistband. *Oh, God, what did it matter what had happened?* And then she remembered the Lady Smith in her purse—*please, please*—unless he'd found it as well as her cell phone. He turned around then, holding up a bottle of white wine and a longneck bottle of beer. "Either one?"

"Wine," she said, barely keeping the frustration from her voice. "But, uh, Jake . . ."

"Huh?"

"I need my purse."

"What? Your . . . uh, sure. Hall closet right next to your briefcase on the shelf. Want me to get it for you?"

"No," she said quickly. Too quickly. *Slow down.* "Pour the wine. I'll be right back."

It was all she could do not to run from the room. It was even harder not to shout with joy when she found the little gun exactly where she'd left it. She brought it into the bathroom, and her hands shook as she checked the chambers to make sure he hadn't found it and unloaded it before putting it back. Remembering that she was supposed to be freshening up, she turned on the water, then leaned against the sink as a wave of dizziness washed over her. Nerves!

She splashed her face with cold water as she pondered the question of whether or not she could actually shoot another human being. She amended the question. No, not just anybody. Jake—a man she'd begun to know. The man who had taken her against her will at gunpoint, yes, but also the man who had fashioned a pillow with his jacket for her head. The same man who had apologized for handling her so roughly after her escape attempt, then gently pulled off her snow-drenched clothing, made her tea, and covered her with an afghan. She smiled at her reflection as she recalled the words he'd uttered as she drifted off to sleep.

Rest, beautiful. Maybe when you wake up, this nightmare will be over. He'd brushed a strand of hair from her cheek, and his face had been so close to hers, she'd felt his warm breath on her brow. And then he'd whispered words that had soothed her like lines from a lullaby. *Forgive me, little one. I'll keep you safe, I swear.*

Tears filled Dinah's eyes at the words she hadn't remembered until now—words she might have believed she'd dreamed if not for the calluses on his fingertips that had made his touch all too real.

No, she couldn't shoot him. She couldn't even hate him.

He's the enemy, Dinah.

She squeezed her eyes shut, refusing to accept the truth of that, denying the tears and wishing with all her being she could allow herself the one emotion her heart was asking her to believe in.

Chapter Twenty-three

❧

Dinah joined Jake on the sofa after freshening up and changing into an oversized Rams jersey, stretch pants, and socks.

"You look comfortable," he said. He smiled, though Dinah noticed that his eyes didn't quite make the connection.

He picked up her hand, running a callused thumb over the silk-smooth skin and staring at the perfectly manicured fingernails.

"What?" she asked, her tone betraying her surprise at the sudden tenderness.

"I want to know why such a knockout isn't married," he said softly. "Why she's a high-dollar, cutthroat attorney instead of some cute kid's mama. Why she's living in Missouri when her accent gives her away as Yankee bred. And why she decided on hiding out in a wilderness cabin instead of staying in the city, where she'd no doubt be surrounded by family and friends. And most of all, what has she got against Christmas?"

Dinah's first instinct was to be annoyed—to refuse him an answer to any question more personal than what the weather looked like outside. After all, how dare he presume she'd give him the time of day, much less the answers to her innermost feelings. And then, damn it, he smiled, and this time it not only spread fully across his face, it reached his eyes, transforming him from a menacing stranger to a man she wanted very much to like and trust.

She found herself laughing self-consciously as she sought to answer him. "I don't know why I've never married, really. I don't have anything against the institution. I think I just married my work instead of a man."

He grinned at that and nodded. "Yeah, I've been accused of the same thing."

"So, you never married either?" she asked.

His eyes darkened briefly, but then he shrugged. "Almost. Got within a few weeks of the wedding."

"I'm sorry," she said, reaching out to touch him, though this time her hand came to rest on his cheek. "I didn't mean to dredge up bad memories."

"They aren't bad. Some are sad, and they tend to overshadow the good a lot of the time, but mostly they were happy. We were very much in love." He grinned as he caught the hand she started to withdraw. "We were kids—twenty-three, both of us—when we got engaged. Too young to know that life is more than making love, planning a big wedding, and setting goals. Anyway, she didn't leave me at the altar. She died."

"Oh, Jake, I'm so sorry."

He grinned. "Hey, it's okay. It was ten years ago. Besides, we were talking about you."

She shrugged. "But there's nothing to tell. Basically, I'm a workaholic. I love what I do. End of story."

He laughed derisively. "Hell, who wouldn't? You've gotten rich on the poor schmucks whose wives you've represented."

Dinah felt her face catch fire with the sudden blast of her anger. It was a moment or two before she could trust herself to speak. When she did, she was proud of the control she heard in her tone. "For your information, Mr. Jacobs, I don't get high on the misery of other people. I'll admit to deriving a certain pleasure out of besting the good ol' boys who make up so much of the legal system. But what really gives me a thrill is the justice I win for my clients with my expertise and skill."

Jake stood up and walked to the fireplace, a muttered "Bullshit" under his breath.

"Wait a damn minute!" Dinah scooted from the sofa and hurried after him. "What do you mean by that? It's true!"

He'd grabbed up the poker and began stoking the fire, but he turned now, brandishing it like a schoolteacher emphasizing a lecture with a pointer. "Is it? True, I mean. Or isn't it really true that you are a ball buster, and that's really what you get your kicks from?"

Hands on hips and left foot tapping an angry tattoo, Dinah let loose an exasperated deep breath. "Oh, brother. What's the point? You really aren't evolved enough to get it."

He watched her spin away and march to the big picture window. He was as annoyed as she, but he grinned when she caught the end of her sleeve with her fingers and pulled it down over her hand to clear a big circle in the fogged-up glass. God, she was a cute little spitfire. He almost laughed, would have if he hadn't worried that she'd march back across the room and wrestle the poker from him to crown him with it. He decided instead to bring the subject back to neutral territory.

"What about the rest? The holiday season and all the parties?"

She hunched her shoulders and answered without turning. "I do the parties. It's a requirement of the job. I'm just not much into Christmas."

Jake looked around the room, which was warmly furnished in country French decor, yet entirely lacking even the slightest holiday touch. "Yeah, I can see that. Not so much as a sprig of holly or a bell to jingle."

There was nothing golden about her silence. Rather, it fell over them as dark and dank as a heavy black cloud. Jake scratched at the two-day stubble on his jaw. He wanted to keep her talking— as much for hearing the utter femininity of her voice as for keeping her mind off the reason they were holed up together—yet he wondered how far he dared push.

"What about your family?" he ventured.

"What about it? My parents are both dead. I have three sisters. Did I mention that earlier? I think so. Anyway, I love them all, but we haven't been close for a long time. I guess you'd say we just never learned to put the fun back into dysfunctional."

"And they don't worry about your Scrooge complex and urge you to share the holidays with them?"

She turned then, surprising him with a wide grin and an exaggerated roll of her eyes. "Oh, Lord, they'd get a kick out of that. Especially Ardath, who hates the season with an absolute passion." She crossed the room to stand beside him in front of the hearth. Nudging him with her hip, she made room for herself and held her hands behind her back to warm them. "Lauren makes a big deal about Christmas, but I've always suspected she was merely better than the rest of us at pretending. She always devotes a lot of thought to the gift giving. Really, though, only Yardley truly enjoys the holiday. She gets into it in a big way—makes fudge and bakes cookies, and decorates her house top to bottom. But that's the way Yardley does everything. She's sentimental about life in general and pretty much manages not to go back into the dark place where the rest of us always end up."

She'd left it out there hanging, ready for him to grab onto, and damn it, Jake knew better, but the next thing he knew, he'd opened his mouth and gone for it, hook, line, and sinker. "So, tell me. Why is Christmas such a big, bad idea that three out of four of you can't stand it?"

She hesitated only a second before looking up at him and catching his gaze. "My mother died on Christmas Eve. She was shot."

Chapter Twenty-four

~

"Ironic, isn't it?" she asked when the quiet that stood between them got too thick and heavy. "Somehow, I never thought the phrase 'like mother, like daughter' was applicable to me, and yet here I am awaiting the same fate on the same occasion."

Un-uh. No way, baby, Jake thought. He wasn't going anywhere near that one. "You didn't say where you grew up."

"Philadelphia. Chestnut Hill, actually."

"I was right about the Yankee accent. So how did you end up in Missouri? And what about your sisters? Do they still live in Philadelphia?"

Casting him a sidelong glance, Dinah frowned. "What is this? The Evan Jacobs's version of *Twenty Questions*?"

Jake laughed. "Sorry. Guess I just like hearing you talk."

She moved to stand in front of him, her head

tilted back so she could look him in the eyes.
"Why?"

*Because all I can think about is making love to you,
and if you stop talking, I'm not going to be able to think
about anything else.* Yeah, like he could tell her that.
The pager he wore clipped to his waistband suddenly chirped, surprising them both and saving
him from answering. Removing the tiny black box,
he frowned as he read the number.

"What is it?" she asked. "Is that from A.J.?"

Jake shook his head, preoccupied. "Huh? A.J.?
No, it's my dad." He looked at her then. "Why
don't you go dish us each a bowl of soup while I
check this out."

She stared at him, searching his face for a long
moment before finally acquiescing. "Okay, but how
are you going to call? My cell phone probably
needs recharging by now."

"The cops will have your frequency, so I couldn't
use it, anyway," he told her as he went to the hall
closet and pulled out his duffel bag. A moment
later, he held up another telephone for her to see.
"I've had mine charging on a battery power pack."

"Well, that's a definite relief," she said, her tone
dripping sarcasm. "At least I got kidnapped by a
pro and not some bumbling, unprepared amateur."

Before he could reply to that, she'd marched off
to the kitchen.

Well, mad was better than scared, he supposed as
he punched in the number. His father picked up on
the first ring.

For the next five minutes, Jake listened without
speaking except for an occasional angry expletive
muttered softly against the mouthpiece. He stood at

the window, his free arm resting above his head against the sill. When he hung up, he turned and found Dinah standing only a few feet away. He met her gaze, but couldn't hold it. "Soup ready?" he asked.

"Something terrible's happened," she said. Her eyes widened in the next instant. "It's about A.J., isn't it? The police have caught him, haven't they? That's why you're so upset."

"No, damn it! I almost wish it was that." He ran a hand through his thick, iron-gray hair, then over his face in an eloquent gesture of frustration and impotence. "My dad was relaying news from A.J."

"Your father is in on this, too?" she asked incredulously.

Jake shook his head. "Jesus, lady, the only thing my folks are in on is trying to keep A.J. safe and anyone else from getting killed."

"Oh, right, that's why they're funneling information from A.J. to you. My God, Jake, at the very least they're accessories after the fact."

"Look, he's their son. They believe in him, and they're trying to help."

"But they know where he is, and they're keeping his whereabouts from the police," she insisted, the lawyer in her tenaciously clinging to the ramifications of their involvement.

Jake sighed, sounding as if the last question had zapped him of the energy to argue further. "Yeah. They own property all over the city. He's hiding out in one of their houses."

"And what?" Dinah asked after a long reflective moment. "I should be reassured, somehow, that your parents are involved in this . . . this horrible debacle?"

Jake didn't answer straightaway. Instead, he began pacing the room. He stopped, finally, to stare out the window again, much like a caged animal viewing freedom. Quiet hung between them for so long, Dinah jumped at the abrupt sound of his voice when he spoke again. "I just thought you might understand better if I explained the faith we all have in—"

"Poor, maligned A.J.," Dinah finished for him. "Yes, I get that. He's your brother and their son, and you all believe in him. But the fact remains that he made threats against four women and one of them is dead now. Murdered."

"Two," he said on a ragged sigh.

It took only a heartbeat for the import of that to penetrate, and then fear began to skitter under her skin, as if a thousand tiny spiders had been turned loose inside. "Oh, good God," she breathed. "Who? When?"

"Judge Bianci. Lucy." Jake turned to face her. "I don't know exactly when. Last night some time."

"Lucy? Dead?" Dinah shook her head, trying to make sense of the impossible. "No, that can't be. They moved her to a hotel with her husband, Tony. State troopers were assigned to protect her."

"I know. Her husband had gone to their daughter's house to deliver Christmas presents. He stayed longer than he intended. Otherwise, Dad said, he would probably be dead, too."

"But how? I mean, how does a wanted man get past armed guards?"

"One," Jake said. Then at the confusion in her expression, "There was one trooper on duty. He was inside the suite with the judge."

"Okay and what? Did he fall asleep? Sneak out for a cigarette? Just decide he needed a break? Why didn't he stop him?" Midway through her string of questions, she'd come to stand in front of him. Panic and anger were quickly overwhelming her, and she was desperate for reassurances, even if the only one who could give them was the killer's accomplice. She squeezed her eyes shut and hugged herself. "Damn it, Jake, at least tell me they caught A.J., that he was calling your folks from jail."

"The officer was killed, too, Dinah. Anthony Bianci found the bodies, and as far as we know, no one in the hotel saw or heard anything unusual."

"Oh, sweet Jesus." She sank against him, clutching his shirt, as the reality of the grim message permeated all the way to her soul. Lucy Bianci, a woman Dinah had known and admired, had been murdered—killed by a vindictive sonofabitch who was going to come after her as well.

Anger washed through her, replacing grief and fear, with the suddenness and intensity of a tidal wave. She pounded Jake's chest, railing at him. "Why? Why did they page you? My God, are the whole damn bunch of you so sick you had to let me know how A.J. had succeeded again? So you want me so terrified—"

"Damn it, Dinah," Jake said, grabbing her shoulders and shaking her. "Listen to me! A.J. didn't kill the judge. He didn't kill Rhonda. He had no reason to hurt either of them. And neither is he planning to kill you or Tori, that conniving bitch he was married to. Think about it, Dinah. Did he make a single unreasonable demand, or was he unusually generous in the settlement he offered? And what about at the hearing? Did he look angry to you? Was he quarrelsome or vindictive? You know the answer to all those questions. It's *no*, Dinah. He didn't fight. Not once. And he could have. He had proof that Tori paid Rhonda Harker ten thousand dollars to get up on that witness stand and lie about an affair with him that never happened. But he let it go, because all he wanted, at any cost, was his freedom."

Dinah shook her head and struggled against his grip. "No! Shut up! I'm not listening and I'm not buying."

Jake picked her up and carryed her to the sofa, dropping her with as much effort and concern as a bored child discarding a rag doll. "Sit there," he said, his tone laced with venom.

Dinah hugged her knees to her chest and buried her face. She was trembling from head to toe, though whether from shock or fear or anger, she wasn't certain. She was weary of the struggle of holding it together, of hoping against hope for a miracle to deliver her from this twisted turn of fate.

She was amazed by the calm that enveloped her in the instant of her decision to give up the fight. She exhaled slowly, and realized she'd let go of the last of her fear. She raised her face to his. "Please, Jake, just get it over with," she said. "Please don't make me wait for him. Go ahead, do it yourself. Shoot me."

Jake stared at the beautiful woman with the heart-shaped face and mesmerizing gray eyes that were now as serene and dark and shiny as lake water on a placid winter night. He looked away as shame welled in his throat as bitter as bile.

"Oh, Jesus, Dinah, didn't you hear anything I just said?" he asked. He stepped over the coffee table and hunkered down in front of her. "Listen to me . . . please."

She nodded, slowly, tentatively.

Jake smiled his gratitude, taking both of her hands in his. "I'm so damned sorry. I never thought it would go this far. I thought Judge Bianci was safe. You have to believe that." He met her steady, unblinking gaze, willing her to believe what he was about to promise: "I'm not going to kill you, Dinah, and neither is A.J. I swear it."

"Oh, God!" she cried, scooting to the edge of the sofa to wrap her arms around his neck. "Thank you, Jake."

When she released him at last, she giggled with happiness and relief for a few seconds before her expression sobered again. "You've just given me the first reason I've had in twenty years to celebrate Christmas. This is a gift I won't ever forget."

She started to stand, but Jake caught her wrist, stopping her. "Dinah, wait."

She laughed and shook her head. "Oh, God, Jake, I can't. I want to pack. I want to load up the car and get back to the city. I know it sounds crazy. I always come here for the holidays to be alone, but for once I want to share the season with people I care about. I want to call my sisters, and visit my friends and wish them all a Merry Christmas."

"I'm sorry," Jake said, shifting his gaze to a Norman Rockwell print that hung on the wall above the sofa.

"What's wrong?" she asked.

"You can't leave, Dinah. You misunderstood. I swore I wouldn't kill you. I didn't say I could let you go."

Chapter Twenty-five

~

Tears shone in Dinah's eyes. She shook her head, comprehension eluding her. "What do you mean? If A.J. is innocent and neither of you wants to kill me, then why? Why won't you let me go?"

"Because *someone* intends to kill you." He wiped a tear from her cheek, sighed, then continued. "And I'm not going to let that happen."

Anger surfaced to mingle with her fear and disappointment. "Oh, right. You kidnapped me—tied me up and left me in the trunk of my car for two hours—because you want to keep me safe. Uh-huh, I believe that just as I believe Santa's going to bring a toy to every deserving child in the world tonight."

"I know it sounds crazy, but it's true, every word of it, I swear to God. I was at A.J.'s house the first time the police arrived to question him about the death threats he allegedly made on the telephone to Tori, Judge Bianci, Rhonda Harker, and you." He stopped, waiting for a response of some kind. When she didn't so much as blink, he sighed, and continued. "We had just arrived home from a business trip to Chicago. We hadn't even taken his bags out of the trunk of the car yet. The cops said the calls were made between nine-thirty and eleven o'clock the night before, when A.J. and I were supposed to be at a dinner meeting."

This time when he paused, her eyes flickered, and her gaze eventually moved to his. "Okay, so?"

"So, we both had come down with the stomach flu. We canceled the dinner engagement and stayed in our hotel suite the whole night. When he settled the hotel bill, there were two long-distance calls, both of them made by A.J. and both of them to the three-one-four area code. One of them was to our folks. The other was to his answering service."

"He doesn't carry a cell phone?"

Despite his desperation to convince her, Jake grinned. "Hey, you know what, lady? You think just like a lawyer."

She didn't smile, and the shadows that darkened her eyes didn't disappear.

Jake swallowed his disappointment and came back to her question. "He owns a cell phone, sure, but the police checked out the telephone calls with Ma Bell, and guess what?"

"The records proved there were no calls made from his phone to ours," she said, her tone as flat as his hopes of making her believe.

"You got it, but you're still not buying, huh?"

She shook her head, whipping the glossy cap of jet hair. "No. I'm sorry. I really am, because I think you believe in your brother's innocence, and because of your love for him and your misguided faith, you've committed a felony that is chargeable as a capital offense, which means you could receive the death penalty. The worst part, though—if it's possible for there to be anything worse than being sentenced to die—is that you are going to have to stand by and witness the folly of your faith when A.J. kills me."

"No!" Jake barked. He stood up and strode away, his anger evident in the ripple and strain of his shoulder muscles against his shirt and the way his hands flexed as he braced his arms on the fireplace mantel. "You're dead wrong," he said with quiet certitude.

Dinah came to stand behind him. "Then prove it to me. Give me anyone else with a reason to make up this particular hit list."

"Victoria Jaffee-Jacobs," he said.

"Tori! That's utter craziness! Why would she threaten me? Any of us, for that matter. As you just pointed out, she got everything she asked for in the divorce settlement. I mean, okay, sure, she had reason to hate Rhonda. Good Lord, the woman broke up her marriage. But Judge Bianci was more than fair in the judgment she handed down, and I was her attorney, for heaven's sake!"

Jake stood with his arms folded over his chest and an odd grin playing across his face. "All fine and good, except for one thing."

Her eyes the color of pewter, she matched his

stance, folding her arms and lifting her chin a notch as well. "Uh-huh, and what would that be?"

"She didn't want a divorce."

"Like hell she didn't!" Dinah scoffed. "He hurt her to the core, and as much as she wanted to forgive him, he laughed in her face when she proposed they see a marriage counselor."

"The last is probably true," Jake agreed. "After all, when he found out that she'd married him for his money, that she never intended to have children, no matter how much he wanted a family, he kicked her out of the house on her proverbial ass."

"Why didn't any of that come out in court?"

"Because he just wanted it over and done with. He didn't care what it cost him, so long as he was rid of her."

Dinah thought about it for a long moment. She remembered her initial meeting with Victoria Jaffee-Jacobs. The woman had been genuinely devastated. There wasn't an actress born who could pull off the kind of hurt Dinah had seen in her eyes. But was it possible that A.J. was the one who'd asked for the divorce rather than Tori as Dinah had been led to believe? Anything was possible, but what about the death threats? She posed the question aloud. "Anyone could have sent the letter I got in the mail. I'll grant you that much. But the phone call is something else altogether. I recognized your brother's voice, Jake."

"It was taped, Di—"

"I know. The police found the tape in A.J.'s house. How do you explain that?"

"I don't have to explain it. A.J. already did. The message was from a call he made to Tori on the day their marriage blew up in his face. The private investigator he hired had just handed him proof of her infidelity as well as several other condemning bits of information. To make a long story short, he lost it. Called her and left a message on their answering machine at home."

"And what? He threatened to kill her?"

"Yeah," Jake admitted. "But it was one of those things people say in a fit of rage. He didn't mean it. It was stupid, but as I said, he was angry—furious, I guess—and at the end of his rope. The point is, the so-called death threat all of you received was actually an edited version of that message." He rubbed a weary hand over his face. "Can you remember the actual wording?"

"Oh, yes! A person doesn't forget something like that."

"Tell me," he prodded.

"Well, he said something like—"

"No, not 'something like.' Give it to me verbatim."

"Okay, he said, 'You bitch! You've ruined my life! I'm going to kill you! Send you to straight to hell where you belong.' He sort of laughed, and then there was a long silence, during which I kept asking who he was. And then he hung up."

"And that was it?" Jake asked.

Dinah nodded. "Yes."

"He never said who he was or used your name?"

"No, but it was him. Tori—"

"Confirmed that it was A.J.'s voice? Yeah, I heard. Rhonda, too, the police said."

"But you're saying A.J. didn't make the calls. Tori did."

"That's exactly what I'm saying."

"But why would Tori threaten us? And why would she kill Rhonda and . . . and Lucy Bianci, for God's sake?" she asked, exasperation ringing in her voice. "What did Lucy do to her except award her everything she asked for?"

"Jesus, Dinah, you're not getting it. Read my lips. Tori . . . did . . . not . . . want . . . a . . . divorce. It was all a game with her. She played you just as she played him. She thought if she got him by the short hairs, he'd reconsider, take her back. My God, the night their divorce was final, she called him at home and begged him to change his mind. When he laughed at her, she lost it, and promised to make him sorry they'd ever met."

Doubt was starting to niggle, though Dinah couldn't help thinking that it was also just as likely that Jake had been duped with a pack of convincing lies. She frowned. "I don't know what to believe."

Jake grinned, and a flicker of hope shone in his eyes. "I know, the whole thing is unbelievable. But just stay with me another minute or two, okay?" He didn't wait for her answer, but rushed on in his defense of an elaborate frame. "Think about the note he allegedly sent."

"I don't have to think about it. I have a copy in my briefcase."

"Get it," Jake said. "Please."

She went to the hall closet, returning a moment later. She laid the note on the coffee table.

A Life FOR A LIFE

you RuiNed Mine

Now I have To

Take your s

LADY Die! Get It?

Ha HA ha

"Do you see anything that proves A.J. sent this?" Jake asked.

Dinah exhaled slowly. "No, but neither do I see anything that would lead me to believe it was Tori who sent it."

"Come on, Dinah, look! Read between the fucking lines. You and A.J. didn't speak to each other more than once or twice, did you? Do you think he would have made a pun with a nickname he'd very likely never heard?"

"But he had, Jake," she said. "His attorney was Stan Rosenthal, remember? Stan calls me Lady Di all the time. In fact, I'd guess your brother never heard me called anything else."

Jake straightened and walked to the fireplace to lean against the mantel again. "Okay, forget it. I can't convince you, so I'll just have to prove it to you."

"By holding me hostage," she stated flatly. "For how long?"

"For as long as it takes her to show up."

"Tori? And if A.J. comes instead?"

"He won't."

She moved to stand beside him and laid a hand on his arm. "For what it's worth, I believe in you," she said, her voice hardly louder than a whisper.

His eyes softened, and he grinned. "Well, that's something. But you'll believe in A.J., too, once this is all over."

"I know you trust him, and I know that's why you went along with his plot to kidnap me. And I heard the depth of your conviction in your passionate defense of him. But I can't forget the menace in A.J.'s voice on the phone that night. It terrified me. And I can't ignore the fact that the police found his fingerprints on the knife that killed Rhonda."

Jake blew out a long frustrated breath. "It was a knife taken from his kitchen, Dinah."

She laid her head against his shoulder and sighed. "Okay, never mind. We'll just have to wait and see who shows up." After a long pause she asked, "But, Jake, if it *is* A.J., will you stand by and let him kill me?"

He turned then, catching her in his arms and pulling her against him. His breath caught in his throat, and shame burned in his chest. "Oh, God, Dinah, what the hell have I done to you?"

"It's okay," she whispered, granting absolution as a sense of peace washed over her like a midsummer ocean spray. "We'll get through this. Now that I know who you are, it doesn't matter who the killer is. I'm not afraid."

Jake sat down on the rock ledge of the fireplace and pulled her onto his lap. His expression tender, he pushed the silky black strands of her hair away from her face, tucking them behind her ears. "You're beautiful."

"Thank you," she said on a whispered breath.

"I know circumstances are all wrong for this, but I want you to know something."

Dinah nodded encouragement, though she didn't speak, didn't trust herself to find a steady voice.

"I'm thirty-three-years old, Dinah. I've waited a long time to fall in love again. I was just a kid the last time, and love was something that evolved slowly out of friendship. I never thought I'd feel the same way again. And so help me God, it isn't even remotely the same. But it's love, Dinah. I know it sounds crazy. Hell, maybe I'm crazy, but whatever it is, I'm crazy in love with you."

She answered his confession with a deep, lingering kiss.

"Oh, Jesus," he groaned as he pulled away. "Uh-uh, babe. We can't do this. Not unless you're willing to go all the way with it, because I've wanted to make love to you for the past thirty hours, and you're driving me over the edge."

"Poor baby." She slid from his lap, grabbed his hand, and pulled him after her as she stretched out on the braided rug that covered the center of the living room floor. She laughed, the sound as sultry and inviting as a cat's purr. "Even though my field of expertise isn't criminal law, it seems to me there are certain entitlements prisoners are due."

He grinned as he positioned himself over her, straddling her hips with his legs. "Well, far be it for me to argue the law with an expert. After all, I'm just a lowly jailer. And you being the owner of this prison, I think it only right that you dictate what liberties an inmate enjoys."

"Well, then, are you going to talk all night or make love to me?"

Chapter Twenty-six

~

Jake was sound asleep in Dinah's bed. She watched him, his features so relaxed and peaceful in repose, and she remembered how different he'd looked when they made love on the rug in front of the fireplace. Her face burned with mingling thrill and humiliation. Jake had been demanding and fierce in his urgency, and she had accepted him with hunger and utter abandon. She recalled how she'd practically writhed on the floor as he stripped out of his clothing, then stood above her, taunting her with the magnificence of his physique and his engorged, throbbing penis. He'd dropped to his knees between her parted legs and teased her with his hands and mouth before finally granting her plea to enter her.

Lying next to him now, she closed her eyes as every wild, wanton moment came back. She recalled looking at the uncovered picture window and almost giggling as she imagined old Gus coming to check on her and catching them in the act.

She sighed with the memory of him carrying her to the bedroom much, much later and making love to her again, this time with tenderness and languor and caring.

Afterward, they'd talked, he about his work, his family, she describing her three sisters, and her pleasure at being the only one named by her father.

"Dinah, because he worked his way up on the railroad, and there was that silly damn song about working on the railroad all the livelong day and Dinah blowing her horn. His name was Clayton—though most everyone called him Clay—and he gave it to me as a middle name." She'd gone on, telling him about her mother, but halfway through the telling, she'd realized that he'd drifted off to sleep.

Ever since, she'd been lying beside him, watching. She hadn't said the words, hadn't admitted to loving him, too, but as crazy as it was, she knew her feelings transcended the lust they'd sated. She'd never believed in love at first sight. From what she'd witnessed, love was an emotion that came with time and began with respect and shared interests. And yet, here she was lying beside a man she had known less than thirty-six hours—a man who had kidnapped her! But, as God was her witness, she'd fallen deeply, profoundly in love with him.

And what's more, she would trust him with her life. Only, she couldn't trust his brother, she thought as she kissed Jake's lips lightly, then slipped silently from the bed and sneaked across the room to pull a heavy sweater and wool slacks from her suitcase.

She dressed in the bathroom without turning on the light, then pulled her hooded parka from the hall closet. She went from there to the living room sofa, where she fumbled in the darkness with the laces of her snow boots.

Last, she searched the pockets of Jake's jeans that he'd dropped on the floor for her car keys. She retraced her steps to the hall closet and patted down his jacket in a hurried search. His duffel bag was secured with a combination lock. No use wasting time there. But where else could she look? And then she heard the faint squeak of the bed springs as he moved.

There was no more time. If she was going to escape before Jake woke up, she had to go now.

She paused only long enough to grab her purse, slip the strap over her head, and zip her coat over it. Then she turned toward the front door.

The last of the fire he'd built hours before still burned low. But, as she made her way across the room, a charred remnant of wood shifted, creating a shower of sparks. In that instant Dinah saw the Glock lying on floor beside his pager. She kicked both of them with the toe of her boot, sending them gliding under the sofa and out of sight. If he woke up any time soon and decided to come looking for her, the search for his missing weapon, at least, would slow him down.

She hurried to the front door.

The dead bolt gave way with a click that sounded as loud as a thunderclap against the silence in the house. Dinah flinched, though she knew the worst was yet to come when the door hinges squealed like a stuck pig. She held her breath, then turned the handle and yanked it open.

She was wrong. It wasn't merely a squeal; it was a piercing screech that started her heart pounding in her ears as she darted outside. She no longer cared how much noise she made. Even the bang of the door didn't slow her. What did it matter? Jake was surely awake by now.

But in her favor he was buck naked. And she knew the backwoods that led to Highway 54. Of course, she'd never been out there in the dark or on foot on a winter night when the wind chill felt well below the zero mark. But even without a flashlight, she was confident she could make the mile-and-a-half trek to safety.

The going was much harder than she'd anticipated, and even with the ridged soles of her snow boots she lost her footing a half dozen times and stepped off solid ground into waist-deep snow drifts.

She kept her head bowed, her chin tucked and buried in the lining of her hood as much as possible, but the cold was biting and the wind unmerciful. Her nose and lips were soon numb. Her lungs burned, and tears spilled over her lashes, scalding her cheeks.

She became turned around a couple of times, but the crescent moon had climbed high in the eastern sky and restored her sense of direction.

The night sounds terrified her. The mournful wind whistling through the trees—the crackle of twigs as they were snapped off by the weight of snow—the howl of a dog or wolf in the distance all made her stop to gaze wistfully over her shoulder where her cabin had been swallowed up in the darkness. She wished she could turn around and return to the safety of Jake's arms.

Of course, that was impossible. Jake might truly love her, as he'd claimed, but he loved his brother first, had put his entire future on the line for him. No, she couldn't risk going back. And even if she dared, she wouldn't put Jake in the position of defending her. Not when it would almost certainly mean hurting A.J.

She plodded on, falling and picking herself up, then falling again. And then, all at once, she heard a startling sound—the crunch of tires on snow-packed pavement.

Dinah stopped dead, fear riveting her. Had she somehow wandered near the edge of Highway H, where Jake would no doubt be cruising by, searching for her?

Wiping her eyes on her coat sleeve, she squinted toward the west, searching the darkness for the beam of headlights. But the night in that direction was as black as ink.

And then she heard car doors slam shut, and voices raised, shouting greetings over the gusting wind.

Dinah laughed with joy as she realized what the sounds meant. She'd made it. Highway 54 was just over the next ridge. There was a truck stop another quarter mile or so to the west. She'd have to sneak across H, but buoyed now by the realization that the worst was behind her, she knew she could make it.

She scampered up a ridge, grabbing hold of a tree limb that snapped off in her hand, causing her to fall hard. Her chin took the impact, snapping her head back. She bit her tongue and tasted blood almost at once. "Damn it," she cried as she picked herself up and spit into the snow.

She wiped her mouth with her gloved hand and brushed back her bangs that were snow-crusted and stiff. Aching everywhere now, she wanted to sit down in the snow and cry. *And then A.J. wins*, her mind taunted.

"The hell he does," she said as she clawed her way to the hilltop with renewed resolution. She stopped with a sharp bark of laughter.

Our Lady of the Lake Church! That's where she was. Parishioners and holiday visitors were gathering for the midnight Christmas Mass. Somehow, she'd gotten off track and strayed a half mile or so farther north than she'd intended. Or perhaps, she thought as a gentle shiver coursed through her, she'd been led to the ideal hiding place, while Jake searched the roads for her. He'd never suspect her of sitting in a chapel when she could be on the road, hitching a ride, or at the truck stop, calling the police for help.

A priest was reading from the Gospel as Dinah slipped into a pew near the back of the beautiful little chapel. She pushed her hood from her head, pulled off her gloves, and with fingers stiff with cold, worked the coat's zipper down and shrugged it off.

Melting snow and ice dribbled from her bangs. Again she pushed them back from her forehead, then reached inside her purse for a tissue to wipe her face. Her hand brushed the handle of the small gun, and she shuddered to think of the harrowing hours she'd endured.

A small smile followed as she recalled the moments passed in Jake's arms, and tears welled in her eyes as she could almost feel the warmth of his breath against her cheek as he spoke in a drowsy whisper. *I love you, Dinah Clayton Smith. I'll keep you safe, I swear to God.*

Oblivious of the priest and the sermon he was delivering as well as the worshipers scattered in the pews around her, Dinah clasped her hands and slid from her seat to the padded kneeler. She bowed her head and closed her eyes.

She was safe now. And by leaving she'd protected Jake, too, assured him that no one would ever know the part he played in A.J.'s sick vendetta. And when everything was over, when A.J. was apprehended, she'd go to Jake. She'd say the words she couldn't speak as long as his brother's threat stood between them.

The chapel was decorated with garlands and poinsettias, but as Dinah opened her eyes and raised her head, she saw only the Virgin Mother in the center of the Nativity. She was reminded suddenly of her own mother, whose beauty and youth had been forever perpetuated by death, and the tears that welled in her eyes slipped free.

In that instant she let go of the anger she'd harbored for so many years. She hadn't known exactly how or why her mother died. She'd never asked for an explanation, and now, even after receiving Ardath's letter explaining that Zoe had taken her own life, Dinah hadn't cared. She'd never believed in living in the past, so what did it matter? But, all at once, she understood that her mother had been a woman in crisis as surely as Dinah had been for the past two days.

"Only I had you helping me," she uttered in an awed whisper of comprehension.

Dinah realized that the congregation was standing, and she pushed herself stiffly to her feet as she heard the priest ask them to turn to one another and offer words of peace.

Dinah smiled at an elderly couple who turned in the pew in front of her, offering their hands and wishing her a peaceful and joyous holiday.

There was no one in the pew with her, so she turned, her hand extended and a smile already spreading.

The smile froze in place as her gaze locked with the deep-set green eyes of the man standing directly behind her. He wore a hooded navy blue parka that successfully shrouded most of his face. It didn't matter. She'd spent too much time with Evan Jacobs not to recognize the man as he covered her hand with his. "Merry Christmas, Dinah."

Chapter Twenty-seven

~

She wouldn't let panic overwhelm her; she had to hold on. In a voice that surprised her with its quiet strength and steadiness, she replied to his greeting. "I pray so, A.J."

"Come with me?" he asked, the words so softly uttered, she might have missed the command in his tone.

She felt her lips part in a smile of agreement, then seemed to watch herself turn away and slide toward the aisle. Every move she made felt exaggerated and slow, like the gestures of a mime.

She paused to genuflect, dipping her chin and using the moment to free the clasp on her purse that hung around her neck. She hadn't thought about what she was doing until her fingers closed around the pearl handle of the Lady Smith.

She felt A.J.'s hand on her elbow as she began to rise, and her heart skipped a beat as she wondered for a horrifying second if he'd seen the weapon in her other hand. But as he steered her out of the chapel, she tucked the gun inside her pocket, exhaling a slow, relieved breath at the same time.

"Where are we going?" she asked as soon as they were outside in the parking lot.

"You could have frozen to death out there," he said as if she hadn't spoken.

"Sorry to disappoint you," she snapped, bitterness barging into her tone. "If I'd known you were coming, I might have made an effort to accommodate you."

Her eyes widened when she saw the car they were approaching. She hesitated, pulling against him as fear bottled up in her windpipe. How had he gotten her car, and where was Jake?

"Get in," A.J. said.

Dinah sucked in a deep breath of frigid, winter air, then hurried to obey him, though only because people were starting to file out of the church. She wouldn't risk their lives. Not when the gun in her pocket gave her the option of waiting until they were out of the parking lot. She slid into the seat.

"Funny, I never pictured you as a churchgoer," a voice said from the backseat, provoking a startled cry of surprise from Dinah.

Her confidence evaporating like helium in a popped balloon, Dinah snapped her head in the direction of Stan Rosenthal's voice. The interior of the car was dark, but Dinah could make out the forms of two people seated in the back. In the next instant A.J. opened the driver's door, activating the dome light.

"Oh, God," she groaned, her attention drawn to

Jake's battered, bloodied face. "What have they done to you?"

"Shut up," Stan snapped. Then in a voice laced with sarcasm, "Much as I hate sounding like a player in an old gangster movie, I can't resist saying, 'Don't make me kill him, sweetheart.'"

Dinah surprised him with a wry smile. "Oh, my God, you really are more of an ass than even I ever realized."

She hadn't seen the gun he held pressed against Jake's side, but he raised it now, pointing it at her face. "I said for you to shut up!" He spat the words like venom.

Dinah's smile widened, and she chuckled. "Or what? You and A.J. will kill Jake and me right here in this parking lot with all these people to witness it? Oh, Stan, Stan, you stupid, little man."

"Close the door!" Stan growled.

The door slammed shut in the next second, and Dinah felt something smash against the side of her head. She thought she heard Jake yell, but it may well have been a protest shouted inside her head just before the world faded to black.

Dinah groaned with the sharp pain of awakening. Her vision was blurred, and even the least move was an agonizing effort. But there was nothing wrong with her memory. She recalled every detail of the past two days since her abduction from the courthouse. "Jake," she moaned.

"I'm right here, babe," he said from a place just above her.

She tipped her head back, ignoring the razor-sharp pain and accompanying waves of nausea.

"You're holding me," she whispered when she found his battered face above hers.

Somehow, despite the swelling and bruises and a deep cut that had split his bottom lip, Jake managed a crooked grin. "You got it."

"Jake, I lo—"

"Jesus Christ, Smith, shut the fuck up!"

Dinah moved her head to the side far enough to make out the face of the man who had struck her, and she realized that they were inside her cabin once again. Tears stood in her eyes from the excruciating pain of every move, but she kept her gaze locked on his. "Go to hell, you little coward."

Stan's face darkened with rage, but Dinah refused to release the grip she had on him with her eyes, and after a moment he recovered his cool enough to force a laugh. "Oh, my, my, well no one ever said our Lady Di didn't have guts."

Her head was splitting, but she had to keep him talking. She'd figured out where she was— sprawled on the floor, her head in Jake's lap as he sat braced against the sofa. Now, if she could keep Stan busy and find out exactly where A.J. was, she might be able to get to the gun in her jacket pocket.

"Did you ... um, help A.J. kill ... the others?" she asked.

The question startled a roar of laughter from the attorney.

Dinah swallowed convulsively. Oh, God, the noise and the pain were making her sick. She gulped back bile as it gushed to her mouth. She had to hold on. Her eyes closed, she worked the fingers of her right hand down the side of her jacket. A soft cry as involuntary as a hiccup slipped from her lips when she discovered the empty pocket.

Stan was talking again, and though her frustration had only exacerbated the nausea and the piercing ache in her temple, she forced herself to listen. If, by the grace of God, she lived through this nightmare, she had to be able to bear accurate witness to the man's guilt.

"You were the catalyst, Di—the reason I came up with the scheme in the first place."

"Wh-why?" she stammered when he hesitated.

"Why? You're asking me *why*? Are you serious?" He was enjoying himself—a monster in his element as he tortured his victims. "Well, I'd think that was obvious to anyone. What about you, Jake? You're a macho man—stud. The brawn behind the brains at J & J, right? Not the sharpest knife in the drawer, but I'm sure you get it, huh? So, why don't you tell your little girlfriend why."

Dinah could feel Jake's stomach muscles tighten beneath her head. She angled her head back as far as she could to meet his gaze, willing him to stay calm, to play along and stall for time.

She saw rebellion flash briefly in his eyes before a corner of his mouth lifted in compliance.

"I'd guess he tried to best you in court several times. When he couldn't, he decided on an 'if you can't beat 'em, join 'em' strategy. Probably asked you out a couple of times. I'd venture you turned him down, further adding insult to injury."

Jake paused, treating himself to a chuckle that opened up the cut on his lip. Blood oozed, and he wiped it away with the back of his hand, then raised his gaze to meet the eyes of the man who had sneaked up on him while he slept and pistol-whipped him. "How's that? Accurate enough? Or was it worse than that? Could you see the distaste and incredulity in her eyes at the very idea of spending even a few minutes outside the court-room in the company of such a slimy little worm?"

Dinah watched Stan's face suffuse with rage as he raised the gun and aimed it at Jake's head. She reached for her lover's hand, silently begging him not to go further.

"I don't understand how you convinced A.J. to go along, Stan," she interjected in an effort to divert attention from Jake.

"Except to come into the church and get you to keep him from killing my brother," A.J. said, his tone conveying weariness and dejection. "I didn't go along with anything, Miss Smith. I'm sorry."

Stan had lowered the gun, Dinah saw. He was leaning against the window in about the same place that Jake had selected as a lookout post. Only Stan seemed to have forgotten the purpose for keeping a vigil at the window and was wiping tears of mirth from his eyes with the back of his coat sleeve as he laughed. "Damn, this is fun. The others, I had to do too fast to really enjoy. But, hey, kiddies, I'm enjoy-ing myself now. First I get to beat the shit out of this cowboy, who almost fucked everything up by get-ting between me and the sweet Lady Di here.

"Next I get to do a little bragging about how easy it was getting to the others. Especially that bitch, Tori." He stopped short, taking in a sharp breath, then let it spill out on a great gale of laugh-ter. "Hey, buddy," he said, his gaze directed at A.J. "Did you know your ex–old lady was getting it on with a lady friend as well as some dude who worked in your company? Perry something-or-other. I mean, wow, I've read about bimbos like her in *Playboy*, but I sure never thought I'd get to peep in on one while she was having at it with another broad, you know. Real sick, but fun as hell to watch."

Dinah absorbed the news that Stan had killed Tori in the same way that Jake seemed to take it: silently, letting it sink in and harden like quick-setting concrete.

"That's where he caught me," A.J. volunteered. "I was sitting in my car just up the street from her place when I saw a shadow dart across her side yard. I got on the phone and called Dad. I was telling him to get in touch with you here, Jake. Let you know that Tori was on the move—" He cut himself off on a ragged sob. "Jesus Christ, I thought it was her sneaking out of there. I didn't know he'd just cut her throat. And all the time, I could have stopped him ... if I just hadn't been so fucking smart and ready to lay the blame on her."

"Ah, well," Stan said. "You win some, you lose some. Them's the breaks. I'll tell you what, though, A.J., you are on one bum losing streak. In fact, I'd say you've just about played your last card."

Dinah had been half listening, half concentrating on feeling under the sofa for the powerful semi-automatic she'd kicked under there earlier. Now, though, she whipped her head in the direction of their captor at the shift to deadly menace in his tone. Her head throbbed. She cried out with the pain, but the sound of it was lost in the loud report of the gun in Stan's hand.

"You son of a bitch!" Jake screamed as A.J. toppled from his chair to the floor, bringing him into Dinah's view for the first time since she'd awakened.

"Hey!" Stan yelled. "He had it coming. Do you know what a pussy he was? Do you know how he forced me to sit there with my thumb stuck up my ass while your hot little lady here gave away the store. Fucking wimps like him don't deserve to live!"

Dinah trembled from head to toe, but she knew she had to pull it together and reach Jake's gun. The muscles in Jake's body were coiled tight, turning him into a time bomb about to go off.

"Oh, God, I'm going to be sick," she whimpered, throwing herself onto her side.

"Look at that, Jake," she heard Stan say. "Not such a nail-'em-to-the-wall hard-ass lawyer now, is she? About to puke, just 'cause your brother's lying at her feet, bleeding all over her oak floor."

Oh, please, Jake, keep him talking, Dinah begged silently as her hand closed around the miniature barrel of the Lady Smith instead of the Glock. The small gun must have fallen out when she fell to the floor. She began inching it toward her, hearing each soft scrape it made as loud as a thunderclap.

It wasn't as good as the powerful semiautomatic, but on the other hand, it was lighter, easier for her to lift, and it would stop him if she could just get herself turned around to fire it at the bastard.

Somehow, Jake seemed to get the message to buy them time.

"Hey, Rosenthal, answer me one thing before you kill us, too."

Stan didn't respond, but she supposed something in his body language conveyed a willingness to at least hear the question, when Jake pressed on.

"How did you fuck up so bad that Dinah managed to slip out of here and get all the way to the church before you knew she was gone?"

"You really don't have much going on up there in that head of yours, do you, pretty boy?" Stan laughed. "It's so obvious, it pisses me off to waste time explaining, but, hey, I wouldn't want to kill you without you being clear on everything."

Dinah pulled the gun in under her chest. She curled her hand around the smooth pearl handle and placed her finger on the trigger. She had to summon the strength to roll over, then fire in the very next instant before Stan realized what was happening. She was breathing deeply, calming herself. She could imagine the gun dangling in his hand as she had seen it earlier. *Steady, Dinah. Hold on.*

". . . So by the time I got A.J. handcuffed to the post on the back porch and had worked the lock on the door, you were all alone. Guess I should apologize for the beating I gave you. But it made me madder then hell when I realized she had slipped off." He chuckled under his breath. "And, hell, you know the—"

Now! Dinah rolled toward the window, her hand holding the gun, already coming up when the world exploded around her.

Another gun fired, followed by the loud shatter of glass and a roar of protest as Jake's body rose above her, catapulting into the air before landing full length over her.

"No-o-o-o!" Dinah wailed as understanding came crashing in on her. She thought she cried Jake's name one last time, but it may have been only a plea shouted in her heart as she let herself go with the darkness that reached for her.

Chapter Twenty-eight

~

Dinah didn't open her eyes again until most of Christmas Day was spent. When she did, Jake, alone, sat at her side in a hospital room. Even his megawatt smile failed to light his eyes. "Welcome back," he said.

"You act like I've been gone forever," she managed in a whispered croak through her parched lips.

"Twelve hours," he told her, reaching for her hand at the same time. "But it seemed like forever." He drew her hand to his mouth and kissed her palm. When he looked up again, she was amazed to see tears welling in his eyes. And then she remembered.

"Oh, Jake, I'm so sorry about A.J." Her eyes widened at another memory, more appalling even than his brother's murder. Jake had been shot! She was positive. She'd heard the gun fire, felt him lifted up by the thrust of the bullet, then fall on top of her. "Oh, thank God, you're okay! You weren't too seriously hurt, or you couldn't be sitting here. You are okay? Tell me I'm right."

"Hey, calm down," Jake said, moving from the chair to the bed to sit beside her. "I wasn't shot. A.J. was, but he's going to be fine. The bullet hit a rib, otherwise he probably wouldn't be here."

She smiled and closed her eyes, suddenly weak from the brief surge of adrenaline that had accompanied the horrific memories. "I'm so glad," she whispered, reaching for his hand and finding it. "I don't understand everything that happened. Maybe I'm confused, but I don't care as long as you're okay."

"I'm fine, Dinah. Now that you're awake, I'm fine."

She still hadn't opened her eyes again. She didn't dare until he told her what it was he was keeping from her. There was something. She'd seen it in the flatness of his gaze, could hear it in the heaviness of his voice. "Tell me," she said simply.

"You have a fractured skull," he said, anger roughening his tone. "The bastard almost killed you." His last word caught on a ragged sob, and Dinah felt tears burn in her own eyes. This wonderful, strong man was crying for her.

She squeezed his hand and opened her eyes as her own tears began to trickle into her hair. "But I'm all right, now. Somehow you saved me, Jake, and that's all that matters."

He pinched the bridge of his nose as he shook his head. "It wasn't me, babe. All I did was almost succeed in getting you killed."

"That ain't exactly right," a new voice put in from the doorway.

Both Jake and Dinah turned in that direction. Gus Abbot stood there, looking uncomfortable holding a potted plant in his hand. "This is from the wife," he said, coming into the room and setting the plant on the bedside table. "She and the kids will be over later on to see for themselves how you're gettin' on. Me, I couldn't wait. Had to find out if you were out of the woods yet."

"The doctor was in here a half hour ago," Jake told the old man. "His prognosis was for a full recovery in just a few days." He stood up to shake the man's hand. He motioned to the chair, then sat again beside Dinah. "Here's your hero, babe."

"Ain't so," the old man disagreed. "Just dumb luck and a knack for being too derned nosy. That's all."

Dinah laughed softly. "Would one of you please tell me what happened. The last thing I remember was thinking you were dead, Jake. I heard a gun go off . . ." She hesitated, squinting her eyes. "Glass breaking, I think, and then you fell over me. Is that the way it happened?"

Jake handed off the question to Gus. "Go ahead. Start with the car you saw on the side of the road."

Dinah's eyes moved expectantly to the old man's, though she held on to Jake's hand.

"Well, let's see. Guess I should explain that my oldest, Maggie, always attends midnight Mass, and most times I let her think she's bullying me into going with her. Last night, though, she decided not to go 'cause the baby has a cold. I almost stayed home myself, rather than let her on to the fact that it's my favorite night of the year.

"Anyways, my grandson, Tyler, suggested that him and me go together, and we took off. The reason I'm telling you all this is to explain about how we even came to notice the car."

Dinah nodded and signaled her patience with a smile.

"Well, I found out real quick that the reason Ty was so hot to go along was so he could coax me into letting him drive—he's only fifteen, not old enough for a license. And damn, if we wasn't just on the road for a couple of minutes when he almost side-swipes this fancy car that's slid off the shoulder. Why, hell fire, I was so mad at how close he come to hitting it, I didn't register where it was parked or stop to wonder why until I seen you come into the church, all covered in snow and your chin all scraped up like you'd taken a bad fall.

"Anyways," he continued, "I got to thinking about that car and wondering if there could be any connection to the way you looked and it being stuck only a few feet from the end of your drive. And just as I'm wallerin' that one around, in comes this feller who sits down directly behind ya. Nothin' strange about that exceptin' the Mass is almost over, and he doesn't unzip his coat or even pull the hood off. The next thing I know, he's got hold of your arm and is steerin' you out of there."

Dinah met Jake's gaze and offered a grin in the hope that the old mountain man's colorful story-telling would ease the tension she could still read in his face.

"Well, I hurried out after ya, and got outside the church just in time to see you bein' helped into your car. For a minute there, I was pretty much convinced that everythin' was hunky-dory, but one of the cars was turnin' out of the parkin' lot just then, and the headlights lit up the folks inside that car just like you was center stage at The Mainstreet Opry, and I seen that weasel in the back hit you on the head."

Gus stopped to pull a handkerchief from the hip pocket of his overalls and mop his face of the perspiration that had beaded there with the reliving of that horrifying moment.

"I ran back inside the church—scared Father Weinert to a near heart attack—and called the sheriff. Related what I'd seen, and told him I'd be waitin' on the road for him to pick me up."

Jake took advantage of the pause to push the story along. "I saw them outside the window, Dinah. There were three or four men, and I saw one of them raise a rifle and aim it at Rosenthal's head. I was so busy trying to keep him talking, I almost missed the instant the sharpshooter closed his left eye and pulled the trigger. I threw myself over you to keep the glass from cutting you when the window exploded."

Dinah covered her mouth with her hand and squeezed her eyes shut as her mind suddenly slammed her back in time to the instant she thought Jake had died.

"Hey, it's all right. We made it," Jake crooned, running the back of his hand over her cheek and wiping away the flood of tears that had started with the memory.

Neither of them heard Gus clear his throat or noticed when he slipped out of the room. Jake stretched out beside her on the bed and slipped an arm under her to draw her close while she wept.

A nurse interrupted them a long while later. "Sorry to bother you, Ms. Smith, but I have to check your vitals."

Jake scooted from the bed and stood at the window overlooking the lake below. A low fog hovered over the water, creating a haunting, surreal aura, much like everything else about the weekend that dusk was bringing to an end.

"Well, you're doing fine, Ms. Smith. I'll just let the two of you get back to your visit," the nurse said as she picked up her chart and started for the door. "Oh, by the way, Mr. Jacobs, your brother woke up and asked me to tell you all Merry Christmas."

Jake turned away from the window, offering a weary smile. "I'll be down to see him in a minute. Would you let him know?"

"Sure," she said, looking back and forth between them with a knowing grin. "And I'll just pull this door closed so the two of you can, ah, rest."

Dinah laughed mildly until she looked into Jake's eyes again. "I wish you'd tell me what's wrong," she said.

"What could be wrong?" he asked, trying for a grin that worked only partway. "We're alive—at least some of us—and the bad guy got his. As soon as you and A.J. are on your feet, it'll be back to life as normal."

"No," she said, shaking her head. "The normal

we all knew is gone forever. Nothing can ever be the same. Not for A.J., whose whole life was turned upside down long before he was shot and his ex-wife murdered. Not for Tony Bianci or Rhonda Harker's parents." She paused, waiting for him to look up from the floor, where he'd been staring while she spoke. When he met her gaze at last, she smiled. "We're the only two who seem to be emerging better off."

He ran his tongue over the stitches in his bottom lip, and his gaze moved to the bandage on her head. "Yeah, well, I guess everyone's perspective is different."

"Damn it, Evan Jacobs, will you stop feeling sorry for yourself and look at me." She pointed at her eyes with two fingers. "Right here."

"Sorry for myself!" Jake shouted. Then softer as embarrassment darkened his face, "I guarantee you one thing, lady, I'm feeling anything but self-pity. I'm pissed off, because I didn't keep you safe. And mad as hell at you for not trusting me. And, yeah, maybe I am a little hurt that you took advantage of my feelings for you—"

"Took advantage!" Dinah shrieked. "I took advantage of your feelings? How in the hell do you figure that?"

"Well, I think that's pretty damned obvious. Jesus Christ, Dinah, you let me make love to you, even let me tell you how I felt, and the whole time it was just a means to an end. A clever ploy to get me off my guard so you could make your escape."

"That's not true!"

"Then why did you leave?" he asked, his voice choked to a whisper by hurt.

"Because I thought A.J. was using you to get to me. I believed in you Jake. It was A.J. I didn't trust."

"And do you forgive me for not saving you?" he asked after a long moment.

"But you did. When you threw yourself over me, you gave Stan an easy target. If he'd managed to pull the trigger even as a reflexive action, he would probably have caught you midair and killed you instantly." She sighed. "Besides, silly, you proved what a hero you are in every gesture, from the moment you kidnapped me to save your brother, to the time you placed your coat under my head so I'd be comfortable, to the kindness you displayed when you covered me with a blanket while I rested, then made soup so I could eat when I was hungry, and later—"

"Okay." He stopped her, embarrassed. "I don't know, maybe I was or maybe I was just . . . never mind. I don't know what I want. Maybe just for this never to have happened."

"Oh, no, Jake. Don't ever wish for that, because we would never have fallen in love."

His head snapped up. "What did you say?"

Dinah smiled. "Jake, look into my eyes and tell me what color they are."

"Blue," he said, amazement ringing in his voice.

"I know! I saw it when the nurse was taking my blood pressure, and I raised the lid on this table and looked into the mirror. They've never been blue in my life! Always gray or sometimes silver when I'm angry, as you noticed. Dull as pewter when I'm sad. But right now the only thing I'm feeling is incredibly, wildly, madly in love." She threw her arms around his neck and laughed. "I'm convinced, the color of love is blue."

"I'll make sure they never change," he promised, then sealed the vow with a kiss.

PART FOUR

~

Yardley

BY
JODIE LARSEN

Chapter Twenty-nine

~

Spring 1998

With closed eyes he relished the dwindling rhythm of the heart pulsing beneath his perfectly manicured fingertips. It grew softer with each beat, until at last, it stopped. He sighed, knowing the screaming, the fighting, were over.

Another dead bitch! he thought as he grabbed his jogging suit from the edge of the nearby Jacuzzi and dressed. Walking across the barren room, he gathered the discarded clothes. With infinite care the black skirt was folded, then the torn scarlet blouse, the satin bra, the ruined panty hose. Collecting the string of pearls and the black sling-back pumps, he placed them gently atop the pile and scanned the room one last time. Almost as an afterthought, he stuffed the digital pager into his pocket.

Resuming the long, rhythmic strides of his interrupted run, he passed the FOR SALE sign planted in the center of the impeccably groomed front lawn. Slipping unnoticed onto the street, he pushed the button on the side of his sports watch to stop the chronometer from counting precious seconds. Distance soon diminished the memory of both the house and the dead woman inside.

With pride he realized exactly twenty-one minutes had elapsed—a full six minutes longer than ever before. A hint of a smile creased his face as he pictured his next test. Young, blond, energetic— sure to be quite a challenge.

Slowly closing her eyes, Yardley Smith lifted her face to the sun to experience the texture of the first day of spring. A satin breeze accompanied tiny ripples of heat, helping to calm the case of rattled nerves that had plagued her all day. Ambling down the sidewalk of her latest listing, Yardley stretched graceful hands toward the crystal blue sky, forcing herself to relax, to ignore the frightening reality of the recent murders.

A cluster of something bright yellow captured her attention. Gathering the skirt of her denim dress in one hand, she stooped to reveal the treasure. With a genuine smile Yardley pushed aside a drift of decaying oak leaves, uncovering a stunning row of pansies that had somehow managed to survive the coldest Oklahoma winter in fifty years.

It was almost three o'clock, and not one soul had stopped by the open house since noon. She reached her four-wheel-drive Rocky and grabbed her well-worn wooden box of art supplies, then twisted her long, blond hair in a knot to keep it out of the way.

Sitting cross-legged just inches from the flowers, the cool stone sidewalk caressed her bare skin as she escaped into her own world—a place where shades and shadows captured life.

In moments, the virgin canvas was washed in pale indigo, then blotted dry with a sponge. After blending a palette of watercolors from zesty yellows to the lightest whispers of green, Yardley started to bring the image on the canvas to life. The tip of the paintbrush skillfully pulled fragile dark streaks from the center of each pansy into its cadmium yellow petals. She added shimmering droplets of water. As usual, she was captivated, lost in nature as beauty was frozen in time.

Out of the corner of one eye, she glimpsed the top of a pair of athletic shoes. Stopping in midstroke, her breath caught as she gazed up at the long, lean body of the man who had appeared just a few feet away. With an artist's eye Yardley absently assessed the color of his hair and eyes as a shade of raw umber. He wore an expensive lightweight jogging suit— navy with cream stripes—and an elusive smile that instantly piqued her curiosity.

"Sorry. I didn't mean to startle you," he said with a shrug. "I wondered if I could look at the house."

Scrambling to her feet, she quickly replied, "Of course, I'm sorry." After fumbling for a business card, she wiped the paint off one hand, then thrust it toward him as she said, "I'm Yardley Smith, the listing agent for McCay Reality. This is a great house; you're going to love it." Following the direction of his gaze, she knew he was staring at the antique pin she always wore—a tiny palette splashed with iridescent drops of color. A slender solid gold paintbrush crossed the palette, its bristles delicately etched to a fine point. Snapping closed her painting supplies, she explained, "I'm a frustrated artist at heart. I was supposed to wrap up the open house a little while ago, but I couldn't resist capturing these gorgeous pansies."

"I'm glad you didn't." Carefully picking up the canvas, he studied it, then said, "You're really quite talented. Are you a professional?"

Laughing, she started toward the house as she replied, "Yes and no. I have a degree in fine arts, but I sell real estate to make ends meet."

"Another starving artist?" he quipped as he gently placed the painting back on the ground and followed her.

"Not if I can help it," she answered. There was something about his voice. Its deep resonance intrigued her, yet at the same time made her uneasy. As she unlocked the front door, he stopped just behind her, so close that when she whirled around, the hem of her dress brushed the front of his legs.

Yardley's face was only inches from his chest. His downcast eyes held hers as she tilted her chin upward to speak. The narrow porch left little room to maneuver. Shifting to one side, she said, "I'll . . . You can look around all you like since the house is vacant. Be sure and check out the master bathroom; they just remodeled it. I'm going to gather my painting things, but I'll be happy to answer any questions you might have when you're finished."

His hand reached out to touch her. Slender fingers plunged into her hair as he roughly brushed his thumb along her cheekbone. "I doubt if this marvelous yellow streak is part of your normal attire," he joked as he boldly wiped the smudge of paint from her cheek.

Yardley was electrified. His touch sent shivers through her entire body, a chill of dreadful anticipation. The rush of adrenaline was unlike anything she had experienced, a strange mixture of alarm and desire. Her cheeks ignited as she held his gaze and shyly mumbled, "I tend to lose myself when I'm painting . . . I apologize for being so . . . unprofessional."

Laughing, he pulled open the door and slyly said, "You can redeem yourself by giving me a personal tour."

Calm down! she silently scolded herself. *You're just nervous. The women who were murdered lately have everyone on edge. You can't afford to blow this sale just because you're afraid of your own shadow!*

Even though she knew it wasn't wise, Yardley Smith nodded and stepped inside.

It was Sunday afternoon and Kim Grant, the receptionist at McCay Realty, was hard at work. With a sigh she stuffed the last file into place, rolled the large cabinet drawer closed, then began to gather her things. When the phone rang, she expected it to be her roommate, Yardley Smith. Instead, it was one of the agency's most prized clients.

After listening intently, Kim replied, "Yes, Dr. Crotty, if you can hold on for a few moments, I'll check." Quickly poking her head into the owner's dignified office, she cleared her throat and muttered, "Excuse me, Mr. McCay."

He was in his late forties, but his black hair, gray eyes, and year-round golfer's tan made him look considerably younger. Glancing up from the stack of closing papers, he merely cocked his head and nodded for her to continue.

"Anne was supposed to show the Stephenson estate at three o'clock, but she still isn't there. Dr. Crotty is waiting. What do you want me to tell her?"

"Have you tried to contact Anne?" he asked.

Kim nodded. "I've been paging her for hours, plus trying her cell phone. Her husband says she left the house early this morning. . . ."

Looking at his watch, he said, "Page Yardley. If she's still at the open house in Maple Ridge, she can be over there in a matter of minutes. And, Kim, when you track down Anne, tell her I need to speak to her first thing in the morning."

"Yes, sir." Kim knew Mr. McCay had been patient with Anne's erratic behavior for several months, but standing up a client was inexcusable. With a slight twinge of guilt she hoped that Mr. McCay would realize she could easily fill Anne's position.

As they passed from room to room, Yardley grew a little more at ease with the handsome man at her side. Normally, she was quite good at reading people's faces, but his was different. At every turn she caught his direct, intense gaze, leaving her momentarily flustered. Yet several times he surprised her with an appreciation of the home's unique architectural details that few clients ever noticed.

When she led him into the newly decorated

master bath, they were surrounded by glass walls, cultured marble, and sparkling mirrors—mirrors that multiplied the image of unyielding eyes following her every move. Quickly stepping back into the empty bedroom, she brightly asked, "Exquisite, isn't it?"

Although his fingertips were touching the marble countertop, through the reflection of the mirrors she knew he was actually staring at her chest as he replied, "Very elegant . . ."

Yardley had the feeling he might be describing her grandmother's antique pin, her breasts, anything except the damned bathroom.

Cocking his head, he asked, "Is something wrong? You seem nervous." Before she had the chance to answer, he swiftly turned toward her and declared, "How stupid of me! It's those open house murders, isn't it? I'll bet there isn't a female real estate agent in the city of Tulsa who isn't terrified of being alone in a vacant house with a strange man right now."

Yardley nodded and smiled with relief. Surely, no killer would raise that subject.

Reaching into his pocket, he pulled out a business card and said, "I apologize. I should've introduced myself the moment I met you. My name is Kyle Baker. I buy older homes, fix them up, and re-sell them. I'm sorry if I unnerved you."

Taking the card, Yardley sighed and flashed a re-laxed smile for the first time. "To tell you the truth, I *was* a little frightened. Is there anything else I can show you?"

Stepping closer to her, he casually said, "Just more of that beautiful smile."

Without furniture to warm the rooms, the house seemed almost as threatening as the man who was once again standing too close for comfort. Backing away, Yardley practically jumped out of her skin at the unexpected beep of a pager. She and Kyle Baker simultaneously reached into their pockets, each pulling out a pager to gaze at its small digital screen.

"Not me," he said, sliding his back into his jogging pants.

"It's mine. Will you excuse me?" she asked.

Nodding, Kyle said, "Sure. I'll check out the backyard, then meet you out front by the pansies."

Even though the breeze was still pleasantly warm, an involuntary shiver ran through her as she stepped onto the porch and dialed her office number. "You rang?"

Kim answered, "Mr. McCay wants you to rush to the Stephenson estate. Anne was a no-show, and Dr. Crotty is there waiting."

"I'll be there in five minutes." After briefly hesitating, she added, "Kim, did he mention any particular reason for choosing me to show the estate?"

Kim laughed. "I'm afraid this time you were in the right place at the right time. Don't worry, sooner or later he'll figure out what he's missing and ask you out again."

Yardley muttered, "Right. See ya," then clicked off. Noticing Kyle strolling leisurely toward her, she felt silly. He didn't seem nearly so daunting in the light of day. In fact, she was ashamed of how spooked she had been as she explained, "I'm sorry, Mr. Baker, but I've got to go. If you have any questions, please give me a call at the office, or page me if you like. I have several listings you might find interesting."

"Listen, I know I frightened you, and I'd really like to make it up to you. How about having dinner with me?"

Extending her hand, she said, "I'm sorry, Mr. Baker, but I don't go out with clients. It was very nice of you to offer." He grasped her hand, making the handshake linger so long that she became aware of the rhythm of his pulse through his palm.

When he finally released her hand, his eyes gleamed as he smiled and said, "I'm sure I'll see you again soon, Yardley Smith. Very soon."

"You must be Dr. Crotty. I'm so sorry you had to wait. If you'd still like to see the estate, I'd be happy to show it to you," Yardley said, relieved to see the doctor was a *woman*, tall, with dark hair and kind eyes.

Smiling, Dr. Crotty replied, "We'll have to make it fast. I've got a four o'clock tee-time at Southern Hills."

Hurrying up the entry stairs, Yardley opened the keybox and unlocked the magnificent crystal doors. Inviting the client to follow, she led the way through the massive formal living area, the kitchen, and the den. Stopping at a staircase, Yardley said, "Upstairs are five guest rooms, each with its own full bath, plus there's an office and a playroom." Nodding to the opposite direction, she added, "The master bedroom wing is down this way. Which would you like to see first?"

"Let's save upstairs for another day," she replied. "I'm almost out of time."

Leading the way, Yardley enjoyed the feel of the plush carpet underfoot as they noiselessly walked down the brightly lit hall. Throwing open the door to the bedroom, she turned and said, "It's quite a magnificent view, isn't it?"

The wide-eyed expression of shock on Dr. Crotty's face made Yardley spin around to look for herself. At first she saw exactly what she expected through the floor-to-ceiling windows—fresh, bright green trees and shrubs dotting the South Tulsa hillside. But she gasped as her gaze fell upon the pair of unseeing green eyes staring directly at them.

Dr. Crotty rushed to the woman's side, quickly taking a pulse. Yardley followed, immediately recognizing her fellow agent, Anne Browne. Swallowing hard, she saw the despondent look crease the doctor's face. A moan escaped her lips as she realized Anne was dead.

Dr. Crotty stood, pulling out her cell phone. "I'll call the police. Don't touch anything."

Yardley merely nodded. An involuntary shiver confirmed that her instincts had been right—again.

By the time the police let Yardley leave, the Oklahoma skies had surrendered to a bank of ominous storm clouds. As she drove home, the rain arrived in clear, pounding sheets. The evening's colors bled depressingly together on the windshield before they were rhythmically pushed aside by the path of the wiper blades.

Exhausted, she waited at the stoplight and tried to remember what Anne was like before. Instead, she was tortured with vivid images of unseeing eyes, fresh bruises, raw violence. Like a still life, she pictured Anne's clothes, neatly folded and stacked. *Did he make her undress? Why would he fold her clothes? Stop thinking about it! Just a couple more minutes until you're home. Kim has green chili enchiladas in the oven. Then a nice, long bath.*

The light turned green, and she drove slowly through the intersection until something caught her eye—a man crudely clutching a helpless puppy in his outstretched arms. "Holy shit!" she cried as she slammed on her brakes. The car behind her honked loudly as it frantically swerved to avoid a collision. Pulling to the curb, she jumped out of the Rocky and into the stormy night.

He stood on the corner, young, very thin and soaked to the bone. Beside him was an old animal crate, and from his extended arms dangled the terrified, wet puppy.

Desperate to be heard over the howling wind, she yelled, "Are you crazy? What do you think you're doing?"

Relaxing his arms, the man cradled the frightened dog like a football as another bolt of lightning ripped across the sky. "He's the last of the litter. You want him, lady?"

Thrusting up her hands, she answered, "Couldn't this wait till tomorrow?"

Thunder cracked as he pushed the puppy at her, shouting, "Come on, he's a great pup. He hears real good, in spite of that maimed ear of his. Just take him, will ya?"

Yardley knew better, but the combination of the man's reckless insensitivity and the look of terror in the dog's huge, sad eyes quickly convinced her to grab him. Tucking the shaking animal safely against her bosom, she rushed back to her car, jumped inside, and slammed the door. Driving slowly home, she glanced at the puppy in the passenger seat and the two of them shivered in unison.

"Kim is going to kill me," she said as she pulled the one-eared baby Doberman against her cheek. As the meaning of her own words sunk in, the horrid mental picture of Anne's body returned. Holding the puppy even tighter against her cold, wet denim dress, she pulled into the garage and parked. The tears she'd fought back for hours finally began to fall.

Within seconds the pup's rough tongue found the salty drops and licked them away. "Everything's going to be all right," she mumbled, as much to herself as to the dog. Looking down, Yardley would have sworn his little nub of a tail was actually wagging.

"How are you?" Chuck McCay asked as he pulled Yardley into a comforting, light embrace the next morning.

With a hesitant nod she answered, "Okay, I guess."

Other agents were filing into the McCay Realty conference room, taking the few remaining seats. Grim faces revealed they had already heard the bad news, that this would be nothing like their typical, optimistic Monday morning sales meeting.

"You look exhausted," Chuck said.

Shrugging, Yardley wearily replied, "That's probably because I am. Besides finding Anne, I adopted a puppy yesterday. Between the two, I was up most of the night. He has a horrible cough, and he's afraid of storms."

Chuck lightly shook his head and replied, "I should've guessed you'd be the type to rescue a sick animal."

Narrowing her eyes, she said, "You say that as if it's a bad thing."

"That depends." Glancing about the full room, he added, "You have to be tough these days. Meet me in my office after the meeting. I've got a couple of deals I'd like to discuss with you."

Nodding, Yardley agreed, even though she wanted nothing more than to be back home, preferably with her head buried under the covers for a long, long nap. Instead, she sipped her steaming cup of coffee, trying her best to appear alert and interested.

Chuck McCay's voice was powerful and authoritative as he addressed his employees. "I'd like to start this meeting by thanking all of you for coming. I know it's difficult for those of you who were closest to Anne, so I'll keep this brief. I've asked Detective Jones with the Tulsa Police Department to speak for a few minutes."

Yardley recognized the officer from yesterday's ordeal at the Stephenson estate. Settling back in her chair, she stared out the window while he spoke.

"I'm sure most of you are aware that this is the fifth time a female real estate agent has been murdered at an open house in Tulsa. The last two have happened this month. The killer seems to be striking more frequently now, so the danger to each of you is very real. Obviously, we're doing everything we can to apprehend the suspect, but investigations like these take time.

"Your help in finding your co-worker's killer is important, but your safety is our biggest concern." His eyes jumped across the faces of each female agent, resting on Yardley's as he continued. "Only well-established clients should be met alone, and even then, if at all possible, take a friend. Open houses need to be conducted in pairs, preferably with a male agent. Do *not* show to walk-ins. A female officer is going to teach a self-defense class here on Thursday night. I recommend each woman agent attend. Any questions until then?"

Kim quietly asked, "Do you have any idea who the killer might be?"

Weighing his words carefully, the detective replied, "We're releasing this information to the press tomorrow, so I suppose it's all right if I tell you. According to the coroner, the suspect is probably a muscular man with large hands. At several of the crime scenes, neighbors have reported seeing an unfamiliar jogger near the time of the murder. He's probably in his thirties and is described as tall with dark hair and eyes."

Yardley's heart started to pound as she instantly made the connection to Kyle Baker. Raising her hand, she gathered her nerve and asked, "What time was Anne . . . ?"

"Between noon and two o'clock yesterday afternoon."

And Kyle showed up at three, on foot, just a few miles away. "Can you tell us what this runner was wearing?" she asked.

"So far, he's always been in a dark blue or black jogging suit of some kind. Yesterday's witness described it as navy."

Suddenly, Yardley felt as though every person in the room was staring at her. Memories of her encounter with Kyle Baker raced through her mind, but as she started to speak, the officer's radio came to life. She watched as he hurriedly excused himself to leave, then she slumped against the back of her chair and silently prayed her instincts about Kyle Baker's innocence were right.

Kim purposely waited until everyone left for lunch before she dialed the familiar number. "Hi, handsome," she whispered.

"Are you alone?" he asked.

"Almost. I'm at work, but Mr. McCay's in his office with his door closed. I can talk for a few minutes."

"I've missed you," he said.

Glancing nervously over her shoulder, Kim whispered, "Me, too."

"Why didn't you call back sooner?" he asked.

"We had a meeting about the open house murders. The woman killed yesterday was one of our agents."

He sounded distracted, almost uninterested, as he replied, "Sorry to hear it. Do the police have any leads?"

Kim strained to listen for the sound of approaching footsteps as she anxiously answered, "None that they're telling us about."

"That roomie of yours still pissed at me?" he asked.

Defensively, Kim replied, "Austin, Yardley is just watching out for my well-being. You can't hold that against her."

"I know Yardley never cared much for me, that it was her idea for you to break up with me in the first place. So do me a favor—don't tell her you started seeing me again. I think we'd all be much happier."

Kim wondered how Austin could possibly have known that Yardley didn't like him. When they broke up, she told him she wanted to date other people, not that Yardley had anything to do with it. Yet she was glad she was seeing him again. He was the only man she had ever dated who made her feel truly loved.

Nodding, Kim decided it was a good idea to keep their relationship quiet for a while. Besides, what Yardley didn't know wouldn't hurt her. . . .

"Mr. McCay asked about you this afternoon," Kim said, stepping onto the balcony outside Yardley's bedroom.

Yardley looked every bit the image of a starving artist. She was wearing paint-stained jeans and an equally splattered plaid shirt. Her blond hair was loosely knotted at the nape of her neck, highlighting the dark circles under her eyes. "Shit!" she muttered through the bushy goat-hair mop paintbrush clenched in her teeth. "I completely forgot he wanted to see me after the meeting. What'd you tell him?"

"I didn't tell him you were taking out your frustrations on an innocent canvas, if that's what you mean." Answering the look Yardley shot her, she smiled and added, "I told him you had two show-ings, and that you were still pretty shaken about finding Anne's body yesterday."

Grabbing the brush, Yardley clearly replied, "Thanks. I owe you one."

Kim stared at the painting—a dark, ominous land-scape of muddy yellows and greens on a black back-ground. "Are you all right?" she asked.

"Pretty gloomy, isn't it?" Yardley said.

"Let's put it this way. It's good, but I wouldn't want it hanging in my bedroom. It gives me the creeps."

"Was that supposed to be a compliment?"

Laughing, Kim replied, "That depends on whether you were actually going for that X-Files look. . . ." Her gaze fell on the puppy sleeping in a box near Yardley's feet. "What did the vet say about our little friend?"

"That he just needs love and care. He thinks he's already almost six months old, so he's not going to be very big, even when he's full grown. Apparently, he's mostly miniature pinscher. They call them min pins."

"Are they vicious?" Kim asked, eyeing the pup skeptically.

Following Kim's gaze to the dog curled into a tiny ball, Yardley asked, "Does he look mean?" An-swering her own question, she added, "Of course not. At least the little guy is feeling better. He hasn't coughed in a couple of hours."

Squatting next to the box, Kim gently stroked the dog's head as she said, "What's with his missing ear?"

"According to Dr. Nida, it was probably ripped off in a fight. Considering his short life, he's had it pretty rough. Maybe that's why I identify with him . . ."

"What's that supposed to mean?"

Yardley sighed, her eyes focused somewhere deep within the painting as she replied, "I just found out my mother committed suicide."

"Oh," Kim said uncertainly. "Are you okay?"

Shrugging, Yardley sighed. "I guess. I think I'd have rather not known. It makes me feel . . . abandoned. Like she didn't love us enough to stick around."

"Oh, Yardley. I'm so sorry."

Brushing away a tear, Yardley nodded. "I know." Looking at the puppy, she added, "See why I love him? Unquestionable love, any time of the day or night."

Kim gently ran her hand down the short, black fur. "He is definitely adorable. Have you named him yet?"

Yardley quickly shook off her gloom, asking, "Promise not to laugh?"

"Why? Did you name him Dammit?" Kim joked.

"No. His name is Vincent van Gogh. Vinnie for short."

"I should've known you'd choose a great artist to immortalize." Softly touching the exquisite red fabric underneath him, Kim asked, "So what've you given our little one-eared friend to sleep on? Pure silk?"

Adding splashes of crimson to her painting, Yardley replied, "It's a scarf my sister sent. Gorgeous, isn't it?"

Nodding solemnly, Kim said, "Too pretty to use as a dog bed."

"I know. I hadn't put it away, and the next thing I knew, he had curled up in it. The box is just his size, and he looked so safe and warm that I didn't have the heart to take him out. Besides, how dirty could he be after spending half the night in a downpour?"

"Good point. You always said you were the only sentimental one in your family. Which sister sent it?" Kim asked.

Concentrating on her painting again, Yardley answered distractedly, "Dinah. She wants me to keep the scarf and the gun—"

"Gun?" Kim asked, incredulous. "She sent you a *gun*? In the mail? Isn't that illegal? What on earth for? Where is it?"

Shrugging, Yardley said, "It's still wrapped in that red scarf, so it's under Vinnie."

"Must not be a very big gun," Kim replied.

"Actually, it's quite small. It's a Lady Smith, with inlaid pearl grips. If it wasn't a *gun*, I might be able to think of it as a work of art. Could you please freshen this for me?" she asked, handing Kim the jar of cloudy water she'd been using to wash her brushes.

Kim left the door open while she slipped inside. From the bathroom she yelled, "What're you going to do with it?"

"If you're asking about the gun, I'll keep it in my purse until they catch the son of a bitch who killed Anne."

Stepping back onto the balcony, Kim handed Yardley the bottle of fresh water as she said, "You're kidding! You know that's against the law."

Shrugging, Yardley muttered, "Technically . . ."

Eyeing her friend, Kim asked, "Does this have something to do with that man you mentioned last night? The one you *didn't* bother to tell the police about at the crime scene or at this morning's meeting?"

Shaking her head, Yardley replied, "I was just nervous—obviously with good cause."

"But you said the guy had a pager. Have you thought about that? Exactly what kind of emergencies do professional remodelers have on Sunday afternoons?"

Shrugging, Yardley answered, "How should I know?"

"You said he was wearing jogging clothes." She paused, then added, "I know I wouldn't want to go for a run without my pager, would you?"

"I know, I know. And he was on foot. Most people looking at houses don't show up without a car."

"Then why didn't you tell the police?"

Reaching into her paint supplies, Yardley replied, "Because I have his business card right here. What kind of murderer hands out calling cards?"

With a scowl Kim asked, "The really psycho kind?"

"Or maybe, just maybe, Kyle Baker is what he says he is. And if that's true, he might turn out to be an excellent client."

Kim read the card. "How far do you think he ran?"

"Why?" Yardley snapped impatiently.

"Did he look like he had just finished a marathon, or was he out for a leisurely afternoon jog around the neighborhood?"

"He wasn't panting or sweaty if that's what you're getting at."

Sticking Kyle Baker's card under Yardley's nose, Kim flatly said, "He should've been. According to this, his home address is about twenty miles from your open house."

Chapter Thirty

~

Kyle Baker was exhausted by the time he arrived at his office on Monday afternoon. His jeans were filthy, his hands crusted with PVC glue and sawdust. Stopping at his secretary's desk, he tiredly asked, "Did you gather that information I needed?"

"Yes, sir." Jewel was nearly seventy, but she could still handle the telephone and do the little typing Kyle required. She proudly gave him the sheet of paper she had obviously spent most of the day working on. "These are all the listings in yesterday's Sunday paper for Yardley Smith, including her upcoming schedule of open houses. Just in case you needed them, I copied all the other McCay Realty listings as well."

Glancing over the summary, Kyle's eyes couldn't help but stop on the Stephenson estate listed by Anne Browne. A grim expression on his face, he wondered if Jewel had made the same connection.

* * *

Yardley poured a cup of coffee, then settled into a chair at the kitchen table to read Thursday's morning paper.

"Did you take Vinnie for a walk dressed like *that*?" Kim asked.

Looking down at her oversized bathrobe and lamb's wool slippers, Yardley yawned and replied, "Nobody's awake at this hour except the two of us and those crazy people who jog before dawn."

"Vinnie seems better, but I hope you don't expect him to be a watchdog," Kim said, tossing the high-strung puppy a rolled sock to chase.

Yardley swept him into her arms when he proudly brought the prize back, playfully scratching behind his ear as she said, "When you look like a Doberman trapped in the body of Chihuahua, you'd better learn to be tough."

As if on cue, the beep of Yardley's pager sent Vinnie flying out of her arms, yelping as he ran to hide under the kitchen table.

Kim laughed. "Oh, yeah! He's *really* tough!" Offering a small piece of her breakfast muffin, she tried to coax him back out.

Scowling, Yardley read the number on her pager.

"Who in the world would call at this hour?" Kim asked.

"I haven't got a clue," Yardley said as she grabbed the portable phone and dialed.

"Hello," a man's deep voice answered.

"This is Yardley Smith with McCay Realty. Someone at this number paged me."

"That would be me, Kyle Baker. I hope I didn't wake you. We met at your open house in Maple Ridge last Sunday. . . ."

Glancing sideways at Kim, she walked into the other room with the phone. "We're early risers. What can I do for you, Mr. Baker?"

"I wondered if I could convince you to reconsider my invitation. After all, I'm not actually a client unless I buy a house from you, right? Besides, I happened to notice another one of your listings is by the Full Moon Cafe. Since you nixed dinner, how about meeting me for lunch today, then you can show me the house."

After only a slight hesitation, she asked, "Is twelve-thirty all right?"

"You bet."

Before she could even hang up, Kim popped around the corner and asked, "Are you crazy?"

Yardley's frustration was apparent in her voice. "More like lonely. Look, maybe he's single. I already know he's ruggedly handsome and owns his own company. What more could I want?"

"You don't see it, do you?" Kim asked incredulously.

"See what?" Yardley snapped.

"You just described Chuck McCay."

Shrugging, she replied, "Maybe it's time I broaden my horizons. If *Mr.* McCay were actually interested in me, we'd have gone out more than twice in the last six months."

Softening, Kim said, "He's just been really busy with this merger. I'm sure when things settle down, he'll come to his senses. The two of you would make a great couple."

"But you know what they say, timing is everything. And I'm tired of waiting. Besides, having lunch with Kyle Baker in a crowded restaurant isn't exactly like agreeing to go to his lair."

Shaking her head, Kim hugged Vinnie tightly and sighed. "Just promise you'll be careful."

Yardley smiled and grabbed her purse. "I've got pepper gas, mace, and by the time I meet him, my pretty little gun will actually have bullets in it. What more could a girl need?"

Yardley and Kyle sat on the balcony of the small cafe, facing west so they could both enjoy the view. Kyle was dressed casually in a pair of stonewashed jeans and a chamois shirt with the sleeves comfortably rolled halfway up his muscular forearms. Yardley had chosen her favorite plaid walking shorts with a hunter green and navy sweater.

Halfway through his bowl of tortilla soup, he paused and asked, "Being with me still makes you nervous, doesn't it?"

Smiling, Yardley poked at her crispy salad and tried to keep her tone light. "Lately, I'm always a little nervous."

Kyle was obviously amused, his eyes searching hers. "I'm not a mass murderer. I'll prove it. Ask me anything. Anything at all."

Leaning back, she said, "Okay . . . Let's see. Why were you on foot the other day when the home address listed on your business card is miles from my open house?"

He answered without missing a beat. "I'm working on a house at 26th and Utica. It was such a pretty day, I decided to go for a short run."

"But you weren't winded—or sweaty. When I finish a good run, I look like someone hosed me down, then whacked me with the hose a couple of times for good measure."

Laughing, he replied, "You probably work at it harder. I do one long run a week, fifteen to twenty miles, usually on Monday. The rest of the time I'm more interested in building muscle endurance."

"Training for a marathon?" she asked.

Smiling, Kyle said, "No. Running just helps me do the sport I *really* love."

"And what sport would that be?" she asked.

With a gleam in his eye he watched her closely as he answered, "Mountain climbing."

Choking on the sip of water, Yardley said, "You're kidding, right?"

"Not at all."

Motioning toward the Tulsa horizon, Yardley announced, "In case you haven't noticed, there aren't any mountains around here."

"True. When I get serious, I fly to the Sierra Nevadas or the Rockies. Where there's a will, there's a way . . ."

"And when you aren't serious?" she asked.

Kyle was obviously in his element. He practically beamed as he answered, "I keep up my skills by practicing at Chandler Park, plus there are some good climbs along the Arkansas and Illinois rivers. I even work in my garage."

She tilted her head, enjoying the banter. "You have a mountain in your garage?"

"Not quite. I've rigged the ceiling so I can train at home in bad weather."

"Unfortunately, the only mental picture that comes to mind is of you hanging upside down like a bat. Am I close?" Yardley asked.

"Come see, sometime." Reacting to the return of her distrustful look, he shook his head and smiled. "Really, you should come with me on Saturday. There's a group of us that meets at the park. I'll teach you some of the basics. From watching you paint, I have a feeling you love nature as much as I do. . . . I promise it'll be a unique experience if nothing else."

Yardley shook her head skeptically. "I think I'd prefer to have my arms and legs in working order for a few more years, even though it might make a good story to tell my grandchildren someday."

"That's the beauty of climbing. If you do it right, you're safe. Of course, you have to learn to trust your lead."

"Lead? As in being on a leash?"

Laughing, he said, "I guess you could look at it that way, but most people prefer to think of the lead climber as a fellow athlete, an integral part of a safe team."

Cringing, she said, "What about snakes? Don't they live in the rocks?"

Amused, he replied, "Most snakes don't slither up the sheer side of a cliff just to find a good place to sun themselves. Seriously, I've been climbing for ten years, and I haven't run across one yet." He sipped his tea. "Occasionally a tarantula might cross our path, but they're generally harmless."

Suppressing an involuntary shiver, Yardley reached out to take his hand in hers. "Your nails are perfectly trimmed and clean. I assume you wear gloves when you're clawing your way up these spider-infested cliffs?"

"No. I had a manicure last night. In fact, I have

one *every* Wednesday night. Between climbing and remodeling, if I didn't, I'm afraid my hands would be a pretty disgusting sight."

Grinning, she couldn't help but raise an eyebrow. "Regular manicures?"

"I know. Real men don't have their nails done. . . . So sue me. I happen to like a good hand massage. Besides, my manicurist is drop-dead gorgeous."

Yardley felt the strength of his hand under her fingertips, and was caught off guard by an unexpected twinge of jealousy.

Kyle pulled his hand free, flipping it to capture hers in his. "Come on. Give it a try. You don't have to tell me where you live. You can meet the group at the park on Saturday morning. Trust me—we're a hard bunch to miss."

"Under one condition," she said.

His eyes locked onto hers. "Name it."

"You honestly tell me if you're interested in the house I have listed near here, or if you just called to get me to go out with you."

Raising his hands, he said, "Guilty as charged. The house on 57th just isn't my type."

Standing, she smiled and held out her hand. "Then I'll see you Saturday morning."

Thursday night, McCay Realty's women agents emerged from the conference room one by one, each looking a little more confident than they had just two hours earlier. Yardley was the last to step out, accompanied by the female officer who had taught the self-defense class. After escorting her to the front door, Yardley locked it and went back to her desk to finish working through the details of a sales contract.

She was deep in thought when she felt two big hands close around her neck, startling her. From behind, Chuck began to massage gently as he quietly said, "I'm glad you took the class, Yardley. Of all my agents, I'd be most upset if anything happened to you."

Turning to face him, she stood. "Really, Chuck? To be honest, I thought we were . . . well . . . *not* involved."

"There are different degrees of involvement. Now that we've closed the merger with Brookside Realty, I've finally got a little free time. I know the last few months have been hell, and I truly apologize for being so inattentive. But I've already started reordering my life. I'm working out and jogging again, and now I think I'm ready to seriously devote time to a little romance." With a wide grin he added, "How about a quick cup of coffee at Java Dave's?"

Glancing at her watch, she said, "It's almost ten o'clock. I'd be up all night."

Pushing her gently toward the door, he laughed and replied, "Then it's decaf for you."

After the short drive, they settled into a corner booth, sipping steaming concoctions topped with whipped cream and chocolate. The next thirty minutes were spent in light conversation about everything from art to work.

They were almost ready to leave when he casually asked, "By the way, how was tonight's self-defense class? Care to fill me in on the latest ways to drop a man?"

Yardley yawned. "The class was . . . informative. Downright scary."

"Scary?" he asked, taking her hand in his as he wrapped an arm around her for support.

Softening at his touch, Yardley replied, "It makes me sick that women have to learn how to gouge out people's eyes with car keys to defend themselves." Yawning again, she added, "I'm sorry. I'm just so tired."

"You've had a rough week. I'll drive you home."

Nodding, she could barely keep her eyes open as Chuck helped her to his car. By the time he slipped behind the steering wheel, she was sound asleep.

Struggling to open her eyes, Yardley was sure she must be dreaming. The pillow beneath her head was encased in crisp, boldly striped sheets, nothing like the soft, pale lavender kind on her own bed. Sitting up slowly, her head pounded as she realized the entire room was totally unfamiliar.

Where the hell am I? . . . I remember going for coffee with Chuck . . . Being so tired . . . He offered to take me home . . . Oh, my God . . . I must be at Chuck's house!

Rolling onto her back, she suddenly realized she was naked beneath the covers. Moaning, she picked up the phone on the nightstand and dialed her own number.

"Kim?" she softly asked.

Hearing her voice, Kim shouted, "Where the hell are you? I've been up all night, worried sick!"

Yardley winced as her head throbbed even harder. Whispering, she said, "I think I'm at Chuck McCay's place."

"What do you mean, you think? Don't you know?" Kim asked, obviously baffled.

"I must have the flu or something. I feel like hell. . . ."

Kim's voice still had a hard edge. "Listen, I know his address. Want me to come get you?"

"And tell him what? Besides, I don't see my clothes, and I can't leave stark naked."

"Yardley! Ever heard of safe sex?" Kim bellowed.

"Damn it, Kim, I told you . . . I have no idea how I got here or what happened after ten-thirty last night." Tears began to well, and her voice cracked. "I just want to come home."

Softening, Kim said, "Okay. Calm down. It's a little after seven. McCay is always in the office by seven-thirty, so he's probably already left. Go check, and call me right back. Okay?"

"Okay." Cradling the phone, Yardley eased out from under the sheets and went into the bathroom. Leaning against the closed, locked door, she fought back a wave of nausea by taking a deep, cleansing breath. Opening her eyes, she was relieved to see her clothes stacked neatly on the bathroom counter.

Gathering her courage, Yardley dressed and peeked out of the bedroom. Listening intently, she waited. Not a sound. Creeping down the stairs, she poked her head around the corner, once again comforted to see an empty room. A note was propped against a ceramic coffee mug in the kitchen. Her feet felt brittle as she crossed the cold tile to read it.

Yardley—
Hope you're feeling better. I thought you might like to sleep in after last night. I'll call around

ten. We can have lunch together if you don't already have plans.

—Chuck

One phrase he had written kept repeating in her
mind, long after Kim had picked her up and taken
her home.

After last night . . . After last night . . .

Yardley wiggled her toes under the covers, teasing Vinnie. Bouncing across the bed, the miniature
dog kept springing back and forth as he playfully
growled and attacked her foot.

Cracking open the door, Kim peeked inside.
"Good, you're awake. Feeling better?"

Nodding, Yardley sat up and stretched. "I must've
had a twenty-four-hour bug or something."

"I vote for 'or something.' McCay is on the phone.
Are you up to talking to him?"

Shrugging, Yardley said, "Guess I can't put it off
forever," and grabbed the extension. "Hi, Chuck."

"I hear you slept all day. Luckily, you have an
understanding boss. Last night's coffee must've had
quite a reverse kick."

Winding the cord nervously around her finger,
Yardley replied, "I'm really sorry. I had no idea . . ."

"It's okay. Look at it this way—at least you were
in good hands. A lesser gentleman might have tried
to take advantage of you in your vulnerable state."

Vulnerable? she thought. "I appreciate your help, I
really do. Listen, I still have an awful headache.
Can we talk later?"

"Sure. Do you need me to have someone cover

your open house this weekend? Or better yet, I could personally assist you."

"I'm sure I'll be fine by Sunday. Thanks for thinking of me. I'll see you tomorrow." Replacing the phone, Yardley leaned back and sighed.

"That wasn't so terrible, was it?" Kim asked.

Growling at Vinnie, she replied, "I guess it could've been worse."

"Such as?"

"Such as him saying, 'Oooh, baby, we were so good together last night. Too bad you don't remember . . .' "

"Speaking of not remembering, I almost forgot. Kyle Baker left a message on the machine. He said you should wear comfortable clothes, but nothing baggy, and that he'd lead you to heaven in the morning. I really didn't care for his metaphor—or should I say threat?" Kim pulled back the drapes to the balcony, then flung open the French doors. The room was instantly flooded by the late afternoon sun and a fresh breeze.

Holding her pounding head, Yardley moaned. "Quit being so melodramatic. Kyle's teaching me to climb rocks, not predicting my untimely demise."

Stepping outside, Kim leaned against the rail. "Okay, okay. But for the record, I still don't think you should go."

Following her onto the balcony, Yardley muttered, "Yes, Mother. We both know it's impossible to see the future. Notice how I've refrained from reminding you how strange Austin turned out to be, even though you thought he was Mr. Perfect. Mr. Obsessive was more like it. Aren't you glad you broke up with him before it was too late?"

Kim immediately stiffened. Turning back toward Yardley, she threw her hands up. "That's enough! I don't want to argue about Austin with you again. It's your scrawny neck at stake this time, not mine. And in spite of your attitude, I can honestly say I'm still glad you were with Chuck McCay last night and not *Kyle Baker*!"

Frowning, Yardley thought Kim had grossly over-reacted, but her voice was much softer as she apologized. "I'm sorry, Kim. I know how much you cared for Austin, and I shouldn't have thrown him in your face. Why are you glad I was with Chuck?"

"Two reasons. First, maybe if you date him a few times, you can get him out of your system once and for all. Second, if you'd been out with a less reputable man last night, I'd be worried he used that date rape drug on you. You have all the signs, you know. Loss of memory, hangover-type symptoms . . ."

Yardley groaned as they headed back inside. But deep down, she couldn't help but wonder if Kim might be right.

On the street below, a man had been watching and waiting for hours. The entire time the women were on the balcony, the expensive camera was pressed against his eye. Grinning, he snapped picture after picture for his growing collection.

Yardley parked the Rocky along the side of the road, certain she was in the right place. The sheer cliffs were already being ascended by five or six climbers, and it was barely seven o'clock in the morning. Glancing at her purse, she knew there was nowhere to hide the Lady Smith, or even the small canister of pepper gas, in the tight, skimpy clothes she was wearing.

Sighing, she hoped her instincts were right about Kyle, who was already in full climbing gear, smiling widely as he walked toward her. She couldn't help but admire the way the skintight black Lycra displayed his excellent physique.

"I can't believe you actually came!" he said.

"I promised I would, and I'm a woman of my word."

He glanced quickly up and down her lean figure. "You're about a size seven shoe, right?"

Shooting him a wary look, she replied, "Oh, God. Please don't tell me you have a foot fetish."

Laughing, he motioned for her to follow. "More like a desire *not* to see you injured. One of the most important pieces of climbing equipment is a good pair of sticky boots."

Cocking her head, Yardley grinned. "You're kidding, right? I don't think I want to know what makes them sticky . . ."

Pulling the shoes out of the back of his Land Cruiser, he handed them to her as he explained, "No, I'm serious. Sticky boots are climbing shoes that have a smooth, sticky rubber sole to help you cling to the rock. Unfortunately, they also collect sand, dust, and dead bugs quite well, too, which ruins their effectiveness."

"Oh, boy. Rock climbing sounds like more fun every minute." She couldn't help but notice the inside of Kyle's car. It was immaculate. Even the box of climbing equipment was broken down into sections, each one containing neatly organized ropes and gadgets. Ignoring the knot in her stomach, she asked, "Your things are so precisely arranged. Are you a neat freak or something?"

"A good climber takes care of his, *or her*, equipment. It could save your life someday."

Leaning against his truck, she slipped out of her rugged hiking boots and into the thin, supple shoes. Stretching, she said, "These fit perfectly, like little leather mittens made for feet."

"As expensive as they are, they should feel like a second skin," he said as he added a few items to his belt.

"So, do you always keep an array of extra sticky boots with you, or do I happen to be your size?" she nervously joked.

Eyeing her, he flatly said, "As a matter of fact, you happen to be about the same size as my ex."

"Ex what?" Yardley asked candidly.

"Girlfriend. We were together for six years. Two months ago I came home and she was gone. However, I must admit she was quite considerate. She actually took the time to leave me a note explaining why she cleaned out my bank accounts and stole several expensive pieces from my art collection before she hit the road."

Yardley grimaced. "Ouch. I'm really sorry." She could almost hear Kim shouting, *I told you to be careful! The murders started about two months ago. It's not too late to leave!*

Coldly, he grabbed the last handful of gear and slammed the door. "Actually, I'm glad she's gone. It gave me the chance to meet you."

Looking up, Yardley cleared her mind and pointed at the impressive rock cliff just a few yards away. "Surely, you don't expect me to climb *that* my first time? Doesn't this sport have something like a bunny slope?"

"You'd be embarrassed to climb the rabbit rock. It's for kids . . ."

"I'm not proud. Actually, the rabbit rock sounds like the perfect place for me to start! Let's go."

Another climber overheard their conversation and burst out laughing. Kyle's eyes met the man's with a quick wink before he looked innocently at Yardley and said, "Sorry. That's an old climber's joke. There is no such thing as a rabbit rock."

"Too bad, there should be," she said, pretending to be irritated to cover her fear.

He handed her a helmet and harness. In response to the look on her face, he added, "Come on. Give it a chance. What makes this sport unique is that each climb is different. Every rock, every movement, every change in the weather requires the climber to react both mentally and physically. You'll use muscles you never even knew you had, and reach places you thought you'd never go."

"Last time I checked, I wasn't a mountain goat. Besides, there's probably a good reason humans don't go to those places."

"But you love nature—I could see it in your eyes the moment I met you." Gazing at her Lycra body-suit, he grinned as he added, "And I know you're in excellent physical shape. So what have you got to lose? If you get to the top, and you don't like it, you never have to climb again."

"Except back down," she grumbled as she stared up at the huge boulders before them.

"We'll go over the basic intricacies of ropecraft, anchors, and belaying, and then we'll get started."

"Excuse me?" she asked, still studying the formidable rocks.

"Ropecraft is nothing more than learning how to tie a few basic knots. Anchors can be natural places in the rock, or artificial like these." He ran his hand along the various items dangling from the waist of his harness. "Belaying is the process of holding, dispensing, or taking in the rope, which is the climbing equivalent of a safety net. Just think of belaying as controlling the net. And by the way, stop doing that."

"Doing what?" she asked innocently.

"Looking at the whole climb. When you see a landscape, do you paint the entire thing at once, or do you break it down into manageable portions? We'll climb the rocks, one step at a time."

"It's not the rocks I'm worried about."

"Then what is it?"

Pointing up to a small overhang at the top, she exclaimed, "It's that! I'm not spiderwoman."

"We call that a roof, and I'll lead you over it. Stop worrying. Take a deep breath. Enjoy the view, and do what I do. What could be easier?"

Almost anything! Yardley wanted to scream.

When the doorbell rang at eight o'clock on Saturday morning, Kim ran to answer it in her bathrobe. Peering through the peephole, she quickly unlocked the door and nervously said, "I wasn't expecting you, Mr. McCay. Is something wrong?"

Smiling, he answered, "Oh, no. Nothing at all."

Kim gathered the collar of her robe around her neck as she added, "I'm sorry, won't you come in?"

From behind his back he withdrew a stunning spring bouquet of daisies and yellow carnations as he walked into the house. "Sorry to barge in without calling first. Is Yardley home? I thought she might like to go on a morning drive with me."

Shrugging, Kim replied, "To be quite honest, I'm not sure. Let me check her room." She scurried past the kitchen and up the stairs to knock lightly on Yardley's door. When she opened it, Vinnie came barreling toward her, his entire rear end wagging to make up for his cropped tail. Sweeping him into her arms, Kim glanced at the perfectly made bed and knew Yardley had ignored her advice—again.

Walking back into the living room, she said, "Sorry. Looks like you missed her."

"Do you know where she is?"

Even though she did, Kim shook her head. "No. Yardley likes to catch the morning sun in her paintings, so she could be almost anywhere."

"What are your plans for the day?" he asked.

"Studying for the state licensing exam. With a little luck in the next few days I'll have a provisional real estate license, and I'll be beating down your door, asking for a chance to become one of your agents."

"I've been looking forward to it," he replied.

The closer Kim was to Chuck McCay, the more agitated Vinnie became. Suddenly he bared his teeth and growled openly. "Vinnie, stop that," Kim scolded.

"It's all right. Would you mind giving these to Yardley when she gets back?" As he handed her the flowers, Vinnie snapped at his hand.

Struggling to control him with one arm as she took the bouquet, Kim said, "He's really a sweet dog. He must've been abused by a man before we adopted him."

Backing out the door, Chuck McCay nodded skeptically. "Obedience classes might be a good idea. Study hard. I'll see you tomorrow."

Kim closed the door and leaned against it. Between classes on Saturdays and working every Sunday she felt as though it had been months since she'd had a life. McCay had promised things would get back to normal after the merger, but he obviously still expected her to work six days a week. Another Sunday afternoon blown, but she supposed she should get used to it if she wanted to become an agent.

"How are you feeling?" Kyle asked as Yardley edged across the face of the rock toward him. By the time she was safely at his side, he had expertly belayed the rope attached to the waist of her harness.

"Great," Yardley answered, relieved that she had actually made it up the last steep incline.

"We've been at this for over an hour. Are your muscles burning?"

"Not bad. My fingers are getting a little raw."

"That's normal. Beginners tend to claw instead of grip; a little practice makes a world of difference. Use more chalk, and if your legs or arms start to bother you, find a good hold and shake them out."

Reaching over, he moved closer to her. His long, tapered fingers curled around her neck as he massaged it gently. "You handled that last wall quite well. Think you'll make it now?"

His fingers were magically melting the tension away. She wished they could stop for a while and talk. "I have to admit, it's more fun than I expected." She looked down, then up as she added, "But I'm still not sure about that blasted roof. . . ."

"Just watch what I do. First we need to conquer this mantelshelf sequence. I'm going to check my grip, spring upward and get my weight balanced over my hands, then bring my right foot up as my right hand seeks a higher hold. Watch closely. I'll anchor you from above, so there's nothing to worry about if you lose your footing."

"You say that every time. Exactly when *should* I worry?"

"When you're gripped," he answered.

Puzzled, she cocked her head. "Gripped, like holding on?"

"No, 'gripped' is when a climber freezes during a very hard move. You either have to calm down and do it, or retreat."

Smiling, Yardley leaned close as she joked, "You mean retreating is an option? You didn't tell me that!"

"There isn't anything to retreat *from* on a rock like this." She watched him effortlessly push up to the next level, then surprised herself by duplicating his moves without any coaching from above.

He proudly said, "Good work! You're definitely fit enough to conquer your first roof. Ready?"

Grimacing, she said, "As ready as I'll ever be. Are

you sure you don't need suction cups to get around that thing?"

"I'm sure. Watch, learn. Basically, do what you just did, and you'll be over the top in a couple of seconds."

She did watch. His long, lean body seemed to be joined to the rock jutting above their heads as he maneuvered horizontally along its bumpy underside. He swung one leg over the edge, then disappeared from sight.

Her mouth was still hanging open when his grinning face reappeared. "I told you. Nothing to it."

Wide-eyed, she gasped, "Oh, no! There is no *way* I can do that. No way! Forget it!"

"I'll admit it's a moderately difficult move, but I know you can handle it. Besides, I'll belay you. You can't stop when you're this close to the top. You'd never forgive yourself."

"And when I'm a pancake"—she pointed to the ground a few stories below—"I'll never forgive *you*!"

His eyes narrowed seriously. "You do realize that you don't have much choice."

Taken aback, she asked, "Is that a threat?"

With a sinister smile he shrugged. "Interpret it however you like. I know the way off, you don't . . ."

"How dare you!" she cried.

Although she could no longer see him, Yardley would have sworn she heard him snicker. Before they started climbing, he had warned her that one of the most important things a climber needed to know was the way off—the route down from the top of the crag. "Kyle! You can't just leave me here!" she shouted.

Silence.

With a worried frown she gave a swift, hard tug at the rope around her waist. In a flash he tightened it slightly and shouted, "Ready up here. Go ahead."

Taking a deep breath, Yardley wedged her feet against the wall, then gripped the small handholds in the cracks of the rock with all her might. Hanging horizontally, she tried to swing one leg over the ledge as Kyle had done, but her bottom foot slipped.

Every climber in the park heard her shrill scream as she lost her grip and fell.

Chapter Thirty-one

~

Disoriented, it took Yardley several seconds to realize the safety rope had worked perfectly, quickly stopping her fall. Although her head had bumped a rock, the helmet, too, had done its job. "Kyle! I told you I couldn't do that damned roof!"

"Actually, you're doing fine," Kyle shouted from somewhere above her.

"You call almost killing myself doing fine?" she yelled back, still dangling a few yards below the spot she had unsuccessfully attempted to climb. Swaying back and forth, she gripped the rope and adjusted her weight in her harness. As soon as she was back in control, he started to pull her up.

Between drags she heard him say, "You were never in any danger . . . falling is part of . . . the adventure. When done right . . . there's minimal risk. In fact, falling on your first climb . . . has definite advantages. It gets the fear out of your system . . . lets you take more chances on future climbs. . . ." As she struggled over the rough edge and into his arms, he added, "You just learned that if you don't get a move quite right, your equipment will protect you."

"Or is it the lead climber who does the protecting?" she asked. Once again he was too close, his heavy breathing making her aware of every beat of her own heart. As he had done the first time they met, his fingers plunged into her hair, and he gently wiped a smudge of dirt off her cheek with his thumb.

Grinning, he pulled her tightly into his arms. "Having a good lead is always important for a beginner. Just wait. Someday you'll lead me."

Relaxing against him, Yardley could feel the sexual energy between them. He was so alive, so virile, she knew she was falling for him—hard and fast. Leaning back, their eyes met. She said, "Considering we met only last Sunday, you certainly have confidence in my abilities."

Without irony he replied, "I'm a good judge of character." His lips met hers in a soft, warm kiss.

All Kim's warnings, everything the police had said came rushing back into Yardley's mind. Lightly pushing away, she tried to break the spell he had on her by slyly asking, "If you're such an expert on people, then how do you explain your ex-girlfriend's little stunt?"

Scowling, Kyle snapped, "I'd be nice if I were you. You still don't know the way out."

Looking down at the ground so far below, she sighed. "Oh, yeah. I forgot. I'm stuck up here."

He laughed softly. "Not exactly. Since you're new at this, we'll rap down."

In mock frustration she nudged him and asked, "Would you mind speaking in English every once and a while?"

Tossing the rope over the edge, he explained, "Rap down means rappel. You know, slide down the rope, occasionally glancing your feet off the face of the cliff."

"I *know* what rappel means!" she said in a fierce voice.

Studying her, he smiled. "You can't possibly be mad. You *did* it! Look around!"

He was right. For the first time she did look around, drinking in the unbelievable view. "It *is* pretty exciting to be up here." Kyle had once again shifted his footing so near hers that Yardley stepped back and defensively asked, "Why do you do that?"

"Do what?" he snapped.

"Stand so close! It really gives me the creeps. I must have a territorial problem, a need for my own space. Or maybe all the stress from the recent murders has left me a little shell-shocked."

Kyle thought for several seconds before saying, "Sorry. It's just that something about you grabbed me the moment I saw you. I can't explain it, but I've never felt like a stranger around you. Besides, you get used to being close to the people you're climbing with. Pretty soon, it'll feel natural to you, too." Growling, he playfully added, "Maybe it's an animal thing—I'm just guarding my territory."

"Meaning *I'm* your territory?" she asked warily.

"Maybe not yet, but I can pretend, can't I?" he replied.

Shaking her head, Yardley didn't know whether to be flattered or worried. Purposely changing the subject, she turned away and said, "The perspective really is worth all the work. The angle is spectacular. I wish I had my paints."

"Then you're gonna love my surprise." Pulling the tail of his shirt free, Kyle reached behind his back and whipped out a folded piece of sketching paper. From his belt of tools, he magically produced three sharp pencils. He handed them over as he wrapped her in his arms and whispered, "Sorry, I didn't know what kind of pencil you like to use . . . and the paper's a little damp with sweat. But I knew once you made it up here, you'd want to remember every detail."

This time, she was glad he was so close. It made it much easier for her to kiss him.

That night, Yardley made it home as the last rays of sun sliced the western sky. Stretched out on the living room floor, Kim was obviously engrossed in her studies. Glancing up, she called, "Check out the kitchen table! Mr. McCay brought those flowers for you this morning. Looks like the two of you finally have a chance."

Yardley slumped into the overstuffed chair beside Kim and tiredly asked, "Why does life always work this way? For a year I've been invisible to anything with a Y chromosome, and now I have two men beating down my door."

Closing her notebook, Kim replied, "I wouldn't complain. I'd love to have several men to choose from."

"Good point. It's just the timing sucks. If Chuck had been interested a few weeks ago, things would be different."

"Kyle must have made quite an impression." Grinning, Kim added, "I never realized mountain climbing was a contact sport!"

Yardley's eyes lit up as she leaned forward. "I've never felt like this about anyone. It's like getting too close to a live wire. There's electricity practically humming between us, and even though I know it isn't safe, I still want to touch it, to see if it really will shock me."

Vinnie curled in Kim's lap and Yardley slid onto the floor beside her. "Is that how you felt about Austin? Like you couldn't stop yourself from seeing him, even though you knew he might be dangerous?"

Kim merely shrugged. "I guess." Changing the subject, she added, "I'm really starved. How about we run over to Goldie's for a big, juicy burger?"

Yardley smiled. "Perfect. Kyle is going to be here in thirty minutes. We'll all go to dinner together. He's anxious to meet you, and I want you to get to know him, too. I'd like an unbiased opinion."

Kim sighed. "That must mean you still have some reservations."

"Believe me, I have plenty of doubts. He seems so nice, so normal. . . . But there's that undercurrent of . . . hell, I don't know how to describe it. Please, come to dinner with us."

After briefly hesitating, Kim nodded. "Okay. I suppose I'd worry a lot less about you if I didn't think you were dating Charles Manson."

Kim was impressed when she pulled open the door a half hour later. Kyle wore crisply pressed Dockers and a casual shirt. His dark hair had a sexy wave, his skin glowed with a healthy tan, and his smile was sincere.

When Yardley opened her bedroom door, Vinnie came bouncing out beside her, playfully running circles around her until he spotted Kyle at the foot of the stairs. The tiny dog stopped in its tracks, growled once, then bolted toward him. Viciously attacking, Vinnie leaped, latching his tiny jaws onto the thigh of Kyle's trousers. The feisty little one-eared dog snarled and dangled uselessly, holding on for dear life.

Even though both women were horrified at the dog's behavior, the sight of him hanging on Kyle's leg was too funny not to laugh. Kim tugged on Vinnie's body, but the puppy had no intention of letting go.

Kyle joked, "I guess he doesn't like my cologne. Next time I promise not to wear eau de Feline."

Kim attempted to pry apart the dog's teeth. "I don't want to tear your slacks. How are we going to convince him to stop?"

"Watch this," Yardley said. She leaned down and pressed one finger over Vinnie's nostrils. It was only seconds before he opened his mouth to breathe. As soon as he did, she pulled him into her arms. "If you'll excuse me, I need to explain some basic house rules to Vinnie. I'll be out in just a minute."

"I'm sure Vincent van Gogh sends his sincere apologies," Kim said as she and Kyle waited on the porch.

Kyle was momentarily baffled, then said, "Ahhh, you named the little beast after van Gogh because one of his ears is gone!"

Bending over, she nodded as she lightly brushed the wet spot on his slacks and added, "Hopefully, when this dries, it won't leave a stain."

"Don't worry about the pants, no harm done. Vinnie's got to learn that just because he looks like a Doberman, he can't necessarily act like one."

Eyeing him, Kim asked, "Meaning, things aren't always as they seem?"

He didn't get a chance to answer, since Yardley emerged from the house. They walked to his car and Kyle opened both passenger side doors.

"I really am sorry," Yardley said. "I guess obedience classes are definitely in our future."

Kim added, "That's exactly what Chuck Mc-Cay recommended when Vinnie attacked him this morning."

Yardley stared at Kim. "You're kidding, right?"

"Nope. But Vinnie never—" She stopped in midsentence when she spotted a dark green Jeep parked at the end of the block. The vehicle instantly pulled away. Glancing at Yardley, Kim was relieved to see she hadn't been watching.

"Vinnie never what? Are you all right?" Yardley asked.

Kim ducked into the backseat. "Sorry, I must be more tired than I thought. He . . . uh . . . Vinnie never bit him or anything."

"You sure you're okay, Kim?" Yardley asked, twisting in the front seat to eye her friend. "You suddenly went pale."

Kim merely nodded. Even though she tried to be good company, she spent most of the evening wondering how she was ever going to get rid of Austin. Again.

* * *

"I hope you haven't been waiting very long," Yardley said as she climbed out of her car and grimaced. Every muscle in her body felt as if it were on fire, and the sunburn on the back of her neck made her wish she hadn't worn a light wool pantsuit.

Chuck McCay smoothed his jacket and straightened his tie as he came to meet her. With genuine concern in his eyes, he quickly asked, "Are you okay?"

She laughed. "Technically, yes. I'm just unbelievably sore. Until yesterday, I would've sworn I was in pretty good shape. Now I realize how much I've been kidding myself."

"What crazy thing did you spend your Saturday doing when you could have gone on a beautiful scenic drive with me?"

Yardley hesitated, then admitted, "I went mountain climbing. Actually, rock climbing to be precise."

Shaking his head, he cracked a smile and said, "I would've guessed skydiving, maybe even bungee jumping. With your daring soul, it's just a matter of time. Who talked you into trying something so dangerous?"

Purposely evading his question, she said, "Right now being a real estate agent seems a lot more hazardous than clinging to the face of cliff."

"Who'd you go with?" he persisted.

Trying to sound casual, she started walking toward the house and answered, "A friend."

"Old?" he asked.

"Meaning an old friend, or an old person?"

He stopped walking and waited for her to turn

back around. "You know, Yardley, I worry about you. That's why I wanted to be with you at today's open house."

"I appreciate all your concern, and I'm looking forward to spending the afternoon with you, Chuck. But really, I can take care of myself."

A Land Cruiser pulled into the driveway, and Yardley's eyes widened. Kyle emerged, smiling broadly. "Beautiful afternoon, isn't it?"

Moving quickly toward him, Yardley extended her hand and said, "Mr. Baker. I'm so glad you stopped by to see the house again. This is Mr. Mc-Cay, the owner of McCay Realty. He's working with me today."

Firmly shaking McCay's hand, Kyle said, "I prefer to be called Kyle." He turned to Yardley. "Actually, I just stopped by to drop off your sweater. You must have left it in my car last night."

Yardley's face flushed as she took the sweater and smiled. "Thanks for bringing it by."

"How are you feeling? You're not sore, are you?" Kyle asked as he climbed back into his car.

"Not at all," Yardley lied.

"Fantastic! I'm looking forward to next time!"

As he drove away, she called, "Me, too." Then she met Chuck's intense gaze. "I know. I should've admitted I was a wimp."

With a broad smile Chuck shook his head, then laughed.

"What's so funny?" she asked.

"You. Actually, women in general. You try to act so tough," he said.

"Like men don't act tough every minute of every day?" Yardley snapped.

Still amused, he replied, "You're comparing apples to oranges. And by the way, I hope Mr. Baker isn't my competition."

"Not unless you plan to start climbing mountains," she joked.

His expression turned dead serious. "No, I mean for your attention."

"It's already Wednesday, and I haven't seen you all week. Where have you been hiding?" Chuck McCay asked.

Yardley was relieved that he didn't seem upset. She'd spent most of the week avoiding him, which was surprisingly easy with Kim's expert assistance. Tossing her purse into her desk drawer, she answered, "I wrote contracts on three houses and listed two more this week. Spring is definitely here! I can practically feel my checking account growing."

"That's terrific. Kim called me from Oklahoma City a few minutes ago. She said she aced the state licensing exam, and wanted to know if she could try to sign a deal for her first listing tomorrow. Seems she's already staked out a good lead."

Yardley grinned broadly. "Kim has worked really hard to make it this far. Are you going to give her a chance?"

Smoothing the lapel of his tailored Armani suit, he shrugged. "Of course I am. Kim's a hard worker. She'll do well because she has the inner drive it takes to succeed. It wasn't that long ago you were in the same position she's in right now."

"I know. And I appreciate all you've done for me," Yardley said sincerely.

He glanced around to be sure they were alone, then pulled her next to him. He whispered, "Good. Then let's celebrate with dinner at the Fountains."

Yardley's face instantly showed her answer. She tried to sound disappointed as she replied, "I'm sorry, Chuck. I already have plans for tonight."

"Really? Something you can't cancel?" He waggled his eyebrows. "I'll make it worth your while."

She briefly considered telling him that she had another date with Kyle, but instead decided only half the truth was better for her career. "I'm taking Vinnie to obedience school. I think you'll agree that's pretty important."

Stepping back, his face turned cold. "By all means, teach that vicious little dog some manners!"

Yardley started to laugh, but quickly realized he wasn't kidding.

Kim spent most of Friday afternoon waiting outside Austin's apartment, mentally fueling her anger so she would have the courage to go through with her plan. When he finally pulled up in his Jeep, she waited in her car and waved for him to come over. Her voice was strong as she gazed up at him. "Austin, you broke your promise. I know you were watching my house last Saturday night, and I spotted you twice this week."

Staring at his hands, he simply stood next to her Honda and nodded. At six-foot-four, it always amazed her how childlike he could be. That was part of the problem—she felt compelled to help him, to make him understand that he was a good person, but not necessarily the right man for her.

Running his hands through his jet black hair, his

dark eyes narrowed as he looked down at Kim. "I couldn't help it. You know how I feel about you."

"If you care about me, you won't push me into a relationship I'm not interested in. I know you're ready to settle down, but I'm not. Don't you want to make something of your life?"

His words were calculated, almost pleading. "Of course I do. But I think we should build our lives together."

Kim's heart started to melt, as it always did when she was near him. But deep down, she knew what was right. "Listen, Austin, I got my provisional real estate license yesterday, and I just finished listing a great house. For the first time in my life I feel like I'm making some progress toward my goals. I'm not ready to commit to you or anyone else right now. When I agreed to go out with you again, you knew I was going to date other people. And you promised you would, too."

"I know. But I love you. And I don't want you selling houses. It's too dangerous. There's a killer out there, stalking helpless women." He leaned close and added, "Women just like you."

Kim suddenly felt her whole body tense. Gripping the steering wheel so tightly that her knuckles turned white, she tried to sound calm. "I have to go now, Austin. Whatever we once had is over. Find someone else."

His jawline hardened, his voice cold as he muttered, "There isn't another woman like you! There never will be. I've tried! Really, really tried! They're all just bitches! Worthless manipulating bitches like your roommate!"

"Bullshit, Austin! You just don't get it, do you? I

tried to care about you, to help you. I'm warning you, I won't let you interfere with my life again. Please don't call. And don't park in front of my house anymore. If you do, this time I really will get a restraining order. Understand?"

Kim didn't wait for an answer. Instead, she violently pushed the accelerator and sped away. After a few miles she finally started to relax, certain he hadn't followed her. Turning on the radio, she punched through the buttons trying to find a song that might lift her out of her bleak mood. When she landed on the deep voice of a local newscaster, she started to keep going, but her hand froze as his words soaked in.

> *Tulsa police are speculating that the sixth victim of the killer now known in Tulsa as the Open House Murderer has just been discovered. The latest victim has not yet been identified, but one source tells us that it is a female real estate broker in her mid-twenties. Although this is the first killing to have occurred on a weekday, like the others the body was found in a vacant house. We'll have more on this story as it develops.*

Pulling into a parking lot, Kim leaned her head on the steering wheel and started to shake. She couldn't help but wonder about her future.

It was late afternoon when Kyle crept up behind Yardley. For several minutes he silently watched her transform the sketch she did at the peak of her first climb from a smudged drawing to a vibrant painting. He had found her at one of her favorite spots, beneath the tall oak trees at the small park within walking distance of her house.

Leaning over, he whispered, "You must have an incredible memory. It's been over a week, and the colors bring me right back to that exact spot."

She tensed, then without looking back at him, she distractedly answered, "I take a mental snapshot. People do it all the time—they just don't realize it."

"Maybe extra-talented, gifted people do, but I don't think the average Joe has a Polaroid hidden in his brain," Kyle said.

Setting aside her palette and brush, she stood. "If I prove it, will you let me work in peace?" Taking a breath, she added, "I'm sorry. We still don't know each other very well, so I'd better explain. When I'm working, I sort of *become* the painting. If I'm interrupted, it takes me a while to immerse myself so the colors flow by themselves again. I know it sounds crazy. . . ."

Holding up his hands, he said, "Then I'm the one who's sorry. I really do admire your work. It's breathtaking." Reaching into his back pocket, he pulled out the same three pencils he had taken to the top of the climb. "I forgot to give these to you the other day. I thought you might be able to use them."

"Thanks, I'd love to," Yardley replied. She gently placed them in her supply box, then straightened and walked behind him. When he tried to turn, she grabbed his shoulders and said, "Don't move." Holding her hands over his eyes, she asked, "What am I wearing right now?"

Kyle hesitated, then said, "A white shirt with

tight, sexy jeans that show off your perfect ass . . . a vest that covers way too much of . . ."

Poking him in the ribs, she added, "What kind of vest is it?"

"Ouch! Blue jean. But with pieces of different jeans sewn together, like a quilt. And you have that old pin on the lapel, the one you said was your grandmother's. Okay, obviously you proved your point."

Yardley nodded, her hand automatically touching the pin as he turned to face her. "This isn't just an old piece of jewelry—it's an *antique*. There's a difference. One is something that's been around a long time, the other has been *loved* a long time."

"It's beautiful, but why do you wear it so often?" he asked.

She shrugged. "I feel a special connection to my sisters, and I suppose this pin is unique because it was our great-grandmother's. I was named after her. She was an artist, too." Grinning, she added, "When I was a kid, I'd say my prayers to her. Like she was my guardian angel or a saint or something."

"So painting runs in your blood, Yardley Smith?" he asked.

"I suppose. By the way, what are you doing here?" she said lightly.

"I heard about the latest murder on the news. I had to be sure it wasn't you."

Her shock was apparent. "Oh, God. Not again."

"I'm afraid so," he said solemnly.

"Did they say who it is?" Yardley asked.

He shook his head. "Only that she worked for Atlantis Realty. Listen, I'm sorry to be the bearer of bad news, but it's such a lovely afternoon. We could go for a run, hike a few miles, you name it. I love playing hookey on Fridays."

For a few seconds she was so absorbed in her own thoughts that she didn't answer. "How in the world did you find me?" she finally asked.

"Your neighbor told me he saw you head this way with your painting supplies."

Yardley mentally noted to have a talk with her neighbors about being so helpful. "Persistent, aren't you?" she asked rather pointedly.

"I never give up until I get what I want," he snapped.

Suppressing an involuntary shiver, she sat back down. "Neither do I, and I want to finish this painting. If you can be quiet for five or ten minutes, that is."

"Mind if I watch in silence, oh great one?" he asked, bowing before her.

"Yes, you may." She laughed. "Would you hand me my purse? I need the tube of Alizarin crimson I bought yesterday"—she indicated the splash of color across the middle of painting—"to get just the right shade on these wildflowers."

Kyle reached for her oversized brown leather handbag and dug inside it. He finally located the tube of paint in the bottom, next to something he obviously didn't expect to find. Holding both items in the palm of his hand, he asked, "What the hell is this?"

"My paint and the gun my sister sent me a few weeks ago." Reacting to his intense gaze, she put her paintbrush down and angrily added, "Do you have a problem with a woman defending herself?"

"Not if she's competent," he seethed.

Yardley jumped to her feet. "Did you just imply I'm incompetent? To do what? Choose a decent man to date? Well, for once you just might be right!"

"For Christ's sake, Yardley, this damn thing is loaded. How long have you been toting it around this way?"

The same energy that had attracted them to each other now incited their fury. Yardley didn't care that people were shooting them curious looks as she screamed her answer. "Years, decades, hell, since I was born. What difference does it make?"

"Well, have you bothered to take any safety classes? Do you know how to fire it? What kind of damage it will do? Or did you just toss it in your purse and hope for the best?"

Her eyes narrowed in fury. "Not that it's any of your business, but when I bought the box of .38s, the man at Dong's showed me how to fire it."

"Did he bother to tell you it's against the law to tote it around with you wherever you go?"

"He mentioned something about a concealed weapons law."

"Which you chose to ignore?" Kyle fumed.

"I don't intend to keep it with me all the time. Just until they catch the open house murderer!"

"The least you could do is keep it unloaded."

"And say, 'Excuse me, Mr. Murderer, sir. Could you hold on a few minutes while I load my gun?' Correct me if I'm wrong, but I thought the purpose of having a gun was to be able to actually *use* it!"

"Exactly my point!" Kyle shouted, his red face only inches from hers.

"What? You've really lost it, Kyle. If it's not

loaded, how the hell is it going to help me defend myself?"

"Scare tactics. Because if it *is* loaded, chances are someone will use it on you before you get the chance to use it on him."

Throwing her supplies into the wooden box at her feet, she asked, "Did you come here specifically to destroy my day?"

He rubbed his face and sighed. "Hell, no."

"It seems we both have bad tempers," Yardley said, trying to collect herself.

"I'll say. I'm sorry. I guess I overreacted."

Damn right you did, she wanted to scream. Instead, she muttered, "I'd like to think you'd want me to be safe."

"I do. I just don't believe you're going about it the right way. Besides, guns make me nervous."

She tried to lighten the mood by saying, "Yeah, but you're happy as a clam hanging over a sheer cliff face." He rewarded her with a weak smile. Still, she couldn't help but wonder if he was really worried about someone besides her getting hurt—someone like the open house murderer. . . .

Chapter Thirty-two

When Kim arrived home at six o'clock Saturday evening, she was exhausted. All day, everywhere she turned, she thought she saw Austin. When Yardley and Vinnie popped out to yell "Surprise," she actually screamed.

Setting Vinnie down, Yardley hugged Kim. "Sorry. We didn't mean to scare you."

"I know. I'm just jumpy right now. What's going on?"

"We're celebrating your new job and your very first listing! I'm so proud of you!" Yardley excitedly led her into the kitchen, saying, "I made all your favorites—cashew chicken with steamed rice, baby corn, and a pineapple upside down cake." Holding up a rented videotape and a bottle of wine, she added, "After dinner we'll curl up with *Legends of the Fall*. Booze, Brad Pitt, and a good friend. What more could you want?"

Tears spilled down Kim's cheeks as she answered, "Nothing. Thanks, Yardley. You're the best."

Hugging her again, Yardley said quietly, "Then I'd better confess. I was hoping you'd also let me in on whatever it is that's bothering you."

"It's that obvious?" Kim asked, wiping a tear from her silk blouse.

Yardley nodded. "Why don't you go change, and I'll pour the drinks."

Kim came back downstairs a few minutes later in her favorite sweats. "I feel better already," she said as Yardley handed her a glass of wine and they sat on the sofa. "How's it going with Kyle?"

Sipping her drink, Yardley said, "It isn't. We had a huge argument yesterday. I feel like such a jerk."

"So . . . Call and apologize," Kim said.

"I'm not sure I was *that* big a jerk." She laughed.

After drinking half a glass of wine in one gulp, Kim asked, "What'd you fight about?"

"The gun my sister sent to me."

"Really?"

Nodding, Yardley felt the relaxing effect of the wine. "Really. He doesn't like guns. Especially if it's loaded and he happens to stumble across it in the bottom of someone's purse."

Kim said, "He has a good point. Aren't you afraid it might accidentally go off?"

"Nope. The man at the gun store said all Smith & Wesson handguns are manufactured so that a direct force, I think twelve pounds, on the trigger is the only thing that'll fire them. I'm not going to test the theory, but supposedly you can drop one, pretty much pound the hell out of it, and it won't mis-fire. Besides, I realize how ridiculous it sounds, but

I've been so jumpy lately, having the gun with me makes me calm, as though part of my family is always with me, protecting me."

"Okay, since you've bared your soul, it's my turn to confess," Kim said.

"You started seeing Austin again, didn't you?" Yardley asked.

Shocked, Kim replied, "How'd you know?"

"I've spotted his car down the street a couple of times lately when I was on the balcony, painting. I was hoping he was still just admiring from afar."

"Afraid not." Kim refilled her glass. "You were right about him all the time."

"Mind if I ask why you agreed to see him again?"

Leaning back, Kim rested her head on the sofa. "I was at Woodland Hills Mall a few weeks ago, and I ran into him with another woman. They were holding hands, you know, looking like a happy couple. The next day he called me at work. He didn't ask me out or anything, said he just wanted to make sure we were still friends. We talked on the phone a few more times, then he called one day and said that he really missed seeing me."

Yardley closed her eyes and listened.

"I met him for a drink, and he was a perfect gentleman. He said he broke up with that other girl because he realized he was still in love with me. I thought it would be different this time, until the night I went to dinner with you and Kyle."

Sitting up straight, Yardley asked, "Is that what was wrong with you that night? I was sure Kyle must have molested you on the porch or something."

Kim laughed. "Actually, I think Kyle is great. A

little too intense, sometimes, but otherwise a nice guy. Anyway, Austin followed us to dinner."

Obviously concerned, Yardley said, "And then I saw him parked out front twice this week."

"Yeah, I'm really getting scared."

"Besides following you, has he done anything else?"

Kim was quiet for a moment, then said, "No. It's just that he was violent with me a few times when we were dating and now . . ." She trailed off, then blurted, "Do you think there's any possibility he could be involved in the open house murders?"

Yardley covered her surprise by setting her wineglass on the coffee table. "Why would you think that?" she asked calmly.

Almost babbling, Kim poured out all her private speculation. "The murders started about the time I broke up with him, and he hates you, and you're a real estate agent, and now I'm one, too. . . ."

Yardley was staring at her, deep in thought.

Shrugging, Kim said, "I know. I'm just being paranoid . . ."

"No. In fact, I confronted Austin the day after you broke up with him. He was watching the house. Basically, I told him that if he ever bothered you again I'd kick his scrawny ass."

"You did *not*!" Kim cried in disbelief.

Nodding, Yardley tried to suppress her laughter, but instead of being mad, Kim joined her, both holding their aching sides. "You attacking Austin . . . would be like Vinnie going for the throat of a St. Bernard."

Yardley laughed so hard she could barely speak.

"We are truly . . . pathetic. We both think . . . the guy we're dating . . . is capable of murder!"

Kim twirled in front of the full-length mirror, for the first time happy to be working on a Sunday. Everything was perfect. The new turquoise dress was exactly right for an open house—friendly, yet not too sexy. Grabbing her purse, she headed for the back door. Running after her, Vinnie barked and nipped playfully at the hem of her dress. When she jumped away, her leg brushed against the magazine rack, instantly ruining her hose.

"Look what you did!" she snapped.

Cowering, the puppy rolled onto its side as if to surrender before she scolded. "I know you don't like to be left here alone, but if you don't stop misbehaving, you'll end up staying in the garage most of the time. Understand?"

He whimpered, then rolled back onto his feet. Every muscle in his body suddenly tensed. Pointing his good ear toward the garage, he cocked his head, then growled and bared his teeth.

Kim glanced at her watch. If she hurried, she still had time to change her hose and make it to her first open house on time. Vinnie's eyes shifted from her to the door that led to the garage then back to her. This time his whine was intense, as though he was desperately trying to tell her something.

"Come on, boy. Quit doing your Lassie impersonation," Kim said. "Let's go! I'll race you upstairs." She turned and started to run, but he didn't move. Bending over, she swept him into her arms and headed up the stairs. "You may be the strangest little beast on the face of the earth, but Yardley and I love you anyway."

Vinnie struggled the entire way, his neck craning to watch the door. As soon as she tossed him on the bed, he sailed to the floor, barking at the top of his lungs as he flew back downstairs.

Kim slipped into a new pair of panty hose, yelling, "Vinnie, be quiet!" As if by magic, the barking instantly ceased.

"Good boy!" Kim called, hurrying back down the stairs. As she rounded the corner, she saw him, his tiny black-and-tan body motionless on the kitchen tile. Rushing to him, she started to bend over, but stopped when she saw a man's reflection in the window. Slowly, she turned to face Austin.

"Hello, Kim. Bet you didn't expect to see me this morning, did you?"

"No. As a matter of fact, I'm kind of in a hurry right now. How did you get in here?"

"When Yardley left, I stopped the garage door before it made it all the way down. Pretty clever, huh?"

Kim braced herself, boldly asking, "What do you want?"

"You."

Turning to leave, she said, "We've already been through all this, Austin. I have to go now, or I'll be late."

The telephone rang, and with sickening ease he wrapped one arm around her torso, pushing a knife against her throat with the other. "Answer it, and don't even think about telling anyone I'm here."

Moving with him, Kim reached for the phone on the wall near the refrigerator. "Hello," she managed.

"Kim! I'm glad I caught you at home. I'm going to meet Yardley at your open house, to let you relax a little this afternoon. I know I've been pretty demanding lately, and you deserve an entire weekend off."

"But . . ." For several seconds Kim didn't dare to breathe, afraid Austin would actually slit her throat. Finally, she felt her heart sink as she flatly answered, "Thank you, Mr. McCay. I can't tell you how much I appreciate your help. Good-bye."

"Wise move," Austin muttered.

In tears Kim whispered, "Why? If you really do care about me, why are you doing this?"

Effortlessly, he carried her into the garage and pinned her against her own Honda. Grabbing her hands, he twisted them behind her, then bound them with duct tape. Tossing her shoes aside, he did the same to her ankles. "You've always known it would come to this," he said gruffly. "That's why you came back. Because we have to be together—one way or another."

Kim tried not to panic, straining to stay as calm as she could.

"Now that you don't have to work today, you'll probably want to call your new boyfriend, right?"

"What new boyfriend? Please let me go! We can talk about all this later. I promise."

He shook his head and smiled. Reaching over, Austin pulled a stack of folded sales sheets from the side of her purse. He glanced over the descriptions of the house she was trying to sell. "This must be the place you were going to meet him. Maybe we'll go there together. See if he still shows up."

Yardley is waiting there, and Mr. McCay will be there,

too. Thank God she has a gun! Kim thought. She tried to sound enthusiastic. "That's a great idea. You could go with me. We'll spend the afternoon together, and I can prove I'm not seeing anyone else."

"The newspaper said that until that murderer is caught, all the open houses would be done in teams." Grinning even more, he pulled the cell phone out of her purse and said, "We're calling your bitchy roommate. Tell her your boss is taking your place so she won't get suspicious. And if you don't want me to kill her, don't pull any cute stunts."

Austin dialed the number, then crushed the knife against the side of her throat even harder. Holding the phone between them, they both listened intently for the sound of Yardley's voice.

With the Rocky's windows down, Yardley waited patiently in the driveway of Kim's listing. Anxiously glancing at her watch, she wondered where Kim could possibly be. Just seconds later, her cell phone finally rang. Snatching it, she asked, "Where are you?"

"Yard, it's me, Kim. Something came up. I won't be coming, but Charles will be there soon."

Instantly alert, Yardley asked, "Kim? Are you okay? You sound really odd."

"Whatever. Just cover me, Yard. Do whatever you can to push the sale through, and I'll see you later. 'Bye."

"Yard? And who the hell is Charles?" she insisted, but the connection had already been broken. Yardley held the phone in her hand and stared at it for several seconds. "What sale?"

Shaking her head, she realized that was one of the strangest conversations she had ever had with anyone, especially Kim. Kim never called her "Yard," and neither of them called Chuck "Charles." Quickly punching in their home phone number, she drummed her fingers on the steering wheel and waited. After three rings Kim's chipper voice said, "You've reached Kim and Yardley's machine. She's painting or showing a house, I'm studying or slaving away at the office. We'll call you back if you do your thing at the beep."

After hanging up, Yardley tried Kim's cell phone, which only rang. For several seconds she contemplated what to do. Finally, she dug in her purse, found Kyle's card, and reluctantly dialed his home number. When he answered, she hesitantly said, "Kyle, it's Yardley. I'm really sorry about the other day in the park. I was way out of line."

"Me, too. Can we forget it and move on?" he asked, his voice sincere.

"That'd be great."

"I'm really glad you called," Kyle said. "Believe it or not, I was going to stop by your open house this afternoon. I thought you might want to catch the Gun & Knife Show with me." He laughed.

Relieved that he seemed to be his old self, she smiled and said, "Very funny. Are you busy?"

"Why?"

"I hate to even ask, but I really need a favor."

"Just name it," Kyle replied, apparently eager to help.

"Kim was supposed to leave the house ten minutes after I did to meet me at this open house. First she was late, then she sounded really odd when she phoned just now. Plus, when I called back, she didn't answer either the telephone or her cell phone. Could you stop by our condo and make sure everything is okay?"

"You bet. You're at Kim's listing on 88th and Jamestown, right?"

An involuntary shiver ran through her. "How'd you know?"

"Along with all the other would-be killers stalking the city, I troll the Sunday paper for gorgeous women real estate agents, preferably unarmed ones."

"Good, then no one will bother me since I obviously have two good arms. They come in handy when I try to climb places God only intended bighorned sheep to go."

"Seriously, you shouldn't be at an open house alone until they catch that killer."

"I'll be fine." She resisted the urge to add, *My loaded Lady Smith will protect me quite well!*

"Why don't I check on Kim, then drop by and keep you company?"

Although she still felt a little uncomfortable, the fresh memory of Kim's jittery voice made her certain she needed someone's help, and Kyle was it. The knot in her stomach tightened, but she agreed and hung up. When she suddenly caught a glimpse of a man in her side mirror, she gasped. With a sigh she opened the door. "You scared me half to death, Chuck." She hadn't immediately recognized him because he was wearing casual clothes—a sleek black jogging suit that emphasized his powerful upper body. Smiling, she wondered if he really was giving up his workaholic ways.

With a sheepish grin he said, "Sorry. This is such

a huge estate, I thought I could check the grounds for my favorite agent. I gave Kim the afternoon off."

Yardley hid her disappointment, quickly realizing that Kyle would be there soon. "It was nice of you to come."

"No problem. I'll head around back while you open up the place."

"Do you mind if I set up my paints?" Yardley asked.

"Not at all. I'd love to watch you . . . paint, that is."

Suppressing a shudder, Yardley unlocked the door and led Chuck to the patio doors. After he slipped outside, she walked from room to room. The tension never lessened as she nervously familiarized herself with Kim's listing in case any potential buyers actually did stop by.

The vacant house was an agent's dream—a gorgeous home resting on a well-kept lot in the middle of two wooded acres. Since it was almost entirely made of stone, it would be very low maintenance, plus the neighboring houses could only be seen from the front yard, giving it a secluded, country feeling, even though it was close to the heart of the city.

Climbing up the central staircase, she browsed around the master bedroom, noting the house had a splendid stone fireplace. The rooms were spacious, the entire place clean. Kids would love the surprise she found in the closet in one of the bedrooms—a half door that led to a loft. Walking through it, she descended the narrow staircase that connected the loft to the office on the first floor, and found herself just outside the ranch-style kitchen.

When Yardley felt competent to show the interior, she threw open the patio doors and stepped into the huge backyard. Kim had told her that the gate on the side of the eight-foot cedar privacy fence was always kept locked. It was an attractive fence, unusual because the rails were all on the outside, giving a seemingly endless line of perfectly level pickets to beautify the view from the patio.

As with most older homes in the area, seasons of growth had left the boxwoods and hollies a little overgrown along the fence line, but the previous owners had done an excellent job of landscaping with spring bulbs. Lining the sidewalk that skirted the perimeter of the home were rows of brilliant red tulips. Unable to resist the temptation, she decided to paint the flowers while she waited.

Leaving both the front and back doors open would allow the doorbell to be heard if prospective buyers stopped by. After arranging her supplies just outside the back door, she started to work. Picking up the bundle of pencils Kyle had given her, she pulled one out, sketched the flowers, then placed it carefully back with the others.

Five minutes later, Yardley was so engrossed in capturing the vibrant colors of the flowers, she barely noticed movement at the far corner of the house. Every muscle in her body tensed, even though she was sure it was only Chuck. A rush of adrenaline made the tips of her fingers tingle as she slowly pulled her eyes away from the canvas.

When he drew closer, Chuck smiled and waved. Yardley sighed, relaxing as soon as she realized her shattered nerves were still playing tricks on her.

"Kim landed quite a listing, didn't she? If the inside is half this great, it should sell fast."

"It's even better," Yardley replied.

Eyeing her, he leaned close. "I'm glad I came. I wouldn't want anything to happen to you, Yardley."

Uncomfortable, she blushed. "Thanks."

Nodding toward the house, he said lightly, "I suppose if I'm going to be of much help, you'd better give me a quick tour."

Pushing aside her box of paints, she grabbed her purse. "Sure."

Chuck followed her inside, and although she was walking away, from the corner of her eye Yardley was sure she saw him twist the lock. Careful not to draw his attention, a glance at the front door confirmed her fears—it was closed. Had it too been discreetly locked? *The wind could've blown it closed. . . .*

Yardley's instincts were warning her to run. Instead, she slid her hand into her purse, wrapping her fingers around the pearl handle of the fully loaded Lady Smith as she led the way.

Following the same path she had just taken twenty minutes earlier, Yardley began McCay's tour downstairs. Briskly covering the attributes of each room, she moved constantly ahead to maintain a safe distance from him.

As they made their way upstairs, she suddenly wondered if finding Anne's body, plus all her own crazy fears, had pushed her over the edge. Chuck hadn't done anything threatening—hadn't even acted slightly odd.

After all, locking the back doors could just be his way to make sure we're safe. So no one can surprise us. . . .

Mentally scolding herself for jumping to such ridiculous conclusions, Yardley relaxed her grip on the weapon. She pulled her hand out of her purse as they entered the master bedroom. Casually, she said, "I'm still really embarrassed about that night we went for coffee. I can't understand what could've made me so tired. Would you mind clearing something up for me? It's bothered me ever since."

Stepping close to her, he smiled. "We have no secrets from each other. Believe me."

For several seconds she simply froze. A strange look in his eyes—an evil, detached stare—instantly terrified her.

"Well, what did you want to ask me?" he asked, never blinking or breaking the trance he held her in.

Shaking her head, Yardley tried to clear her mind. "It . . . I . . . I guess it really isn't important."

"Sure it is. Come on. Ask. You'll feel better."

"I just wondered how I ended up—"

"Naked in my bed?"

Blushing, she stepped back and nodded. The sinking feeling grew as she realized she had, literally, backed herself into a corner.

Quite matter-of-factly he explained, "You see, I like to try my conquests out first without a struggle. It allows me to focus better, being well acquainted with each woman's body. In a kinky sort of way, it makes the real event even more challenging."

"The real event?" she echoed, wishing she still had the gun in the palm of her hand instead of buried in the purse dangling at her side.

"Now. The next few minutes. We're going to have the wildest sex you can imagine. Not like the first time. Today you'll move with me, moan when I thrust, beg for more. Like Anne and the others did, for a while at least."

Not like the first time! Fighting a wave of nausea, Yardley remembered waking in his bed and realized Kim had been right—he had drugged her!

Willing herself not to panic, she tried to remember the self-defense class. There was no time for hesitation, only the strong survived. Gathering her courage, she said sternly, "No way, Chuck. Find another playmate." Pushing past him with long, confident strides, her head was held high as she hurried toward the door. Groping for the nearest weapon, her fingers closed around the pager clipped on the pocket of her slacks.

For an instant she thought her bluff had worked. But before she reached the door, he caught her from behind, his long, strong fingers grabbing her hair, jerking her to a stop. Clean, short nails dug into her flesh as he clamped his hands fiercely around her neck from behind. Yardley tried to hit him with the pager in her hand, but it merely glanced off the side of his face and slid across the floor. She swung her purse over her head, relentlessly pounding him with it until she lost her grip and it, too, fell to the floor.

Clawing and twisting, she exhausted every ounce of strength, trying to pry loose from the deadly grip on her neck. Her lungs desperately fought for even the smallest gasp of precious air. As they struggled, she saw his crazed reflection in the mirror of the master bathroom, and she instinctively knew—one of them would die that day.

Chapter Thirty-three

~

Kyle parked the Land Cruiser, then jogged to the front door of Yardley and Kim's condo. Barely able to hold still, he rocked cheerfully back and forth as he rang the doorbell and waited. When there was no answer, he peeked inside a nearby window, then tried again. Still nothing.

Walking into the small yard, he looked around. Several cars were parked up the street, but everything seemed peaceful. He quickly jogged to the back door, then knocked loudly, calling, "Kim! Are you in there? Kim! Answer the door!"

Cupping his hands to block the light, he pressed his face close to the window and stared inside. The kitchen and living area were empty, making him certain Kim wasn't home.

In the garage Kim felt her heart sink at the sound of Kyle's car starting. He had given up. A tear slid down her cheek and fell on the blade of the knife still at her throat. The weapon pressed against her skin no longer felt cold and threatening. In a strange way she wanted to push against it, to try anything, even bleeding, to throw Austin off guard and regain control of her life.

His lips were so close to her ear that Kim cringed when she felt his hot breath. "That's him, isn't it?" he seethed. "He's the one you dumped me for. Probably came to give you a ride to your open house. Maybe I'd better prove what happens when you screw around on me." Shoving her toward the trunk of her car, he pushed her inside. "We'll find him, and you can see exactly what I've got planned for you if you ever even look at another man again."

With a sob she cried, "No . . . that's Yardley's friend. Really, I barely even know him."

"Yeah, right. I have a nice zoom shot of the two of you practically screwing on the front porch. Your face is just inches from his dick, and you're rubbing his thigh! Besides, if he's only a friend, what the hell was he doing practically breaking down your door just now? In case you didn't notice, he was shouting *your* name, not Yardley's."

"I don't know why he was here!" she pleaded as the trunk slammed closed. "Please let me go, Austin. Please . . ."

Lack of oxygen blinded Yardley, creating a spectacular array of bright flashes that floated like fireworks inside her eyes. In her light-headed state she thought the colorful spectacle must be the path to heaven, or maybe hell.

It had been months since she thought much about her family, yet suddenly there her mother was—drifting in the distance. Yardley strained to find comfort in the woman's presence, but the vision faded as abruptly as it had materialized.

Surrounded by a black void, Yardley felt everything slipping away. Her struggling hands relaxed, then fell as she realized how futile it was to fight him. *It's over . . . I can't . . . He's too strong.*

As fast as they had disappeared, the blinding lights returned. They danced around the phantom woman's pleading eyes, abruptly making her message clear. *It's not your time! Life is too precious! Fight!*

The palm that had just brushed lifelessly past her grandmother's antique pin suddenly flew back up. Grabbing it, she ripped the piece of jewelry from her dress and brutally stabbed the back of Chuck's hand with the sharp point of the gold paintbrush.

Screaming, he let go. Finding a shred of strength somewhere deep within, Yardley managed to whirl around. Slashing wildly back and forth, she gouged deep lacerations across his face. Barely able to see, she grabbed her purse off the floor and ran down the hall. Remembering the back staircase, she stumbled toward it, groping for the gun hidden inside her purse as she ran.

Her throat was on fire; every gasp for air sent shivers of pain through her entire being. Slowly the brilliant lights faded, replaced by the grim vision of reality. In the closet she ducked to squeeze through the half door that led to the loft, slamming the door closed behind her.

Yardley turned to face the door, clutched the Lady

Smith, and tossed aside her purse. Desperately trying to steady her shaking hands, she watched and waited.

Each breath burned; every moment seemed to drag for hours. Almost in slow motion, she saw the doorknob move. The trigger beneath her index finger jerked and several deafening shots rang out, blasting through the half door.

Having no intention of waiting to see if any of her bullets struck home, Yardley turned and ran. Her ears rang from the gunfire, so she had no idea if he followed her. Tearing down the stairs, she slid across the cool tile of the kitchen in her stocking feet, realizing she must have lost her shoes at some point in the struggle. With shaky hands she managed to unlock the patio doors. Flinging them open, Yardley escaped into the backyard.

The Lady Smith was still in her hand, but she had no car keys, no way to distance herself from his madness. Hesitating, she wondered how many shots she had fired. *Were there two bullets left, or three?*

Keeping low, she crept behind the bushes, then rushed across an open area until she was at the gate. It was locked! *How did McCay get in?* she wondered, but quickly pushed aside the irrelevant thought when she realized there was no place to hide. Retracing her steps, she hurried to find cover near the bushes along the back fence. While she crept along, her eyes never left the windows, as if the huge, vacant house could somehow warn her. In a way, it did.

Movement in the kitchen made her freeze. Chuck McCay was at the sink, casually washing the blood from his face and hands. When he looked up, he stared out the window and smiled.

She knew he had spotted her, yet surprisingly, he didn't seem to be in any hurry. Suddenly, everything was clear. *He kills women for sport, and the bastard thinks he's won! He's giving me a head start to even the odds. This is a game to him!*

Darting off, Yardley tried to boost her courage by saying angrily, "Big mistake, Chuck. Never underestimate your enemy, especially a woman who's really pissed off!"

The trunk of the Honda was dim, musty, and completely free of anything Kim could use as a weapon. As Austin drove recklessly through town, she tried to find a way out of her predicament. Closing her eyes, she took deep breaths until she suddenly remembered seeing a show Oprah had done on child kidnappings. They had shown kids what to do if they were ever trapped in the trunk of a car.

Kim's eyes flew open. Enough light came through the taillights that she could see what she needed to do. Even though the move was difficult, she wiggled into position and began furiously kicking the inside of one taillight, hoping to knock the entire fixture out so someone in a passing car might see her trapped inside. Since she was barefoot, each kick sent pain shooting up her entire leg, but she kept trying, until warm, sticky blood running down her feet finally convinced her to give up.

Still determined, she rolled over and twisted until she was positioned directly over the back tire. Her hands tied behind her, she felt along the inside of the trunk until she found the thick cord of wires she hoped powered the brake lights. Wrapping her fingers around the cord, she waited until Austin sped around a corner, then rolled with the centrifugal force. It slammed her brutally to the opposite side of the trunk, but she didn't care—the wires had snapped loose. Twisting around to the opposite side, she repeated the process, knowing the odds of being stopped by the police were much greater for a car without signal and taillights.

By the time Kim finished, she was drained, but hopeful. Blood ran from gashes on her forehead and her feet, but she worked over to the passenger side, refusing to give up. She managed to open the compartment where the tire jack was stored. If she could only get it out, she might be able to free her hands by rubbing on its sharp edge, then use it to beat the hell out of Austin.

Yardley knew she wouldn't get far without shoes, and that the eight-foot privacy fence surrounding the property would be impossible to scale, since the rails were on the outside. Screaming wouldn't help—neighbors were too far away to hear. Even though Chuck hadn't used a weapon on her yet, she knew he might easily have a hidden gun or knife. Moving carefully so the bushes wouldn't betray her, she worked her way around the house. Her heart sank when she realized there was no easy escape.

As she leaned against the rock house, she gazed over, then up, an idea forming. The end of the house was made of large stones that rose from the ground to the top of the second story. The rocks jutted far enough out from the mortar to be easily climbed, yet it was a long way up.

"What the hell," Yardley muttered as she stuffed the Lady Smith into the pocket of her jacket. Stepping carefully over the row of bloodred tulips, she began her ascent.

Remembering everything Kyle had taught her, she found footholds and handholds as she worked her way up. It wasn't easy. The mortar left only an inch or two of clearance, and it gnawed at the tips of her fingers and toes until they were raw. Without chalk on her hands and sticky boots on her feet, climbing wasn't much fun. Yet, faster than she'd dreamed possible, the top of her head bumped the bottom of the eave.

Kyle would say it's just a little roof, a tiny obstacle between me and the top. Find a good handhold, swing a leg up, and pull yourself over.

The sound of McCay's voice floating causally from the backyard gave her the mental push she needed. Holding fiercely with her left hand, she curled her toes into the stones and swung her right hand out. Groping, she suddenly felt it. *A nail!* Grabbing it, she prayed it would hold her weight as she pushed with all her might. The hem of her slacks caught another nail, and she struggled to work her leg over the edge. Suddenly, she was on top of the eave, sprawled on the roof and panting.

Chuck McCay walked slowly along the narrow path beside the house, holding his bullet-grazed upper arm as he searched. For months he had waited for this day, knowing Yardley would be his biggest challenge. Blotting his fresh facial cuts with the back of his sleeve, he knew he'd been right.

Stopping in his tracks, a slow smile creased McCay's face. Next to his blood-stained athletic shoe lay a bright red calling card—a broken tulip. At its base the iridescent pearl grip of a small hand gun gleamed in the afternoon sun. Picking it up, he felt her warmth radiate from it. She was close, very close.

As McCay retraced his steps, he didn't bother to glance up. He knew Yardley was up there waiting. *You're every bit as clever as I thought . . . I promise, you won't be disappointed . . . And neither will I . . .*

The warm shake shingles snagged Yardley's hose with every step as she inched toward the chimney. She knew if he was inside, even the slightest noise would give her away. The rock chimney towered three feet above the adjoining roof, offering protection from being seen from the yard below. Behind her the peak of the roof made her invisible from the street side of the house—it was the perfect hiding place!

Moving toward the chimney, she was within a few inches when her foot slipped on a loose shingle. Staggering sideways, she lost her balance, falling and sliding until she abruptly collided with the rocks and mortar on its edge. Finding a handhold, she struggled to keep from teetering off, then scooted to the center of the rocks. Grimacing, she spotted the loose shingle that had almost cost her everything.

Closing her eyes, Yardley rested her head on her knees and tried to listen. Faint ringing in her ears reminded her of the shots she had so recently fired. She dug in her pocket, reaching for the Lady Smith, only to find the pocket empty. Yardley barely recognized the hoarse voice that whispered, "Oh, no . . ."

Even though it seemed like hours, she was certain only a few minutes had passed. Gathering her nerve, she peeked around the side of the chimney. The backyard was empty—he was nowhere in sight. But the relief she felt was short-lived.

As she turned back around, she noticed a pair of hands reach over the peak of the roof. Her gun was in his right fist, his index finger on the trigger, ready to fire.

Breaking free the loose shingle, Yardley recklessly bolted up the roof. Just as his evil eyes appeared, she swung the shingle, whacking him across the face with all her might. Stunned, his fist opened, and the Lady Smith slid down the roof, bumping to a stop when it hit the chimney. McCay fell across the peak, his arms and head on one side, his torso and legs on the other.

Steadying herself, Yardley stepped back and watched. He was still breathing, but she was sure he was unconscious.

"Yardley!"

She froze, hearing Kyle's voice from somewhere below. Sighing, relief washed over her as she turned and yelled, "Help! I'm up here!"

Then, instantly, she felt McCay's hand wrap around her ankle. With a sudden jerk she fell flat on her stomach on the steep roof, her head well below her feet. With surprising agility, McCay jumped on her back, his weight crushing her against the splintering wood as they began sliding toward the edge.

Yardley focused on the gun and prayed the chimney would stop her from falling. Stretching out her hand, she reached for it as they crashed into the rocks, but it was just beyond her grasp as they stopped.

McCay grabbed her arm, twisting it painfully behind her back. Brutally rolling her on top of her own arm, he straddled her torso as he clamped one hand around her throat. A sick grin lit his face as he shouted, "I win!"

"What the hell is going on up there?" Kyle yelled.

McCay froze, then leaned slightly forward to look over the edge of the roof. The shift in his weight gave Yardley the momentum she needed. With all her might she bucked him off, sending him flailing over her head to the ground two stories below.

Although she was instantly relieved, the rapid movement made her skid to the edge of the eave, where she quickly groped for anything to stop her fall. Dangling from the roof by one hand barely gripping the gutter, she heard Kyle's calm voice call from below. "You're okay! There's a great foothold just a few inches from your left foot. That's it! Now, ease your right hand over to the chimney and push against it until you can feel your weight shift onto your foot. Perfect! Do you want me to help, or can you make it down alone?"

Her face inches from the rock, she tried to stay focused. "Where's my next foothold?"

"Down and to the left. Keep the pressure on the right. Good! Now release and shift . . ."

When she was five feet off the ground, her strength was gone. Missing the last step, she fell into Kyle's arms.

Holding her tight, he whispered, "You're a fast learner."

She didn't answer. Instead, she spent several seconds enjoying the feel of the ground under her feet, the fresh air in her lungs, and being wrapped in Kyle's protective embrace.

When she finally looked up, she drew strength from his smile. Out of the corner of her eye she could see Chuck McCay sprawled facedown on the sidewalk, his head surrounded by tulips. From the odd angle of his neck she suspected it was broken by the fall. Kyle made sure she could stand alone before he squatted beside him to check for a pulse. Shaking his head, he stood. "He's dead."

"Good," Yardley said.

With an expression somewhere between amazement and alarm, Kyle asked, "Who the hell is he?"

"His name is Chuck McCay. He is . . . was . . . my boss, the owner of McCay Realty."

"So why'd you toss him off the roof?" Kyle asked, trying to lighten the horrible reality of what had just happened.

Her eyes met his as she said flatly, "He's the open house murderer."

Kyle and Yardley stood a few feet from McCay's body for several seconds. Finally, she said, "I need to get the cell phone in my purse and call the police. It's upstairs."

He nodded, supporting her as she tried to walk. Obviously concerned, he asked, "Are you sure you're all right? Your neck looks pretty bruised, and your feet are bleeding. We should get you right to a doctor."

Yardley's free hand touched her swollen neck. "That bastard tried to choke me to death, and I guess I've got a few splinters and cuts from the shingles."

"I wouldn't doubt it. How'd you get up there, anyway?"

With a sly grin she replied, "I climbed."

"Impressive. Have any trouble?"

"I had a good teacher, and a lot of luck getting over that eave." Proudly, she pointed up and explained, "I grabbed one of the nails they must've used to hang their Christmas lights on, then swung one leg up. The other followed, just as you said it would."

Pulling her back into a hug, he shouted, "All right! But why did you need a handhold on the roof?"

She looked at him as if he were insane. "To get over the eave. It's just like the overhang I fell from at the park, remember?"

"Why didn't you just move over four feet and scale the outside of the chimney to the top, then step onto the roof? That way you wouldn't have had to conquer the eave at all."

Yardley instantly realized that he was right, and her cheeks flushed. Chuckling, she poked him in the ribs. "Even though I took a harder route than necessary, learning to climb saved my life. I can't thank you enough."

They walked past the canvas of bloodred tulips as Kyle asked, "By the way, where's Kim?"

Stopping, Yardley's face fell. "She never came. You mean she wasn't at home?"

"If she was there, she didn't answer. Nothing seemed out of place, so I assumed she was just running late and came over here."

"She said Chuck told her not to come. I'll bet poor Vinnie went nuts when you rang the doorbell. It makes him so crazy."

She saw Kyle's face tense. Tentatively, she asked, "He did bark at you . . . didn't he?"

Shaking his head, he grimly replied, "I never heard a sound, or saw him. And I rang the bell over and over . . . I even pounded on the back door."

Kyle followed her inside as they rushed to find her purse. Since Yardley couldn't remember where she lost it, she said, "I'll take the back stairs and check the loft if you'll look in the master bedroom."

They split up, Kyle bolting up the central staircase as Yardley limped in the opposite direction. In the vacant bedroom there was no purse, but as he turned to leave, something caught his eye. Stooping down, he gently picked up Yardley's antique pin. The clasp was broken, and the solid gold paintbrush was bent and covered with blood. As he tucked it into his pocket, he heard Yardley call, "I found it!"

Meeting her in the kitchen, he eyed the purse and asked, "Where's the gun?"

"Chuck had it on the roof, but he dropped it when I whacked him with the shingle." Responding to the twinkle in his eye, she added, "Don't you dare say I told you so!"

With a sly grin Kyle replied, "After all you've been through, I wouldn't think of it."

"The gun is still up on the roof. It slid and stopped against the edge of the chimney. Do you think we might need it to help Kim?" she asked.

"I certainly hope not. Why don't you call the police on your cell phone? I'll climb up and get the gun . . . just in case."

As he left, Yardley pulled out her cell phone. The digital display was blank, so she pushed the power button. Nothing happened. Tapping it lightly against the countertop, she tried again, then realized it was dead, probably broken in the struggle with McCay. "Damn!" she muttered.

Grabbing her purse, she hurried out the back door. Before she could shout to Kyle, she heard a noise behind her and whirled around. She found herself face-to-face with Austin.

"Where is he?" Austin shouted. "I know you're hiding him for Kim. Always trying to protect her, aren't you, bitch?"

Yardley noticed he had one hand behind his back. Moving slowly away, she practically tripped over her box of paints. "Where's Kim? What have you done to her?"

"You didn't answer my question. Where is he?" His right hand appeared, wielding a long, gleaming knife.

"I don't know who you're talking about, Austin. Really. I was here, waiting for Kim. The only other person who showed up was the open house murderer." She hoped that revelation would distract him from his insane jealousy.

Brandishing the weapon just inches from her face, he replied, "Yeah. Right."

"No, really. He's around the corner. Dead. I killed him." Holding up her cell phone, she added, "I just called the police. They'll be here any minute."

He lunged at her. "Then I'd better hurry . . ."

Kyle had no trouble scaling the rock chimney. The Lady Smith was exactly where Yardley had said it would be, and he quickly unloaded it, surprised to see only two of the five bullets hadn't been fired. Stuffing them in his pocket, he tucked the gun into the waist of his jeans and started to climb back down the chimney. Voices from the yard below made him instantly freeze.

Crawling onto the roof again, he silently crept across it until he was directly over Yardley and a man brandishing a knife. Peering down, he watched in silence, shocked when the tall man suddenly pounced on her. Ready to jump, he waited for an opportunity that wouldn't endanger Yardley's life. She struggled, but in a matter of seconds the man easily had her in his control.

Two stories above them, Kyle watched the man plant the knife against Yardley's throat and scream, "I know you're here somewhere! I'll kill this bitch if you don't show your ass right now!"

For the second time in less than an hour Yardley found herself wondering how much longer she would live. Tears of rage and sheer exhaustion stung her eyes as she pleaded, "Austin, you don't have to do this! Really. The man you're looking for is already dead. I killed him. He's on the sidewalk, right around the corner. He has a broken neck."

"You're not big enough to break anybody's neck," he scoffed.

"I took a self-defense class. I'm sure Kim told you about it. They made all the women in the office go—"

With a snicker he painfully tightened his grip. "Did you a lot of good, didn't it?"

Raising her voice, she said, "Look at me! No shoes, my slacks are ripped, my hands and feet are bleeding. Believe me, I killed him, because he was going to kill *me*!"

Austin's voice was a raspy whisper against her ear. "Okay. But I'll slice you if you even *think* about lying to me. Which way is the bastard?"

Her hand shook as she pointed in the direction Kyle had gone just minutes ago, praying that he knew what was coming. Austin squeezed her tighter, half carrying, half dragging her. When they rounded the corner, she was relieved to see only Chuck McCay's body.

She spoke as firmly as she could. "See . . . I told you. His neck is broken. Now will you let me go?"

Austin was obviously studying the body on the sidewalk carefully, slowing his approach. Yardley feared if he got too close, he would realize it wasn't Kyle.

Without tilting her head she glanced up and saw Kyle on the roof. Knowing he needed a distraction, she quickly pretended to be hysterical, screaming at the top of her lungs, "He tried to kill me! Don't make me go near him again! Please!" With a rush of adrenaline she managed to break free of Austin's arms.

Over her shoulder she saw Kyle leap off the roof, his fall partially broken when he landed on top of Austin. Both men rolled into the grass, yet somehow Austin managed to hold onto the knife. For several seconds she numbly watched them struggle, until she realized she had to find a way to help Kyle.

Running as fast as she could, Yardley searched the yard for anything she could use as a weapon. All she saw was her box of painting supplies, so she ran to it. Pure adrenaline pulsed in her veins as she threw aside paintbrushes, tubes of watercolor, sponges. She smiled when she finally saw something even remotely dangerous—the three newly sharpened pencils Kyle had given her, still bound tightly by a rubber band.

Rushing back, she gasped when she rounded the corner. Somehow, Austin had managed to gain the advantage. Kyle's arms were shaking as he fought to keep the blade of the knife from stabbing his chest.

Without hesitation Yardley ran across the soft grass, raising her dubious weapon overhead as though it, too, was a lethal blade forged of fine steel. She stopped just behind Austin to be certain she had the precise angle. Sliding onto her knees, she grimaced as she ruthlessly rammed the pencils into his back, just below his rib cage. She knew her aim was true when she felt the pencils plunge deep into soft tissue. An inhuman scream ripped through the air as Austin fell on his side. Writhing in pain, he threw the knife at her.

Yardley ducked, the blade missing her by only a few inches. She went to Kyle and wrapped her arms around him. "Are you all right?"

"I hurt my shoulder when I jumped"—reaching behind him, he pulled the Lady Smith out of the back of his jeans and handed it to her—"plus I'm gonna have a hell of a bruise from landing on this damned thing. Otherwise, I'm okay."

"Sorry . . ." Yardley was too weak to go on.

Crawling to his knees, he shook his head and muttered, "Holy shit. Are there any more lunatics lurking around trying to kill you?"

Her eyes never left the growing circle of blood around the pencils protruding from Austin's back. "Actually, he was trying to kill *you* not me."

Kyle stared in Austin's direction. "But I've never seen him before in my life!"

"He's Kim's ex-boyfriend. It's a long story. Right now, I think we really need to find Kim. He might have hurt her before he came after you."

Even though Austin seemed unconscious, Kyle disconnected a garden hose. Yardley helped him wrap it around Austin's feet and hands, just in case he regained consciousness. When they were finished, he asked, "Where the hell are the police?"

"My cell phone was broken, so I never got through."

Wrapping his good arm around her, Kyle sighed. "Then let's use the one in my car."

After silently walking through the house, they both stepped onto the front porch and froze. An odd thumping sound came from the driveway. Rushing down the sidewalk, they could hear Kim's muffled voice.

Kyle popped the lock on the trunk, using the release latch on the driver's side. Yardley quickly pulled it open. "Kim! Are you hurt?"

Her voice hoarse, she cried, "Where's Austin? We've got to get away! Get me out of here!"

Kyle rounded the corner as Yardley explained. "It's all right. Austin is . . . no longer a problem."

"And neither is Chuck McCay, the open house murderer," Kyle added.

Kim murmured, "That's not funny!"

Helping her out, Yardley said, "Believe me, it wasn't intended to be."

Chapter Thirty-four

~

"Relax, Kim. It isn't as hard as it looks. Concentrate on each move, one step at a time."

"Easy for you to say! You've probably climbed this thing ten times in the last month. Trust me, it isn't as simple as you claim!"

From the top of the cliff Kyle laughed and called, "A few weeks ago Yardley swore she'd never climb again. Now she's your lead."

"Which means you have to trust me, Kim," Yardley joined in. You'll make it over the roof just fine. Just watch what I do!"

"I should've stayed home and cuddled with Vinnie," Kim muttered. "At least he doesn't expect me to do anything but walk on nice, flat land."

"Quit whining! We're almost there," Yardley snapped.

Kyle asked, "How's Vinnie doing?"

"Dr. Nida said he's recovered from his concussion,

but it'll probably be a long time before he learns to trust *any* man," Yardley replied.

As she crept along the edge, Kim mumbled under her breath, "If the two of you hadn't saved me from Austin, I wouldn't be here now. Which, come to think of it, might be a good thing. How in the world did I ever let you talk me into this?"

"Watch closely!" Yardley conquered the overhang as though it were just another piece of rock, smiling broadly at Kyle as he greeted her on top. Spinning to face the ledge, she turned her head and whispered back to him, "Think she'll fall?"

Kyle wrapped his arms around her waist so she could still belay Kim as he replied, "Probably."

Yardley asked, "Have I done everything right?"

Kyle had watched her every move. "Of course," he said. "You had a great teacher."

Raising her voice, Yardley called, "Ready when you are!"

They both heard Kim mutter, "Shit. I'm gonna die." Seconds later, the sound of her screams filled the air.

Together, Yardley and Kyle peered over the edge. Kim dangled from her harness a few yards below, struggling to upright herself. Yardley shouted, "Are you okay?"

Kim screamed back, "Do I look okay? I'm hanging off a friggin' cliff! Get me outta here!"

Laughing, Kyle used his good arm to help Yardley hoist Kim up and over. He said, "You know, some people just aren't cut out for mountain climbing."

Flopping onto solid ground, Kim said, "No kidding! Never again! Not in a million years!"

Yardley shook her head and looked at Kyle. "Are you going to tell her, or should I?"

"I don't have the heart. She's your best friend. You tell her."

Kim bolted upright. Her eyes wide, she asked, "Tell me what? Oh, God! There's more, isn't there?"

Yardley bit her lower lip and grimaced. "The way out . . ."

"What the hell does that mean?" Kim moaned.

Kyle nodded toward the ground several stories below. "Going down is much, much harder."

Kim paled. "Call Lifeflight. Tell them I had a heart attack. Tell them anything, just make sure they bring a helicopter to fly me out of here. I am *not* climbing back down this . . . this horrible monstrosity!"

Yardley and Kyle broke into laughter, unable to maintain their ruse any longer. Kim immediately relaxed. "Very funny. How are we really going to get off this thing?"

Kyle replied, "We'll rest for a while, then rappel down. It's simple. Really."

Rolling her eyes, Kim muttered, "I've heard that before!"

Yardley wrapped her arms around Kyle and whispered, "Ignore her. She'll be fine once we're back home." Gently rubbing his lower back, she added, "I noticed last night that your bruise is finally gone. Did I mention that I got rid of the Lady Smith, permanently?"

He hugged her. "Thank heaven!"

"You have to admit, it did come in handy."

He smiled at her wickedly. "You don't really want to start that discussion again, do you?"

Grinning, she kissed him. "As long as I'm eating crow, I suppose I should admit you were right about something else, too."

"Really? What?"

"Remember that horrible day we were talking about the visions of people I saw when I was, well, you know . . ."

Kim supplied, "Dead. Deceased. Just as I'm going to be in a few minutes when I try sliding down that stupid rope!"

Kyle chuckled. "So you finally dug out your family album?"

Yardley said softly, "I'm still not sure I believe it. It had to be my mother I saw in the light. . . ."

Kyle held her tightly. "That reminds me! I have a surprise for you! I thought this would be the perfect place to give it to you." Unzipping a small pouch that dangled from the belt of his harness, he pulled out a velvet jeweler's box and handed it to her.

Yardley beamed as her eyes met his, seeing his unmistakable love. Opening the box, she gasped. Nestled inside was her grandmother's antique pin. "Kyle! It's as good as new!" She narrowed her eyes. "You told me the police had to keep it as evidence."

"So I pulled a few strings. The jeweler put a new clasp on it, straightened it out, and cleaned it. You'd better look it over closely to make sure it's absolutely perfect."

Picking the pin up, sunlight caught the diamond ring nestled underneath its palette. Tears came to her eyes as Kyle dropped to one knee. "I fell in love with you the moment I saw you painting yellow pansies. Will you be my bride, Yardley Smith?"

"Of course I will!" Yardley cried.

"Looks like Vinnie will have to learn to trust at least *one* man." Kim laughed. Gazing apprehensively over the edge of the cliff, she added, "Please tell me you're going to get married on nice, flat ground."

Epilogue

∼

Even in a congested airport bar such as the one in St. Louis's Lambert International on Concourse C on a Friday evening, it was not a common sight to find four exceptionally beautiful women huddled together. People stared, and the four men sitting on the far side of the room enjoyed every single flirtatious gawk, whistle, and grin.

"They're something, aren't they?" The man, who only some thirty-odd minutes before had been introduced to the others as Jake, asked.

"They certainly are," Peter agreed, including them all in the enthusiastic compliment, though fixing his gaze on his bride of only five short months.

Ethan, swirling his brandy absently, studied each of the women with his artist's eye. "You know, it's odd. They're each exquisite, uniquely so, even though, of course, Dinah and Lauren share the same coloring. But I mean, Dinah is petite, while Yard-ley's beauty is more ethereal, or maybe angelic is a

better word. And Lauren is very much the Audrey
Hepburn or Jacqueline Kennedy type."

"And that gal of yours just exudes sensuality,"
Kyle put in.

Ethan laughed appreciatively. "That she does.
My Rita Hayworth, I call her. But if you take a
minute to study them all, there's an underlying resemblance that is really startling."

"I think it's in the eyes," Peter Cain suggested.

"Really?" Jake asked. "I disagree. I think it's their
mouths. Watch 'em as they laugh. Awesome."

"I think it's their bones," Kyle said. "And not just
the face, the whole structure thing. What do you
think, Ethan?"

"I think you're right, all of you, but it's more than
the sum of any one thing you've mentioned," Ethan
said, accepting the mantle of authority. "It's in their
carriage and the innate sense of pride, of strength, if
you will, that even tragedy and years of separation
couldn't diminish."

"Well, all that baggage has finally been discarded,"
Kyle said. He picked up his beer, drained the last of
it, and signaled the bartender for another round.
Then he looked at the other men, who would soon
all be related to him through marriage. "And speaking of baggage, I made sure Yardley got rid of that
damned gun."

"Oh, yeah, the famous Lady Smith. Me, too, once
I found out she'd had it in her purse the whole
time and could have killed me with it," Jake said,
frowning with the awful memory of their Christmas debacle.

"Uh-huh, so Yardley gets it all wrapped up in a
fancy silk scarf with a little note about her being the

keeper of family treasures. Some treasure! Kind of like hanging onto a pair of rattler's fangs because it was the snake that bit you and almost killed you," Kyle Baker said with a shake of his head, amazed. "Sorry, I just don't get the sentimentality there."

"I understand what you're saying, Baker. However, I've got this sense that in some weird way I don't think any of us could ever explain, it actually brought us all some very good luck." Peter, the debonair millionaire, beamed as he focused on his wife again. "At least, in my case I can certainly testify that it played a significant part in the peace and love Lauren and I have found together."

"Well said," Kyle told Peter with a firm clap on the shoulder and a wink directed at the other two men. "Maybe I should have had Yardley send it back to Lauren since you're so fond of it."

"Wait a minute," Ethan said. "I know all about the gun's history—only too well, in fact—and I know why Lauren sent it to Ardath, and then why Ardath insisted Dinah carry it, but if Dinah sent it to Yardley for safekeeping, why did you insist she get rid of it?"

A shadow fell over Kyle Baker's eyes as he recalled the harrowing ordeal with the man who had killed several real estate agents, and very nearly succeeded in murdering Yardley. He tried for a smile as his eyes focused on the woman he loved more than he could ever express. The smile succeeded, though he didn't quite manage to keep the strain from his tone. "Dinah sent it to Yardley all wrapped up in the scarf ol' Jake here used to tie her up. Yardley knew the whole story, and as I found out much later, thought it all very romantic, like a

Shakespearean tragedy." He sighed, sipped on his beer for a moment, then related a dehydrated version of the real estate murders.

"Whoa," Ethan said. "No wonder you made her promise to lose the gun."

"Now, hold on, don't get me wrong," Peter said. "If I never saw that little gun again, I wouldn't lose a wink of sleep, but in a strange way I'm convinced it played a part in bringing all of us together. And I'm curious, Baker, what did she do with it?"

"Yeah, I'd like to know, too," Jake agreed. "No matter how we feel about any of them carrying a gun around, Dinah put a lot of faith in Yardley by sending it to her. If she's told me once, she's told me a half dozen times, how Yardley is the sentimental one they all entrust with the safeguarding of family history."

"She definitely is sentimental," Kyle agreed, and then he started to laugh. "And I think you're gonna appreciate the way she handled my orders to get rid of it." He pointed to the far corner of the room, where the four women were all opening small black velvet boxes. "You can't tell what's in 'em from here, but you'll see what I think is so funny as soon as they've finished celebrating their private reunion."

Peter pushed back the sleeve of his cashmere jacket to glance at his watch. "Which I'm afraid we're going to have to interrupt in just a couple of minutes if Lauren and I are going to make our flight to Paris."

"That reminds me," Jake said. "Why a second trip to France in only, what, four or five months since your honeymoon?"

"Because Paris is even more glorious in the spring

than it is in the fall." Peter paused, treating himself to a satisfied grin, then leaned forward to confide, "Besides, we figure since this may well be the last chance we have to travel for a while, as well as the last opportunity for quite some years to travel as a couple rather than as a family, we should do it."

"Hey, you mean . . ." Kyle began.

"That we're pregnant," Peter confirmed, his forest green eyes gleaming with pride.

"Well, congratulations, man!" Jake said, raising his glass and motioning with a thrust of his chin for the others to join in. When their glasses clinked, he proposed a toast: "Here's to you, Peter. As one of the four luckiest guys on earth, I can honestly say, you done good, pal." He paused on a chuckle, then added, "I'd tell you to keep it up, but I guess you've just proven you know how to do that without any coaching from us."

They were all laughing as Peter dropped a couple of twenties on the table, refusing the others' offers to chip in. "The next one's on you, Ethan," he said. "We'll be back in time for your wedding next month."

"Just see that you are," the handsome writer said. "And then it's off to Oklahoma in June for Kyle and Yardley's big day, which I'm particularly excited about since she's promised to show me her artwork. Ardath says she's quite talented."

"Gifted," Kyle corrected.

"Well, I was about to ask if you're nervous about making it all legal, Baker, but I can see from that shit-eating grin that would be a stupid question."

"But one I'll answer, anyway. Hell, no! I can't wait! If I had my way, I'd have a judge marry us just as Dinah and Jake did on New Year's Eve. Yardley's adamant, though. Insists on a traditional wedding with the church and flowers, the whole thing. Even has her heart set on June." He looked to where his bride-to-be and her three sisters were all making their way out of the lounge, causing gridlock as passersby literally stopped in their tracks to stare. "She said there's no way she's going to miss the chance to show off the most beautiful bridesmaids in the world. And just look at them. How can I argue with that?"

"Don't even try," Peter cautioned. "No way in hell you could win."

The four men made their way out of the crowded room through the clutter of chairs and carry-on luggage strewn about the floor. Jake stopped short a few feet from the door to draw the other men's eyes to the pendants that hung from silver chains around all four women's necks. "Don't tell me," he said, his gaze fixed on Kyle.

"Hey, I don't have to. You can see for yourself."

The others tightened the space between them to have a better look at the unusual heart-shaped necklaces. They were beautiful, with intricately crafted silver-gray backing. In the center of each dull cast metal heart, another, smaller one caught the light that played over the mother-of-pearl.

"Son of a bitch," Ethan muttered. "They're wearing the gun around their necks."

"Yeah, but you gotta admit they wear it well," Jake said.

"In a way, it's a part of each of them, I think," Peter said, his voice soft as he caught his wife's gaze and smiled.

There were hugs all around, and Kyle rocked on his heels, feeling pretty smug about how clever his fiancée's idea was. "Yep, what better way to keep it in the family, and who better to wear it than a Lady Smith?"

ABOUT THE AUTHORS

KATHERINE STONE is the bestselling author of twelve novels, including *Happy Endings, Pearl Moon*, and *Imagine Love*. A physician who now writes full-time, Katherine Stone and her husband, novelist Jack Chase, live in the Pacific Northwest. Her new novel, *Bed of Roses*, has just been published.

ANNE STUART has been writing since the beginning of time, specializing in her own brand of romance, suspense, and black humor. She's won every major award in the romance genre, and publishes historical romances for Zebra as well as contemporary romantic suspense for Dutton Signet. She lives in Vermont with her carpenter husband and two splendid children.

DONNA JULIAN is the bestselling, award-winning author of eight novels including her January 1998 Signet release *Bad Moon Rising*. Donna's passions are her family, pets and writing, dance, travel, and reading—in frequently changing order. She makes her home with her husband Jerry in a St. Louis, Missouri suburb.

JODIE LARSEN is a native of Tulsa, Oklahoma, where she currently resides with her husband and two children. Before she discovered her love of writing, Jodie practiced as a Certified Public Accountant for over fifteen years. Her novels include *Deadly Company* and *Deadly Silence*. Jodie would like to thank Mark Nida for his technical assistance with *Sisters & Secrets,* as well as D. L. Larsen and R. T. Jones of the Tulsa Police Department for their expertise and advice.